THE
FIFTH VOTE

THE FIFTH VOTE

David Pepper

St. Helena Press

The Fifth Vote

Published by St. Helena Press

Cincinnati, Ohio

Library of Congress Control Number: 2023934751

ISBN (paperback): 9781662937538
eISBN: 9781662937552

WEDNESDAY

Chapter 1

Four words stopped him cold.

Councilman Dylan Webb had planned to buzz right past the raggedy-looking figure. Rocking back and forth, waiting by the entrance to the community center in torn jeans and a frayed gray T-shirt, the man bore the makings of a ten-minute, meandering conversation. Already rushing from his parked Jeep to the aging center's front door, Dylan couldn't afford the interruption. He lowered his head to avoid eye contact, focusing on his polished brown shoes.

The man missed the hint, stepping forward. Dylan looked up at the worst possible moment—just as the man's ash-gray, deep-set eyes pierced into his. His thin lips quivered as he prepared to speak, his prominent Adam's apple lifting a half-inch.

"You saved my home."

Dylan stopped. While quiet, the words commanded a response.

"Pardon me?" Dylan asked politely.

The man first reached out to shake his hand, but then he leaned in for a full embrace, holding Dylan's six-foot frame for a good five seconds. The first bear hug from a stranger in his short political career. Not a hugger, Dylan waited patiently.

"I said, you saved my home," the man said after taking a step back. "Just after Christmas, I heard you on the radio talking about how to avoid a foreclosure. I had just gotten my second notice from the bank. I'm a single dad—three daughters—and had no idea what to do. But I called the number you mentioned, did everything they said to do, and it worked! We're now in our home for good."

He brushed a tear from his stubbly right cheek.

"I'll never be able to thank you enough."

Dylan nodded, pleased. More confirmation that his little program was working. He'd come up with it on the fly to avert foreclosures that had been sweeping through Cincinnati's poorest neighborhoods. Few others at city hall even paid attention, while he knew from monthly reports that the approach was saving thousands of homes. But this was the first time someone had thanked him in person.

"You're so welcome, sir. Just doing my job. And I'm so glad you and your daughters are okay. Keep up the fight."

They stared at each other for a few seconds more, shook hands, and then Dylan walked into the community center, a broad smile across his face.

"You saved my home."

The fundraising. The glad-handing. The interminable speeches drawing out the countless meetings. The social media and talk radio vitriol.

In his short time in office, he'd experienced the innumerable downsides of politics.

But the man's four words showed what a difference he could make. What public service could be. What it should be. And why he'd joined its ranks.

* * *

The rusty metal chair creaked as Dylan took his place behind one of three foldout tables at the front of the community room, which doubled as a gym after school. It was damp inside, and a good ten degrees hotter than the parking lot. Flakes of paint hung from the walls, and a musty odor pervaded the place. Unlike the city hall chambers he'd just left, there was nothing stately about the center, nor was there any media present. But the crowd was almost as big and impassioned as the one at the weekly city council meeting.

Exactly as Dylan had planned.

After two months on the council, Dylan had insisted that zoning hearings take place in the communities actually impacted by the projects in question, and no longer buried within the inaccessible

3

bowels of city hall. Big money in town had a storied history of barreling over community concerns when it came to developments that made fat profits and prettied up the street but drove the poorest residents out of their own neighborhoods. And an explosion of even bigger money of late was making things worse—sleek projects popping up all over made Dylan wonder who was actually demanding all this new development. Either way, locating hearings in those neighborhoods at least forced developers, lawyers, and politicians to face the people their projects would most impact. It gave the residents a fighting chance to be heard.

Today's throng provided a case study of why he'd done so.

Nestled below the steep hills that rose a few miles west of downtown Cincinnati, the neighborhood known as Lower Price Hill had been saddled with crippling poverty for generations. Old buildings, many abandoned. Run-down streets and vacant lots. Abundant hunger and drug use matched with little hope and scant opportunity. A dumping ground of decaying industries. On hot days, thick, dirty air hung over the community—Dylan's lungs would ache after only thirty minutes. He'd cringe thinking about the kids who grew up breathing that air all day, every day.

On the zoning committee's agenda was a plan that, in theory, would change all that. A combination of new and renovated housing and a modern commercial district. But as the packed room made clear, that plan would also force most of the current residents to leave.

Thirty-five people testified over the next ninety minutes. Many more who didn't speak cheered on comments they agreed with. Except for the developer, his pin-striped lawyer, and two younger lawyers, all were poor. Most were Black, and those who were White spoke with strong Appalachian twangs. A few of the speakers represented new immigrant communities that had been settling into Cincinnati in recent years—largely from Nigeria and Guatemala. A rare diversity in a city whose fifty-two neighborhoods were largely split along racial lines.

To a person, all opposed the project. Their neighborhood needed help desperately, they all agreed. They liked some of the new features.

But they shouldn't be the victims of that progress—forced out for new businesses and high-end, hillside condos they couldn't afford. After all, they'd been the ones who'd stuck it out all this time before the urban core's real estate market had taken off. They'd been the loyal city dwellers when the rich people had fled.

Yes, their comments were scripted. And repetitive. And Dylan had a lot of other things to do. But phone buried deep in his pocket, he made a point of looking directly at each resident who spoke. Of listening to every word. As he did at every hearing since his first day on the council.

His attentiveness fulfilled a commitment he'd made to himself years before. He'd once testified before the council as an everyday resident—fighting a proposed new building in his own neighborhood that would've killed the views of the river. He'd been shocked by the experience. For the entire three minutes, all he saw were the tops of five heads. Every council member was looking down, scrolling through their phones. At first, he waited for the panel to look at him, but they never did. The sight was so distracting, he stumbled through his remarks. At one point he'd paused, prompting two of the council members to look up, assuming he was done. But by the time he was five words back into his remarks, the two were back in their phones. The council ultimately approved the project despite overwhelming opposition. And Dylan never forgot those three minutes.

So now, at every meeting, he made sure to look directly into the eyes of every person speaking. Inevitably, this made him the only council member *not* on his phone, which spawned the corollary effect that for ninety minutes, each resident testifying looked at *him* as she spoke.

On the one hand, it was draining to be the only one paying attention. He resented his colleagues for placing the entire burden on him. It was a public hearing, for God's sake. The entire point was to get the public's input. To listen.

On the other hand, his effort also meant he heard their words. The pain they were expressing cut through. And the fear. And even if what they said was similar, and predictable, each told her story differently—through expressions as much as words. Outside of knocking on doors, he never felt more in touch with communities than he did by listening at these hearings. Really leaning in. These good people lived tough lives. Hard lives. No one fought for them. Hell, their own elected representatives didn't even bother listening from ten feet away when they were speaking, through nerves and sometimes tears, about their lives being turned upside down. But those same representatives would listen for hours to developers and lawyers who didn't even live in the city, in fancy rooms all over town, phones nowhere in sight.

It was that experience that drove so much of how Dylan Webb ultimately voted. All other things being equal—and they usually weren't equal—he'd side with the people every time.

Closing in on two hours, after lots of testimony and little discussion, the committee's clerk called the roll. The crowd fell silent, the fate of thousands in the hands of the four people in the front of the room.

"Mr. Thelan . . ."

Thelan was the mayor's appointee and committee chair, there to do the mayor's bidding.

"Aye."

A murmur from the crowd.

"Ms. Busken . . ."

Laurie Busken was the other member of the city council on the Zoning Committee. An independent.

"Aye."

The murmurs evolved into scattered boos. Heads shook with disappointment. They had spoken so clearly. So overwhelmingly. Yet were being ignored.

"Ms. Gonzales . . ."

Ann Gonzales occupied the "community seat" on the committee, an appointment that Dylan had spearheaded in a close vote.

"Nay."

A few claps. Someone had listened.

"Mr. Webb . . ."

For Dylan, it wasn't a close call. This project was overkill, and it would upend far too many lives in the room and many more *not* in the room. He leaned into the microphone and pushed the red button. "No!"

Applause broke out. A few whoops balanced the nasty glares coming from the developer and his hired guns.

"The vote is two for advancing the plan, and two against," the clerk announced.

More chatter from the crowd. Confusion. What did a tie mean?

Dylan knew the answer. The decision would go before next week's full city council meeting. Another close vote in the offing, with those lawyers and developers digging in deep to get it passed. In addition to legal and policy cajoling would come the promise of large contributions for council members who went along—something they'd stopped offering Dylan months into his term when it was clear he couldn't be swayed.

But Dylan was confident his "no" vote would prevail. It always did.

As the meeting ended, he snuck a quick peek at his phone—both at the time and the calendar. One reception to go, then he'd be free. But as he stood up, residents surrounded his table, gushing with thanks about his vote. And the fact that he'd actually listened to them. That he'd heard them.

He had to run, but he was glad they noticed.

They always noticed.

Chapter 2

They looked out of place.

Not as trouble, necessarily. But out of place for sure.

Two teenagers on a weekday evening. In Mount Adams—an upscale, hilly neighborhood of condos and tall, brightly colored townhouses where few families lived, and hours before the bar scene up top got going. And in jeans and sweatshirts, the duo was ambling down a steep hill where they surely didn't live.

Dylan Webb had owned his home on Hill Street for eight years, ever since moving back to his hometown. He knew everyone on it, mostly empty nesters and a few young professionals. No teenagers among them.

The taller of the two teens had darker skin, in a neighborhood that was painfully, entirely White. And the college kids that partied at the top of the hill tended to be all White as well.

And because the hill bottomed out at a highway entrance into downtown Cincinnati, unless you lived on it, there was no earthly reason to be walking *down* it.

So the young, diverse, walking, talking duo stuck out as Dylan drove past them after turning left down Hill Street.

But he didn't slow down.

He'd been chasing his schedule all day. The mid-morning groundbreaking had run long, making him late for lunch, which meant he'd had to hustle to make the 12:30 city council meeting. The meeting's formal agenda had been short, but the most recent police shooting generated two hours of tense testimony and discussion, causing him to arrive late to the zoning meeting. It took him ten minutes to navigate away from the throng at the community center, which of course meant he'd arrived late to the reception for a local nonprofit. And he hadn't been able to duck out of the reception early because he was the guest of honor. So he'd sped through his remarks, then raced home to change for his sole nonwork event of the week.

A date.

An actual date.

It was Wednesday, and early enough in the evening that a gap in parked cars remained in front of his front door—large enough to squeeze his Jeep into. Looking down at the imposing twenty-percent grade, he pulled the parking brake as high as it went, an essential step many Mount Adams visitors skipped to their and others' regret.

This was going to be a five-minute stop, trading out his navy-blue suit for the more casual khakis and sweater fitting for a first date on a fall evening.

Dylan hopped out of the Jeep, locked it, and jogged to the front door of his yellow townhouse. Twisting the key in the lock, he opened the door and stepped inside.

Now dusk, the lights of the Kentucky side of the Ohio River shimmered through the townhouse's arched back window.

But what mattered to him more was that the digital clock on the kitchen counter flashed 6:51.

Which meant he was late.

She lived twenty minutes away, north and east, and he was supposed to pick her up at 7:00. Better to let her know in advance than keep her waiting.

He reached into his pants pockets in search of the torn-off corner of the lunch program where she'd written down her number. In his left pocket, where his keys had been, there was nothing but some lint. In his right pocket, he pushed his wallet to the side to see if the paper was there. Three coins. Nothing else.

He took out the wallet and rifled through it. A few receipts, some business cards accumulated over the last week, no actual bills—and no scrap of paper.

He shut his eyes, thinking.

"That's right," he muttered.

She'd passed the number to him through the Jeep's passenger window just before he'd driven away from the city's annual economic development lunch last week. He'd placed it on the dashboard and must not have moved it since.

He plucked his keys off the kitchen counter and stepped back outside, pressing the unlock button on his Jeep key to the sound of a short beep.

He stepped across the red-brick sidewalk and opened the passenger door.

Bingo.

A scrap of paper lay folded under the windshield, halfway across the car. He stretched, grabbed it, and unfolded it. Between the creases, the key information was still legible:

Can't wait. Steph. :)

Her phone number was written below.

He grinned.

Stephanie Walker was a tall brunette, impressive professionally, funny as hell, and confident enough to date one of the city's most recognized politicians. He couldn't wait either.

Dylan tucked the note into his right pocket and turned around.

His smile collapsed.

The two teens stood only inches from him, pinning him against the open door.

One stood over him—6'1, or maybe taller since he was slightly down the hill. The other was well shorter. Both were wearing oversized sunglasses, masking much of their faces. The tall kid in back had a Bears baseball cap on, tilted low. The tall kid was Black, the shorter one White.

Both were skinnier than he was. Not too imposing.

But the squarish black cylinder pointed right at his stomach did the trick, paralyzing him.

Chapter 3

"Give us all your money!" the shorter kid holding the gun said.

Dylan's heart pounded like it was going to shatter a rib from the inside.

He'd fork over hundreds of bucks if he had them. More, even. But he remembered his empty wallet.

"Guys, I don't have any money," he said slowly, lifting his hands palms out, trying to project calm. The gun's barrel looked enormous as it faced him. "I swear. If I did, it'd be yours."

"Bullshit," the taller kid said, spitting on Dylan in the process. "Waste his ass!"

"Wait! Wait!" he yelled without meaning to. "I'll show you."

"Do it," the shorter kid said, gun not budging. "Slowly."

Dylan reached into his right pocket and removed his brown leather wallet. He opened it with both hands, fumbling through the business cards and smattering of receipts.

"See," he said. "Nothing."

"Bullshit," the tall kid said again. "What about your pockets?"

Dylan reached in and pulled the lining of both pockets out. Some lint fell out, and that was it.

"Empty too."

The guy with the gun shook his head, thrusting the barrel hard into Dylan's abdomen.

"Don't fuck with us, dude. I saw a lot of plastic in that wallet. Any of those ATM cards?"

With both sets of eyes inches from his face, lying wouldn't work. Dylan had a terrible poker face.

"Sure. One of them is."

"Well let's go use it then," said the shorter kid.

"Take it! Take my whole wallet if you want."

A gun to the gut had a way of making nothing else matter.

The short kid chuckled.

"Right. We're taking *you* too. Get in the car. *You* drive. And hand over your phone before you get any bad ideas."

Chapter 4

To their eternal credit, Cincinnati's forebears insisted on building among its seven hills and fifty-two neighborhoods a system of parks that rivalled any city in the nation. Nestled along the first few hillsides east of downtown, Eden Park stood out as a crown jewel of that system.

The park's vertical array of lush lawns and thick copses of oaks and elms, dotted with sculptures, monuments, trails, and lakes, made it a favorite of runners and lovers alike. But amid these features, the capstone was the wide panoramic view of the mighty Ohio below, as it curled in from the east, meandered west past downtown, then veered south in the far distance.

And the view was dynamic, varying by the hour.

Most mornings, the park offered the perfect vantage point of the sun rising upriver. As day broke, red and orange streaks interrupted the faint glow of dawn, illuminating the dark water below. Then came the sun itself, initially a beaming neon sliver above the water, gradually expanding into a wider arc before rising into a full sphere of glimmering yellow, lighting the water below with a kaleidoscope of bright colors.

In the evenings, the park offered witness to the journey's end, the falling sun painting the river's western side orange and red while lighting up downtown's storied skyline. Whenever he could, this was when Dylan Webb took his daily jog. While his eight-minute miles kept him at his target weight of 190 pounds, the stunning view from the overlook rewarded him for another busy day. His rare moment to relax.

Tonight was one of those perfect evenings, the sun setting as Dylan drove up and through Eden Park, passing to the left of the storied overlook.

Which made having a pistol only inches from his stomach all the more jarring.

"Don't even think about it," the guy in the passenger seat said as they passed a crowd of park visitors to the right, enjoying the evening's natural show. A police officer directed traffic at the entrance to the overlook's driveway, only yards away from the Jeep. Dylan racked his brain for any option to break free, but none came to mind that didn't involve gunfire.

As they exited the park and entered Walnut Hills, Dylan tightened his grip on the steering wheel. Initial panic was calming to nervous resolve.

He was the adult. They were kids. Jumpy, maybe, but neither seemed high nor nuts. *Take control*, he told himself. *Gain their trust.* Which meant giving them advance notice of issues and obstacles, and doing all he could not to piss them off. And if they ever seemed on the verge of killing him, he could always ram the Jeep into a tree, gambling that he'd be injured the least.

"There," the kid in the passenger seat said, pointing forward and to their left. "Go in there."

Dylan slowed as they approached the First American Bank in Walnut Hills.

"Guys, there's a limit on how much you can take out at one time."

"Bullshit," the tall kid yelled from the back seat. "Put a cap in him."

Thank God he wasn't the one with the gun.

"Listen," Dylan said as he pulled into the bank's driveway. "I want to give you what you want. I want to help you. But banks have limits on how much you can withdraw from an ATM."

For instances such as these, he felt like saying. But didn't.

"Which makes sense, right?"

He turned to the shorter kid in the passenger seat. The one who'd called every shot so far.

"Don't look at me!" the kid yelled, lifting the gun a few inches from his lap with his right hand while adjusting his sunglasses with his left.

"Okay! Okay!" Dylan said, looking forward as his new calm disappeared.

Moments of silence passed.

"I'll tell you what. You tell me what amount you want to ask for, and I'll type it in. If it works, great, and then we ask for more. But best to start at a few hundred bucks. Too much, and you'll get nothing."

The guy in the front seat moved the gun back to his lap, still clenching its grip.

"Okay. Start at $250."

Dylan pulled up to the drive-through ATM, took out his card, and typed in his four-digit PIN. He then pushed the button marked, "Withdraw from checking."

"$250, right?"

"Yeah. $250."

He typed in the three numbers and pushed enter. The kid in the passenger seat peered over Dylan's shoulder, his breath warming the back of his neck.

His heartbeat spiked as the small monitor displayed the word *Processing* for what felt like minutes. Forking over $250 would be much better than explaining why the request had been declined.

The whirr of bills whisking through the machine came at the same time the word *Approved* flashed on the screen. His nerves eased as he reached into the dispenser and pulled out a bunch of $20s and a $10.

"$250," he said, handing over the stack of bills. "Here you go."

The kid let the gun lay in his lap as he counted the bills.

"Now $100 more," he said coldly.

Dylan kept his face blank as his moment of hope faded.

"You sure? That might break the limit. Maybe try—"

"Quit talking and do it!" the guy in the back yelled, kicking hard against the back of Dylan's seat, jolting his neck forward.

The guy in front jammed the gun hard into the side of Dylan's stomach.

"I said $100! Now."

"Okay!"

Frazzled by their bursts of anger, Dylan struggled to reinsert his card into the slot. When he got it in, he requested $100.

Another long pause. No whirr this time, but a beep as the machine spit the card back out.

Declined.

Dylan's mouth went dry.

"Guys, I'm sorry to tell you, you hit the limit."

"Bullshit," the kid in the back yelled, kicking again. "You did that!"

"You're full of shit, dude," the kid in the passenger seat said, jamming the gun even harder into his now bruised abs.

"I'm not. I swear. I typed in exactly what you told me to."

He racked his brain.

"I'll tell you what. Let's drive to another ATM. Maybe the limit only applies at each location."

He doubted his own words, but they needed to see that he was trying.

"Yeah. Do that. There's one by the courthouse. Go there!"

Dylan pulled out of the bank and drove back to the edge of Eden Park, but this time he turned down toward Columbia Parkway, the scenic highway that cut between the hillside and the river to take Cincinnati's East Siders downtown. It was the same route he drove to work every day.

No one spoke for a few minutes. The silence frayed Dylan's nerves—outside of driving off the road, talking was his only lever of control.

"Hey, guys, have you ever heard of Dylan Webb?"

"What are you talking about?" the kid in the passenger seat asked.

"Dylan Webb. The council member."

As odd as it felt to introduce himself, he needed a better rapport with these guys. *Make them like you.*

The kid in the back spoke up. "Is that the guy with all those yard signs?"

"Sure is."

Dylan had insisted on four thousand yard signs. Running for city council was all about name ID—the top nine vote-getters out of a field of dozens win the nine seats on the council. First-time candidates almost never broke through, especially if they'd only spent time on one side of town. And Dylan, raised in Mount Lookout and a graduate of the Catholic high school that the East Side's elite flowed through, was certainly guilty of that. He may have known a ton of people on the East Side, but when he started the campaign, he was a complete stranger everywhere else. And that wouldn't break the top nine.

So even though his Gen-Z campaign team thought he was nuts, he figured a yard-sign blitz in every part of the city would be a key part of winning. And the gaudy signs with the spiderweb graphic on them, which they'd planted in thousands of yards in one weekend blitz, had done the trick. His number of social media followers exploded as people wondered who the hell Webb was. And on election day, voter after voter—West Side, East Side, central, and north—recited his slogan back to him. That's when he knew he was going to win.

"Wait," the guy on the right said. "You're a councilman?"

"I am," Dylan said. The bright lights of downtown were now right in front of them, meaning time was running out.

"Shit," the guy in back muttered.

"Don't worry," Dylan said, working to build the same bond he'd forged with so many skeptical voters at their doors, where you only have seconds to win them over. "I'm only a politician because I want to help kids like you."

"Shut up, dude," the guy in the back said. "You don't know us."

"Yeah, you don't know shit," the guy on the right said. "Don't even try to be our friend. You're all the same."

"I get it. I don't know everything that you guys have been through, but I ran for office because I know people like me have gotten all the breaks in the world, and kids like you haven't."

"You think?" the kid in the back asked, deadpan.

Then silence.

"Where do you guys live anyway?" he asked.

It was the first thing you'd ask a voter. Everything in Cincinnati flowed from what neighborhood you grew up in and where you went to high school. But as soon as he asked the question, he wanted to take it back.

"Shut the fuck up," the kid to his right said. "We ain't telling you where we live."

"Okay, well my guess is it was tough," he said, talking slowly, trying to recover. "And I'm doing everything I can to help."

In less than one year on the council, he actually had. Dylan had fought for new investments in the city's most poverty-stricken neighborhoods—investments that actually helped those who already lived there. He'd killed the types of projects that had done so much damage—high-priced homes and condos that were tearing apart families and communities who couldn't afford the exploding costs. And he'd beaten back road expansions that valued traffic engineering mathematics more than community well-being. He'd also fought for better police-community relations and real reform, and for the types of social supports—childcare centers, higher wages, youth jobs, health clinics—long overlooked by the powers that be.

Of course, these two wouldn't know any of that. Most didn't. Crime, ribbon-cuttings, and political infighting diverted the media's attention from real substance. Like that foreclosure program, even city council members didn't appreciate all he was doing.

"Nah. It's all about the rich people. Never seen anyone down there do shit for people like us."

"That's why I ran for office, and that's why I work so hard every day."

Like at a voter's door, Dylan never gave up. And neither of his captors said a word as he continued. Maybe they were listening. A few times, the guy on the right even appeared to nod.

As he walked through initiatives he'd championed, the parkway merged into Fourth Street, a few blocks up from the river. He shook his head at the timing. In Cincinnati, "Fourth Street" didn't just refer to the wide, one-way avenue of medium-sized, aging buildings that ran the length of downtown. The term also signified the elite leaders of Cincinnati's business community, where all the biggest shots were called. *The rich people.*

Dylan slowed at a light, then took a right onto Main. Three stoplights later, heading north and away from the river, he pulled over half a block from the county courthouse.

The door clicked as Dylan pulled its handle.

"What the fuck you doing?" the kid on his right said.

"Going to the next ATM," Dylan said, pointing out the passenger window. "It's right there."

"I know. But you're not going alone."

The kid looked into the rearview mirror.

"Go with him," he said to the guy in back, waving the gun in a small circle. "And if you try anything, you're dead."

Dylan stepped outside. The kid in back got out and clutched Dylan's right elbow with a tight grip. Now on even ground, he was definitely over six feet tall.

"No bullshit," he said.

Dylan considered running. But the gun in the passenger seat kept him from straying. Yes, the odds were he'd get away—but one lucky shot could end things quick. Not worth the risk.

The tall kid stuck right with Dylan as they both walked to the ATM, a strong breeze blowing from left to right.

Two people going to an ATM together would've looked suspicious if anyone had been there to see it, but this part of downtown was a ghost town after work. Only a bearded man stood nearby, likely one of the many homeless people who used Courthouse Square as their night-time home.

With the kid watching over his left shoulder, Dylan inserted his card into the machine, then typed in his PIN.

"How much this time?"

"Um, try $50."

He typed in $50, then hit enter.

Processing.

A long pause.

The card spit back out.

Declined.

"Damn. The limit must've applied here too."

"Bullshit, man. Try again."

"You saw me type it in. The limits kicked in, like I said they would. We might lose the card."

"Let's try again."

Dylan lifted the card to put it back in, but the kid squeezed his elbow firmly.

"Not here. Another—"

"Hey, can you guys spare a five?"

They both jumped as a gruff, deep voice interrupted them. The bearded man had eased a few feet closer, and now he looked at them with round, wide-set, and intense eyes.

Dylan normally conversed with panhandlers, handing them a card indicating where they could get help for addiction or a roof over their head.

"Sorry, we've got nothing," he said quietly before the two walked back to the car.

Chapter 5

"We've hit the limit."

The third ATM, a drive-through on the other side of downtown, near city hall, had just declined their request for $50.

"Bullshit!" the guy from the back yelled, angrier than when they were standing outside.

But the guy in the passenger seat knew better. "He's right."

Stay in control. Help them end this peacefully.

"Listen, you've got what you can get," Dylan said. "I can drop you off wherever you want and we can forget this ever happened. Even take my car if you want."

"I don't think so."

It was the guy in the passenger seat. Bad news.

"I'm going to drive now. Pull over up there."

Dylan did as he was told, and the councilman and the abductor walked around the front of the car. He weighed running, but the gun again held him back. One lucky shot and all he had planned in life would be cut short. Dead on a city street. A headline.

"Find something to cover his eyes," the new driver said as he pulled away from the curb.

Some rustling in the back seat.

"Here," the kid in back said, passing something white forward. Dylan opened it up to find a T-shirt he'd been given at a community event a few days back.

Fearing he was losing complete control, Dylan pushed back.

"Guys, think about how this looks. People are gonna see me sitting here, blindfolded, and know exactly what's going on, then call the cops."

Now he was imagining being catapulted into the windshield at the end of a high-speed chase gone awry.

"That's true," the kid on the left said, raising the gun again and pointing it at Dylan's head. "So wrap that thing around your head and duck down."

"Okay. But still—"

"And stop talking, bitch!" It was the kid in the back seat. "You talk too much."

Dylan wrapped the T-shirt around his head, then ducked forward, limbs shaking.

He was no longer at the wheel. And for the first time, he couldn't see what was happening.

But worst of all, again, was the silence. His primary lifeline, gone.

All he heard now was the sound of the Jeep's engine. Accelerating. Slowing. Shifting into higher and lower gear as they navigated the hills of Cincinnati. The squeaking of brakes and squealing of tires. The repetition of it all—one sound after the next—made time disappear.

After climbing a steep and curvy road, the Jeep took a right, then another right, then went back down a hill before coming to a stop.

"Where's your wallet?"

"But there's nothing left—"

"Give us your fucking wallet."

Dylan pulled it from his pocket and held it out to his left. It was promptly snatched away.

"We now got your driver's license, your credit cards, and your phone. We also know where you live. If you call the cops, we'll be back."

"I would never—"

"Shut up! Now lean over. If you move or say a word, you get a bullet in the head."

Dylan ducked down, a chill running down his spine.

This was the moment where they'd make their decision. About him. About how to best end this without getting caught—whether it was better to let him go, or kill him, or beat him senseless. And there was absolutely nothing he could do to influence that decision.

His life was fully in the hands of two teenage strangers, one of whom seemed trigger-happy.

He tried to reassure himself. *They aren't high. They aren't nuts. They listened.*

Still, he took the final step of resistance he could think of. He wrapped his arms around his head in a way that covered as much of his skull as possible. If they pulled the trigger, at least make the bullet go through his arms first. Maybe bone or muscle would stop it. Or at least slow it.

Seconds passed, with furtive movements and some rustling both to his side and behind him. The car door to his left opened and slammed shut, followed shortly by the one behind him.

He suddenly felt light. Giddy.

They were leaving.

Then came muffled voices through the door. But they weren't directed at him.

"What the fuck? The dude is a councilman. If we let him go, he's gonna have the cops all over us."

"You need to chill."

"I'm chill. But be smart. He'll talk. And he runs the damn police."

Silence. The other guy was making up his mind.

Frozen, face only inches from his knees, Dylan was breathing hard. Panting. His stomach churned. Listening to two kids hash this out was like watching a coin flip—heads you live, tails you die.

"Did you do everything I said?" the front passenger finally asked.

"Yes."

"Then they'll never know who it was."

Silence.

Dylan waited for the tall kid's rebuttal, but it never came. Seconds ticked by.

He remained frozen in place, heeding the driver's warning. Maybe they were gone—maybe they were watching him. Still deciding.

He started counting in his head, his numbers coinciding with the thumping of his heart.

One . . . two . . . three . . . four . . .

At one hundred, he raised his head and pulled off the T-shirt, squinting as a streetlight blinded him.

Once his vision adjusted to the light, he looked around. He was near the top of another steep street in Mount Adams, facing downward. A large building of high-end condos towered above him.

The Celestial.

He was on Oregon Street. After all that driving, just a quarter mile from home.

But far more important, not a soul was around. His abductors were gone.

The sight of the perfectly barren street—the realization that he was free, that he would live—didn't make Dylan laugh. Or even smile.

Even though every limb suddenly felt lighter than before, he didn't move.

He simply stared down the steep hill, a liberating giddiness overcoming him as if he'd just sucked the air out of a helium balloon.

He couldn't recall anything feeling so good in his life.

Chapter 6

"I almost got killed trying to get your phone number."

The quip had come to Dylan Webb riding the elevator up to his law firm. Given what his two abductors had said, heading home was not an option.

"Is this Dylan?" asked Stephanie Walker, who'd picked up after one ring.

"It is." He was calling from the firm's landline after pulling her scrap of paper from his left pocket. "I'm so sorry to keep you waiting, but—"

"Where've you been? And what the hell are you talking about?" she asked.

"I wasn't joking. I went to my car to get your number, and two kids mugged me at gunpoint. Obviously they let me go, but not before taking my phone and wallet, and making me drive to some ATMs. But I still have my car and would absolutely love to have dinner."

"Are you kidding me?" she asked, her tone growing angry.

"No, it all happen—"

"Oh, I believe it happened. But you've got to be kidding about having dinner. And think about it, Dylan—your car's a crime scene. You need to call the cops right away."

"Oh, I'm going to call them and deal with all that too. But for now, I'm just relieved to be alive. Wired, to be honest. And starving. A nice dinner will settle me back down. But you're right—maybe we should use your car."

His computer monitor showed that it was 8:22.

"Let's say I grab an Uber and get there at 8:45 or—"

"Dylan, dinner can wait. You need to call the cops. Then call me back afterward."

They hung up.

Although hard to explain, Dylan had described exactly how he felt. The helium high was still there.

Dylan dialed his chief of staff, leaving a message. Then he called his parents, who'd retired to Florida, and filled them in.

"Honey, that's awful," his mom said. "Thank God you're okay. Do you need us to come home?"

"Thanks, Mom. I'll be fine. Just glad to be out of that car. But since they know where I live, can I stay at your place?"

"Of course, Dylan," she said, reminding him of the code to get into their East Walnut Hills condo. "What are the cops saying, anyway?"

"I haven't called them yet. I wanted you guys to know first."

"Well, we know now. You need to call the cops right away."

So he did.

"911. What is your name and your emergency?"

"Hi, my name is Dylan Webb."

"As in the council member?"

"That's me."

"Are you in a safe place?"

"I am. I'd like to report a mugging. A kidnapping, I guess."

"A kidnapping? Of whom?"

"Of me."

"Oh. One second, Councilman . . ."

The phone clicked as she patched him through to a supervisor. He walked through what happened for five minutes, then answered a rapid-fire series of questions. The supervisor told him detectives would meet him in the lobby in ten minutes.

After hanging up, he called Steph back, the high now gone.

"Steph, you were right. We'll have to reschedule dinner for another time."

Chapter 7

Of course, the media monitored police scanner traffic 24/7. It's how they got to crime scenes almost as soon as the cops did.

It just didn't dawn on Dylan that the radio call of his mugging would mention that *he* was the victim. But when the elevator doors opened on the ground floor, that fact became instantly clear.

Bright lights blinded him from multiple angles. He squinted as he stepped out, bringing into focus faces three deep, all ogling him. TV news cameras were filming live while still cameras chirped like crickets.

"Dylan!" a voice yelled out.

"Are you hurt?" another yelled. "What did they want?"

Once out of the elevator, his path was blocked.

"Did they know you were on the council?" a woman asked as she shoved a microphone just inches from his face.

"Folks!" A deep voice he recognized boomed from the main lobby of the building. "For God's sake, give the man some room."

He looked toward the voice to see the immense, hairless head of Deputy Police Chief Patrick Prince. Amid many duties, Prince served as the chief's liaison to the city council—with the exception of controversial incidents—so it wasn't surprising to see him there.

Nobody moved.

"I said, let him through!" the square-jawed Prince barked. "That's an order."

The cameras gave way, allowing Dylan to reach Prince, whose 6'2" athletic frame looked even more imposing in street clothes than in his standard uniform. Prince reached out with his bear paw of a hand, shaking Webb's with a crushing grip.

"Glad you're okay, sir. You're in good hands now."

He turned to a stern-looking woman standing next to him in her police whites. She was a few inches shorter than Dylan. Her jet-black hair, which plunged in a straight line to just below her shoulders, contrasted with skin that was nearly as pale as her uniform.

"This is Detective Shawna Moses. We're gonna take you to headquarters."

While he'd met a lot of Cincinnati cops, Dylan didn't recognize her.

"Nice to meet you, Detective."

"You as well, Councilman," she said with a flat expression and no handshake. All business.

"And what about my car?" Dylan asked.

Prince raised an eyebrow as he gazed over Webb's right shoulder, prompting Dylan to turn and look in the same direction. The round, spongy end of a microphone hung only a foot behind him, recording every word of the conversation.

Detective Moses answered formally, her narrow mocha eyes fixed on his. "Sir, we will arrange for your car to be transported to our lot, where it will be processed for evidence and fingerprints. Please hand me your keys"

"Makes sense," Webb said as he handed his keychain over.

"Thank you, sir," she said.

Her formality was comforting.

"Let's go," Prince said, stepping toward the lobby entrance while jutting his right arm forward, elbow out, daring the reporters to stand in their way. Outside the large windows of the building sat one unmarked SUV, and one marked cruiser, both with their sirens flashing.

Camera clicks and a shuffling of feet followed them as the press captured every movement of their brisk walk to the door.

No doubt, he would be the lead story of the eleven o'clock news. They had their B-roll already. But they'd still need some sound, which was why the questions came quickly.

"Were you targeted, Councilman?"

"Did they hurt you, Dylan?"

"What did they take?"

The politician in him knew to look pleasant in front of cameras. One bad expression would be splashed all over the next TV ad against him or turned into some viral meme. And he hated dodging questions, which would look sketchy. But if he stopped now to talk, things could unravel quickly.

Still, he needed to say something, so he turned back their way just in front of the revolving door.

"Guys," he said, trying to appear calm, "I'm going to sit down with these detectives tonight and walk through what happened. Happy to talk through any questions you have tomorrow."

He turned back around and followed Detective Moses through the revolving door, with Prince tailing behind.

A dozen people gawked from the other side of the street as Prince opened the curbside back door of the unmarked SUV. Dylan took his seat while Prince circled the vehicle and sat in the front passenger seat. Moses joined Dylan in the back.

They drove off, siren still on.

"Captain, I can't thank you enough for getting here so fast."

"Of course, sir."

They'd always had a mixed relationship. Polite and professional but accompanied by the tension that always existed between the department and the politicians. Dylan learned in his first few months that unless you wore a badge, no matter how polite on the outside, the police higher-ups weren't interested in your views on how to keep the city safe. Or on their efforts to do so.

Still, the by-the-book professionalism felt like stability now. These guys knew what they were doing.

Chapter 8

The first red flag shot up high enough to jolt Dylan upright in his chair.

He was in a windowless, squarish room within the bowels of police headquarters. Detective Moses had been running through basic questions as two other detectives took copious notes while interjecting their own follow-ups. Deputy Chief Prince looked on quietly, standing along with the two detectives, while Moses and Dylan sat in chairs facing each other across a small wooden table.

"Does this type of crime happen a lot?" Dylan asked after describing the initial confrontation.

"Not really," said a salt-and-pepper-haired detective, thin as a stilt and sporting a thin brown mustache that made him look like a Civil War soldier. He didn't look at Dylan as he spoke. "But that's not to say people don't *say* it happens."

Dylan laughed out loud.

"*Say* it happens?" he asked. "As in, report it when it doesn't?"

The detective looked at Prince as he responded, making the next words more jarring.

"Yep. And *that* happens more than you'd think."

Dylan chuckled, trying to appear casual. But the implication was clear.

"Why would anyone make something like this up?" he asked, stomach quivering.

"Oh, any number of reasons," the other detective said, looking down at Webb with a flat expression that perfectly matched his sunken eyes, short buzz cut, and wrestler's stocky build. His crooked nose looked like it'd been broken multiple times.

Webb wasn't interested in delving any further, but Mustache jumped right back in, holding up his thumb.

"An unexplained absence . . ."

He paused, then lifted his index finger. Counting.

"An attempt to get attention . . . an unexplained expenditure of money—"

"A drug deal gone bad," Buzz Cut chimed in, bemused, holding up three fingers.

"Maybe a lover's quarrel," Mustache added. "That may be the biggest reason of all."

Buzz Cut chuckled. "Google the words *abduction* and *staged* sometime. You'll see how often people make shit like this up."

Dylan cast a false smile as he heard the words but said nothing back.

"So why'd you get in the car?" Buzz Cut asked seconds later.

"Like I said, I had no money, and they wanted to go to ATMs to get some."

"Was that your idea, or theirs?"

"Um, theirs. After they saw I had no cash on me, they asked me if one of my cards was an ATM card, and I said yes. I told them to take it if they wanted."

"Was it your idea to drive?"

The rapid-fire, leading questions felt like a deposition from his law practice.

"No, that was their idea."

"Yet you agreed to drive? To get in the car?"

Worse than a deposition. More like being in the principal's office, as if he'd done something wrong.

"Yeah, I got in the car. But I'm not sure I'd use the word 'agree.' It wasn't exactly a fair negotiation—you know, gun and all. What would *you* have done?"

Detective Moses spoke up.

"Getting in the car took this from a routine mugging to an abduction. So it matters legally how it happened. A much bigger sentence for them. But getting in that car was a huge mistake—half the people who get in that car never live to tell about it."

Dylan shuddered at the statistic.

"But I thought you said this didn't happen that much."

"It doesn't," Moses said. "But when it does, the statistics are grim for those who get in the car. Fatal mistake."

Back to the principal's office.

"Well, like I said, I offered them the card. They demanded we drive, and since they had a gun and there were two of them"—his volume rose in frustration—"I felt like I had no choice."

Both detectives jotted down more notes as if this was critical evidence.

"Then what happened?"

Dylan described arriving at the first ATM and informing the abductors about the limits on withdrawals.

A heavy knock shook the wood door, interrupting him.

"Come in," Moses said.

The door whisked open, and in stepped Chief Buck Reinhart. The chief stood about 5'11", with short-cropped wheat-blond hair that was graying on the sides, intense hazel eyes, and a square chin with a pronounced dimple. A pink scar ran from below his right eye, diagonally down his cheek, to the corner of his thin, colorless upper lip. That, his leathery skin, and a pronounced Roman nose made him look like a warrior. Which was fitting, since he always carried himself with a field general's bearing, ramrod straight and formal in every way.

The two detectives turned his way, backs straightening.

"Sir," Moses said, standing up.

Dylan followed her lead.

"Sorry to hear this happened to you, Councilman," the chief said, always a few decibels louder than necessary. "But you're in good hands—the best detectives on the force."

"Honestly, Chief, it was just a mugging. I'm fine. They took a few hundred bucks, and in the end, they didn't even hurt me. You've got bigger fish to fry than putting your top people on this."

"Dylan, you're a member of the city council," the chief said, flashing a crooked smile. "This is as serious as it gets for us. We need to send a loud and clear message. Bottom line, this team will take care of it. It'll be a long night as we gather every detail while it's fresh, but then we'll spare no expense to get to the bottom of this."

"Thank you, Chief. But please, no special treatment."

The chief nodded back, cryptically, but said nothing. He looked at both Buzz Cut and Mustache, then turned and exited as quickly as he entered.

In the minutes that followed, Dylan described withdrawing cash from the first ATM, making the failed second attempt, then driving downtown.

"So they wanted to try other machines?" Mustache asked, chuckling. "Obviously that wasn't going to work."

"No, that was my idea."

"*You* told them to go to more machines?" Mustache asked, smirk disappearing.

Anger billowed up within, which Dylan knew would show up as red splotches on his cheeks. From his childhood on, he'd never had a good poker face.

"Yeah. I had a guy behind me telling a guy next to me to put a bullet in my brain. So it felt like a smart way to keep them happy. I didn't think it would work either."

The detectives jotted down more notes.

"But you at least offered to get them more money?" Buzz Cut asked.

Dylan shook his head. "I wouldn't put it that way."

"Well, how would you put it?"

"I wanted to convince them not to shoot me."

* * *

For an hour, Dylan answered question after tedious question, all the way through to the saga's end. As he described peering up from the passenger seat to see an empty Oregon Street, he shifted in his chair.

Almost done.

But the detectives kept right on going, alternating between standing and sitting as if playing a game of musical chairs.

"So you went right to your law firm after?" Mustache asked.

"I did. Home didn't seem like a good idea."

"And what time did you get there?"

"I guess around 8:15."

The detective tilted his phone, reading something from the screen. He frowned as he looked back up.

"You didn't call 911 until 8:32. What did you do in between?"

"I made a couple calls to let people know what happened. But what does that have to—"

"Who'd you call?"

"Well, you know the woman I told you about? The number I was getting from my car?"

Mustache paged back through his notes. "Right. Stephanie? Your girlfriend?"

"Yes, Steph. But, no, not a girlfriend. Like I said, it was gonna be our first date. Anyway, I called her to tell her."

Buzz Cut now looked up from his notes, eyes coming to life. "Just a first date, huh? And she's the first call you made after thinking you were going to die?"

"Well, I had kept her waiting—"

"And you wanted to explain why you were so late."

Recognizing the echo from the beginning of the interview—the first reason they'd listed for why people falsely report abductions—Dylan nodded.

"I did."

Frowning, Buzz Cut jotted down more notes before looking back up.

"Did you tell her what happened?"

"Yes. The basics, at least."

"And how'd you leave the call?"

Dylan grinned. "I told her I still wanted to have dinner, which was true."

Mustache's sparse eyebrows danced.

"Really? What'd she say?"

"To call you guys."

Buzz Cut spoke up. "So it was *her* idea to call 911? Not yours?"

Dylan leaned back in his chair.

"Initially, yes. I was going to call, of course. But all I can tell you is that at that moment, I was so excited to be free, I just wanted have a good steak and some wine. That may sound strange, but I guess you don't know how you'll react until it happens to you."

Mustache spoke again. "With respect, sir, we talk to victims every day. We know how they react."

"Fair enough."

"So *then* you called 911?"

"No, I called my parents. Told them what happened."

"And what did they say?"

"Mom freaked out. And then said—"

"To call the cops," Mustache said.

"Exactly. So I did."

"At 8:32."

"If you say so."

"I do. And what did you do after that call?"

"I waited, then came down the elevator."

"So no more calls?"

"No more calls."

"You text anyone?"

"My phone was taken, remember?"

Mustache smirked, his mustache lifting on both sides. "That's right!"

Detective Moses stood up and leaned against the back of her chair.

"Councilman, I know this is not a fun process," she said with a sympathetic tone. "But we need to get a record of every detail when they're most fresh in your head."

She was a master of the "good cop" role.

"I get it."

"Is there anything else you can remember that we should know?"

Dylan paused. Thought.

"No. That's it."

The two other detectives stood up and walked out of the room, not saying a word.

Before the door closed, in walked a new woman in uniform. She looked far younger than the others, with light umber skin and a short Afro of curly black hair parted halfway across her forehead. Unlike everyone else he'd encountered thus far, she gave Dylan a warm smile, her round, chestnut eyes sparkling.

"Councilman, this is Officer McKee, our forensic artist. She'll be sketching pictures of the guys who grabbed you."

Chapter 9

"I never got a good look at either of them."

The fact that Deputy Chief Prince was still watching over it all, stone-faced and silent, had evolved from a source of comfort to a cause for concern. But Dylan tried to ignore him.

"Do your best, sir," Officer McKee said politely. "Think about any specific details that stuck out. Anything distinctive."

Dylan had already described his abductors' heights, builds, and attire, which he'd taken in as soon as the two cornered him.

But the details of their faces were fuzzy.

"They both wore dark sunglasses. And the kid in the back had a Bears cap pulled down pretty low."

"Okay. Well, my job is to help you remember key features. Let's try this. I'm going to show you some heads. Try to pick out the one that most resembles each of them."

She leafed through several pages of photos, all with different head shapes.

Dylan picked out one round head—the kid with the gun. Then a long face—the kid in back.

"His head was smaller too," Dylan added.

With a thick pencil, Officer McKee sketched broad strokes on one piece of paper, then did the same on a second. She tilted her head as she worked, with one strand of her tight curls plunging past her left eye.

"Skin color?" she asked, showing him several pages of options.

He picked a pale hue for the kid in front, and a dark hue for the kid in back. More sketching followed.

"What color hair?"

"Dark brown on the White one—the kid in front."

"Style?"

She showed him several options.

He pointed to a close-cropped style.

"Sort of like that. But shorter on top."

"That's a fade."

"Yes. Close to that."

She sketched on one piece of paper.

"And the other?"

"He had that hat on, remember."

"That's right." She paused, sketching again.

"You didn't see the color?"

"I'm afraid not."

Prince scowled like this was the wrong answer.

"And no hair fell below the hat?"

"Not that I saw."

"Noses?"

"Pretty plain."

"Like any of these?" she asked, showing a number of photos, varying from bold Romans to sharp hawks.

"Sort of like those two," he said, pointing.

Dylan didn't feel confident enough to pick anything but nondescript, plain shapes. The last thing he wanted was for the cops to pick up some innocent kid because his nose resembled something he'd pointed to on the fly, exhausted.

She sketched some more.

"Mouths?"

Nothing had really stuck out, so he again went with plain. Average. He did the same for foreheads, cheeks, chins, and ears, but still, Officer McKee kept sketching away.

"Any other features? Scars, birthmarks, or anything?"

"Honestly, one guy was behind me the whole time, and the other—the one time I looked over at him, he barked at me to look forward. So I never got a great look. I guess I'd say he had higher cheekbones, and a chin that receded a little bit."

Prince exhaled loudly.

"Didn't you say the kid in the back walked you to the second ATM?" he asked.

McKee kept drawing.

"He did, but it was dark, and I never got a good look at him. Trust me, I wish I had."

Prince sighed. For minutes, the furtive scraping of graphite along paper was the only sound in the room, interrupted by the softer rubs of an eraser. Office McKee tilted her head at various angles as she sketched, the strand waving to and fro.

A new detail flashed in Dylan's mind—the profile of the kid in the front seat.

"Peach fuzz!" Dylan blurted out.

"Pardon me?" McKee asked, looking up.

"The guy in the front had some peach fuzz on his chin. And above his lips. Oh, and some pockmarks on his cheeks."

Without looking up, McKee nodded and kept sketching, wide eyes glimmering as she pursed her lips tightly.

A minute later, her expression relaxed as she laid her pencil down. She lifted both pieces of paper up, squinting as she assessed them one last time. Like an artist revealing a masterpiece, she flipped them over so Dylan could see them.

"How do these look?"

On the one hand, he was impressed. They captured pretty accurately what he saw and remembered.

"Not bad."

The problem was, they also captured the fact that he hadn't recalled much detail. Two faces, one Black, one White, hidden behind sunglasses, one wearing a Bears hat, the other with short brown hair and some peach fuzz.

"Any adjustments?" she asked.

"No. That's pretty much as I remember them."

Dylan grimaced, imagining dozens of kids being picked up because these drawings were so nondescript.

"Sorry I couldn't be more specific. These could be any one of thousands of kids this age."

Officer McKee nodded. "It's fine. You were driving, it was dark, and you thought you might get killed. You saw what you saw, and I did my best to capture it. Narrows it down at least."

"Thank you."

She looked at Prince.

"I'll go ahead and file these."

His thick arms folded, Prince watched as she stepped out of the room, drawings in hand.

He stood up, towering over a seated Dylan.

"We're almost done. Only one more task for the night."

"What's that?" Dylan asked, failing to suppress a yawn.

Prince lifted a packed ring of keys out of his pocket.

"We're going for a ride."

Chapter 10

With a young officer driving the dark, unmarked SUV, Dylan, Moses, and Prince retraced the entire route.

Prince expressed skepticism at every stop.

First they headed up one side of Mount Adams, through the now hopping bar district, then down the quieter Celestial Street, where townhomes on one side faced the steps of Immaculata, the Catholic church that towered over the entire neighborhood.

"Nice places here," Prince said, looking to his right.

They pulled up to a stop sign at the bottom of Celestial.

"So where did you first see them?" Moses asked, polite as always.

"Right after you turn down Hill," Dylan said, pointing down and to the left.

The SUV turned left, now aiming straight down the steep grade of Hill Street, like a ski jumper in the gate. Then inched down the hill.

"I parked there. Right in front of my house. That yellow one there."

"So even though you thought they looked suspicious, you parked and went in?"

"I didn't say suspicious, per se. More that they stuck out."

"Okay. And once you got inside, you were basically safe from these two people who, as you say, 'stuck out.'"

"I guess I was, I just didn't know it."

"And two minutes later, you walked *back* outside, *right in front* of them?" Moses asked.

Prince spoke up. "Sort of like seeing a shark fin in the water, then diving in anyway."

41

After a few more loaded questions about that decision, they moved on.

"So this is where they first attacked you?" Moses asked, the car idling a few yards down from Dylan's house.

"More like confronted. I reached into the car through the passenger side door, and when I turned around, they were both right on top of me. And the one had a gun pointed right at my chest."

Prince grunted. "I thought you said stomach before."

"Well, sort of mid-level—lower chest, upper stomach."

"Gotcha," Moses said. "And that's when you told them you had no money and offered to drive them to ATMs."

"I didn't offer—they insisted."

* * *

Minutes later, after driving up and through a now dark Eden Park, they pulled up to the First American ATM machine Dylan had visited four hours before.

"How much did you take out?" Moses asked.

"$250, the first time."

"Then you tried again?"

"Yes, I asked for $50 more, and that was declined."

"And you handed the bills to the guy in front?"

"Sure did."

"And what did you do with the receipt?"

Dylan froze.

"I don't recall. Obviously I took the card back. But I don't remember grabbing the receipts."

"Do you usually take receipts?"

"Of course. They build up in my wallet pretty quick."

"Hey, Jimmy," Prince said, looking over at the driver. "See if you can find the receipts out there."

Jimmy backed the SUV up a few feet and got out, a small flashlight in his left hand.

"So after you were declined, you proposed trying other machines?"

"I did. They were pretty upset. I didn't want them taking it out on me."

The beam from Jimmy's flashlight danced around all parts of the ATM. The machine itself. The ground below it. The driveway within several feet of it.

"But you say you knew it wouldn't work?"

"I knew it was unlikely, but I wanted them to see I was trying to help them. I wanted to stay in control. Honestly, it worked pretty well."

"Until they blindfolded you."

"Right."

The driver door opened, and Jimmy got back in the SUV.

"Any luck?" Moses asked.

"I actually found two . . ."

Good, Dylan thought.

"One still in the dispenser from, like, a half hour ago."

"And the other?"

"On the ground. A withdrawal at 7:32 . . ."

Dylan knew that couldn't be it. Too late by a few minutes.

"Some woman named Tammy something-or-other."

"So no receipts from the councilman?" Prince asked.

"Nope."

* * *

"So what did he look like?" Moses asked.

They were pulled over on Main, a block south of the courthouse, the SUV idling as Jimmy searched the second ATM. After grilling Dylan on why he hadn't run away once out of the car, they turned the subject to the man who'd asked for money.

"The panhandler? White guy. Big beard. Knit cap. Wrapped in a big jacket or blanket of some sort, so hard to say too much else. Bigger than a lot of the folks you see out here."

"As in overweight?" Moses asked.

"No, bigger as in built, from what I could tell. Not skinny like most of the people you see on the street."

43

Moses wrote this down.

"He also had pretty distinct eyes," Dylan added.

"Distinct how?"

"Wide—like spaced far apart. Intense, almost bulging."

She kept writing.

"Maybe he's still up there? Don't about a dozen or so sleep there most nights?"

"Not lately," Prince said. "We started clearing them out a few weeks ago, at 10 p.m. on the nose. Mayor's orders. It's empty now."

Made sense. The judges and lawyers had been complaining about the stench of urine at Courthouse Square, demanding the mayor do something. He'd come down hard on the chief for letting it go on for so long. Publicly.

Webb thought it was all overblown, but he hadn't wanted to fight about it. These poor people needed help, not harassment. That's why he always gave them that resource card. But you had to pick your battles.

* * *

Ten minutes later, they were heading back up to Mount Adams— the part of the route that Webb hadn't seen the first time.

"At least you're consistent," Prince quipped. "No receipts at any machine."

Dylan didn't bother responding, but Moses broke the silence.

"Councilman, you had an hour with these two. What did you talk about with them?"

Dylan chuckled.

"Well, up until this point, I was trying to give the best political speech I could muster. I figured if they'd want to vote for me, they wouldn't want me dead."

"And how'd you make them want to vote for you?"

"Oh, I talked about my work on the council. How I was trying to support youth in our city. Pushing for investment in some of our poorest neighborhoods. Filled them in on the reforms I've been pushing for . . ."

Oops. Not a good topic, but he couldn't stop now.

". . . better police relations."

Reinhardt and Prince were livid about the measures Webb and his colleagues were pushing, campaigning against them publicly. Changes to use-of-force guidelines. Requiring outside investigations of police-involved shootings and citizen complaints. Tracking how many times officers pulled their weapons. And other changes. It was all an invitation to more crime, Reinhardt had been telling the media with great effect, Prince always nodding at his side. But since the recent spate of police-involved shootings and national headlines, the council was poised to enact them in the coming months. The big question was whether the mayor would veto them.

Prince chuckled.

"You gotta love the irony of you telling two armed thugs, as they *kidnapped* you, how hard you're working to reform *us*."

"You gotta do what you gotta do to stay alive."

"Don't we cops know *that*," Prince replied. "Yeah, I bet they loved hearing about you tying our hands."

Webb said nothing.

After more awkward silence, Moses pivoted back to their conversation.

"So they knew who you were?"

"What makes you say that?"

"You said you told them about your council work."

"Yes. But that was after I said who I was."

"Wait a second, you *told them* you were a councilman?"

"I did. Like I said, I wanted to win them over."

Prince's shadowed head shook in disbelief.

"Is there something wrong with that?" Webb asked.

"Well, yeah. For a lot of criminals, that would've put a much bigger target on your back," Moses said. "Either because they would assume you were loaded. Or because it meant we'd pursue the case far more seriously."

"Or both," Prince interjected.

* * *

"Down there?" Jimmy asked from the top of a steep hill.

"Yes, maybe fifty feet down."

They turned a slight right and headed back down Oregon, the road where they'd left Dylan in the Jeep—blindfolded, arms wrapped around his head, counting one hundred heartbeats.

"Right about here."

The SUV stopped. As before, a bright light illuminated the street as well as the inside of the SUV.

"So they told you to stay here, and ran off?" Moses asked.

"They weren't sure what to do at first. Argued a little bit. Then left, thank God."

"You should consider yourself one lucky man."

"I do."

"Funny," Price interjected, although he wasn't laughing. Not even smiling.

"What's that, sir?" Moses asked.

"Just how well lit this street is. With a large condo tower looking right down over it. About the worst place you'd want to bring a kidnapping to a close."

Dylan's mood darkened again. They'd now raised doubts about every part of his story—even how it ended.

"At least it means there may be more witnesses who saw what happened from one of the condos," he said.

"It sure does," Moses said. "We'll be sure to knock on those doors in the next few days. Any witness would help you at this point."

Dylan sunk further in his seat. Even the "good cop" now doubted him.

THURSDAY

Chapter 11

"Show of hands? Who believes him?"

Not a single hand went up in the WKYC-TV newsroom in answer to news director Rick Temple's question. Instead came a few laughs, and one sarcastic, "Right!"

Maggie Coyle sat quietly but wasn't about to raise her hand.

Several copies of the *Cincinnati Enquirer* front page lay in the middle of the station's conference room table.

The large photo of Councilman Dylan Webb leaving his law firm was a tough look for a politician known for valuing his good looks. His sandy blond hair, usually parted neatly to one side before flaring back, was disheveled. His blue suit was a crumpled mess. And the frown across his face was only made worse by the shadowy lighting. He was sandwiched between two cops, like a perp walk for some rich guy who'd done something very wrong and very embarrassing.

But the coup de grace was the headline above the photo. It was accurate, of course. But a single loaded word tainted Webb's entire narrative.

Councilman Says He Was Abducted.

Says.

On the surface, none of it added up. And the *Enquirer* headline wouldn't have read that way if police higher-ups hadn't signaled off the record that it was all bullshit.

Cops who'd been around knew what she knew—people make shit like this up all the time, for all sorts of reasons.

"Okay. Who wants to cover it?" the stout, square-jawed Temple asked.

This time Maggie lifted her hand high in the air, as did four hungry young reporters seated around the table.

If this was a beauty contest, Maggie thought, she'd surely finish in fifth. But the story was right up her alley—a great break from the dreary crime stories that took up most days.

Temple pointed her way.

"You guys know the rules around here. If Coyle wants it, Coyle gets it."

A former police detective with the wrinkled forehead and scattered gray hairs to prove it, she knew how to dig into cases better than the young'uns who were in town for three-year stints before leaping to bigger markets. And she was friends with a lot of cops. That combination made her the best investigative reporter in town, and from reporters to cops to criminal defense lawyers, everyone knew it.

"Thanks, Rick. I'll let you know if I can use anyone's help."

"Please do. We want to be the station that breaks this thing wide open."

"Get that guy, Maggie," growled one producer from across the table, grinning from ear to ear.

She understood why he said it. And why none had raised their hands to the first question.

It wasn't just cynicism.

Sure, Dylan Webb was smarter than most local politicians, and he had stood up to powerful people in his short time on the council. He had chutzpah and charisma, maybe without even realizing it. She was fine with all that. And others would be too.

But it was the way he did it.

He came across as a pretentious, privileged prick. In how he treated reporters, cops, and just about everyone else.

It wasn't intentional. Other politicians were rougher, or ruder, or more pompous. But Webb—he was always in a rush, as if the person right in front of him never mattered. The smartest guy in the room. And absolutely terrible at hiding it. Something about his cleft, dimpled chin and chiseled jawline only made it all worse.

It was a never-ending performance of earnestness bordering on self-righteous. Like he was some sort of Lone Ranger. A self-appointed savior. And in proud Cincinnati, no one turned people off more than a self-righteous know-it-all, no matter how well-intentioned.

Cincinnati didn't need saving.

Most assumed he was doing it all to be the next mayor. Or maybe Congress. So a lot of people would be celebrating this morning, hoping to take him down a few rungs if not knock him off the ladder completely.

But that wasn't how she felt. She'd seen too many falls to take glee in them anymore. Including her own.

If he had fucked up as bad as it looked, it was just plain sad.

Either way, how she felt didn't matter. Her job was to get the facts. To expose the truth.

And if that meant Dylan Webb's career crashed and burned, so be it.

Chapter 12

"Wild guess, Maggie. You want the skinny on the Webb abduction."

Calling from her desk, which in the crammed newsrooms of today amounted to no more than a cubbyhole, Maggie Coyle chuckled as Sergeant Shirley Meadows answered her home line. They'd been in the same recruit class, then later overlapped as homicide detectives for a few years.

"Wait, you don't even say hello anymore?" Maggie asked.

"What's the point? I know you too well for small talk when you're on a case."

"I plead guilty. But since you brought up the topic, what's the word?"

Meadows' tone changed. "I think you know."

"Know what?"

"How shaky it looks."

"Looks, or is?"

"Both. I mean, how many of these have we seen made up in the last couple years? Even that one actor in Chicago—sent cops on a wild goose chase, then totally ruined his career."

Maggie's eyes widened. They really didn't believe him.

"Did Shawna interview him?"

"Yes, but Prince sat through it all. Even drove the route with them."

"Wow. They're not fucking around."

"That, and babysitting as well."

Detectives hated top brass looking over their shoulder. And Prince was the chief's personal pit bull.

"For sure. Who else talked to him?"

"Jeffress and Vogel."

"Jesus."

Maggie had had run-ins with both when she'd been their supervisor. Both assholes. But also badass investigators. Close to the chief. If she'd done something wrong, that's the last duo she'd want asking her questions. Or watching her as she answered.

"Well, how'd he do?"

"I don't have the full lowdown yet. But I gather from that headline, not well."

"I thought the same. That had to have come right from the chief."

"You know it."

A long pause, then Meadows added more.

"Word is he talked a ton. No lawyer. He offered up lots of details. If they don't check out, he's screwed."

"Babe in the woods."

"Indeed. I almost feel bad for the guy."

"Almost?"

"Yes. Almost. But not quite. He sort of has it coming."

"My guess is a lot of people think that."

"So many, including his own colleagues," she said.

"On the council?"

She nodded.

"More than anyone. People get tired of a Boy Scout."

* * *

"I can't give you those, Maggie. You know that."

Police departments leaked like sieves. But private companies like First American Bank had walls thicker than Fort Knox. And no one was tighter-lipped than First American's head of security, Tommy Dean.

"Tommy, I don't need the tapes myself. But have you sent them over at least?"

He didn't answer.

"You can tell me that. They'll be out soon enough."

"Yeah, we sent them over first thing. Maybe half an hour after they were requested."

"Did you see them?"

"Honestly, I didn't. Just sent them over."

Honestly was usually a tip-off that the opposite was on its way.

"C'mon. You didn't watch them?"

"I didn't. That's a few levels below my pay grade. We do things by the book here. I told our tech guys to get the footage over as soon as possible, which they did."

"Okay."

Once in public hands, she could get them.

"And no one else watched them?"

"Maggie, they didn't. We don't want to have any part of this."

Smart.

"It's in your hands now."

"You mean the cops' hands," Coyle said.

"Same difference."

Maggie shook her head, her straight, toffee-brown hair falling off her shoulders.

It's what they all assumed. If they only knew how complicated things really were.

* * *

"Jason, you're about to get an email requesting the Webb 911 call," Maggie Coyle said as she made the short drive up into Mount Adams.

"10-4."

Maggie's big journalistic advantage was her deep connections into the bowels of the Cincinnati Police Department. The cops who knew everything, but who no one else in the media knew. Old, trusted friends she'd come up with in the department—at the academy, working shifts, closing cases.

But when it came to the formal interaction with the communications section, she had no better standing than other reporters. Probably worse. Jason Day, the department's communications director, was close to the chief. And the chief was still mad at her—always would be. So she did her best to avoid him and his tight coterie of loyalists.

As she'd learned painfully, tangling with the chief wasn't worth it. If she ever crossed the line, he had the power to cut her off completely. And if that order ever came down from headquarters, that'd be the end of her career. A second time.

"I'd like to get them as soon as possible today."

"I hear ya. We'll send them to you when we send them to everyone."

"Gee, thanks. As in by noon? I'm trying to provide an update then."

"Probably."

"Oh, and the email also requests the tapes from the bank cameras."

"Not sure we have those—"

"I confirmed that you've already gotten them."

"*I* haven't gotten anything yet. If our tech guys got them, they're processing them now. Which means you're not getting them till they're done."

This was code for waiting weeks or months.

"We've been through this before. Those are the bank's tapes. They made them. Which means once you have them, we get them when we ask."

"You can ask. You'll get them when you get them."

She let a long pause serve as her protest. Then upped it a notch.

"By the way, the request is coming directly from our lawyer."

"But of course."

Maggie hung up as she parked on Hill Street, next to the house that voting records indicated Dylan Webb resided in. And a damn nice house at that.

Chapter 13

Having slept in at his parents' condo high atop East Walnut Hills, Dylan Webb drove their Cadillac into town and parked it at his designated spot a block from Cincinnati city hall.

As he did every time he approached city hall, Dylan gazed upward. While its main structure was only four stories high, almost everything about the 130-year-old building was far more imposing. From its perch on the western end of downtown, the building's nine-story clock tower, tall steeples, and triangular roofs peered out over the city like a fortress. And its columns, high arches, and hefty auburn and ochre stones, set against small windows in the upper floors, created the illusion that the building was taller than it actually was.

Dylan walked below the looming tower and up the building's gray front steps. Security guards watched over his entrance as they did any other day. He nodded and waved like always, then trudged up two sets of grand marble stairs, past large panes of colorful stained-glass windows.

The third floor was always crowded early in the week, building up to Wednesday's council meeting. But come Thursdays, the place emptied out—not only the chambers where the council met but most of the offices too. So Webb walked down the hallway and into his small office without encountering a soul.

Gabby Moore, his diminutive chief of staff, looked up at him as he shut the office door behind him, her usual warm smile replaced by a long frown.

"I called and texted you for hours. You okay?" she asked.

"They took my phone. Can't imagine how many messages I haven't responded to. But yeah, I'm okay."

"You've gotten tons of calls here too. So many people sending their love and prayers. You're a blessed person."

Dylan shrugged.

"I'm not feeling very blessed."

He sat down in a small metal chair across from Gabby, who sported the same chin-length bob of long black curls she'd had when she'd first volunteered on his campaign. While most volunteers came and went, her tenacity and fearlessness quickly propelled her to be his most trusted counsel. Gabby's dad was a civil rights lawyer, so she'd spent her life breathing the politics Dylan was still learning. And growing up in Bond Hill, a predominantly Black, middle-class neighborhood north of Cincinnati, she knew the parts of the city he rarely encountered from his genteel East Side stomping grounds.

"I can imagine. It's all over social media and talk radio."

"Is it?" Dylan asked. "So what are they saying?"

Her round, copper eyes widened further.

"Oh, Dylan, you don't want to know."

* * *

"You're damn right I was calm," Dylan said after Gabby explained the immediate skepticism that his 911 call was too subdued. "I was free and not in danger anymore, so I've never been calmer."

"People expect 911 callers to be freaking out. And you obviously weren't."

"Those callers are in the midst of the crime taking place," Dylan said, agitated. "Mine was over. I'd been trapped in a car thinking I was a goner—but when I called I was free. So yeah, I admit it—I couldn't have been happier."

She let a few seconds pass before delivering more bad news.

"And, Dylan, they're saying the same about what you said to the cameras last night. At your law firm. That you looked too pleasant."

His temper flared as if he were back with Mustache and Buzz Cut.

"I may be new, but I've been around politics long enough to know you don't want to glower in front of TV cameras. Hell, people already accuse me of being too serious. So yes, I tried to look pleasant without saying much."

"I know, Dylan. Somehow we're gonna have to explain that."

Dylan picked up the phone on her desk.

"Which station is talking this way? I'll explain it right now."

"Dylan," she said sheepishly.

"Yes?"

"They *all* are. Conservative and liberal. Black and White. We're going to need a plan way beyond you calling in and getting mad."

He put his head in his hands, trying to calm down.

"And there's one other piece of bad news," Gabby said.

"What's that?"

"You're trending on Twitter and TikTok."

To save himself from distraction and wasted time, Dylan had stopped tweeting after the election. Gabby managed the accounts for him, with license to fire away day and night, only seeking Dylan's approval for the most edgy tweets.

"How bad?"

"Terrible. It's exploding. And all with the same awful hashtag." She tailed off.

"What is it?"

"Okay. But you're gonna—"

"Just tell me!"

"Okay. It's #Webboflies. And it's gone totally viral."

Chapter 14

"That doesn't sound like someone who feared for his life."

Rick Temple smirked as he said it. He and Maggie Coyle were reviewing Webb's 911 call in his office, with the recording about to lead their noon broadcast.

Maggie nodded but didn't say anything.

First, she was concentrating. Running late, she was applying the blush that kept her round cheeks from appearing too pale and her arched nose from looking too pointy, realities of her face that the camera would magnify without small touch-ups. Last week's round of Botox at least meant she didn't have to worry about her forehead.

Second, she'd learned early on that victims reacted in a variety of ways to the trauma of crime. So she resisted assuming how a victim should respond or judging how they actually did.

Temple replayed the tape a third time, pausing after each sentence, as Maggie brushed her hair out to its full length below her shoulders, trying to extract a slight curl at the ends. After weeks of close observation, the station's consultants had said that was the look viewers best responded to, along with lower-cut shirts and blouses that accentuated her "hourglass figure," as their report officially termed it.

"At least he didn't name-drop his title," Maggie said. Public figures usually expected special treatment when they called the cops. But here, the call-taker was the one who identified Webb as a member of the council.

But that one positive was drowned out by other odd aspects of the call.

He spoke slowly. Methodically. Nearly monotone.

He didn't sound alarmed. Or scared. Or even excited.

Instead, he came across as detached emotionally from the events he was describing. Calm as can be—as if he were reporting what he'd had for dinner or worn to work that day. Not that he'd just faced the deadly end of a gun for an hour.

The way he said, "That's me," bordered on chipper.

His tone left the impression that the call itself was a chore. That he'd made it because he *had* to. Not because he wanted to.

She resisted telling Temple she agreed with him. She'd withhold judgment.

But airing this tape would only heighten the doubt. And it was about to air on every television station in town—and likely far beyond that. This was the type of raw human drama that went national, especially if people suspected someone famous made something up.

And after hearing this tape, that's what everyone would think.

Chapter 15

Gabby stepped into Dylan's doorway.

"It's a Detective Moses on the phone."

The good cop.

"Great."

She transferred the call to Dylan, who'd spent the prior hour on the phone with his parents and younger sister, close friends, and the city manager, all while responding to the hundreds of emails that had overwhelmed his inbox overnight. His calls to his council colleagues and the mayor had gone to voicemail.

"Hey, Detective. Hope you got some rest. Anything to report?"

"We've got your phone and wallet back."

"Already?"

"Sure do. They were in a garbage can at the top of the street."

"The one they left me on?"

"No. Hill Street. Where it levels out at the top."

Maybe twenty yards from his house.

"Weird," Webb said. "Why would they have . . ."

He stopped asking.

Moses didn't say a word.

Webb then remembered the conversation in the car.

"Any ATM receipts?"

"I'm afraid not."

"Anything else?"

"Just have a few guys checking with neighbors. Another asking around at that condo above where they left you. Seeing if anyone saw anything."

"Did they?"

"Nothing to report yet. Will let you know."

They hung up.

Ten minutes later, Gabby called through the open doorway again.

"Dylan, it's your neighbors. They say they need to talk to you right away."

"My neighbors?"

"Yeah. The Schunks. They say it's urgent."

He barely knew the Schunks, who had moved in two doors down the hill the prior year.

"Okay. Patch them through."

Chapter 16

Over several decades, one house at a time, Mount Adams had morphed from a run-down, gritty neighborhood of poor Irish and German immigrants to a high-end urban enclave of yuppies and empty nesters. As the new wave moved in, refurbished homes and higher property values pushed the old working-class families down the hill into Cincinnati's East End, abutting the river, or even further.

The Schunks' property was the last on Hill Street to be upgraded. The old two-story house had sat empty for years, trash piled up to the windows—an eyesore obstructing a perfect view of the Ohio. Their whole-house rehab had taken more than a year, annoying the neighbors with noise and a hulking gray dumpster that took up precious parking space. But when it was done, it was the grandest house on Hill, modern and cascading four stories down the steep hillside.

Dylan had always wanted to see the inside, but today was not the day for the grand tour.

George and Linda Schunk, in their late fifties, answered the door together, both looking fit in trendy-looking athletic gear. After friendly introductions, they led Dylan into the living room, where the bay window opened out to the river. A far better view than his.

They sat down on a dark leather couch while he sat in a black chair that looked like a piece of modern art.

"Thanks for calling. What's happening?"

They hadn't shared anything on the call.

"We called you right away," Linda said, alarm in her voice and a frown weighing down her usually sprightly face. She took a sip from a teacup, but as she moved it away from her lips, it shook in her hand.

"I appreciate that. Did you guys happen to see anything last night?"

"No, it's not that," George said through a grim look that matched his wife's. "The police left about an hour ago."

Dylan nodded casually. "Yeah, they told me they'd be talking to neighbors to look for any leads."

"Well, I'm afraid that's not what happened here," George said.

"What do you mean?"

"We did spend the first few minutes on whether we saw anything last night," Linda said, looking uncomfortable. "But we didn't. We got home after nine. And that's what we told them."

"Okay."

"But then they spent the next hour asking about *you*."

"Me? For an hour? What about me?"

"Everything. How well we know you. Any habits you have. When you get home at night. If you ever didn't come home. If we ever see you with other people at night or in the morning."

"Other people?"

"Yeah. They asked about women. Men." A long pause. "Teenagers."

"Teenagers?" Dylan asked, simmering with anger.

"Yes, teenagers," Linda said, grimacing. "The whole line of questioning felt totally out of line."

"Okay. I get the picture. What did you say?"

"The truth," George said. "That we didn't know you that well. That you basically came and went like everyone else. Left home before we did—"

"When I work out."

"Which was our guess. That you seemed to work all the time and not have much of a social life—"

"Sad but accurate."

Linda took another sip of tea, then continued.

"George finally got annoyed and asked them what kind of investigation this was."

"What did they say?"

"They got shitty. Said all these facts were relevant to the case . . ."
Dylan rolled his eyes.

"And that's when they said the part that so upset us."

She looked over at her husband, who cleared his throat.

"They said we shouldn't worry about crime on this street. That this looked more like a lovers' quarrel than a real holdup."

"Lovers' quarrel?" Webb asked, an echo of Buzz Cut's words from the night before. "And who are the so-called lovers?"

"They didn't say exactly. Either the person or people in the car with you, or someone who was waiting for you—"

"Or some combination of both," Linda interjected.

Dylan ground his teeth, raging inside.

"See why we called? We thought you should know."

"I do. And I appreciate it."

"I mean, if they say that to others, and it got out, you'd—"

"Trust me, I know. Did you get their names?"

Chapter 17

Slated to stop by police headquarters at 2:30 to retrieve his phone and wallet, Dylan stormed into the building twenty minutes early. He paced in the public lobby until a young officer ushered him into a small conference room, where Detective Moses and Deputy Chief Prince awaited.

Moses reached out, holding a plastic zipper bag containing both his wallet and phone.

"What the hell is going on?" Dylan yelled, glancing at Moses as he snatched the bag, then at Prince, who looked more familiar in his white uniform.

"Calm down, tiger," Prince said, both hands high in the air.

"You try being calm when cops are walking down your own street smearing *your* reputation."

"Wait! What happened?" Moses asked.

"Your two pit bulls from last night knocked on my neighbors' door, telling them I made this all up due to some lovers' quarrel," Dylan said, spitting out the last two words. "What the hell is that? Total bullshit. Who else are you guys saying that to?"

"Nobody," Moses said. "And if they said that, I'll be sure it doesn't happen again."

"*If?* They said it. I just left my neighbors' house, and they were sick about it."

Prince stepped forward.

"Councilman, I'm going to need you to sit down. We need to talk."

"We've done enough talking. All night, I recall."

"I'm afraid we haven't. Take a seat."

It was a tone he hadn't used before. Not sarcastic. Not snarky. But deadly serious. And it stopped Dylan in his tracks.

He sat down. Moses and Prince did the same on the other side of the cheap, oval-shaped table.

"Councilman," Moses said gently, "your story isn't checking out."

Dylan shook his head, eyes widening as he clenched his right fist. "What do you mean it's not checking out?"

"Nothing you described is adding up."

"*What's* not adding up? It happened exactly as I said it did."

Prince jumped in. "Nothing we've found confirms it. And I mean nothing."

Dylan sat in silence as Prince walked through the list. He wasn't playing the bad cop anymore. Worse. More like a disappointed father.

"First, so much of the story makes little sense. We told you these things are rare to begin with—"

"But—"

"But if it happened as you said," Prince interrupted back, "there'd be evidence confirming it. Something. But there isn't squat."

"You mean the ATM receipts? They could've been taken by someone else. Or blown away, for God's sake. Hell, I might've declined to receive them."

"We're not just talking receipts," Moses said softly. Frowning.

"What else?"

"The bank tapes."

"You have them? What about them?"

"We do."

"And do you see me?"

"Yes. You're there, front and center."

"See?" Dylan said, buoyed.

"But you're the only one. Just a guy, by himself, withdrawing money."

Dylan recalled the scene. The kid was right behind him in the car, literally breathing against his neck.

"In the car? Well, it was dark by then—maybe it was hard to see the passenger."

"And by the courthouse. It's well lit, and you're there standing, typing away. But you're alone."

"That can't be true. He was right there. Walked up next to me."

"No one's in the video, Councilman. No homeless guy. No teen next to you. Just you."

"What about evidence from the car? You've had it all day. Nothing in the car?"

"We looked for hair or prints in the front and back seat. Door handles too. And for any other evidence they were there."

"And?"

"Nothing but yours."

"Maybe they wiped it all before they left the car."

Prince shook his head, his bald scalp shining from the light above.

"The way you told the story, they would've hardly had time for that. Plus, two amped-up teens wouldn't have pulled that off—wouldn't have even thought of it. They were with you for a whole hour. We'd have found smudges at least."

A long pause.

There was more.

"Sir," Moses continued, "where we found your wallet and keys—right up the street from your own house? That also makes no sense."

Dylan shrugged.

"I can't explain that."

"We can't either. Why would anyone circle back that way?"

"Where they left me isn't that far from that spot. Maybe—"

"Why go in that direction, that close to your house again? That would risk being seen or caught. Criminals do all they can to avoid the scene of the crime."

Dylan couldn't disagree.

"And we found no prints—except yours—on either of those as well."

Dylan slumped lower into his seat.

"So what are you going to do?"

Prince looked at Moses to answer.

"Sir, at this point, it's best if you find yourself a good lawyer."

Dylan re-clenched his fist.

"I don't need a damn lawyer. Hell, I *am* a lawyer. And everything happened exactly as I said."

"We see no proof of that, sir," she said. "And unless that changes, we will have to announce that to the public. As I'm sure you're experiencing, the media is all over this story. They're demanding answers."

Dylan stared at her, speechless.

"And," Prince added, "we'll have to communicate to the prosecutor about charges."

"Charges?"

Jesus. Dylan had been publicly critical of the prosecutor, A. J. Magwood, for locking up too many young Black men and throwing away the key. Magwood would be licking his chops.

"Yes. You can't make up a crime like that and walk away. Really doesn't matter what—"

"I didn't make anything up," Dylan said, leaping to his feet. "It happened exactly like I said it did."

As he uttered the words, Dylan caught a glimpse of his reflection in the one window of the conference room. On his feet. Steel-blue eyes ablaze. Hair messily stretched back over the top of his head from having run his hand through it repeatedly. Shirt untucked. The wild image shocked him so much that he started to question himself.

Did it really happen the way he recalled? The way he described? Had he gotten things wrong?

He shut his eyes.

Details of the entire hour flashed by vividly. The same details he'd described the night before, and again to Gabby and his parents.

He sucked in deeply, then exhaled. He let his breaths slow, and his pulse along with it. More details replayed in his mind.

No, he assured himself. *It happened. He hadn't lost his mind. He'd done nothing wrong. It happened just as he said it did.*

"Councilman, you need to calm down."

Dylan opened his eyes. Moses was now also standing.

"It's best if you call a lawyer. As a lawyer, you know that. You shouldn't say anything more."

He turned back to Prince.

"Forget the damn lawyer. I want to talk to the chief."

Chapter 18

"Come on in, and shut the door."

Dylan stepped in, pulling the heavy door closed behind him.

In his pressed white uniform, with his thick, wiry hair combed perfectly straight, Chief Buck Reinhardt stood up behind an immense oak desk. Symbolic of his role in city government—ruling over the biggest budget by far, outlasting all the elected officials—the chief's office was as large as the mayor's, and better furnished. Plaques and framed newspapers adorned three walls and bookshelves behind him.

Above his shoulders, two prominent framed photos faced all visitors. The first was of Reinhart taking the oath as chief, fully blonde then, with far paler skin. The other was of a young Reinhart, standing in the middle of a photo of the scarlet-clad St. Timothy high school football team, holding a helmet against his right side. The twin images summed up why Reinhardt was the hero of the city's West Side, famous for populating both the NFL and the city's police force.

They were two floors up from where Dylan had met with Prince and Moses. The Deputy Chief had escorted the Councilman to the office but hadn't followed him in the door.

Dylan pulled the door closed, then turned back around.

"Have a seat."

The chief was an imposing figure, more so now than ever. They'd never met one-on-one before. And Dylan's entire career now rested in this man's hands. Reinhardt's credibility was untouchable in this town, so even a hint of doubt from him would be devastating.

Dylan sat down, his stomach in knots.

The chief rubbed his hand through his hair without shifting a single strand out of place.

"What a mess, Councilman," he said, frowning, as if Dylan had already pled guilty to a crime.

No choice but to push back.

"I'll say. Eighteen hours ago, I thought I might be shot, and now your people are threatening to ruin my career."

The chief slowly shook his head, pursing his lips tightly. Calm, but disappointed.

"I'm not sure what you want me to say. I put our best people on it. People I trust with my life." He paused. "I told them to do their best on a case that would get a lot of attention. To spare no expense to ensure we got it right."

He paused again. Then lifted his hands in the air.

"And after all that, they tell me your very unique story doesn't check out."

Dylan felt his body heating up. From the chief especially, the words struck like a punch to the face.

"Chief, it doesn't matter what they say. And unique or not, it happened exactly as I said it did. Cops should know better than anyone that victims don't conjure up the circumstances of their crime."

"Criminals don't disappear into thin air, either. Or do the things your story claims they did. At least, that we've ever seen."

He'd clearly been briefed.

"Chief, why would I make this up?"

"Only you know that, sir. It happens more than you think, for reasons I think were explained to you."

Fully briefed. And he'd made up his mind.

Dylan felt nausea setting in.

"Chief, I'll take a lie detector. Answer every question. Anything else you need. I did *not* make this up."

"Dylan, no need for any of that. Do yourself a favor. Get a good lawyer."

"The moment I get a lawyer is the moment I've announced to the world that it didn't happen. And that's the end of me. You know that!"

The chief's hazel eyes stared back for a few seconds, thumb and forefinger on his chin as if deep in thought.

"You really don't have a choice. Hell, we shouldn't even be having this conversation. What other suspect would be in this room right now?"

"Right, but I'm also a member of the city council."

The chief leaned forward, his small lips contorting into a snarl that twisted his scar into a zigzag.

"And for purposes of this case, that doesn't count for shit." It was the first time the chief had sworn in his presence. "From this point on, we're going to treat this like any other case. No special treatment."

The statement felt off, giving Dylan an opening.

"Chief, precisely because I'm on the council, it's *not* being treated like any other case, is it? It's a reality show at breakneck speed. And my impression is you guys are about to make some kind of statement."

The chief nodded.

"We plan on it. This afternoon, in fact. The media is going nuts. They know it's fishy. And I'd rather say it the right way—through a formal statement—than have things leak out through gossip."

His bushy eyebrows danced up and down as he said it.

"I think you yourself were complaining about that, no?"

He'd already heard about the Schunks.

"Yes. But just because your guys can't keep their mouths shut about a councilman they don't like doesn't mean you should rush some premature pronouncement. *That* is treating this different than other cases."

"They don't *like?*" the chief asked, angry for the second time.

"Sure. It's no secret that you guys hate the council's reform eff—"

"Don't you dare suggest that has anything to do with our response here," the chief said, lifting a few inches out of his seat.

The charge had struck a nerve. As Dylan had hoped.

"C'mon, Chief. Prince made a smart-ass crack about it only hours after I feared for my life. I'm the fifth vote on the reforms you guys hate so much, and you and everyone who works for you knows it."

The fifth vote, he heard himself say. The decisive vote. On a vote scheduled to take place in weeks. On changes the chief hated.

It was the first time the timing had dawned on him. If he were gone, the reforms probably would be as well.

The chief's face turned beet red, as it had at a few council meetings. He *hated* politicians telling him how to run his police department. That was his job.

"Now you sound downright delusional, Webb. You really think we're letting your reforms drive—"

"Some of the attitude I've gotten clearly stems from that."

"Don't flatter yourself. My team couldn't care less about your so-called reforms, as dangerous as they may be. My men answer to me, not you. Plus, we'll be here long after you're gone, even if you serve all eight years. Either way, they are handling this by the book."

"Right. Just speed-reading through it to get ahead of the internal gossip," Dylan said back, smiling. "Sounds completely standard."

The chief leaned back in his chair, looked down at his watch, then back at Dylan.

"Today's Thursday, right?"

Progress.

"Yes, sir."

"I'll tell you what. We'll hold back on saying anything until Monday."

Big progress.

"And what are you going to say in the meantime?"

"Nothing except that we're investigating every detail as best we can."

"And what about your uniformed gossips?"

"I'll be sure they keep their mouths shut. As I've already made clear to them."

"Thank you—"

"Before you thank me, know that there are public materials about the investigation we have to release. And they're not gonna look good."

"I get that. I've always been a stickler for public records. But thank you on the gossip."

"Don't thank me. *Listen* to me. Get yourself a lawyer by Monday. Hard to see anything changing in three days."

Chapter 19

"He met with investigators again today, along with the chief. Alone."

With her cameraman setting up outside city hall for a 6 p.m. hit, Maggie sat in the passenger seat of their van, filling Temple in as she reapplied blush and a fresh coat of red lipstick. The breeze outside meant that neither her hair nor her puffy windbreaker would satisfy the consultants' standards, which made this like most other live shots.

"And?"

"They don't believe him. And they told him as much. But now they're going to sit on that through the weekend."

"But we're not, right?"

"I think we're best off releasing the facts and evidence we've got so far. Some at six. Some at eleven. Then more tomorrow. They'll speak for themselves."

She'd gotten the camera footage from the ATMs mid-afternoon, where Webb looked to be withdrawing money all by himself. Shirley Meadows had told her that neither receipts nor fingerprints were found anywhere. And the drawings of the two suspects were uselessly generic.

"And what do they say?"

"Nothing good for Webb. Either he's got one hell of a creative streak, or he's got the worst luck of anyone I've ever seen."

"Where is he now?"

"He's been holed up inside city hall since getting back here around three. We have B-roll of him parking and walking inside."

"I saw it. It almost made me feel sorry for him."

She didn't say it, but she *did* feel sorry for him. TV cameras everywhere, including a CNN team. Talk radio going nuts. And on Twitter, the hashtag #Webboflies had gone viral, linked to painful close-ups of Webb alone at the ATMs. All that and the most recent shooting were putting a terrible spotlight on Cincinnati.

Her phone buzzed in her pocket.

"It's from inside city hall. Let me grab it."

"Okay. Break a leg."

"Is this Maggie?"

It was a woman's voice.

"It is. Who's this?"

"Gabby Moore."

Webb's chief of staff. Like her father, a tiger in a tiny body. But while he sued the city, she worked for it.

"Hey, Gabby, how can I help you?"

"We want to talk to you."

"Who's we? A lawyer? The councilman?"

"The councilman."

"On the record?"

"Eventually. And on air too. Stop up when you're done skewering us out there."

Chapter 20

Dylan Webb looked nothing like he had the last time they'd interviewed, when he was proudly touting his police reforms.

His eyes were glazed over. Exhausted.

The usual light-beige hue of his skin was now a grayish pallor.

His shirt was wrinkled, and his youthful sandy blond hair—always parted to the side—tumbled over his forehead in an unkempt mess.

Even in their casual greeting, his usually confident voice was weak, his always cocksure posture sagging.

Maggie couldn't blame him for the atrophy. She'd been through the wringer once herself. Less high profile than this, but she knew what he was going through, and what a toll it took. It's why she'd left, and why so many of the top brass still scorned her.

"You sure you want to do this?" she asked after Gabby fussed to get Webb in camera-ready shape.

"I'm damn sure," Webb said.

"No lawyer?"

"Nope. No need."

Usually a terrible decision, even if it made for better television.

"The cops will be watching everything you say. They'll replay it again and again, looking for inconsistencies. Same with the prosecutor."

He shrugged.

"You know what they say—if you're telling the truth, you don't have to have remember what you said."

"Or something like that," Maggie said, while thinking he was naive as hell. Memories of the truth aren't as clear as people think.

She'd seen plenty of cases go awry when human recollections didn't square with documented or recorded facts.

Gabby sat a few feet to Dylan's right, nervously thumbing her phone. This was clearly Webb's decision.

"Okay. Let's roll, Sam."

The bright light of the camera lit the small office, which barely contained the four of them along with the equipment.

"Councilman, thank you for agreeing to sit down with us. Obviously, our viewers have questions about what happened last night. And this is the first time you've addressed anyone in the media about it. Why are you choosing to talk now?"

"Thank you, Maggie. I've listened to enough talk radio today, and seen enough tweets, to know people are questioning my story. So I figured sitting down with you was the best way to set the record straight. I appreciate the opportunity."

She leaned forward.

"Dylan, it's not just social media or talk radio. Our understanding is that the police are struggling to find evidence backing up your story. Is that true?"

He wouldn't have expected a tough question this early, but he responded calmly.

"I've spent hours with the detectives, describing it all. I've been very impressed with their professionalism. And they're following up now. Let's see what they come up with in the coming days. It's been less than twenty-four hours."

That respectful answer confirmed what she'd heard—the chief had given him the weekend.

"Let's start at the top, then. Tell us what happened."

She let him go on at length about how it began, interrupting only at key moments that begged obvious questions, or when he left out a key detail.

"So why'd you go back outside then?" Maggie asked early on. "Seems like a careless decision."

He turned pink in the cheeks. "I was supposed to go on a date and needed the woman's number. I'd left it in the car."

This was new ground.

"I see. So you're single?"

"I am. I go out on dates occasionally, but usually work comes first."

"Can you tell us who the date was with?"

"For her privacy, I'd rather not say."

"But it was a woman?"

"Yes, it was."

"And only a first date?"

"Yes."

This was about to get painful.

"Have you heard the rumors that this was some type of spat with a girlfriend? Or even a boyfriend? Maybe even with multiple people? You know that's often why people make up being abducted."

He shook his head as his broad shoulders slumped forward.

"I've heard all of them," he said, sighing.

"And how do you respond?"

"That it happened just like I said it did. Others may make things up for all sorts of reasons, I get that. I didn't. This has nothing to do with personal relationships."

He looked right into her round, turquoise eyes as he said it. Not a blink, nor a moment of hesitation. And unlike on the 911 call, his matter-of-fact tone was boosting him here.

"And you're not gay?"

He shook his head calmly.

"I'm not."

She'd say he'd been well coached, but he hadn't had time for coaching.

He walked her through the drive to the ATMs and the conversation with the two abductors.

Maggie chuckled. Classic Dylan Webb.

"Did you really walk them through your policy work at city hall? Were you trying to get yourself killed?"

He smiled back.

"Honestly, I did. I'd always heard you should make a connection with anyone who kidnaps you. I figured explaining what I've been trying to do to help people was the best connection I could make."

He sat up straighter, chest forward, gaining confidence.

"If I could convince them to vote for me, maybe they wouldn't want to kill me."

Maggie nodded. Not a bad plan, actually. What a hostage should do.

"And who chose which ATMs to go to?"

"They told me where to go, and I went."

"Did anyone see you at any point of the hour?"

He learned forward in his chair, blue eyes beaming back to life.

"One person did. At the ATM near the courthouse, a man saw us. He didn't know it was a mugging, but he definitely saw us."

"How do you know?"

Webb chuckled. "Because he asked us for money."

Maggie chortled back. "Wait . . . Someone asked you for money *while* you were being robbed?"

"Like I said, he didn't know."

She wrote down the word *panhandler*. Would be an odd detail to make up, making it an important one to confirm.

"And what did you say back?"

"I told him I couldn't help him."

"What did your abductor say?"

"Nothing."

She moved onto other details.

His description of the final minutes—being blindfolded, then covering his head with his arms as if that would slow a bullet—brought mist to her eyes. In her twelve years as a cop, she'd talked to so many who'd survived ordeals like this, or worse. You never forgot the conversations, or the looks on their faces as they recounted the grimmest details. The moment they feared death.

"So when you got to your law firm, you didn't call 911 right away?"

"I didn't."

"Why not?"

"I know it's the first thing people expect you to do, but I was so excited to be alive, I wanted to celebrate. So I tried to keep my dinner date."

"Do you understand why people question that?"

"Trust me, I get it. Before last night, I'd probably have questioned it too. But all I can say is that's how I felt at the time. Of course I was going to call the police to report it, but it didn't feel as urgent. In my mind, it was no longer an emergency. It was over. It's not like they were going to catch them that night anyway. I was just so relieved to be alive."

He looked directly at the camera.

"My guess is some of the victims watching this will understand."

Maggie guessed he was right.

"When you called 911, you sounded so calm. As if nothing had happened. Why?"

"Same reason. The emergency was over. I felt like I was simply reporting it at that point."

"Same—"

"Let me put it this way—if I'd called from the car, when it was happening, I would have sounded a lot different."

"Same with your rather pleasant demeanor in the lobby of your law firm?"

He shrugged.

"Politicians are told to smile for cameras. That's habit."

She'd saved her toughest questions for the end, unleashing them now in a barrage.

"Councilman, how can you explain the fact that we can't see your two alleged abductors on any of those ATM videos? Your story made it sound like they were near you."

"The videos you guys have been airing nonstop?"

"Yes. Those ones."

"I have no idea. Maybe they were careful to avoid being seen. Criminals try to avoid getting caught, you know."

"Two teenagers?"

"Maybe. I have no idea. They were there, believe me."

Now for the doozies.

"No fingerprints either?"

He blinked rapidly. That hadn't been reported yet. He started to say something, then stopped. No doubt annoyed that the cops were leaking.

"None found *yet.*"

"How about receipts from the ATMs?"

He grimaced.

"They haven't found them," he said. "Yet."

"And is it true they found the wallet and keys back near the house where it all started?"

"They did."

"How do you explain that?"

"You'll have to ask my captors after they catch them. I can't begin to explain it."

"As you said, criminals try to avoid being caught. Going back near your house isn't consistent with that."

"That surprised me as well—maybe they were parked near there."

He was getting more comfortable with each hostile question. Selling it well.

Time for her toughest shot.

"And Councilman, do you use drugs?"

He leaned back in his chair. Torqued his head while flashing an uncomfortable grin she hadn't seen before.

"Now why would you ask that?" he asked, his tone of voice slightly higher.

"Well, another thing people are speculating is that this was a drug deal gone bad. You owed these guys money. Hadn't paid. So they were making you pay up."

He simply stared back, perspiration gleaming from the dimple of his chin.

Maggie kept going. "Trust me, crazier things happen every day on the crime beat. Especially in the drug world."

"I bet."

He didn't want to answer.

"So, Councilman, do you yourself use drugs? Have you recently?"

He looked right at her for a few seconds.

"No, I don't."

But as he finished, he averted his eyes. Just enough to make clear he'd lied.

Trying not to overreact, she let some seconds pass. She'd squeezed hard enough. It was time to give him his say.

"So after all this has happened, can you tell us how you feel now?"

He closed his eyes, shook his head, then opened them back up.

"You really want to know how I feel?"

"I do. I'm sure the viewers do as well. Your constituents."

His eyes narrowed. It was a look she'd never seen before—from him, at least.

"Angry."

"Angry?"

"Yes, angry."

Not the answer she expected from a politician. But his low tone *sounded* angry.

"Because people doubt your story?"

He shook his head, then waved his right hand.

"No, not because of that. That's frustrating, but that's life in today's crazy world—in politics, especially."

He paused again, then spoke slowly—carefully choosing each word.

"Those who know me know I'm not an angry person. But I have to admit there's a rage—raw, visceral rage—boiling up deep inside me. All day, and all night, I keep seeing the black barrel of that gun pointed at me from inches away. I keep hearing the violent talk from the kid in the back seat, like a bad movie script but so real at the time. I hear myself trying to convince two strangers—two kids—not to kill me. Trying to win them over. Begging, really. I relive wrapping my hands around my head to slow down a freaking bullet."

He looked up, no doubt recalling those images again. His eyes bugged wide, his pupils dilated, projecting the fury he was describing. This was all coming from a place far deeper than his other answers.

"Two other human beings were debating whether I should live or die." He paused. "I actually *heard* the debate. Think about that. My life was totally in their hands, forcing me to win their favor so they'd let me live."

He stammered for a second, clearly unsure what was coming next.

"The sheer audacity of it. People placing themselves in the position to decide another's fate—no one has a right to do that."

He slowed his words.

"No one."

He paused a final time.

"Putting someone in that desperate position is such a personal violation. I can't stop thinking about it. And it makes every cell within me boil with rage."

Maggie stared back, letting it all come out.

It was incredible testimony. Incredible footage. Raw and real. Oprah-level.

If it were up to her, this would lead the news.

Webb let out a long breath.

"I guess that may sound a little unhinged," he said, calming quickly.

"Not at all," Maggie said. "Thank you for your sharing it."

Chapter 21

As he drove back to Mount Adams, Dylan tapped his fingers against the cushioned leather steering wheel of his parents' Cadillac.

The interview had felt like the four-hundred-meter hurdles he'd run back in high school. For almost the entire hour, he'd cleared every hurdle Maggie Coyle had thrown in front of him, gaining confidence with each stride.

Then, with the finish line in sight, the last one had snuck up on him. And he'd crashed right through it.

He hadn't expected such a direct question about his own drug use. And the way she asked it—at the end of a battery of other questions he'd easily slapped away—had trapped him. After a series of "nos," and within the context of the "drug deal gone bad" speculation, saying yes felt like a confession, tainting everything else.

So he'd panicked, hesitated, then fudged a little. And once he had, he couldn't take it back.

It wasn't a lie exactly. But no doubt that's what they'd call it. Which would kick-start a whole new round of questions.

Distracted, he barely made the exit from Columbia Parkway to Mount Adams, veering over to the right lane just in time. The exit ramp lifted cars like a roller coaster, bearing up and to the right, high in the air, then arching left back over the parkway before forcing traffic to an abrupt stop at the bottom of Hill Street.

He checked for oncoming cars, then turned left up the steep hill.

Halfway up, growing unease boxed out his simmering frustration. The thin, blonde hairs on his forearms stood on end as nerves gnawed in his abdomen.

We know where you live, the voice echoed in his head. *If you call the cops, we'll be back.*

He was planning on staying at his parents' again, but he needed a few things first. Several days' worth of clothes, toiletries, a book or two. Plus the mail. Just a quick in-and-out to get some bare essentials.

But from deep within, raw survival instincts objected to even this short visit.

Unease grew to fear, his clammy hands moistening the Escalade's steering wheel.

We're taking your license . . .

Dylan hadn't been intimidated when they'd said it. He was more focused on getting free. But now each word played back in his head. What if they followed through? What if after all the coverage, with his muggers' sketches splashed all across the news, the kid in the back won the argument this time?

He slowed as he reached the hill's halfway point, about five houses down from his own.

If you call the cops, we'll be back.

His heart pounded even faster.

He glanced into the rearview mirror to see if anyone was following. Nothing stuck out, either vehicles or people. So he drove up further, slowly, scanning the seats of each parked car he passed. They appeared to be empty. No lights. No movement.

He pulled to the right side of the street, into a parking lane tucked beneath the steep hillside. A landslide a few years back had taken out six cars, so residents knew you parked here at your own risk.

Now directly across from his house, he lowered the Cadillac's window halfway and yanked the parking brake up to its maximum level. He turned the engine off to hear what he could hear, but cars whizzing by on Columbia Parkway drowned out most everything else.

One final look at the cars parked around him revealed nothing. And the sidewalk on the street's other side was empty.

As ready as he was going to be, he opened the car door and began to step out.

Then he froze, his arms and legs shaking so hard he worried he couldn't stand. A grim reality set in: If the duo were anywhere nearby, watching, once he stepped a few feet from his car, he'd be in their hands for a second straight night. Trapped again.

Plus, he was a sitting duck. The bright sky in front of him obscured the cars above, but those cars enjoyed a perfect vantage point down to the entrance of his house. The two could be watching him right now. If they were going to make good on their threat, that's exactly where they'd be, posted up.

Better off driving past to be safe, then circling around.

He climbed back into his car and climbed the rest of the way up. Not a soul was on the street, and all cars appeared empty.

Breathing slightly easier, he continued up, around, and down the narrow streets of Mount Adams. No one followed. He approached Hill Street a second time, ascended it again, then parked in the same spot as before. Other than a neighbor walking a collie down the street, still no one around.

Even with all those precautions, he was as nervous getting out this time.

Of course the fear was irrational. But he couldn't reason with it.

They said they'd come back. Nothing was stopping them. And if they were somehow hidden now, watching and waiting, he was a dead man.

* * *

Dylan stepped through his front door and into the kitchen, legs weakening beneath him.

It had never occurred to him how much its hillside location made his house a death trap. But now he *felt* it. With the single entrance from the street, the only other way out was the deck facing the river—at least a thirty-five-foot drop.

He took one step, then another, then another. Each stride further into the house, away from that front door, felt like a risk. As if he were underwater, diving deeper, with one eye on the surface but unsure if he could hold his breath long enough to swim back up.

He crossed from the kitchen into the small living room that looked out over the river. The point of no return.

Time to move fast.

He rushed into his bedroom, then his closet. He grabbed two suits, two shirts, and a handful of ties, then tossed them on the bed.

He rifled through a few drawers, throwing blue jeans, a sweatshirt, boxers, socks, and some workout clothes into the small duffel bag he traveled with. Then he dumped toiletries and gym shoes on top of the clothes and zipped it shut.

If they entered now, he was done for.

Heart pounding, he glanced around the rest of the bedroom and living room for anything else he might need—books, magazines, papers for work. But none felt necessary versus the all-consuming urge to escape as fast as he could.

With the suits and shirts over his right shoulder and the duffel in his left hand, he raced back through the living room and kitchen and out the door. He locked it behind him then scampered across the street back to his car.

Only when he drove off, up the hill, did his breathing steady.

Chapter 22

"The poor guy." Sam, Maggie Coyle' long-time cameraman, spoke as they drove back to the studio after packing everything up.

"Was it that bad?" Maggie asked from the passenger seat.

"Well, yeah! He nailed the entire interview. Then he up and lies about not using drugs right at the end? So dumb."

"It was that clear to you?" she asked, confirming her own instincts.

"You forget—I see it all close up. He looked away. His eyes widened to the size of quarters. Hell, even his chin was sweating. I'm surprised his nose didn't start growing."

"And you got it all?"

"Yep. Zoomed in tight. It's not gonna be pretty."

Sam was enjoying Webb's fall, but Maggie couldn't stop thinking about the final moment of the interview.

"You know, there's an interesting corollary to what you just described."

"What's that?" Sam asked, turning into the station's parking lot, which stood high atop Mount Auburn and looked out over the back of a well-lit downtown.

"That one answer—everything you described as being so obviously false—stuck out so much from the rest of the interview."

More silence.

Sam nodded.

"That's true. It did."

Chapter 23

"Dylan, we shouldn't be talking."

After a quick shower, Dylan sat down on his parents' living room couch and called Steph, almost twenty-four hours to the minute of their scheduled date.

"I wanted to see how you're doing amid all the craziness. I've kept your name out of it all."

"Well, the police sure knew it."

She sounded exhausted.

"I meant with the media. Yeah, I had to tell the police every detail."

"I know. They came by my office today to confirm them all."

His moment of calm ended quick.

"They did?"

"Sure did. They peppered me with questions for more than an hour."

"An hour? What did you say?"

"Exactly what happened. But I don't think we should be talking. Anything you say to me now makes me a witness. And I don't want my name caught up in this."

She'd clearly consulted a lawyer.

"I'm not going to say anything except that it happened exactly as I said it did, Steph," Dylan said, annoyed. "And if they ask, that's what you can tell them."

A long pause through the phone. Then a sigh.

"Dylan, they were deadly serious. They wanted to know how well we knew each other. If we had a relationship. If we'd ever had sex. If I was angry you were so late. What else I knew about you. They weren't fucking around."

"And?"

"I told them the truth."

A few seconds passed. The cops, or a lawyer, had really spooked her.

"They also focused on what we talked about when you finally called."

"What, that you yelled at me to call the cops?"

"Yes. That was a major deal for them—your calls prior to calling 911. And to be honest, it was a little startling."

"What was?"

"Your call to me."

"Did you tell them that?"

"I *had* to. Because it's what I thought."

Jesus. Now she was undermining him.

"Steph, I was just—"

"There's no point in arguing. I get it. I wasn't in your shoes. But most people would've called 911 right away. I sure would've. Still wanting to have dinner felt bizarre—at the time, and now that I know what you're claiming happened, even more so now. And I wasn't about to tell the cops otherwise."

Claiming?

Dylan took a long breath. No reason to dig any deeper.

"They also seemed bothered that you called back."

That's right. He'd forgotten he'd called a second time.

"Oh, my call cancelling dinner?"

"Yeah. That's what I told them."

He tried to make light of it.

"Did they think we still should've *had* dinner?"

"Dylan, you can joke, but they weren't kidding around. My free advice is that if things didn't happen exactly the way you—"

Dylan could feel his temperature skyrocket.

"It happened like I said, Steph. Sounds like I should call you after all of this is done."

"That makes the most sense. Good luck getting through all this."

"Tha—"

The phone clicked.

Chapter 24

Just how much Dylan Webb screwed up became clear once Maggie Coyle opened her inbox after getting home.

She and Temple had pored over every moment of the interview, splicing it into three segments. Overruling her, Temple had insisted that the drug question run in the first segment released. And as Sam had predicted, the close-up on Webb's face—capturing the councilman's pained expression as he heard and answered the question—was devastating. They'd run the story for the first eight minutes of the 11 p.m. news, after which she'd headed straight home. It only took her ten minutes to reach her hilltop condo in Price Hill. As she did every night, she changed into sweatpants and a T-shirt, sipped her favorite cab and relaxed for a few minutes, enjoying the city's best view of the downtown skyline.

At 11:30, she checked her email.

The subject lines of the three most recent emails told the story:
WebbofLies.

Webb is a dope fiend.

Liar.

The last two emails—one arrived at 11:21, the other at 11:24—were clearly dummy accounts, set up simply to send her the information. Both were unsigned but included phone numbers to call.

The first email, sent at 11:13, was an open book. A man named Marco Sheets used his Gmail account, the address of which was his own name. And he included his name at the top of the email, and again at the bottom.

Worse for Webb, the email provided five long paragraphs detailing the councilman's drug use at a party. And below that detailed narrative came three attachments, which Maggie opened.

All three were photos showing a midsized social gathering. The lighting was dim, but Dylan Webb stood out, at the center of a semicircle of men and women. One couple looked to be making out in a corner, adding a seedy feel to it all.

But far worse for Webb, each photo captured various stages of the councilman smoking a joint.

FRIDAY

Chapter 25

Detective Moses glared at Dylan as he entered the same conference room where they'd last met. It was 8:30 a.m. Friday morning. Her hair was stretched back into a tight ponytail, and her deep-set eyes looked uncharacteristically tired.

"You think it's a good idea to play this out in the media?" she asked, gesturing toward a metal chair.

Dylan stayed on his feet.

"Oh, Detective," he said, trying to project calm, "it was already playing out in the media. Your leaks. The avalanche of tweets. Media gossip. You name it. All day long yesterday, they were on TV, radio, and social media, killing me. So I figured it was better to get my side out too."

"That's your call, sir, but you aren't helping yourself any. Have a seat."

She sat down, opening a manila folder on the table in front of her.

"You told us you made two calls the night you were mugged, outside of calling 911."

The Steph conversation.

"Oh, I meant to tell you, I forgot I had called my date—"

"Stephanie—"

"Yes. I called her back after I called 911. I told her I could no longer meet her for dinner."

He was still smiling. Moses wasn't.

"Is there a reason you didn't mention that Wednesday night?"

"I completely forgot. It lasted a minute or less."

She jotted that down.

"And there was another call you made, wasn't there?"

He lifted his eyes to the ceiling. Trying to remember the night, and what he'd told them.

"I said my parents and Steph, right?"

"Yes."

Those were the only conversations he could remember.

"I think that's it."

"Well, who'd you call at this number?"

She read out a number that started with the area code 513.

He tensed up, realizing they must have gotten the call log from his law firm.

"That's right. I called my chief of staff and left a message. I bet it's a short one."

She looked down.

"Thirty-five seconds," she said, then looked up again. "Is there a reason you didn't mention *that* call?"

"I guess I only thought of the ones I had actual conversations. Not a message."

"So you made four calls from your office, but you only mentioned two to us?"

He exhaled, his body tensing.

"Detective, for God's sake, these are harmless oversights. One was a message. The other was me canceling dinner. And our interview was late at night, only hours after I thought I might die."

She shut the folder.

"Okay, so let's talk about your interview last night. The reporter asked you a question we hadn't asked you."

A chill went through him. *Here comes the drug use.*

"What about?"

"She asked if you ever used drugs."

He nodded.

"And you said you didn't? Or hadn't?"

"I did . . ."

She wouldn't be asking if she didn't have evidence to the contrary.

"And Detective, I will admit it to you, it's more complicated than that."

Her eyes bore into him.

"We know."

"You have to understand—"

"Not a word more, sir. This is when you *really* want to reconsider getting yourself a lawyer."

Chapter 26

"Jesus Christ, Webb. Whah didn't ya call me Wednesday night?"

Rusty Grimes, the best criminal defense lawyer in the area, hailed from eastern Kentucky. So in a fierce battle of unique features, what stuck out the most was his deep Kentucky twang. In close second came a bowl cut of dark brown hair that could've played a starring role in any bad comedy, followed by drooping red cheeks that jiggled as he spoke.

Despite the accent, they were meeting in the cradle of establishment Cincinnati: Fourth Street. Grimes had defended enough rich kids, professional athletes, and Fourth Street big shots to afford the prime-time Cincinnati real estate otherwise reserved for those businesses and clients.

"Because I thought I was helping *them* solve a crime *against* me. Not that I was the damn suspect."

The two were seated in a large conference room, on one end of a long, off-white marble table. In front of Dylan, a floor-to-ceiling window stretched across the length of the room, providing an unobstructed view of the Ohio River. Behind him, a wood-paneled wall displayed four mounted trophies: a moose, an elk, and two bears. The far end of the room boasted a large portrait of the girthy Grimes, rifle in hand, standing over what appeared to be the larger bear.

A younger woman, mousy with short auburn hair and thick glasses, occupied a third seat, slightly behind Grimes. She'd brought Dylan from the lobby to the conference room but hadn't said a word since.

"Well, that was your first fuckup right there. What'd ya tell 'em?"

"Probably too much."

Grimes, who weighed at least three hundred pounds, glanced down at the hulking gold Rolex that encircled his thick, fleshy wrist. "Ah've got time. We need every detail."

Dylan spent thirty minutes walking through the abduction and what he'd told the cops. While Grimes listened and asked questions, his young associate took down every word. Dylan was at the point where he wasn't sure if he still remembered the actual hour in the car or was just repeating conversations where he'd *described* the hour. They were all running together at this point.

"And then ya did that damn TV interview?"

"I did."

"Well, that was fuckup number two, especially with a reporter who used to be a police detective. What'd ya tell her?"

Dylan walked through his back-and-forth with Maggie Coyle.

"So you lied about the drug use?"

"Not sure I'd call it a lie, but I understand why people might say that."

Grimes winked at his associate, like he was somehow entertained.

"Well, that's all that fuckin' matters. Why don't you give me the actual truth then?"

Dylan took a sip of water.

"The truth is that I smoked a lot of pot in college."

For him and his friends, it was basically the same as drinking, without the hangover. Took the edge off all the stress. So a few days a week, he'd happily passed the bowl around the dorm room, or out on a Lake Erie beach somewhere.

"And where'd you go to college?"

"Oberlin."

"So in Ohio."

Dylan nodded. "Yeah, why?"

"It's only a minor misdemeanor here. You smoke since? Law school?"

"Some there too."

"Where?"

"Northwestern."

"Illinois. Clearly illegal when you did it. And since you've been here? And in office?"

"I stopped for a while. But then started again. Then quit again when I ran for the council."

"In public?"

"Usually at home. But I did at a few parties."

"How big?"

"How big what?"

"How big were the parties?"

"Small."

"Let me ask it this way: Did you know everyone at them?"

"No."

"Then that's fuckin' public."

"Okay."

"And you thought it would be a good idea to lie to the whole city about it?"

"This might be a generational thing, but when I think of drug use, I think of hard stuff. Cocaine. Heroin. Not pot. So that's why my first answer was no."

Grimes laughed.

"You really think that's gonna fly?"

"All I can tell you is that's how I thought about it."

"Son, I watched that part of the tape before you arrived. You looked like you were lying through your teeth. I mean, it was so bad, my four-year-old grandson would've called it out."

"The minute I said no, I knew it was off. But I couldn't walk it back either. And yes, I have a bad poker face."

Grimes' jowls wiggled as he shook his head.

"By far the worst I've seen. You agree, Sadie?"

She looked uncomfortably at Dylan, then back at her boss.

"I'm afraid so," she said perkily. "It was pretty obvious."

Dylan pushed back. "Listen, at least I've been consistent. I'm for full legalization, and I've voted that way at the council. The toll the drug war takes on cities like Cincinnati—and an entire generation of young Black men caught up in it—is an outrage."

Grimes waved away Dylan's words with his hefty right hand.

"Son, yer right. And most folks agree with you. I sure as hell do. I've spent a lot of time defending against bullshit pot charges. But the problem is that you lied—not about drug use, but about *anything*. You're in the fight of your life. In the public, or in front of a jury, your credibility is everything right now. And that lie killed it."

Dylan slumped in his chair.

"Where'd you get your drugs?"

"Through different friends."

"You don't have a dealer?"

"No."

"Do you know who your friends' dealers were?"

"No idea."

Grimes sunken eyes narrowed. "Ya don't look like you're lyin' to me."

"I'm not!"

"Sadie, does he look like he's lyin' to me?"

She looked at Dylan, then back at Grimes.

"He doesn't," she said, smiling.

"Best lie detector at this firm," Grimes said. "Do you even know how your friends got their supply?"

"I never asked them."

"Any other fuckups we should know about?" Grimes asked.

"Not that I can think of."

"Radio interviews?"

"Nope."

"Tweets?"

"Nope."

"Facebook posts?"

"Nope."

The associate was writing feverishly.

"Call anyone since?"

Shit.

"I've called my parents, a few friends, and my staff. And . . ."

He knew this was bad.

"I did call the woman who I was going on the date with."

Grimes shook his head again.

"You didn't."

"I'm afraid so."

"Tell me exactly what you talked about."

Dylan walked through the call.

"The cops will be all over that," Grimes said. "So will Magwood."

A. J. Magwood was the long-time county prosecutor the cops were planning to talk to.

"Do you know him well?" Dylan asked.

"Who?"

"Magwood."

"Yeah. Too well." He chortled, pointing around the ornate office. "But I gotta give him credit—he's helped me build a very lucrative practice, along with some expensive hobbies."

Grimes again winked at Sadie.

"Listen, son, you've got pretty big ambitions, don'cha?"

"I don't really think about it that way. I just want to make a difference for Cincinnati."

The truth was more complicated.

"Whatever," Grimes said. "Let me put it differently. You're off to a good start, right? I mean, *I've* heard of ya, and I couldn't give a shit about politics on this side of the river."

Dylan had finished second out of thirty candidates in the council election, surprising the whole city in his first run for office. It fueled immediate speculation about a bright future. Congress, or mayor. And more down the road. So while he'd started out with no ambition beyond getting on the council and serving well, in recent months he'd begun having conversations about running for mayor.

"I'm holding my own."

"Well, all that hype puts a big target on yer back. It's a lot easier to crush your career now, while it's still in the cradle. To taint you forever. And your fuckups are only making it easier, so I suggest you quit fucking up."

"Honestly, I don't even know what my career is. That's not how I think about it."

Grimes slapped the table while cocking his head in a way that made clear he didn't buy it. "You can say that all you want. But ah'll tell ya what—A. J. Magwood sure does. Along with anyone else you've pissed off along the way."

Chapter 27

"Turn on the TV."

Gabby called as Dylan returned to his parents' condo.

"What's up?"

"Just turn it on. Channel 5."

Of course. Maggie Coyle's station.

He grabbed the remote and turned on the television in the kitchen.

He recognized the guy talking. Local lawyer. Around the same age. Big law firm. He'd donated to his campaign at some point.

"Marco Sheets. What about him?"

Usually calm, Gabby yelled back into the phone.

"He said he witnessed you smoking pot. Apparently he has photos."

Seconds later, a dim photo appeared on the screen. Some kind of party.

Dylan squinted. Sure enough, there he was, smoking a joint.

"Holy shit," Dylan said. "What a scumbag."

"Why, Dylan?" Gabby said. "Why?"

"I have no idea why! I've never been anything but civil to him."

"I don't mean him. I mean *you*. Why did you lie? In that interview? About drugs." She paused. "That photo—it looks so awful."

"I choked, okay? I messed up."

On cue, the story switched back to yesterday's interview. Like a dagger to the gut, they aired his stammering response to Maggie Coyle's question about drug use.

Then back to Sheets.

"As you can see, the councilman denied ever using drugs," Maggie Coyle said in the pretaped interview. "So you're sure that was him at the party?"

"Hundred percent. Just look at it."

He held up a printed version of it with his left hand, pointing to Dylan's head with his right index finger.

"That's him right there. Mr. Clean!"

"And that's not a cigarette?"

"No, ma'am. He lied to you. That's pot. It was all over the party."

"You too?"

"Not ashamed to say it," he said, chortling. "Me too."

Chapter 28

"Son, we need to talk."

Even though in the same party, the mayor only called on the most serious occasions. Police-involved shootings. The budget, when Dylan stood as the tie-breaking vote. A controversial development deal that hung in the balance. A toxic gas leak from a railway car.

But that was it.

Willie Ames was in his final term. The old populist firebrand was now casual, bordering on checked out. But Mayor Ames, a labor lawyer for years before becoming a council member, still had the sharpest political instincts in the city. And after a few scandals himself, most due to heavy drinking, his greatest instinct was for survival.

So when Ames's number popped up on Dylan's phone minutes after Maggie Coyle's story ended, he picked up right away, eager to hear the old pol's perspective.

"Thanks for calling, May—"

"I don't know what the fuck you're doing, son, but it ain't workin'."

While the mayor dropped f-bombs every other sentence, he'd only called Dylan "son" a few times. And none had been good conversations. Now he'd done it twice.

"I admit, I don't know what I'm doing either. All I can tell you is I got mugged at gunpoint and now I'm the bad guy."

"Stop, son. Feeling sorry for yourself isn't gonna help. You're in deep shit at this point."

Dylan bit his lip, hungry for details. The mayor would have a good sense of what the cops thought. The chief respected him more than anyone else, largely because he funded the department generously then left it alone.

"How deep?"

"Up to your neck and splattered on your fuckin' chin. If the cops can't verify what happened, Magwood will be all over this. You'll be his biggest trophy in years. And Magwood always bags his trophies."

"What should I do?"

"Hire the best fuckin' lawyer you can."

"I brought on Grimes earlier today."

"There you go. No one better. And you're not gonna want to hear this, but you should resign."

"Excuse me?"

"I said, you should resign."

Dylan forced a laugh.

"Resign? Are you kidding me?"

"Listen, if they bring charges, you'll need to." He was now talking like the old lawyer he was—all business. "I've seen other politicians go through corruption cases—"

"Corruption? I got kidnapped!"

"It doesn't fucking matter!" he yelled. "Once the wheels of justice start grinding you, they don't stop. Their number one goal is your scalp, and in your case, the knife's already drawing blood from your forehead. Your number one goal is to stay out of prison and to keep from being found guilty—a stain you'll carry the rest of your life."

"Of course," Dylan said. "That's why I called Grimes."

"Yes. But you're going to find out quick—the best defense requires you to do things that may be the worst politics."

"Like what?"

"Gee, I don't know," he said, irony dripping from his voice. "Like admitting you used drugs because you're not worried about the political consequences."

Dylan grimaced. A damn good example.

"You need to do whatever you can to win that case. Don't let political ambition trip you up, or you may end up in a jail cell."

"I hear you," Dylan said. "Let me think about it."

He pivoted to a question he'd pondered for the past day.

"What are the others on the council saying?"

Dylan had worked hard to develop good relationships with his colleagues, no matter the party. On a council of mostly big personalities who were often fractured, they called him "the Diplomat," which is one reason he'd gotten so much done in a short time. And stopped things that needed to be stopped.

"They have no idea what to think. But count your blessings—no one's thrown you under the bus yet."

"Yet?"

"Yes. Yet. But I've seen this before: When the politics turn, they turn quick. And they're turning damn quick."

Dylan wrung his hands.

This was why the mayor had called. Not a friendly check-in with free advice. But a warning: The politics are turning. Resign before we all throw you under the bus.

"Mayor, how long do I have?"

"Let me put it this way," the mayor said, his voice all business. "I wouldn't set foot in next week's council meeting if you haven't cleared your name."

Chapter 29

In her last two contracts with Channel 5, Maggie Coyle had negotiated getting off at 4 p.m. on Fridays. It gave her an early start to her weekends, when she had Emmy.

But this Friday, she might as well have stayed at work, because it was all she was thinking about.

Dylan Webb in particular.

As she whipped up some pasta for Emmy before she met up with friends, Maggie stewed about the leak from city hall. The mayor and majority of the council planned to call on Webb to resign next week.

Not a surprise. Politics as usual, really. But so brutal. So quick. It reminded her of her own rapid, painful exit from the department after she'd done the right thing.

After she sipped her cab, her thoughts wandered back to the lie. Webb's sloppy, unforced error, which she'd exposed so harshly. He'd deserved it—she couldn't stand being lied to. At the same time, she sympathized. He was a politician on the fast track, likely paranoid that confessing to drug use would undermine his entire trajectory. So he'd fucked up. He was human.

She poured herself a second glass. It was a warm September night, so in her sweatpants and workout top, she stepped outside onto her small deck.

The low wail of a horn blared out from the right side of her building. With the sun descending, the dark silhouette of a long coal barge, dotted by dim lights from bow to stern, moved gracefully in front of the steep Kentucky hillside. It neared the sharp bend that would lead it southeast, to the bright lights of downtown, before heading along Cincinnati's East Side, parallel to Columbia Parkway.

Which brought Maggie back to Webb's journey. And his story. And specifically, the last ten minutes of the interview.

She hadn't said anything as he was speaking, nor after he was done. Not a word to Sam the cameraman on the drive that followed, nor to Temple as they'd spliced the interview into the three segments.

But now, those final ten minutes—an open window into Webb's rage—were etched in her mind, replaying again and again. Not only the words themselves—anger at having his life in the hands of strangers. But his tone as he expressed them. Raw. Real.

And how he'd looked as he'd uttered them. Fury blazing from his eyes. Nostrils flaring, even seconds after he finished speaking. And for most of the ten minutes, his right fist clenched into a tight ball on his lap, the tendons along his wrist taut like wires. Unconsciously, his inner tension spilling out everywhere. Right in front of her, in a way viewers couldn't see or feel through a TV screen.

It was a startling level of anger from a councilman who otherwise came across as mild-mannered. Buttoned-up to a fault.

This was trauma. Textbook trauma. Not an easy thing to fake.

But what consumed her now was how familiar it was, even if it had been a few years.

It brought her back to the first woman she'd ever interviewed as a detective—both eyes bruised into a deep purple, one arm broken, by an ex-boyfriend who'd beaten her for twenty minutes before she'd gotten away. As a rookie detective, she'd expected the tears. The shock. The trauma. The fear.

But not the anger. That had surprised her. "He made me beg for my life," the woman had said, shaking, with eyes narrowed and fist clenched. "Like he alone should decide if I should live or die."

Over the years, she'd conducted thousands of such interviews. Debriefing victims in the hours or days following violent crimes was the most important part of the job. And as with that first victim, visceral anger became a telltale of a victim who'd truly feared whether they'd live or die. More reliable than any lie detector or other investigatory tactic.

So if her experience from all her years was any guide, one of two things was happening when it came to Dylan Webb.

He either instinctually understood the trauma that follows someone threatening your life and had an uncanny ability to mimic it.

Or he was telling the truth.

And if he was telling the truth, then he was being railroaded.

Gaslit.

And *that* would be the far bigger story.

Chapter 30

Dylan searched back through his text messages.

Mostly prayers and good wishes from all over the country, which he'd been answering for days. Despite all the political skepticism, it was a needed reminder that most people had responded with kindness and sympathy. It was the same lesson he'd learned when he'd knocked on thousands of doors—that most people were nice!—but one so easy to forget once you're in the thick of politics.

But he scrolled past those, looking for eight messages in particular. He'd read them once, but he wanted to review them again.

Suddenly, the sentiments from these eight people mattered in a big way. As with the chief and the mayor, his fate was in their hands.

The first came at 11:08 p.m. Wednesday night.

My God, Dylan, I hope you're okay. Saying a prayer.

It was classic Curtis Jackson, a fellow Democrat who'd served on the council for three terms. Dylan knew that when he said he was praying, Curtis Jackson, a deacon in his church in addition to running a local nonprofit, actually was. When it came to raw charisma and inspiration, Jackson was the star of the council, which made him the favorite to replace Ames as mayor. In private, like that message, he was always a gentleman.

Two other Democrats and a Republican had reached out by 11:15 p.m.

Praying for you, the Republican, Michelle Easley, wrote. The daughter of a famous pastor, she, too, meant it. *Let me know if I can help.*

Thank God you're alive. Hang in there.

Just saw the news. So glad you're okay.

The other four all came through by 9:00 a.m. the next morning.

So before the public doubts emerged, all eight council colleagues had been gracious and supportive. They'd believed him.

Yet only days later, if the mayor was telling the truth, at least some of them wanted him gone.

Dylan dialed Curtis Jackson first.

"Dylan," he answered, gentle as always. "How are you?"

"I'm fine."

"Well, I can't imagine that's true. It's pained me to watch you go through this. How can I help you?"

"Curtis, the mayor called. He said that there's talk on the council about calling for me to resign. Is that true?"

Another pause.

"Curtis?"

"It's the truth, Dylan. They're drafting something up to see if we'd all sign it."

"'They're'? Who are 'they'?"

"Roberts, for one."

Dylan sighed heavily.

Thad Roberts was no surprise. The guy was rabid, the council's most conservative member. Looking to run for Congress whenever the aging incumbent retired, he'd had it out for Dylan from his first day on the council. But it wasn't only Dylan. Whenever Roberts could use the city or city hall as a prop in burnishing his right-wing credentials, he'd do so with gusto. No program or person was safe once in his political crosshairs.

"Who else?"

"The rumor is Kane. But I haven't talked to him directly."

Of course.

Even though a fellow Democrat, Christian Kane was the sleaziest pol on the council. A guy, Dylan joked privately, who watched the show *House of Cards* in search of role models and best practices. Every time Dylan struck a deal with him, he felt dirty afterward. Kane always wanted to know what was in it for him and couldn't care less about the public good.

"And the mayor?"

"What about him?"

"Is he involved?"

"You know city hall. This wouldn't be happening if he hadn't given them the green light."

Dylan nodded. Of course that was true.

"Who else?"

A pause. "I'm not sure."

"C'mon, Curtis! Did they call you?"

"Yes."

"Who?"

"Laurie."

Laurie Busken was one of the council's two independents. A successful entrepreneur and former beauty queen, Busken had no long-term political ambition beyond city hall. She'd moved to town following grad school out West, and rocketed up the commercial real estate world, running for office at the encouragement of the local chamber of commerce. She sincerely cared about her adopted hometown, as well as her reputation within it. Dylan and she had built a cordial relationship, teaming up on a number of issues.

"Laurie? Jesus. What did she say?"

"She'd talked to the mayor, who said the cops were laughing about your story. That you were about to blow up, and we should get ahead of it."

"So is she on board?"

"I'm pretty sure she is." He paused, then a sigh came through the receiver. "Dylan, you must know that we're all being flooded with emails about you. Saying that you're embarrassing the city. That you made all this up. Not a few dozen emails, but hundreds. And calls too. And my staff say the tweets about you have gone viral. I hate to tell you this, but I don't think people are going to withstand the pressure."

Gabby had filled him in on the emails and calls. Usually, a controversial issue led to dozens of citizen emails. Curtis was right—this blew that volume away.

"Are *you*, Curtis?"

A long breath.

"As I told Roberts and the mayor, I'm thinking about it."

Dylan shook his head. He'd whipped enough council votes to know that "thinking about it" was a bad sign. But he held his fire, given that Jackson was sharing so much.

"So you've got Roberts, and maybe Laurie and Kane. Anyone else?"

"Pete may be with them too."

"Jesus. Pete?"

"I'm afraid so."

Pete Stack was a fellow Democrat. Another rising star before Dylan had leapfrogged over him in the last election. An in-your-face idealist versus Dylan's wonkishness, they'd worked on a lot of issues together. But when they disagreed, Stack put up a ruthless public battle. Having come out in his first run for the council, Stack had a passionate following among city progressives. More than anyone but Jackson, his demand for Dylan's resignation would be a gut punch.

"Is that it?"

"Firm ones. Yes. Everyone else is—"

"Thinking about it," Dylan interrupted.

"Exactly."

Dylan put his head in his hands. If a bipartisan majority came out for him resigning, there was no way to stay on.

"Is there anything I can do to stop it?"

"Prove that it happened like you said it did. And soon."

Chapter 31

Even though Ma's cooking was the best, Kai Brewer hadn't held down a meal in two days.

And now, for the second straight night, he couldn't sleep, tossing and turning in the small room he shared with his younger brother, Jamelle.

He'd never committed a crime before. And now he was damn sure he'd never do it again.

Kai had felt like puking the entire hour he'd spent in the back of that Jeep, his hands jammed deep into his pockets. The tough talk had helped channel his nerves, but they'd still eaten away at his insides the whole time. Thank God the sunglasses and hat hid how petrified he must have looked.

It was more than the guilt of holding up someone at gun point—made only worse by how nice the guy had been. It was the stress of knowing even a single mistake might get them caught. And then he turned out to be a freaking city council member.

Now, as he tossed from one side of the small bed to the other, each word of the original conversation echoed in his head.

It had been after basketball practice, two Wednesdays before.

"Kai, I've got a way we can make some good money, quick," Slay, the team's backup point guard, had said.

Money was the biggest stress in Kai's life. He'd just gotten into Miami, his top choice, located an hour north of Cincinnati. But his hardworking parents—dad a firefighter, mom a nurse—were already struggling to pay the bills, so it wasn't clear if he'd be able to go. He knew Slay was trouble—bought and sold drugs, got in lots of fights, hung with a tough crew outside of school—but the money would help. And once he showed even a small interest, Slay was all over him. In the days after, he'd talked him into it, then reviewed the basics of the plan.

Except for the homeless guy, they'd carried it out perfectly.

Still, he'd thrown up minutes after they'd left the guy in his Jeep, lowering the window of Slay's car just in time. And he'd thrown up after every meal since, including twice in the school bathroom. But he'd kept it all to himself, as Slay had sworn him to do.

"Did you know he was a councilman?" he'd asked as they'd driven away, still shaken by the revelation.

"Of course not!"

"I told you, they're gonna be all over this now."

"Maybe."

"What do you mean, maybe? Of course they will. The police work for him."

"But you said you didn't touch anything, right?"

"Yes. I even used my sleeve to open and close the door."

"Then we should be fine."

They'd driven the rest of the way back to Silverton—a quiet, diverse bedroom community immediately north of Cincinnati—in silence. As he'd dropped Kai off, Slay issued one final warning.

"Not one word to anyone. Or no money."

"Of course," Kai had said back. He'd meant it. Forget the money—if he got caught, his life would be over. No Miami. No job. No nothing. And for all they'd done to get him to this point, his parents would never forgive him.

As he'd feared, the abduction of the councilman had led every newscast since. Both mornings, as Jamelle slurped his cereal and Ma drank her coffee while standing by the television, he'd had to watch coverage of the crime *he'd* committed. See close-ups of *his* victim. Then even a sketch of himself.

"That's terrible," Ma had said Thursday morning at the footage of the councilman walking to a police car. "Why would anyone rob that nice man?"

He'd tried to agree, but no words came out. If anyone could see through him, she would.

By Friday afternoon, Kai had felt a little better.

The drawings the police circulated, which the TV stations showed nonstop, were a joke. They could be anyone. And the most prominent features in the drawing—the Bears hat and glasses—were long gone. Slay had bought them just for the robbery, then gotten rid of them.

Plus, while the cops were saying the taller suspect was around 6'3", Kai was barely over 6 feet. Stuffing the heel of his sneakers to add some height had worked well.

Miraculously, neither of them was in the camera footage from the ATM machines. He'd hung pretty close to the councilman by the courthouse, but apparently still far enough to be outside the camera shot.

"Told ya it'd be fine," Slay had said after today's basketball practice, which Kai had struggled through because he felt so physically weak.

"Yep. Seems like it."

"They're even saying it may not have happened," Slay said, smirking.

"Crazy. Do you know when I get my money?"

Slay said he'd managed to get more money from one of the credit cards the next day.

"Keep your mouth shut for a few more days, and I'll get it to you. Maybe Monday."

"Okay."

"Have you told anyone?"

"Of course not."

"Keep it that way. Not a word."

Maybe Slay had been right all along. They'd been careful, and it seemed to have worked.

While Kai felt bad that people were questioning the councilman's story, it also was a good sign. Maybe it would all go away soon.

Still, he stirred for another two hours before finally falling asleep.

SATURDAY

Chapter 32

As they did each month, Shirley Meadows and Maggie sipped coffee in a Frisch's Big Boy in the West End, near downtown. Same back corner booth as always. Out of view.

They caught up on kids—Shirley had two, bracketing Emmy by one year on each side—and their polar opposite dating lives. Unlike most cops, two decades on the force had not aged Shirley physically. Her straight black hair, emerald eyes, and warm, dusky skin looked as striking as they had the first day of boot camp, and a morning regimen of boxing and yoga kept her in top shape. So while Maggie's social life rivalled that of her nuns from grade school, Shirley dated several times a week and was happy to spill all the details.

With no romantic updates of her own to share, Maggie soon pivoted to the Webb investigation.

"Any leads?" she asked.

"None, Maggie. None."

"Not even chatter?"

People beyond policing never appreciated how many crimes were solved through chatter. Street chatter. And usually that street chatter originated with the perpetrators themselves, who couldn't help but brag about their feats back in the neighborhood. A perpetrator tells a friend about what happened. That friend tells another friend. Who tells another. Before long, the cops—always listening for that chatter through their sources on the street—hear about it and track it down.

"None," Shirley said.

"Strange."

"They think so. If these were kids like Webb described, no way they wouldn't have talked to someone."

The younger and greener the perpetrators were, the more likely they were to gab.

"Especially the kidnapping of a council member. That would spread like wildfire."

Maggie sipped at her coffee when Shirley suddenly stood up.

"Hey, ladies," a deep voice boomed from behind.

"Morning, Chief," Shirley said.

Maggie turned to see the unmistakable bald head and tight-end build of Patrick Prince, who stepped within feet of the booth. The warm smile he cast Shirley's way faded as he met Maggie's eyes.

"Getting the inside skinny, Coyle?" he asked.

Maggie's stomach churned. Prince had been the chief's eyes and ears for years, so everything she said now would go straight to the top.

"Just catching up with an old friend," she said.

"Right," Prince said, with the same smirk he'd had back when they were on SWAT together. He'd sported blonde hair back then. "We know you're digging into the Webb case. Heck of a job getting him to lie like that on camera."

"Yeah, he really screwed that one up."

"He sure did. And right when you were letting him tell his story too."

"That's what we do in my business," Maggie replied, trying to stay positive in the face of Prince's sarcasm.

Prince looked back at Shirley. "Have a good day, Sergeant. And try to keep her out of trouble."

"Yes, sir," Shirley replied as Prince stepped away.

"Still the asshole, I see," Maggie said as they both sat back down.

"Always," Shirley laughed.

"Hope I didn't get you in trouble, Shirley."

"Nah. They know you talk to some of us. For the most part, they seem to like your stories. Trust me, if they didn't, I'd know fast."

While Maggie knew this was the reality, Shirley's reminder gave her chills. The chief still kept tabs on her. And he could pull the plug on her sources whenever he wanted—whenever he didn't like a story.

She took another long swig of coffee to move on.

"So, what's the department's theory?" Maggie asked after putting her mug down. "That he just made it up?"

Shirley swallowed a bite of her egg whites.

"That he was hiding something, then lied once, then had to keep lying. Y'know, like those movies where things just keep getting worse."

"But lying about what?"

"Not at all clear. He needed cash desperately. But he couldn't get as much as he needed, so he went to multiple machines. That made him so late, he had to lie to the girl about why."

"And then she made him call the cops."

"Exactly. He didn't want to call them—something they both said—but she pushed him to. Once she did, he couldn't take back the story. And it went downhill from there."

"Why do they think he needed the cash?"

Shirley shrugged. "Drugs? He clearly buys and uses, as you showed. Or a hooker in the back seat? Who knows? It's never a good sign when you desperately need hundreds of dollars in cash."

"So why tell the girl he was robbed? There are so many easier excuses for being late than that."

"Other excuses wouldn't have added up. He didn't text her that he was late. And in this day and age, an hour of going completely dark, unexplained, is weird. So he needed something more dramatic than 'sorry I'm an hour late.'"

"Well, if he was driving around to get money, it would've been easy for him to have texted her."

Shirley winked. "Not if the hooker was in the back seat. Or the drug dealer you'd stiffed was watching from the passenger seat."

"So they think someone was with him, just not two abductors?"

"Yes. Which kept him from reaching out to tell her while it was happening."

Maggie spread strawberry jelly on her last piece of toast. Thinking.

"That's a lot of ifs. Why is this all more plausible than what he's saying?"

"There's so much evidence—or lack of evidence—undermining his story. No prints in either seat. No images in the camera. The strange place his stuff was found. No chatter."

She took a bite, chewing for a few seconds before swallowing. "True."

It wasn't a crazy theory.

She'd seen people do far dumber things than this to keep a secret. And once they started down that dishonest path, people did the most irrational things not to get caught in that original lie, only making it all worse. Then they had keep covering, lie after lie.

Plus, almost no evidence confirmed Dylan's story.

With one exception—which only she'd seen close up. The interview. That rage. She still couldn't erase it from her memory. The chief wouldn't appreciate it, but for her, that was as strong a piece of evidence as there was.

Chapter 33

"Honey, what's going on with you?"

Kai walked across the kitchen, up an hour later than usual for a Saturday morning.

"Nothing, Ma. Just tired."

She grimaced. Ma always knew when something was up.

"You haven't been yourself for days. I hear you tossing around in there all night. Goodness, you look like you've lost ten pounds. What's wrong? Something at school? Or someone?"

She'd smell out any bs. So lying a second time wasn't going to work.

"Just worried about Miami and the money. That's all."

She frowned.

"Kai, you worry about your grades. And getting some rest. And basketball. Dad and I will figure out the money part. We've told you that over and over."

He sat down at the kitchen table and poured Cheerios and milk into the bowl that always awaited him.

"I know, Ma. But that's what kept me up."

She eyed him for a few seconds. "Ma's death stare," they called it.

"You ready for practice?"

He sat up.

"Sure am."

"You think you're going to start?"

It was down to him and a freshman to be the team's center.

"We'll see."

"Well, if it's that close, you better get your rest, young man. And you'll need to put some meat back on those bones."

She leaned down and pinched his cheek. He smiled, hoping she wouldn't see through it. Hoping she wouldn't see the shame.

The doorbell rang.

"I'll get it," Ma said, walking out of the kitchen.

The front door creaked open seconds later, then Ma called out.

"It's Slay. You didn't tell me he was going to drive you to practice."

Kai shook his head, butterflies tingling in his abdomen. They hadn't discussed that.

"Whoops, I forgot to mention it. Tell him I'll be three minutes."

Chapter 34

The light turned red as Maggie reached Vine Street, so she stopped and waited as groups of mostly White twenty-somethings crossed in front of her into the neighborhood called Over-the-Rhine.

As often as Maggie drove by Vine Street, she still couldn't get used to it. The north-south boulevard that marked the official boundary between Cincinnati's East and West Sides was now dotted with hip restaurants, boutiques, and breweries as it headed out of downtown and into Over-the-Rhine.

When she was a cop, Vine Street had been synonymous with crime. Back then, those now-chic Vine Street blocks had served as the region's open-air drug market, a drive-through corridor of abandonment where White buyers converged from Ohio and Kentucky suburbs to buy every drug imaginable from poor Black kids from the city, then raced back to highway entrances to get home. The young sellers hadn't lived there either—when they were done selling, they'd go home too.

It was but one street of a large city that still suffered from far too much crime. But symbols mattered. And that turnaround alone was one of the reasons the chief was so untouchable, even if all he'd done was move the problem elsewhere, out of Fourth Street's line of sight.

The light turned green.

Maggie drove two more blocks east, turned right, then parked. She was chasing down a hunch. One striking detail from her interview.

If things happened as Dylan Webb described, the guy may have had the worst luck on the planet.

With one exception.

If he was telling the truth—and the detail was so vivid, it would be an odd thing to make up—the councilman had caught one break. At the second ATM. The one by the courthouse.

Two breaks at once, actually.

First, a man had interacted with Webb and his abductor at the ATM.

Second, that man may have been homeless.

Her years on the force had taught Maggie that the next best thing to a security camera at the scene of a crime was a homeless person witnessing it.

Time and again, a homeless man or woman had helped her crack any number of cases, for a whole host of reasons.

For one, like everyone else, criminals looked right past the homeless as if they weren't even there.

But they *were* there, Maggie knew from experience. And since many considered the public space their own personal turf, they keenly observed the goings-on around them *more* than others, not less. If something was out of place, or irregular, they'd spot it first.

Some even got into the habit of reporting to the police what they saw, so they kept an even closer eye on things.

Maggie parked at a meter on Court Street and walked to the base of the hulking marble courthouse to check out the councilman's one potential stroke of good, dumb luck.

The courthouse was closed for the weekend, so the usually long line out front was gone. The entire concrete plaza in front of the grand entrance was empty.

But to the left, in the corner, was a small gathering of homeless men.

Maggie walked over to three men huddled in a small semicircle. A fourth sat on a blanket a few feet behind them. In her day, she would've known them by name. But this was a new generation, and there were a lot more homeless people now than back then.

The man on the blanket looked up. Dark-skinned, with a few white splotches on his face and arms, a tangled mess of a beard, and shoulder-length dreadlocks matted so intensely they looked like cloth.

"Leave us alone!"

"I'm not here to bother you," she said softly.

"Cops have been shooing us away for weeks. And you look like a damn cop."

She nodded.

"I was once, sir. But I'm not anymore. And I'm not here to make you go anywhere. In fact, I'm here to ask for your help."

The shortest of the standing men spoke up. Freckled, with his reddish hair in a ponytail, he was so young, he looked out of place.

"Help how?"

"To see if you guys saw anything."

He chuckled, revealing wide gaps from missing teeth across the top of his mouth. One consequence of rampant drug use.

"We see lots of stuff."

"I know you do. Why do you think I'm here?"

They waited.

"A couple nights ago, a councilman was held up. He was forced to take money out of a bunch of ATMs, including the one right over there." She pointed toward it. "Had a tall guy next to him. About eight at night."

They nodded along but said nothing.

"The councilman said that a man with a long gray beard was standing only a few feet away. Saw the whole thing. Even asked for—"

"Fritzy," the man on the ground yelled out.

"Fritzy?" Maggie asked.

"Yeah. It was Fritzy. He mentioned it later that night."

"What did he say?"

"What you just said. That it was weird."

"What was weird about it?"

"That one guy—a Black kid—was watching over a White guy in a suit taking money from an ATM machine. Like Fritzy said, who does that?"

Another of the standing men spoke. The oldest of the group, with half his teeth gone along with his right forearm.

"A few news vans came by the next day. Pretty young things with their microphones walking back and forth. Same reason?"

Maggie grinned.

Pretty young things. Her competition, in such a hurry to move to a bigger market, wouldn't bother talking to these guys—wouldn't even know what good sources they could be.

"For sure. According to the councilman, it was a holdup. The second guy and a guy in the car were robbing him."

"So Fritzy was right!" the guy on the ground declared.

"Yes, he was."

She looked around the courthouse grounds.

"Is he here?"

"Nah," the guy on the ground said.

"Do you know where he is?"

"I don't. He sort of moves around. Hell, we all do." He looked around. "Especially lately."

"When was the last time you saw him?"

"Well, they've started clearing us out by around ten each night. So that would've been when."

"He didn't come back the next day?"

"No, ma'am." He looked up at the other three. "Any of you guys seen Fritzy since?"

All three shook their heads.

"No, we ain't," said one.

"You know where he spends time when he's not here?" Maggie asked.

"Sometimes down by the river," the guy on the ground said. "Under the purple bridge. A bunch of us sleep there."

"He wasn't there last night either," the short guy with the ponytail chimed in again.

"Anywhere else?"

"Nah. I'd check there. He has a lady friend who's there every night."

"What's her name?"

"Sandy. Good lady."

"And do you know Fritzy's real name?" Maggie asked.

"Nope. Just Fritzy. But Sandy might know."

"Thank you for your help. And stay safe."

"We're safe, ma'am. Just keep your old buddies from pushing us around."

She played along. "I'll do my best."

Chapter 35

If Dylan Webb had learned one thing in his first year on the city council, it was how to count votes. But the counting usually ended up at the same number.

Five.

For whatever side Dylan was on.

He hadn't aimed to be the swing vote on the nine-person body. He'd just wanted to get on the council, learn the ropes, then make a difference. But within a few months, the pattern became clear. The math kept working out the same way. At least on the most important issues.

If he was for something, it happened. Five votes.

If he opposed it, it didn't. Five votes against.

With a block of four Democrats who generally viewed things as he did, or slightly left, and another block of independents and Republicans on his right, Dylan Webb had quickly emerged as the decider. The paper even wrote a whole story about the phenomenon months into his term, when he'd driven almost every major decision in the city's budget.

At first, he wasn't comfortable being the swing vote. It added to the pressure. And it guaranteed that he was flooded with calls and emails before every major vote, along with another round of angry calls after.

But then he got used to it, appreciating the power that came with his unique position. He was able to get big things done, again and again. Far more than most first-term members of the council, *his* agenda was shaping the city. And his vote was decisive in helping colleagues pass what they wanted, allowing him to get even more done through the deals he cut.

But he'd also learned never to take that central role for granted. And the way you took nothing for granted was to count votes. And always know how to count to five.

So from the kitchen of his parents' condo, Dylan spent the morning checking in on his colleagues from city hall. Were there at least five who stood with him?

His calls made the answer clear: not even close.

Three Democratic colleagues called him back. But only one— Verna Spiller, a retired teacher—said the words he needed to hear.

"I told them no," she said. "Not interested. Innocent until proven guilty."

The way Dylan counted votes, that kind of explicit commitment counted as a tentative vote. He'd have to confirm it two more times to consider it locked in.

The next call back was from Jackson, who was still "thinking about it."

And the third—Pete Stack, usually an ally—sounded too much like Jackson.

"I hate that you're going through this, Dylan."

"Thanks, Pete. It's been a whirlwind."

"I can only imagine."

"I know Roberts is trying to turn up the heat. I hope I can count on your support."

Uncomfortable laughter.

"You know I'm pulling for you, Dylan."

"But are you with me?"

"Dylan, I want to support you. You know that."

"But?"

"I'm waiting to see what the cops come up with."

"Thank you. But you believe me, right?"

"Of course I believe you. I know you're gonna get through this. Let's see what happens with the investigation."

That was as much as Dylan got before they hung up. Under his system, weasel words like that didn't count as a vote. When someone's for you, they said it—and neither Jackson nor Stack was saying it.

No one else called or texted back. Not Christian Kane, a fellow Democrat, nor Laurie Busken. And not the other independent, or the two Republicans.

When counting votes, silence was the loudest message of all. A hard no.

After a morning of calls, he had one vote. One tentative vote. And five nos.

Chapter 36

"They tell me you're Sandy."

She was a tiny woman, short and emaciated, with stringy gray hair, fierce green eyes, and sharp cheekbones pushing against her pale skin.

"That's me. What's it to ya?" she asked through thin lips that didn't have a trace of color in them. "You ain't kicking us out, are ya?"

Maggie looked around. They were standing in the shadow of a pedestrian bridge that spanned the Ohio River into Kentucky, painted purple when they converted it from vehicles a few decades back. You'd never know it from driving past or walking nearby, but tucked underneath the underside of the bridge was a permanent encampment of homeless people.

It was far bigger than Maggie expected, another reminder that there were far more homeless people now than when she'd been on the force.

"I'm not. I'm looking for someone, and I was told you and he are an item."

Sandy's eyes opened wide.

"You talkin' about Fritzy?"

"I am."

She shook her head.

"Ma'am, he's gone."

"Gone?"

"Yeah. Gone. Haven't seen him in days."

"Is that odd?"

"Hell, yeah, it's odd. He'd come here most nights. Sleep right over there." She pointed at a spot behind her. "He'd check in more than that. But I ain't heard from him in days."

"Did he mention what he saw the other night?"

"When?"

"Two nights ago. He might've seen a robbery."

"Didn't you hear me? He hasn't been here since then. That was the first night he didn't show up."

She sounded frantic, her eyes dampening.

"Have you said anything to anyone about it?"

"Just people here."

"Not the police?"

"Ha!" she said, spitting the words out. "Like they're gonna help find him."

"I used to be a cop. We'd treat it like a missing person like anyone else."

"Well, ma'am, things have changed since. They push us around like we're garbage, the same way the mayor talks about us."

"Well, Sandy, you may not believe me, but I want to help find Fritzy. He witnessed something the other day that we're looking into."

"What?"

"A robbery."

"Well what's new about that?"

"He saw people robbing a councilman. Up close."

"Ohhhh. Well, shit, that's probably why he's gone missin' then."

Maggie didn't want to say it, but of course she was right. What were the odds that he hadn't made it from the courthouse over to his usual resting place on the same night he'd witnessed Webb at the ATM?

"Maybe so. Can you tell me his full name?"

Her eyes narrowed as she looked at Maggie, sizing her up.

"Fritz Ventre. From a big West Side family."

"Cops?"

She'd worked with a bunch of Ventres over the years.

"Yep. Several of his brothers are."

"You have any more information on him?"

"He kept his stuff over here. C'mon."

She led Maggie over to a corner beneath a rusted girder, where several boxes, a sleeping bag, and a canvas backpack were strewn together. Sandy unzipped the front pocket of the backpack.

"I'm not sure why, but I trust you."

She pulled out a wad of cards and papers bound together with rubber bands and handed them to Maggie.

"Here ya go."

The pieces of paper on top looked like junk—dog-eared, creased, with scribbles all over them. Maggie leafed through them quickly, moving them to the bottom of the small pile.

Then came what she needed. Real identification.

A VA card.

"FRITZ P. VENTRE."

"He was a veteran?"

"Oh yeah. Army. Went to Iraq a bunch of times. Saw some terrible stuff. Still can't sleep through the night without nightmares. Why do you think he ended up on the streets?"

Maggie shook her head. The same sad story replayed again and again.

She took a photo of the card, then kept going through the stack.

Again, mostly junk, in varying shades of yellow.

But at the bottom, she came upon a long-expired driver's license.

"FRITZ PETER VENTRE."

The faded photo showed a good-looking guy, clean-shaven with a narrow face, wide-set eyes, and a toothy grin. He was listed at 6'1", 215 pounds—and enough of his upper body was visible to show he'd been fit at the time. The old address was not far from where she lived, further up into Cincinnati's expansive West Side.

His birthdate indicated he was now fifty-five years old.

She took another photo, then handed the cards back to Sandy.

"This is so helpful. Thank you."

"What are you gonna do with it?" Sandy asked.

"I'm going to see if anyone's seen or heard from him. And I'll be sure to let you know what I find out."

Chapter 37

"Hey, where we going?" Kai asked as Slay turned onto the north entrance to I-75—when the basketball gym was the other way.

"Just a quick pit stop, then we'll head over. We're a little early anyway."

They got off the highway two exits north, made three right-hand turns, then pulled into a series of driveways among some old, gray warehouses on the side of the highway.

"What are we—"

"Just sit tight," Slay said without looking over. "This will only take a few minutes. We'll be there on time."

He parked the car in front of a large warehouse, next to a gray van.

"Get out," he said, using the same gruff tone he'd used throughout the robbery. "And follow me."

The roar of trucks and cars whizzing by drowned out everything else as they headed to a black metallic door at one corner of the warehouse. Slay knocked twice, and the thick door creaked open.

A short, stout man with a stubbly beard stepped in the doorway, his meaty hand still holding the rusty metal door handle.

"You're late."

Kai did a double take. No one at school talked to Slay this way.

Slay shrugged. "We're here, aren't we?"

"C'mon in."

The man nodded at Kai but didn't say anything as he scooted past him.

They were on the far side of a cavernous space, must hanging in the air, shadows of large equipment and boxes to their right. Once the door closed behind them, the only light in the place came from a hallway straight ahead. They walked along the side toward the light, their basketball sneakers squeaking with each step.

"Take a right," the man said as they reached the lit hallway. They turned down a second hallway. Another man stood outside a door about ten yards away.

"You're late," the new man said as Kai and Slay reached him. He was taller, in jeans and a brown leather jacket, with shiny black hair slicked back over the top of his head.

"He still in there?" Slay asked.

"Of course he is. That's why you're here." The man looked Kai up and down as he said it.

"You ready?" he asked.

Slay nodded.

"For what?" Kai asked.

"We need your help," the man said. "Will only take a minute. But heads up—he's a little roughed up."

As Kai tried to make sense of the words, the man opened the door and flipped on a light inside. Grunts came from the far end of the room.

Slay walked past the man and into the door as Kai stood frozen.

"What're ya waiting for? Get in there."

"Okay."

Kai stepped into the room.

It was mostly empty. But in the far corner, a man sat in what looked like the desk of a school classroom—where the chair and a small, oval desk in front were attached. His head was slumped down, only a mess of tangled gray hair visible. His arms were tied to the desktop with some type of cord, while his legs were fixed to the front legs of the chair.

A larger man—tall and thick like an NFL lineman—stood behind the desk. Bald with a short brown goatee and narrow, close-set eyes, he folded his thick arms as if they were interrupting.

"So, do you recognize that guy?" the man in the doorway asked Kai.

Kai, still confused, squinted back. "Me? Why would I recognize him?"

"Step closer and tell me if that was him. Your buddy here says he can't say."

Kai stood still.

"Step closer, kid."

Slay nodded, then turned to Kai.

"Kai, remember the second ATM machine? There was that guy who was right next to you and the councilman. Remember?"

"The homeless guy?"

"Yeah. The homeless guy."

The big man grabbed the hair at the back of the man's head, yanking back hard to lift his face.

The man grunted in pain as his large eyes opened, revealing sockets that were bruised a deep purple. Fresh blood oozed down his right cheek, starting not far below his eye, while his entire left cheek was puffed out and blue. His upper lip was a bloated, bubbly mess of blood and saliva.

But it was the beard that gave him away. Long and gray, with strands of hair twisted and knotted together. The injuries didn't obscure the familiarity of it.

This man had stood feet away from them at the ATM. The homeless guy who'd asked for money.

Kai suddenly felt dizzy.

"What the—"

"No questions," the man in the doorway asked. "Is that him? Is this the guy?"

"Kai?" Slay asked. "If we want our money, you need to tell them."

Kai's heart drummed as he processed what he was looking at and what it meant. How had they found this guy? *Who* had found him? And why was he here, tied up and beaten?

"Yeah. That's him."

"You sure?" the man asked.

"Yes. I'm sure. That's the man who saw us."

* * *

"What was that? Who are those people?"

They were back in Slay's car, speeding south to get to basketball practice, Kai's mind racing from what he'd seen.

"Just people, dude. That's all you need to know."

Kai thought back to the robbery. The original idea from Slay. The talk of big money. The exactitude of the planning, and the timing. Slay hadn't once mentioned anyone else being involved. He'd left the impression that only the two of them knew about what they'd done.

"And why are they holding that homeless guy captive? In that condition? What the hell is going on?"

"The less you know," Slay said, still not looking over, "the better."

SUNDAY

Chapter 38

"They want you to resign."

The call came in at 10 a.m. Sunday morning. Dylan, still sweating from his morning run through Eden Park, was watching the Sunday political shows.

"I know," he said. "Well, five of them do, at least."

"Five?" Rusty Grimes asked, sounding confused. "Who are you talking about?"

"Five council members. And the mayor."

"I'm not talking about the council. I'm talking about the prosecutor's office."

Dylan turned down the volume so Grimes could fill him in. Prosecutor Magwood had called back the night before.

"The good news is Magwood doesn't want some drawn-out trial. Would be ugly all around, and with his election in six weeks, he's thinking about the politics. So he's willing to cut a deal—you plead to a fourth-degree misdemeanor, you resign, do some community service, and that's the end of it."

"Plead guilty? A deal?"

"Yeah."

"I will *not* say I made this up when it happened just like I said it did. I'm the damn victim here."

"Well, I've dealt with Magwood a lot over the years. This is about as good a deal as he offers."

"What's the alternative?"

"Trial."

"And the worst case from a trial?"

"He says he'll go for filing a false report. That's a third-degree felony. So worst case is 180 days in jail and you're forced out of office anyway, with some judge picking your successor."

"So he'd let me pick a successor if I resigned?" Dylan asked.

"He said he'd abide by who you've already designated to make that decision."

Cincinnati had a peculiar process to fill council vacancies. At the beginning of the term, each member listed other council members to make the decision after they left. As a rule, the Democrats all agreed to each list their Democrat colleagues as their "successor designees."

"Well, that's better than a judge, I guess." He paused. "Still, I'm not budging. It's one thing for people to accuse me of making it up. Heck, resigning isn't the end of the world. But I'm never going to falsely say I lied when I didn't. *That* would be the lie!"

"Welcome to our justice system, Councilman."

"Well, it's bullshit."

"Yes, it is. But to be clear, he'll go for broke if we don't take a deal. As he said, he could make an example out of you."

"An example of what, exactly? It's going to take a lot more than idle threats to convince me to falsely claim I'm guilty of something."

"We'll fight like hell for ya, but these threats are about to become real, and right quick."

Chapter 39

"Kai!"

Distracted, Kai had had a terrible practice. Coach had yelled at him throughout, capping it off by benching him for the opening game.

"Kai!"

But that's not why he'd been unable to hold down last night's dinner. Or why he still didn't eat breakfast this morning.

"Kai! Do you even hear what I'm saying to you? We need to be at church in twenty minutes."

Kai had felt weak all afternoon, the image of the pummeled homeless man locked into his mind. And then before dinner, Channel 5 had aired more of the interview with the councilman, sending his stress level skyrocketing further.

It came up only in passing. But in the interview, the councilman had explained that a man had asked for change during the robbery. The reporter mentioned that she was doing her best to find the man, to verify the councilman's story.

The exchange was one of the light moments of the interview. And of the mugging. He and Slay had laughed about the homeless guy as they'd driven home—a guy begging for money from a guy being held up.

But the reporter's update made it clear that those few seconds were now critical. The homeless man was the one person—outside of Slay and Kai themselves—who could verify the councilman's story.

And now Kai knew that neither the reporter, nor the cops, would find the man. Based on how badly he was beaten, odds were he wouldn't be alive much longer.

Ever since Wednesday, he'd felt shame for having been involved in a crime. But now that shame had grown into fear. This was much bigger than just going along with a friend's stupid idea.

Someone had put Slay up to the robbery.

And those same people were working hard to ensure the councilman's story wouldn't be believed.

"Kai!"

He looked up.

"Ma, I heard you. And I'll be ready just fine."

The truth was his parents usually needed to drag him to church. Now he was eager to get there.

He needed a good sermon, and some forgiveness.

Chapter 40

"There's been another shooting."

Huddled in the booth of a Walnut Hills Frisch's, Dylan was nibbling at a crinkled French fry when the call came through.

Captain Jayson Humphrey only called with the worst of news. Humphrey was the third-highest guy on the Cincinnati police totem pole, and the highest-ranking Black officer. Friendly, polite, and professional. Respected in the community because he was from the community. Which explained why the chief always assigned him mop-up duty for department messes, when the chief himself didn't want to be the face of a problem. When the chief didn't want to answer questions from the public or, God forbid, elected officials.

"By a cop?" Dylan Webb asked, although he already knew the answer.

"Yes."

"Any details?"

"Little so far. Early this morning. Near campus."

"Let me guess," Webb said. "He was unarmed."

A pause.

"It's a she. And I'm afraid so."

"Was she Black?"

"Yes," he sighed. "This one's going to be rough."

Dylan's young server stepped in front of the booth.

"Like the last one wasn't?" Dylan asked, remembering the tension of last week's long and packed council meeting.

"Nothing compared to this."

The server remained standing in front of him. She eyed his mostly empty plate, no doubt wondering if he was done.

"How old was she?" Dylan asked as he waved her away.

"Nineteen."

"And the circumstances?"

"I'm still getting the details. But basically a traffic stop gone haywire."

Always in the passive voice.

"Haywire by who?"

"That's what they're still trying to figure out."

"Bodycam footage?"

"No. The camera was turned off."

Dylan put his head in his hand. This was the third time this year that the camera "was turned off." A key aspect of his police reform bill was to make it impossible for the small cameras on officer's lapels to be manually switched off.

"Terrible," he finally said, picking at one of the remaining fries on his plate.

"You're telling me."

"'*You're telling me?*'" Dylan yelled back. "You're in the position to do something about it!"

A pause, then something happened for the first time. Humphrey pushed back.

"You're the member of council. *You're* the one in the position to do something about it."

"In theory, sure, but we both know that's not the reality."

A chuckle. "Councilman Webb, that pretty much sums up my situation as well. Look for a press conference at two."

"I will."

"And Councilman?"

"Yes?"

"The chief wanted me to know how disappointed he was by how you talked to me the other day."

"Excuse me?" Dylan asked, nearly choking on the final fry he'd swallowed. He'd asked a few tough questions about the most recent police shooting, but nothing out of the ordinary.

"The chief considered your grandstanding an attack on the whole department."

"Did *you*?" Webb asked, shaking his head.

"Did I *what*?"

"Did you consider my questions an attack on the department?"

Seconds passed.

"I'm only telling you what he told me to tell you."

The server returned, picking Dylan's empty plate off the table.

"Funny. He didn't mention that when we talked the other day."

"I can't speak to that. But he wanted me to be sure you knew that. Oh, and that he expects better this time."

Chapter 41

"Thanks for venturing across the border."

Dylan Webb shivered as an evening breeze blew upriver. He and Maggie Coyle had agreed to meet in Eden Park. They were sitting awkwardly—a few feet apart on a wooden bench, both looking out to the dark hills of Kentucky.

"Happy to," Coyle answered, "even if the view is worse from over here."

One of the many things East and West Side Cincinnati debated was who had the better view. Dylan chose not to engage.

"Well, you owed me after nailing me so badly."

Coyle laughed off the dig.

"You nailed yourself, Councilman. I just taped it as it happened."

He shook his head. She was right.

"So, you have something you wanted to show me?"

Despite Grimes's warnings, the tone of her voice when she'd called had compelled Dylan to meet.

"I do. One minute."

She took out her phone and held it up.

"Recognize him?"

She showed two photos on the screen. An old VA card, and an even older driver's license.

Clean-cut guy. Parted brown hair. Square jaw. Well built in the shoulders and neck.

Both IDs had expired long ago.

"Those are pretty dated."

"They are. They're the best we got."

Dylan squinted. There was something familiar about the man's round, wide-set eyes. The shape of his face. But he couldn't place him.

"Ventre?" Dylan asked, looking at the name on both forms of identification. "As in one of our cops?"

"Forget the name. Do you recognize him?"

"I've definitely seen him somewhere."

"What if I told you that you saw him in the last four days?"

He smirked.

"I haven't seen a soul in the last four days but you, your cameraman, a bunch of cops, and my lawyer."

"I'm talking almost exactly four days ago." She looked at her watch. "Let's call it three days and twenty-three hours."

He looked at his phone. Six o'clock. She was talking about the time of the mugging itself.

"Focus on the eyes."

Not only were they larger and spread wider than most, the eyebrows topping them were distinct—wide, bushy, and angled close to his nose. A combination he'd seen not long ago.

He replayed the mugging in his mind. The two muggers . . . and . . .

His heart skipped.

"The homeless guy! The one who asked me for money. You found him?"

"Does that look like him?"

"He hasn't aged very well, and he was hidden beneath a mop of hair and a wild gray beard. But those eyes and eyebrows look the same. He looked right at me when he asked for money."

She nodded. "Well, a few of his buddies said he came back going on about you at the ATM. That the scene looked suspicious."

"I assumed it did. Just like I said!"

"Well, he figured it out."

His shoulders felt lighter. Finally, a break.

"Have you talked to him? Will he talk?"

She pursed her lips.

"I'm afraid not. He's disappeared."

Dylan winced as his mood crashed back down to earth. His big break already gone.

"Disappeared?"

"Yes. He stays under the Purple People Bridge but never returned that night. And his courthouse buddies haven't seen him since."

Dylan ran his hand through his hair, then stood up.

"What the hell are the odds that he just disappeared? The same night that he's a witness to a crime?"

Coyle shook her head.

"Not good. Which is why I called. I've got the cops from the downtown unit on it, and they're looking for him now."

"Cops? Like they're gonna help with this."

"It's someone I trust. And he has no idea of the connection back to you. Just trying to find a homeless guy who's missing, and apparently, he was someone they knew and liked."

"Maggie, something is going on. I swear it happened like I said it did. But nothing shows up in any cameras. And now the one eyewitness disappears?"

"I get it. You either have the worst luck going, or someone really has it out for you."

MONDAY

Chapter 42

Monday morning's committee hearing marked the first time since the abduction that Dylan would face a crowd. So he'd prepared himself mentally. For questions. For conversations. Maybe even some heckling.

But as he pushed open the thick wooden double doors to the city hall chambers, the initial response was none of those things. It was silence. Every face turned his way, staring.

Then came something Dylan also hadn't anticipated. Something he hadn't heard since middle school.

Laughter. *At* him.

He'd finished second in the city not one year ago, and now people were laughing at him.

"It's Webb of Lies," a regular council gadfly yelled.

"This is a stickup," another shouted to chuckles all around. "Put your hands up!"

Dylan lowered his head and walked up the center aisle, determined to get to the dais without saying something he'd regret.

As he reached the first row of pull-out chairs, an elderly Black woman stepped in front of him, inches away, jolting him to a stop. Before he could step back, the woman's soft, warm hands grabbed his. She squeezed them twice, then shook them up and down softly. He studied her quickly—coffee-brown eyes magnified through wide circular glasses, tight curls of white and gray hair clinging closely to her head, and full lips sporting bright red lipstick—and concluded he'd never seen her before.

"Mr. Webb, we prayed for you when we saw what happened," she said, eyes moist with sympathy. "My husband was robbed in his store several years ago. They pointed that gun right at his head and cleared out all the cash registers. They caught them, but it took him years to get past it. So we know what you're going through."

For a few moments, in that packed room, the only thing Dylan saw was the smile before him. The cacophony fell silent, only her voice cutting through. He'd never cried in public before, but her sincerity and kindness were pushing him to the edge.

"Thank you, ma'am," Dylan said, lip quivering. "I can't tell you how much that means to me."

He reached out and hugged her, holding tight for a good five seconds. She pulled him tight, patting his back like a mom would do.

Behind her, another woman waited. Younger—maybe in her thirties. Beige skin and frizzy caramel hair, misshaped as if she'd been wearing a hat. Dressed in the unmistakable blue and yellow uniform of a Skyline Chili server, she stepped forward.

"Mr. Webb, I was so sad when I saw what happened. But then I thought, now you know what some of us have been through. Now you understand what it's like. Maybe that's why it happened to you. So someone who can do something about it actually knows what it's like."

Dylan eyed her through dampening eyes, speechless. Her words had conjured up a whirlwind. Of his raw anger the next day. Of driving around the block to be sure he wasn't being watched. Of feeling trapped in his apartment. Even the jolt seconds ago when the first woman blocked his way. That split second of fear before her warm smile had eased him.

He grasped her right hand with both of his.

"What's your name?" he asked.

"Portia."

He smiled.

"Well, Portia, I hadn't thought of it that way. But you're right. I do know what it's like now—or at least I'm learning. And I won't forget. Thank you for seeing that."

* * *

As Dylan expected, the chambers were packed even though the agenda of the morning's Law and Public Safety Committee was light. Which was why it was a meeting he couldn't miss.

He'd slept poorly, weighing what to do. Resign. Lobby council members. Let Grimes cut a deal. Many options, all bad.

But as he'd stewed, two moments wouldn't leave him.

"Mr. Chairman," Webb said into his mic seconds after Christian Kane gaveled the meeting to order.

One thing that had kept replaying in his mind was something Grimes had said. That the prosecutor didn't like the politics of prosecuting a councilman so close to an election.

"Yes, Councilman Webb?"

The crowd went quiet.

"I'd like to say a few words."

The other conversation that wouldn't go away was the call with Captain Humphrey.

The warning.

"Mr. Chairman, before we get to our regular agenda, I'd like to ask the department to address the latest shooting."

Apparently, the chief didn't want him asking tough questions of Humphrey. No more grandstanding, as the captain had put it.

"People deserve answers. And to start with, I'd like to know why, for the third time this year, an officer's bodycam was turned off before a citizen of this city was shot dead."

After a brief murmur, the crowd erupted in cheers.

Captain Humphrey, sitting in the front row, rose from his seat.

Staring at Webb, clearly taken aback by his tone, Kane pushed the button of his mic.

"Point taken, Councilman. Captain Humphrey, will you please—"

"Mr. Chairman—"

"Yes, Councilman Webb?"

"We've heard from Captain Humphrey on this. And on every other one of these. Isn't it time the chief answered our questions? He is in charge, after all. The buck should stop with him."

Chapter 43

Council meetings aired live across the region, so Maggie Coyle had the meeting streaming on her monitor to see any Webb announcements.

Based on their conversation the evening before, she had no idea what he might do.

But of all the possibilities, a public grilling of the chief would not have made her top ten.

It went on for an hour.

From fifteen feet away, Webb peppered the chief with questions about every aspect of policing. And he did it so directly, the chief was, unusually for him, off his game.

Why had officers turned body cameras off in three cases?

Are officers disciplined for doing so?

What would his objection be to council passing an ordinance requiring they never be turned off?

Why was he opposed to a strong and independent panel of police oversight?

Why was he opposed to the other reforms they'd proposed?

On it went, in a tone that Maggie had never witnessed before and wouldn't dare to use herself. No kid gloves, for once.

After Webb asked questions for forty minutes, other council members—feeling liberated—fired away along the same lines. Again, as directly as she'd ever seen.

It was must-see TV, the first time in years the chief had faced tough questions. Out of practice, he stumbled as those in the chamber watched in silence. Even lost his cool a few times.

For the first time, the chief looked old. Fallible.

Temple came over to Maggie's desk minutes after the meeting ended.

"Anything happen?" he asked. "Any big announcements?"

"Not about his case."

"So, any follow-up? Are the police still going to announce something today?"

"Not now."

He did a double take.

"But I thought today—"

"Not after that. Not this week. It would look like retribution. I gotta hand it to him. Dylan Webb played the only hand he had, and he played it well."

Temple stepped away just as Maggie's name reverberated over the station's intercom: "Maggie Coyle. Call on line four."

Maggie picked up right away.

"This is Maggie."

"You the one covering the councilman story?"

It was a young voice.

"That's me."

"And you're the one asking around about that homeless guy?"

Her chest tightened. Who would know that?

"What homeless guy are you referring to?"

"Don't play dumb. You're asking about the homeless guy who saw the mugging."

"I've been looking for him. Yes."

"Wanna know what really happened?"

"Of course I do."

"Then we need to meet. Off the record."

"Okay."

They agreed on a time and a location, then hung up.

Chapter 44

"So what's the plan? Let us all look like assholes for weeks on end?"

White socks poked through the holes at the bottom of the mayor's shoes. His arms were crossed, and his long legs were stretched across the oak desk that anchored one corner of the spacious office. Unless he was too hung over, the mayor golfed weekday mornings, so he was dressed in his usual khakis and a golf shirt. Despite all the boozing, smoking, and steak dinners, the former Ohio State pitcher remained athletic, even as a noticeable gut swelled his midsection. A lifelong bachelor, his wavy salt-and-pepper hair, sky-blue eyes, and natural charm attracted a revolving door of women that hadn't slowed even in his sixties.

Surrounded by oil paintings and maps capturing Cincinnati's growth over the centuries, the mayor remained as informal as ever, as if they were talking the Reds' playoff prospects and not Webb's entire future.

In a blue suit and red tie, Webb sat erect in his wooden chair. His stiff posture masked his racing pulse. He was both fired up from the committee meeting and winded from fending off reporters afterward.

"I'm not gonna resign, Mayor. It happened like I said it did."

With a thud, the mayor dropped his feet from the table to the floor. He then leaned forward over the desk as if he were about to grab Webb by the lapel.

"Well, son," he said, glaring, "you're the only one who believes that."

"True. And I was also the only one who was there."

"The cops don't buy it. And your little stunt upstairs won't change that. The brutal fucking truth is that if they don't buy it, no one buys it, and then you're through."

159

Webb stared back, unable to deny that reality.

The mayor slumped back in his chair, which squeaked under his weight.

"Have you looked at your emails?" the mayor asked calmly, as if the outburst from a moment ago had never happened.

"Not since Friday."

"See that folder?"

He gestured toward a thick manila folder lying on the corner of the desk.

"Yeah."

"Good. Because I had Janice print out every email we've gotten about you since last week. Wanna read 'em?"

"No."

"Wanna guess what they say?"

"Not really."

"Well, I'll tell ya what they say. The good people of Cincinnati don't believe a goddamn word of it."

Webb said nothing.

The mayor lurched forward again, pounding his fist on the table.

"You're making a fucking fool out of yourself. And you're making fools out of the rest of us every day we keep quiet."

It was the most energy Webb had seen out of the man since he'd met him. Which got him thinking.

"Mayor, honestly, why do you care?"

"Why do I care?" the mayor repeated, his narrow eyes widening.

Dylan leaned forward.

"Yeah. Why do you give a shit? This is your last term. You have no idea what happened to me. You're a laid-back guy, and we've always gotten along fine, so why are you so mad about this?"

The mayor's face was now only inches from Dylan's, his smoky breath all too pungent.

"Because this is coming back on all of us, that's why. I didn't spend years moving this city forward only to have my final year squandered by some two-bit scandal. Have you watched CNN? It's gone national. They're all asking for us to comment. Your colleagues

160

and I have all kept our mouths shut, scampering to and from the parking lot, heads down, for God's sake. Like we're part of it! It's a fucking embarrassment. But that dam's about to burst."

"When?" Dylan asked, refusing to pull back from the eyeball-to-eyeball showdown.

"When what?"

"When's it gonna burst?"

"Oh," he said. "One sec?"

The mayor leaned back, turning to his left.

"Janice?" he hollered, far louder than necessary.

"Yes?" a voice replied from the other side of the half-open door.

"Bring me that resolution, will ya?"

Seconds later, the door opened another foot and in walked Janice, a petite brunette and middle-aged mom of three who'd put up with the mayor's temper for years.

"Here it is," she said, handing it to the mayor.

"Thank ya."

He plucked a pair of glasses out of his shirt pocket and placed them on the end of his hawkish nose.

He held up the paper, cleared his throat, and began reading. Loudly.

"We hereby resolve—"

From his youngest years, Webb had despised being read to.

"Honestly, Mayor, you really don't need to read—"

The mayor cleared his throat again, more loudly this time.

"WE HEREBY RESOLVE . . ."

He paused, looking up from the paper and above his glasses directly into Webb's eyes—making clear he would be reading the whole thing. Then he looked back down.

"THAT COUNCILMAN DYLAN WEBB IMMEDIATELY RESIGN HIS SEAT FROM THE COUNCIL OF THE CITY OF CINCINNATI, AND THAT THOSE MEMBERS HE HAS DESIGNATED TO NAME HIS SUCCESSOR DO SO WITHIN TWO WEEKS OF PASSAGE OF THIS RESOLUTION."

"Who's on the resolution, Mayor?"

"Not me," he said, holding his hands up.

The mayor never put his name on resolutions, although he was clearly part of this one.

"Who is?"

"It's not my place to tell you who is. But they shared this with me as a courtesy, so I knew it was coming." He flashed a nasty grin. "And as a courtesy, I'm now sharing it with you, so *you* know it's coming."

"How many have signed it?"

He looked down at the piece of paper, then shrugged.

"This is just a printout, but my understanding is they have a supermajority at this point."

Five or six, as Webb suspected.

"And," the mayor said, again glaring straight into Webb's eyes, "they're hoping to get to all eight. That may be why the nastier version I saw earlier has been so watered down."

Dylan shook his head as his chest tightened. People he'd worked with closely for the past year—some of whom he'd helped immensely—were abandoning him overnight. While complete strangers upstairs had felt so moved, they traveled down to city hall to share their empathy with him.

What a shitty business politics was.

"But you know as well as I do," the mayor continued, "there's an easy way to get ahead of this. Before it's got one signature on it that can't be erased."

Chapter 45

"Hey, Kai. Why you avoiding me today?"

Class out, the two were heading to the school gym from the high school building, Slay jogging to catch up to Kai.

Not slowing down, Kai kept his gaze forward.

"What do you mean? I'm not avoiding you."

"Don't bullshit me, Kai."

Kai kept walking, Slay now a foot behind him.

"Not sure why you'd say that."

A strong grip squeezed Kai's right shoulder, then a powerful tug spun him around. Slay looked up at him through eyes narrowed in anger.

"Don't play dumb with me, motherfucker. You avoided me in classes today. Walked over for practice before I could catch you. Now you're lying to my face."

"We're late to practice," Kai said as he turned back around, certain his weak poker face would betray his doubts.

"You're gonna be late to a lot of things, bro."

Kai stopped and let Slay draw even.

"What's that supposed to mean?"

"You getting cold feet, bro?"

"I'm not getting cold anything."

"Then why you been avoiding me? All day."

"Wanna know why?" Kai asked, his temper flaring.

"Yeah."

"Because you didn't tell me everything. And now you won't tell me who those thugs were. They're gonna kill that homeless dude.

Probably already have. And we caused it. If they catch us for the robbery, we're in a lot more trouble because a guy is now dead."

"No one's catching us. And you're better off not knowing all of it. You should be glad I didn't tell you shit. So stop thinking about it."

Kai started walking again.

"And don't think about saying a word to anyone."

"I won't. I need that money. And I don't need to get myself arrested."

Slay let out a cackle that stopped Kai in his tracks.

"Arrested?" he asked. "If you talk to anyone about this, you'll be better off if they arrest you. Safer in a jail cell. Just ask your buddy the homeless guy."

Kai whirled around and grabbed Slay by the shirt. He wasn't a fighter by nature, but he was both bigger and stronger than Slay.

"Don't you threaten me. I won't talk. I'm not an idiot. But don't you ever threaten me."

"Or what?"

He let go of the shirt.

"I did the robbery. I identified the man as they asked. Let this be the last time we ever talk about him. Or any of it. With anyone."

"That's all I want to hear."

"And get me my money. Then we're done."

For the first time Kai could remember, Slay took a step back.

"Sounds like a plan."

Chapter 46

It felt like crashing a party he wasn't invited to.

Still, Dylan was determined to attend all his afternoon committee meetings. If they wanted to call on him to resign, fine. But until then, he was going to keep doing his job, even if it meant hours of awkward looks from uncomfortable city staff and cold stares from council colleagues.

In the Budget Committee, they passed a series of small spending resolutions. The major work of the committee would begin in October as they kicked off deliberations on next year's budget.

The Neighborhoods Committee produced more drama, due to the next step of the prior week's zoning fight.

To move forward, the project had to advance from the Zoning Committee to council's Neighborhoods Committee, and then on to the full council later in the week. Several community members showed up to testify against the project, while the developer's attorneys—with a second bite at the apple in the more friendly confines of city hall—lined up a spate of witnesses in favor of the project. After lengthy debate among the council members—regurgitating last week's talking points—the committee voted three to two in favor of the project. But Dylan remained confident that it would go down five to four at Wednesday's full meeting. With his opposition, that's how the numbers always turned out. He wasn't any more powerful than anyone else. He just happened to be the fifth vote, right in the middle of a split council.

Two other projects moved forward as well. Unanimously. Since Dylan was for them, they would happen.

As the meeting was about to adjourn, the city's community development director leaned into her mic.

"Council members, remember that we have our first of several zoning meetings for Pristine Village in two weeks."

Webb groaned.

Pristine Village.

A perfectly awful name, but also perfectly fitting. He'd been briefed on it a month back.

Decades ago, at around the same time that the federal government was ramming highways through historic Black neighborhoods, the feds erected a major public housing project known as English Woods on the city's near West Side. Not far up the hill from the project they'd just voted on.

At 160 acres, it was a huge site. When completed, it housed eighteen apartment buildings, and at its peak, crammed thousands of lower-income and elderly residents together, many of who had been displaced by Interstate 75 when it destroyed the previously vibrant West End neighborhood.

Because of its hilltop location, English Woods enjoyed a near-perfect view of the Ohio River. But with the middle class abandoning the city for the suburbs, no one cared at the time. The city was in decline, especially its West Side. So even a perfect view didn't matter.

But once the Cincinnati economy began turning around a decade ago, with people flocking back into the city, developers ogled English Woods as a huge opportunity. It was by far the largest contiguous site remaining in Cincinnati to develop, with the bonus of a river view. Nothing else came close.

The project was called Pristine Village because it would essentially be its own new neighborhood. Thousands of poor people would be pushed away from a stunning river view so a new generation of wealthier residents could enjoy it in their place. Not only new homes and condos, but new commercial space as well. The embodiment of the new city, cleansed of its old urban problems. Suburbia within city limits. And of course, billions of dollars in contracts to make it all happen. For years.

When he'd first heard the concept, Dylan had thought it was a pipe dream. That it would never happen. This was the kind of project you'd see in New York. Or Florida. Or California.

No one in Cincinnati would throw this amount of money into a project this gargantuan. Not even close.

But to his surprise—and disgust, as he did the math on how many people would be displaced—it was now moving forward. Fast.

Dylan pressed his mic.

"The hearing will be out in the neighborhood, correct?" he asked.

"As always," the community development director said impatiently. "We'll get you all the details."

Chapter 47

"You're not the kid who called."

The man was in his thirties, at least. Maybe early forties. Short and thick. A five o'clock shadow darkened his fleshy round face, the top of which was obscured by a gray cap. His tan skin was dotted by tattoos running up and down his bulky arms. One tattoo—some kind of snake—crept out of his dark sweatshirt, halfway up his neck. The gray-silver hue of the snake's head matched the distinct color of the man's eyes.

"Yer quick, lady," the man said gruffly, shutting the Escalade door, then locking it with his remote key. "The kid works for me."

"Like for armed holdups and such?" Maggie asked.

He winked back, grinning. Cocky guy. Clearly had been around.

"Funny. Let's go."

He stepped away from the parking lot and toward the entrance to the park, which ran east and west along the river below Columbia Parkway. Maggie caught up to him. While the well-walked and well-jogged trail offered a safe pathway, her loaded Glock weighed down the purse hanging off her right shoulder. The rendezvous reminded her of her days flipping street thugs into confidential informants. Usually uneventful. Occasionally hairy.

They entered the first section of perfectly manicured gardens, river to the right and a large metallic sculpture to the left. Twin paved paths wound in extended curves in front of them, merging every fifty yards or so before curving back out. They stayed to the right.

"Nothing this nice on the West Side, is there?" he asked, looking at the river through the trees.

"Not unless you're into potholes, railroad tracks, and chemical plants," Maggie said. Her retort was a West Sider's reflex, but the truth was that Mount Echo Park was one of the city's best.

A new sculpture, so shiny she could see their reflections in it, welcomed them to the next set of gardens.

"Yer boy's in a lot of trouble, ain't he?" he asked as a stiff breeze almost sent his cap flying.

"He's not my boy. I just cover the news."

"Sure," he said, pulling the cap tighter over his head. "You were pretty friendly when you interviewed him. And now you're trying to prove that he's telling the truth."

He was goading her for some reason. No point in taking the bait.

"Just doing my job. What do you know about it all?"

They were about a foot apart as the two paths curved back into one again. A couple walked past them the other way, so he stopped talking. They then bore right again, back on their own.

"I know that he hasn't been a good boy, and it's coming back to haunt him."

"What did he do wrong?"

"Well, you touched on it when you ran the story on his drug use."

"Okay?"

"But that's just the start. His real problem is money."

"How so?"

"He doesn't want to pay."

"For his drugs?"

"Yeah."

"Pretty risky to stiff your dealer," she said.

"Oh, he paid for a while. But then the dealer figured out who he was and demanded a premium."

"Who's his dealer? You?"

When flipping informants, the direct approach always worked best.

"I'm not. But we know each other."

"How? Are you a dealer for others?"

He stopped walking and turned her way, forcing her to stop as well.

"This isn't about me. So no more questions about me. Got it?"

"Okay."

They started up again, passing a young couple taking selfies in front of the river.

"So his dealer began to extort him?" Maggie asked.

"Call it what you want. His dealer calls it a premium. Since he's a high-profile client, doing business with him is more risky. Does that with others too."

"Others? Like who?"

"Other politicians. Local businessmen. Some athletes. I think even a couple judges. Guys like that need sellers too, but they also need to be more careful."

She nodded. A good story to tuck away.

"How much was this premium?"

"Double."

Definitely extortion.

"So what happened?"

"Webb refused. Said he'd start buying from someone else."

"So they kidnapped him?"

"Ultimately. When he refused to agree one too many times."

"Did he know the muggers?"

An older woman and her leashed collie walked past. She looked twice at Maggie, recognizing her. The collie studied the man.

"I don't know. But he definitely didn't expect it. His dealer's very professional—comes across like a businessman. Seems harmless. So Webb thought he could just say no and move on. But that was naive. This guy's not going to let him walk away that easy."

"So you think that Webb's story actually happened? The robbery? And abduction?"

He chuckled.

"I have no doubt he was in a car at gunpoint. He may have even been shocked by it. Probably scared the hell out of him. But he still has a problem—he knows exactly *why* it happened. Which is also why he didn't want to call the cops."

"So why is there no trace of his kidnappers? Not a whiff of evidence anywhere."

"Oh, they planned it all out. Remember, this was not some random robbery, so the usual evidence cops would find won't be there. They were trained to stay out of sight of the cameras and leave no prints in the car."

He smirked, clearly enjoying the story.

"And since Webb can't tell the cops why he was robbed, they're treating it like a normal robbery."

Thick bushes and a tall, obelisk-like structure marked the park's end. The path curled around and took them back toward the lot. Just as they finished the 180-degree turn, loud engines roared to their left. Two cigarette boats, zipping along the river. They sounded like the souped-up motorcycles that haunted city streets on summer nights, except the sound revved up and down as the boats bounced along the dark, choppy water.

Maggie waited for the roar to die down.

"So why are you telling me all this?"

"I've watched you for years. And I know what happened to you as a cop. So I've always liked you, but I worried you were going astray on this one."

"So how do I know you're telling the truth?" she asked, ignoring the odd reference to her past.

"Give me a private email address."

She recited the one she gave sources when she wanted to keep information out of the station's email system.

"I'll send stuff that will make it very clear."

They walked back upriver, the breeze picking up and the speedboats roaring back the other way. As the parking lot appeared in the distance, rows of tall, colorful townhouses peered down from the right, with the iconic Immaculata Church towering above.

They looked up simultaneously. Fittingly, the first row of houses were the fancy homes of Hill Street itself, where Webb's drama had begun.

"And how did you know I was looking for the homeless man?" she asked, remembering the phone call.

The man chuckled. "You asked the department to look into it, right?"

"Yeah." One cop in the department, she thought. Someone she trusted.

"You of all people know that cops chatter as much as any guys on the street. So yeah, I heard about it."

The man reached into his pocket, a move that always made an ex-cop jittery. But then the lights of his Escalade lit up in the parking lot, the vehicle beeping twice.

Five minutes later, Maggie was back on Columbia Parkway, heading downtown. Right around the spot where Webb regaled his two kidnappers about his proudest policy achievements.

Chapter 48

"They still want a deal. But they're pissed."

With wind gusts whipping against the glass windows, Dylan was back in Grimes's conference room after his long day of committee meetings. Grimes's glare matched those of the dead animals on the wall.

"I bet they are," Dylan said, grinning.

Grimes looked over at his assistant, whose name Webb had forgotten. "Do you mind letting the councilman and I speak in private?"

She nodded, got up, and left without saying a word.

Grimes leaned forward in his chair, grunting.

"Listen, cowboy. Attacking the chief might've bought you some time, but I wouldn't recommend pulling that shit again. He's got a lot more standing than you at the moment. Or at any moment, for that matter."

"They backed off the announcement, didn't they?"

"A very short-term victory for ya. Inconsequential." He paused. "They'd like to have you accept a—"

Dylan shook his head. "Not doing it. It happened like I said it did. I told you—I'm not lying about it."

"Would ya let me finish?" he asked, unusually annoyed. "They sweetened the pot. They said you don't have to say a thing. Plead no contest. They'll urge no jail time to the judge."

"But I still have to resign?"

"Of course resign. With the drug use and this, they say there's no choice there. Say you need more time with your family—"

"I guarantee you half the council smokes pot. And I don't have a damn family."

Grimes chortled. "True on the family. Well, we'll think of some other ways to spin it."

"This isn't funny, Rusty. This is my entire career going up in flames."

Grimes's face tightened.

"I thought you told me you didn't really think about your career."

Called out, Dylan didn't respond.

"Either way, they go for a lesser charge, and you plead no contest. They walk away; you walk away. That's it."

He leaned back, proud of himself.

"Believe me, it's as good a deal as anyone could get in this situation. No contest is a gift. No jail time is the wrapping."

Webb thought about the resolution the mayor had waved in his face. It could leak any day. Any hour, really. If it was unanimous, it would be a crushing blow. And if he resigned after that, it would look like he'd been forced out by his colleagues, including fellow Democrats.

"What about the homeless guy I told you about?"

Webb had filled Grimes in on Maggie Coyle's tip.

"I told ya, I've got my best PI on it. Nothing so far. But that has no impact on this deal."

"But if he's missing after—"

"So what if he's missing? Hobos like that go missing all the time. That's not gonna change a thing. Not in how this looks, and not in a court of law."

"But your guy's looking into it?"

"He is. And he's confirmed that the guy went missing. That's all, at this point."

Grimes looked at his watch.

"But here's the problem: We're not gonna find out what happened to yer homeless guy anywhere near in time to resolve this. The council and mayor will have screwed you by then. The police won't wait that long. Neither will Magwood. If you want to get in front of all this, and do it on your own terms, you need to strike that deal soon."

"How soon?"

"Next day or two, tops."

Chapter 49

Tracking down a missing homeless guy felt like a pointless assignment to Rodney Stone, but it still offered a nice break from stalking wayward, horny husbands. Plus, Rusty Grimes paid a lot more than divorce attorneys.

"That reporter is right," Stone reported to Grimes as he drove his black Ford Mustang into downtown from the Purple People Bridge. "The guy up and vanished."

After six years as a corrections officer in county jails, a decade on road patrol, and another decade in investigations—the department's first Black investigator ever—Rodney Stone had retired from the sheriff's office on his first day of eligibility. Thanks to his peak overtime years, he'd secured a hefty pension. Throw in the private eye gigs he took on almost immediately, and Stone raked in far more by leaving public service than sticking around.

"Doesn't that happen a lot with the homeless?" Grimes asked.

"Not really. These guys have patterns like everyone else. He basically lived at the bridge and socialized and begged for money at the courthouse. Hasn't been seen at either place. To just disappear— after that night of all nights—is pretty bizarre. No one can explain it."

Private work rarely stoked the rush of the old job, but not worrying about being punched, stabbed, or shot was worth the boredom of long stakeouts and the fact that his most potent weapon was a Nikon with a high-powered lens. But beyond the pay, he was an older dad, and it gave him a lot more time with his wife and three sons. The highlight of his life was baseball practice, and mornings at the gym, where he still bench-pressed four hundred pounds. Those workouts were part of the lifestyle of strict discipline that had lifted him from the rough streets of the West End. Which was the same reason why Rodney Stone never drank, smoked, or let his Afro grow more than a quarter inch from his head.

"His brothers are all cops. But they haven't talked to him in years."

"And he's not dead?"

"All I can tell you is his body hasn't shown up at the coroner's office."

Every once in a while, Rodney got an interesting case like this one. The so-called abduction was all over the news. If he solved it, business would really take off. Enough, he hoped, that he could bring on help.

"Okay," Grimes said, impatiently. "So how do you find him?"

"Gonna check the psych ward at UC as well as the Comfort Center."

"Sounds like a plan. Keep me posted."

* * *

"We can't say too much about our clients," the young woman with the silver nose ring and green, tousled hair said across the rickety table. They were sitting in the cramped, cluttered office of the Comfort Center, the city's busiest homeless shelter. At 6'3" and 225 pounds, most of it muscle, Rodney Stone could barely fit in the cheap plastic seat she'd offered him.

Stone clenched his jaw, dousing his quick temper. On more than one occasion, the center had shielded known criminals, citing privacy concerns. Once, he'd chased a mugger here, only to be barred at the door by kids like the girl he was now negotiating with.

"Honestly, it's for his own good. He's a veteran. And we believe he's missing because he witnessed a crime."

The woman's black-rimmed eyes widened.

"Really?"

He nodded. "Really."

Naive do-gooders from the suburbs had no clue.

"Well I can't say much, but give me his name and I'll see what I can do."

He repeated Ventre's full name, then added, "He goes by Fritzy."

The young woman did a double take.

"Aw, Fritzy's a legend around here. One of our best supporters. I'll be right back."

Ten minutes later, she returned with a slightly older man Stone recognized: thin, with a mop of blond hair, and a stringy goatee. Like Shaggy from the old Scooby Doo cartoon, but always yelling. He'd been on TV a few weeks back protesting city hall's new courthouse policies.

"I'm Micah Jansen, the executive director here," he said, neither smiling nor offering a handshake as he sat down next to her. "Lori tells me Fritzy is missing."

"I'm afraid so. Has he been here recently?"

"No, but he'd only come here on the coldest nights, and we haven't had those since last winter."

Lori, the young woman, spoke up. "Micah, remember? He was a no-show at our Saturday rally. He never misses those."

Micah nodded as he looked back at Stone.

"He was a pretty self-reliant guy, so he didn't use our services much. But Fritzy was one of our most passionate activists. Definitely weird that he'd miss a rally."

"You didn't hear from him at all?"

"We didn't. Which was strange, because no one was more pissed about how they've been shooed away from the courthouse. A lot of the guys there are veterans who feel they deserve better."

Micah leaned forward.

"And of course they're right."

Stone nodded, again holding his tongue. The mayor's effort to clear them from courthouse grounds was well overdue. The teeming enclave generated a daily stench, making the place downright unsanitary after the weekend. No one knew the odor better, nor heard more complaints, than the sheriff's deputies in the courthouse. For years, the city had been too politically correct to do anything about it, leaving the deputies to deal with the mess.

"You check with his courthouse buddies? Or the bridge?"

"I did. They haven't seen him in days."

"How about the university?"

"The psych ward?"

"We call it the mental health unit."

More political correctness.

"Right. The mental health unit. They have no record of him *ever* being there, let alone in the last week."

"Not surprised. He basically had his shit together."

"Okay, where would you look for him if you were me?"

"Well, you've been to the places I'd go. Outside of the coroner."

"No report of him there either. That was the first place I checked."

They stared at each other for a few seconds. Then Lori spoke up again, tapping Micah's elbow.

"How about his payments? Who was his payee?"

Micah looked at her, then back at Stone. "Not a bad thought."

Stone sat up straighter, impressed. Most homeless people were eligible for Social Security payments, but without a home or a bank account, they needed a place to receive the funds. And for selfish purposes, a handful of institutions were willing to be their designated "payees."

"You know which his is?"

"Most of them use check cashing stores these days," Micah said.

Stone chuckled. "Back in my day, it was the corner liquor store. Great business for the stores, terrible for everyone else, especially the addicts who blew their new checks on the booze and cigarettes that surrounded them."

"Well, now it's the payday lenders getting a cut of the action."

Stone shook his head. The system was beyond broken.

"You know where Fritzy would have gone for his?" he asked a second time.

"I don't," Micah said. "But a lot of the courthouse guys go to the check cashing place up on Central. Just a few blocks away."

Lori nodded. "Yep. Queen City Cash. They all use it. Open twenty-four hours."

"Great."

Micah shook his head.

"Only one problem," he said, looking down.

"What's that?" Stone asked.

"Their money comes through the first of the month, and that's when they line up to get it . . ."

It was mid-September.

"Not sure why he'd be there last Wednesday."

Chapter 50

"You gotta give us something, Dylan. Anything."

It was time to count to five. Face to face, where they couldn't hide.

"I'm doing all I can, Curtis."

The two were in the back corner of Legends, a decidedly glass-half-full name for the old, seedy bar on the border of the Walnut Hills and Evanston neighborhoods. Curtis—Councilman Jackson—had picked the place, clearly not wanting to be seen with Dylan. Even here, he was dressed to the nines, in a light-gray suit and vest, white shirt, with a light-blue tie. And as always, his perfectly manicured wave rippled across his head, fading at his ears. A close-cropped beard completed a look that had earned Jackson the title "most stylish" public figure by a local magazine.

"Yeah, and so are the cops."

"The cops? How so?"

"They briefed us."

The thwack of a pool stick against a cue ball echoed through the small dive. Then came the carom off another ball.

"On *my* case? Jesus, they haven't even briefed me since Friday, and the crime happened to *me*."

"Well, we were all asking so many questions, the mayor had them brief us two at a time this afternoon."

Dylan groaned. *How nice of him.*

"And?"

He took a long sip from his glass, then reached across and squeezed Dylan's left shoulder.

"Dylan, my friend, it looks terrible. They walked us through what you'd expect to see in a case like this, then they reviewed what they're actually seeing in your case. Basically, there's no evidence supporting your story. Nothing at all. Hell, the cameras only showed you. All alone!"

"I'm giving you my word, Curtis. Same exact thing could've happened to anyone."

Jackson shook his head.

"Dylan, you need to wake up," he said, using a far lower tone than before. Borderline angry. "This 'I'm innocent' bullshit isn't gonna work anymore. Even if it's true. This is politics now. Rough politics. You need to bring some goods."

It was the first time his devout colleague had ever cursed. Or spoken so crassly about politics. He was basically saying he didn't give a shit what had really happened,

"And is it true you hired Grimes?"

"I did."

He slapped the tabletop.

"Sheesh. Everyone knows when you hire Grimes, you're admitting you're guilty."

"Curtis! My freedom's at stake. Of course I'm going to hire the best guy I can get."

"I'm just saying: it's the perception of hiring someone like Grimes. I mean, when's the last time he had a client you thought was innocent?"

"That's not what the mayor said. He thought it was a good choice."

"The mayor? If you're taking advice from the mayor, then I'm even more worried about you."

"So what can I do? What will it take to convince you guys to hold off?"

Jackson took another long sip.

"Not sure if there's anything. But what can you give us?"

"*Give* you. Like what?"

"Like enough to give us cover? We're getting blasted for saying nothing. It's guilt by association. They're saying city hall is a joke, and especially us Dems. Do you know how many pictures of you and me together are now bouncing around Twitter and Facebook?"

Dylan gulped. "I hadn't seen those yet."

"My point is, we need something big. Something that shows the whole world, very clearly, that what you said really happened. Then the council will be fine standing with you."

Cover, Dylan thought, fuming inside. Political-speak for "too cowardly to act on principle."

"So I'm guilty until I prove my innocence?"

Another thwack in the background.

"Dylan, this is politics. So, yes."

Dylan tried to calm himself by taking a long swig of beer.

"There was one witness," he said, putting his glass down, "but he's disappeared . . ."

Jackson rolled his eyes.

"We have a PI tracking that down, but it could take a few days."

"That's not gonna cut it, and you don't have that much time anyway. Maybe do or say something to show that you're sorry for it all. Acknowledge you need help."

"Help? What kind of help?"

"You know. Like with your drug issue. Maybe say you're gonna get rehab. Take a month's leave or something. Show some contrition. Maybe that will get a few of us in a better place than we are now."

"But I don't have a drug issue, Curtis. That would be more of an admission of guilt than hiring Grimes, for God's sake!"

Jackson shrugged.

"All I'm saying is you need to give us something. We need cover. And"—his eyes narrowed—"while I agree with everything you said to the chief today, that ain't it."

"C'mon, Curtis. That's not why—"

"Dylan, don't treat me like a fool. Nor is the Black community full of fools. It's no accident why today was the first time you went there. That was more about you than us, and you know it. We know it."

Ten minutes later, they drove their separate ways.

No other council members returned Dylan's call. Not even Verna Spiller.

His in-person count to five now didn't even reach one.

Chapter 51

Even at 7 p.m., Rodney Stone had to wait twenty minutes to get to the front of the line.

"How can I help ya?" a young man asked from behind the counter, with a twang similar to Grimes's. Located on the edge of Over-the-Rhine, only blocks from the courthouse, the small lobby of Queen City Cash felt like a bank long overdue for cleaning. And in a ratty, faded golf shirt and jeans, the clerk was dressed far more casually than your typical teller. At least the place had personalized the shirt. Small script indicated that the clerk's name was Kev.

"Hey, Kev. I'm here to inquire into a homeless man who might have been one of your regulars."

"I'm sorry. Can't help you if it involves another client." He looked over Stone's shoulder. "Next?"

"But I waited twenty minutes in that line."

"I don't care how long you waited. We don't talk to people about our clients. It would be totally inappropriate. I'm sure you understand."

He again looked over Stone's shoulder, as if this was the final word.

"What if I told you the client might be in danger, and you could help find him?"

"Well then I'd tell you I wasn't born yesterday and repeat for the third time that we *can't* help you if it involves a client." Now he looked right at Stone as he barked, "Next!"

Tennis shoes squeaked behind Stone, the person behind him stepping forward. But he didn't budge, glaring back at the clerk.

"Hey, kid, what's your problem?"

"What's my problem? I'm tired of taking your guys' shit! We all are!"

"Wait—who are '*my* guys?'"

"Cops. We're so tired of you going after our homeless clients. They need to get their money somehow, for God's sake. You can push them around elsewhere, but we're not gonna let you harass them through us. No more!"

"You think I'm a cop?"

"Well, ain't ya? You guys are in here every few days, asking the same questions you just asked. And no offense, but you definitely look like a cop."

Stone held his hands in the air.

"I'm not a cop," he said, softening his tone. "Retired deputy, but I'm now a private detective. And I really am trying to solve a crime. And it could involve one of your clients . . . as the victim."

The kid went quiet, giving Stone a chance to flash an updated photo of Fritzy—beard and all—that Micah had given him at the Comfort Center.

"Here's the guy I'm trying to find. He goes by Fritzy."

The clerk's eyes and open mouth gave him away. He recognized him.

"Yeah, he comes here. Part of that courthouse group."

"Well, he's the one who's gone missing, and I'd love to know if you guys have seen him lately."

Kev looked at his watch, then shook his head.

"Those guys nearly knock those doors down on the first of each month. But that was a few weeks ago . . ."

Stone pursed his lips.

"But give me a minute. I'll see if anyone saw him more recently."

* * *

"I'm the night manager. They tell me you're looking for Fritzy."

Raven-black hair pulled back in a ponytail, dark eyeliner contrasting sharply with her pale face and hazel eyes, the young woman looked no older than green-haired Lori from the Comfort Center. Like her colleague, Barb was dressed in jeans and a frayed Queen City Cash golf shirt, but hers was tucked in at least. She reached out and gave Rodney Stone a firm handshake.

"I am. You know him?"

Barb walked him over to the corner of the room as they talked.

"Yeah. He's been a customer since we first became a payee. Always a smile on his face."

"I'm afraid he's gone missing."

"That's what Kev said. Terrible. But I'm not sure how *we'd* know where he is."

"Well, I've checked every other place he frequents, and there's no sign of him. So yes, we're grasping for straws at this point."

Barb's thick eyebrows danced up and down.

"Kev said you swear you're not a cop. So when you say 'we,' who exactly are you referring to?"

"It's a long story." Stone didn't want to reveal his client.

"Well, my shift doesn't end until one, so I've got time. We don't just talk to anyone about our clients."

Stone took a few minutes to walk through Fritzy's connection to the Webb abduction, after which Barb pepped up.

"That poor councilman. Imagine getting robbed at gunpoint, driven around the city, worried you're going to die, and then in hours, the whole world says you were lying. Or that you're a drug addict!"

"So you believe him?"

"Well, I know nothing about it, but why would anyone make something like that up? Especially the part about running into Fritzy. How would you make that part up?"

Stone nodded along.

"Plus, while people in the burbs wouldn't know it, crazy shit happens all the time around here."

Stone nodded again. He'd seen a lot of crazy shit himself.

"When did that happen again?" she asked.

"Wednesday night."

187

Barb looked at her watch. Then looked up at the ceiling, bobbing her head. Thinking. Counting.

"I know," Stone said. "It's not the first of the month."

She shook her head.

"No, it's not. But it doesn't have to be."

She counted some more.

"Last Wednesday was the fifteenth, right?"

Stone did some quick math.

"Yes."

"Well," she said, smiling, "you may have found that straw you're grasping for."

"How's that?"

"Fritzy's a veteran."

"Okay?"

"He's been getting veterans assistance payments for years."

"Okay. Do they come here as well?"

"They sure do. Twice a month. The first and—"

"The fifteenth!"

"You got it. That's why we see him here more than the others."

"When does the payment get here?"

"We get it early on the fifteenth, process it, then customers can access it by the end of the day. So he very well could've come in that evening. He explained to me once that they wait to come here till after downtown clears out."

"Less busy?"

"No. By then no one's left in the streets to give spare change, so they don't lose money coming here."

Stone smirked. True entrepreneurs on the streets these days.

"How can we confirm that? Records of some sort?"

"Sure," the young woman said, growing as excited as he was. But then she pointed at the different corners of the office. "But security also records everything, so we can check the tapes. Give me one moment."

Stone tried not to get too hopeful during investigations, which usually involved long slogs around repeated dead ends. But his heart skipped a beat now that he was finally getting somewhere.

She walked away from Stone, back to Kev's counter. They exchanged a few words before Kev began typing on the computer in front of him. Then she walked to the back of the lobby and disappeared. Five minutes later, she returned with a smile on her face.

"Come on back, sir."

They walked to the back and entered a small, cramped office. Barb picked a piece of paper off her desk and handed it to him as he sat down in yet another undersized chair.

"Looks like Fritzy stopped in around 8:40 last Wednesday to withdraw funds," she said.

He scanned over the paper. Basic documentation of the transaction, high fee and all. Less than two hours after witnessing Webb at the ATM.

"Nothing peculiar about his visit?"

She swiveled her monitor around so he could see it. Two separate windows were open on the screen, each showing a view from a different camera. One outside, one inside.

"You're the detective. Take a look for yourself."

She moved the cursor to the first window, in the screen's upper left corner. It was a wide shot, with a view of the street, sidewalk, and parking lot outside the building. A digital display showed the time to be 8:39 and 40 seconds.

She pushed the small arrow at the bottom of the window. Seconds ticked off.

"Here he comes," she said when the time hit 8:40 and 15 seconds.

They both leaned in as a bearded man appeared from the upper right corner, walking along the sidewalk, into the entrance of the parking lot, then up to the foot of the building before disappearing at the bottom of the screen. He strode with a confident, soldierly gait. The angle of the final seconds also brought into view a small backpack slung over his right shoulder.

"Go back one more time, if you don't mind," Stone said after Fritzy disappeared from the screen.

She played the tape again. This time, Stone watched everything but Fritzy. Nothing stuck out. One car pulled out of the lot a few seconds after he arrived, but no movement or activity took place otherwise.

"Thank you. You have footage of him inside?"

"Of course. That's next."

She pointed at the other window on the screen, which showed the inside lobby of Queen City Cash from its back corner. She pushed play to start it at the 8:41 mark.

When the digital clock hit 8:41:16, Fritzy appeared from the upper left, walking to the only open counter and taking his place, third in line. As he stopped walking, he gave a slight wave to someone in front of him.

"Was he waving at the teller, you think?"

"For sure. Like I said, he's always very friendly here. It's one reason we want to help."

A few minutes ticked by as Fritzy, rocking side to side, waited patiently behind two people. He faced forward the entire time. At 8:45, he stepped up to the counter, chatted with the clerk, signed a piece of paper, then reached out to take an envelope the clerk was offering him. At 8:48, he tucked the envelope into the side pocket of his backpack and walked out the same door he came in. At 8:48:50, he disappeared from the camera shot.

"One more time, please," Stone asked.

She played the tape a second time, Stone again scanning everything but Fritzy. The two customers in front of him walked out of the lobby, and two other people walked in while he was at the counter, lining up behind him. That was it.

Barb returned to the other open window, fast forwarding to the 8:48:50 mark, then slowing to normal speed.

"You'll see he walks out and goes back in the direction he came from."

Stone nodded as they watched.

"As casual as can be."

On the second viewing, Stone keyed in on the lot itself. As Fritzy walked across the parking lot, an SUV drove into the lot and turned right to park. When he reached the sidewalk, several cars whizzed past on the road. And as he disappeared from the screen to the right, one customer walked out the door, crossing a new customer who was entering.

A whole lot of nothing.

"Pretty uneventful visit, I'd say," Barb said.

Stone nodded, scolding himself for having gotten hopeful in the first place. What the hell was he going to tell Grimes?

TUESDAY

Chapter 52

It reminded Maggie Coyle of the pinata from Emmie's tenth birthday party.

But Dylan Webb was the pinata.

She'd been tipped off thirty minutes prior, but so had everyone else in town. With four local stations airing live from the city hall chambers, all eight council members stepped to the podium to support the resolution calling for Webb's resignation.

None sounded angry. None attacked Webb personally.

No, they were far more brutal than that.

They were "disappointed." They felt let down. The city deserved better, they said. The words from his fellow Democrats were especially damaging, with Jackson saying he'd pray for Webb—as if his friend from only a week ago was morally damaged, in need of salvation.

Maggie cringed throughout. It was why she hated politics.

Allies one day turned into enemies the next.

And not one of them had any idea what had actually happened.

None of this was about principle or truth. Because the truth wasn't yet clear. She'd dug into it more than anyone, and she still had no idea.

This was what their politics demanded. None of these eight cowards could stand the political heat of simply waiting for the truth to come out. Too many emails. Too many calls. Tagged in too many tweets. Too many questions from the press demanding that they say something. And apparently not one had the spine to offer the basic answer: "We're going to wait for the facts."

So here they were, kneecapping him. Hyenas gnawing at a carcass, as the whole city watched.

For their own political gain.

It reminded her of her own downfall—thrown under the bus for telling the truth. A sting operation gone wrong—an innocent civilian dead and a young officer shot in the leg. They'd thought they were breaching a drug den on Vine Street—the *old* Vine Street— but it turned out to house nothing but a poor, young family in an apartment building. Maggie was on the SWAT team then, in addition to her homicide duties, and she'd known they'd violated several protocols. When she testified to that to internal investigators, the entire line of command had turned against her, starting with the now-chief, who'd led SWAT at the time. Prince, who still had blond hair back then, had been the breacher that night, the one who'd knocked the door down. To protect their own hides, they'd ripped her to shreds, digging through her file and killing her credibility through repeated leaks. Weeks later, she'd walked away.

It all still ate at her. But her fall also served as a brutal reminder of how much damage the chief could do when he wanted. As much now as then.

Disgusted by the political pile-on, Maggie convinced Temple that the details of the press conference weren't newsworthy. Just soundbites. And politics. No need to recap it later.

The *new* news came minutes after the conference ended, in the form of an email from Dylan Webb's office.

He had no plans to step down. Unlike Maggie's decision years ago, he was fighting back.

Chapter 53

For a split second, Rodney Stone's chest felt like it might cave in.

"Shit," his spotter yelled out as he reached down and grabbed the metal bar, stacked with 180 pounds in plates on each end.

"Thank you," Stone said.

"Sorry I was late," the spotter said. "Normally you do a lot more than three."

"I know," Stone mumbled as he sat up. "I'm distracted."

His wife had already asked him what was wrong as the family ate breakfast. He'd continued to stew as he dropped his three boys off at school, and he almost ran a red light as he made the short drive over to Westwood, at the far western edge of the city. And now he'd given out just on his third press.

He'd get paid either way, but Rodney Stone was dreading the planned 10 a.m. call. Nothing was worse than sharing bad news with his best client.

He showered, dressed, and drove to his cramped one-room office in Westwood. For the next hour, through two cups of coffee and a can of Monster, he pieced through everything he'd learned in the case, racking his brain for any other avenues to pursue.

And after all that brainstorming, he came to the conclusion that in the end, he had nothing.

He opened another Monster.

In one way, having absolutely nothing told him something was up. Sure, people don't get abducted with no evidence. But people also don't up and vanish with no trace either. Combine both unlikely scenarios, and the odds were that some type of shenanigan was underway. By people who knew what they were doing.

But without more, speculation alone wouldn't satisfy anyone. Not Grimes, and definitely not the higher-ups of the Cincinnati Police Department itching to put the high-profile case to bed.

At 9:55, the theme song from Hawaii 5-0 blasted out from his phone. His youngest son had programmed it as his ringtone months before.

He picked up.

"Rusty?"

"No. It's Barb."

He drew a blank even though the voice was familiar.

"Barb?"

"Yeah, from Queen City Cash. We met last night."

"That's right. Thanks again for trying to help."

"Oh, you're gonna thank me more in a second."

Stone shut his eyes. *Don't get hopeful.*

"Oh, really? And why's that?"

"Fritzy's disappearance was nagging me, so I went back and called the associates who worked last Wednesday night."

"And?"

His pulse started racing.

Don't get hopeful.

"One of them remembered Fritzy coming by later."

"Later?"

"Yeah. Like fifteen minutes later. But then he left without even coming in."

"How strange."

"Yes. Very."

"What—"

"Can I send it to the email address on your card? You can watch for yourself."

"Wait, you have it on video?"

"Yes!"

Just as she said it, his phone beeped.

"Send it right away! And thank you. I gotta get this call."

He jumped to the other call.

"Rusty?"

"Yeah. It's me. Got anything?"

Rodney held the phone away from his mouth, taking a deep breath. He needed to maintain his cool as he walked through things.

"Yeah, I do."

As he filled Grimes in, he opened his email inbox.

"I checked everywhere, and my best lead was with the payee of Webb's Social Security and veterans benefits."

"With the who?" Grimes asked.

To give himself time, Stone drew out his explanation of the role Queen City Cash played in disbursing payments to Fritzy, leaving out that it had been someone else's idea. As he concluded, an email arrived from a barb@qccash.com.

"Pretty smart, Stone. This is why you make the big bucks."

Smiling, Stone clicked on a file attached to the email. A circular arrow began spinning in the middle of the screen, indicating that a large file was being downloaded by his dinosaur of a desktop.

"Stone?"

"Yeah."

"Well, whatd'ya find there?"

The arrow was still spinning. Stone shook his head—he should've upgraded the desktop years ago, but he didn't have the money.

"At Queen City Cash?"

He didn't want to admit that the only thing he might've uncovered was in an email he still hadn't reviewed.

"Well, yeah! You said you had something from there."

"Yeah. It looks like Ventre stopped there *after* witnessing Webb at the ATM."

"Looks like? How do you know?"

The arrow was still spinning away.

"Um, I saw some security footage. He came by and got his money there."

"And? Did something happen while he was there?"

Still spinning.

"Well, at first . . ."

The spinning arrow disappeared, replaced by the now-familiar view from the outside security camera overlooking the parking lot at Queen City Cash. The digital clock indicated it was 9:04:14.

Stone pushed play.

"Stone?"

"Yeah?"

"What the hell's going on? Should I call back at a better time?"

Nothing happened for seconds. But then, reappearing from the top right part of the window, Fritzy walked briskly, hunched slightly forward. No backpack, and not the calm presence of his prior stop.

"Stone!"

A sharp beam of light lit up the top right of the screen. Then the dark shape of a van appeared, taking a quick left into the parking lot.

"No. Now's good, Rusty. One sec. I'm checking my notes."

At 9:04:40, Fritzy hustled to within feet of the door into Queen City Cash. He reached out his right hand to open it.

"Nothing out of the ordinary took place on his first visit," Stone said slowly, trying to maintain calm. "At least from what I could tell."

"Okay," Grimes said impatiently.

At 9:04:42, Fritzy froze, his right arm dropping to his side. He slowly turned around.

"But then he came back a few minutes later . . ."

Fritzy took a step away from the door, back in the direction of the van, which had come to a stop just inside the parking lot. The vehicle's passenger side was lined up parallel to the entrance of the office, about twenty feet away.

Fritzy slowly stepped toward the van, which in the light, looked to be gray.

"And that's when they grabbed him," Stone said, far louder and quicker than he'd meant to, like a play-by-play announcer describing a home run.

"Wait," Grimes said, "they grabbed him at the Queen City Cash?"

Feet from the car, Fritzy's head spun around. Whether intentionally or not, he looked right at the camera, eyes now wide with alarm. At 9:04:50, he stepped into the back seat of the van, the door closed behind him, and the dark vehicle drove off, turning left onto the dark street.

"They sure did. In the parking lot."

"And how do you know?"

Stone scrolled back a few seconds on the video, then advanced forward again in slow motion, looking closely at the back of the SUV as it left.

"Because, like I said," he declared, no longer hiding his excitement, "it's all on tape."

He leaned into the screen as he froze the video.

"And I've even got a license plate of the vehicle that drove him off."

"Well, hot damn, Rodney. Way to go!" Grimes said. "What dumb luck!"

"Luck? Like you said, this is why you hire me."

What he didn't say was that this was all on tape for only one reason, and it wasn't luck: Fritz Ventre wanted it to be.

Chapter 54

As soon as the bell rang, Kai left the classroom, put his calculus books in his locker, and slung his backpack over his right shoulder. He walked amid a stream of juniors and seniors toward the cafeteria. Not spotting Slay nearby, he darted down a short hallway and opened a door into a small outside courtyard on the side of the school.

Five minutes later, he hopped in the Uber he had summoned right before class ended.

"Playing hooky?" the older woman at the wheel asked as she pulled the old white Volkswagen out of the school lot.

"No, I'm a senior, so we can eat lunch off campus if we want."

"Well then, why d'ya look so nervous?"

Two reasons, Kai knew. One, he hoped Slay hadn't seen him duck out, but couldn't be sure. Two, where he was going.

"Big game later, I guess," he said.

They got on the highway and headed north.

"Where is this you're having me go?" the driver asked, looking at the small console in front of her. "I don't recognize it."

"Just a warehouse where I work on weekends. I left something there and need to pick it up for school."

"Right," the woman said, her scrunched up face visible through the mirror.

They drove for fifteen minutes in total silence.

He had done his best to guess where the warehouse was, but as she pulled up to the address he'd typed in back in math class, he didn't recognize the building.

"This isn't it."

"But it's the address you put in."

"I know. I must've gotten it wrong."

"But you said you work here," she said.

"I do," he said, feigning annoyance. "But a buddy usually drives me, so I've never paid attention to the actual address."

The driver shook her head.

From what he could remember, they'd been closer to the highway. The cars had been loud as they'd raced by.

"Head down there," he said, pointing to a road that took them right alongside I-75. "I think it's that way."

She slowly drove to the end of the road, trucks whizzing by from left to right in front of them.

"Now turn left."

She did, and the building appeared. Up and to the left. As he recognized the doorway they'd entered, his heart fluttered.

"That lot there. Actually, maybe pull over here."

He reached into his backpack and pulled out a Green Bay Packers hat and an old jean jacket he'd swiped from his dad's closet, putting both on.

"On the street?" the driver asked. "Before the lot?"

"Sure. That's better."

He took a pair of sunglasses from the backpack and put them on.

Eyes narrowing, she glared at him through the rearview mirror.

"Young man, I'm a mom myself. My son's about your age. What exactly are we doing here? And don't tell me you work here!"

Chapter 55

Rodney Stone looked down at the notepad in his passenger seat.

Diego DeLeon, 182 McPherson.

An old friend in the sheriff's traffic unit had tracked down the license plate captured by the Queen City Cash camera. The owner's address was in East Price Hill, one of the first communities up the hill as you head up Cincinnati's West Side.

"Enjoy Little Guatemala," the friend had joked as they hung up minutes before.

He wasn't kidding. As Stone approached McPherson from West Eighth, there was a life to the street that hadn't existed back when Stone patrolled the area in a squad car. A completely new vibe. A bakery. A couple restaurants. A small grocery. Two bars. All with Spanish signs on top of each storefront and decals in the windows.

Cincinnati's population was finally growing again—the first time in seventy years. But as all the politicians took credit for it, they rarely mentioned that waves of immigration accounted for most of the turnaround.

As he made a left onto McPherson, things quieted down. Small single-family homes and multifamily rentals, one after the next. Tiny yards. No driveways. Some well-taken care of. Others run down.

190.

186.

Stone pulled over in front of a two-story apartment building. With a twisted gutter hanging from one corner of the roof and a smorgasbord of junk piled up against the right side of the building, it was the most run-down place on the street.

Black paint on the sidewalk was the only indication of the house number.

182.

Stone got out of the Mustang and approached the building. A rusted metal door was cracked open a few inches. He pulled it open and entered a small rectangular hallway. A door was on each side of the hallway, neither with a number on it. Coupon booklets, papers of all sorts, and a few plastic bags were strewn about, mainly on the hallway's right side.

Worst of all, the place reeked. Something was rotting inside.

The door to his left cracked opened, and an older Black woman peered through, large glasses taking up much of her round face.

"About time you showed up," she said, an annoyed edge in her voice to go along with a sneer. "I told them it smelled to high hell in here, and it's still been days."

Stone rolled with it.

"You know who lives here?" he asked, gesturing toward the closed door.

"It's been someone new each year for the last twenty or so."

"I mean now."

"I know what you mean. Nice man. He told me to call him Leon. Moved in about a year ago. But he up and disappeared a few weeks back. Not sure he's livin' at all anymore."

From the stench, Stone worried she was right.

"What do you know about him?"

"Not much. Was always polite. Seemed like a dedicated worker. My guess is he was working hard here, then sending money home, like a lot of the new people around here. Construction, maybe, from how he dressed. But like I said, haven't seen him for weeks."

She pointed at all the papers on DeLeon's side of the hallway.

"And it wasn't like him to leave such a mess. Whenever he got home, he'd even mop off any mud left from his boots."

"You ever see him with anyone?"

"Nah. Some other guy would pick him up most mornings. They'd go to work together."

"What kind of car?"

"Different ones. But last I saw, a gray van."

Same one that followed Fritzy, no doubt.

"Are you sure it wasn't Leon's van?"

She shook her head.

"Damn sure. Never parked here. Always picked him up."

She sneered again.

"What's with all these questions? Ain't you gonna go in there? Figure out what that smell is, and where Leon went? I mean, that's why I called all those days ago."

"Sure," Stone said. "But I've got to call it in first. I can't walk into someone's place like that."

She guffawed. "Cops do it all the time," she said. "You health people aren't allowed to? Hell, yer big enough to break down the door with your bare hands."

Stone laughed. "Once I call it in and get authorization, then I can. Open the door, at least."

She nodded.

Feeling nauseous from the odor, he opened the main door again to let some air in. She had to be right.

"Now tell me again the last time you saw Leon?"

"Two Sundays ago. He'd come back from church all dressed up. And I remember that the last time I saw him he had a suit on. Then I never saw him again, and the smell started."

Stone stepped outside and called back his friend in traffic.

"You track him down?"

"I did."

"And?"

"Send a unit to that address as soon as you can and notify the coroner. Call me later and tell me what they find."

Chapter 56

Even though it was midday, the warehouse parking lot was empty. Not a soul in sight.

Kai walked toward the door he'd entered days ago, his stomach knotted as the image of the beat-down bearded man flashed in his memory. Worried about triggering an alarm, Kai didn't go within feet of it.

Ever since they'd driven away a few days back, the guilt had eaten away at him. Maybe he could help find the man if he were still alive. Atone for the mugging. He needed to try, at least. Not even trying went against everything Ma and Dad had taught him. And maybe trying would help him sleep through the night again.

He walked slowly from one end of the front side of the warehouse to the other, but the metallic gray external wall facing the parking lot displayed no markings. A few small, square windows appeared high above. Not at all helpful.

He rounded the corner on the warehouse's far side to encounter another door, smaller than the first, followed by a window. Kai approached the pane and looked in. It was dark inside, but he could make out the basic shape of a small, barren hallway. With tall grass and brush to his left, he walked toward the highway along a path of weeds and loose rocks that abutted the building.

He turned another corner and paced along the warehouse's far side. The ground shook from large semis barreling down the highway to his left. Along the way, he kicked a few soda cans and other trash that had been discarded along the interstate. He stepped around a few stray tires, almost tripping on one obscured by weeds. But still nothing identified what was inside the warehouse, or who owned it.

He finally turned the next corner, keeping close to the warehouse's external wall to avoid thick tangles of branches, brush, and thorns to his left. Still no markings the entire way. Head down, he walked back to the Uber.

"You find what you're looking for?" the driver asked as he sat back down.

"No, ma'am," he said. "No one's there."

She eyed him in the rearview mirror, then looked down at her phone.

"The building's owned by Tri-State Storage."

"Yeah, I know."

She shook her head as she pulled out.

"Young man, be careful. Fibbing is not your strong suit."

Chapter 57

"You're the second person asking for him in two days," the young manager named Barb said to Maggie Coyle.

It was a few minutes after one. They were sitting in the small office in the back of Queen City Cash.

Shane Kramer, an old friend and commander of the downtown unit who she'd called a few days back, had reported back in the morning. While he'd had no details on Ventre's whereabouts, he'd mentioned that many of the homeless guys from the courthouse used this check-cashing store as their payee, so Maggie headed over after grabbing a sandwich.

"Another reporter?" Maggie asked, surprised anyone else would think to check here.

"No. Some kind of private investigator." She leaned forward and picked up a card from her desk. "Rodney Stone was his name."

Coyle nodded. She'd overlapped with Stone over the years, when they were at the city and county, and since. He was a capable investigator. Smart of Webb to have someone that good looking into this.

"He actually visited twice." Barb typed on her keyboard as she spoke.

"Stone did?" Maggie asked.

"No, the guy he was looking for. Who you asked about. The whole thing was really odd."

She typed again, then swiveled the monitor around so Maggie could see it.

"Twice when?"

"The night Mr. Stone asked about. Last Wednesday, I believe. Here, look for yourself."

Over the next five minutes, Maggie watched both videos. The first, when Fritzy stood in line and picked up his money. And the second, when he approached the door outside before a gray van appeared.

"Pause there," Maggie said, heart racing. "Zoom in."

Perfect. The van's front plate was visible. She wrote down the number.

"Can I also have Mr. Stone's number?"

"Sure."

The girl handed her the card.

Chapter 58

"You were right."

Stone chuckled as he walked back into his mess of an office, Subway sandwich in one hand, phone in the other. Of course he was right. Decomposing human tissue stank like nothing else.

"How long?" he asked his buddy in traffic.

"They said a week at least."

"How?"

"Either a heart attack or foul play. No obvious external injury beyond some basic bruises that could've been caused by anything."

Poor guy, Stone thought. And his poor family back home.

"It wasn't a heart attack. This was part of something bigger."

"I hear ya. Speaking of, they want to know how you knew."

"I told ya. The place stunk of death."

"Not how you knew he was dead. How you knew to go there in the first place?"

"Who's they?"

"Homicide."

"Cincinnati PD homicide?"

"Yes. It's their jurisdiction, of course."

"It's a long story, but I'm in the middle of a private job. I can't say anything at the moment."

Stone knew the police department was all over the Webb abduction, with what Grimes said were mixed motives. Too close for comfort.

"Well, they may give you a call."

"Wait, do they know I'm the one who reported it?"

"C'mon, Rodney. You know I couldn't keep that from them."

"Can you at least keep me out of any paperwork?"

"I'll do my best. But it would help if you told me what triggered your suspicion."

"Can't right now. But I will when I can."

Seconds after hanging up, another call came through.

"Is this Rodney Stone?" a familiar woman's voice asked after he picked up.

He rolled his eyes. Homicide calling already.

"This is he."

"It's Maggie Coyle. From—"

"*The* Maggie Coyle? How are ya?"

He'd always respected her both as a police investigator and as a reporter. But he also knew that an interview with her would be huge for business.

"I'm great. You and I are chasing down a similar story, I believe."

They talked for the next five minutes, then agreed to grab coffee at four to swap notes.

Chapter 59

Head tilted, the receptionist looked askance at Dylan Webb from the moment he stepped off the elevator. After he said his name, she did a double take.

"Is she expecting you?" she asked through a full scowl.

Her question made clear Laurie Busken was in.

"She's not," he answered back as the receptionist pressed a few buttons on her desk phone. "I was down the street after lunch and thought I'd drop in."

She leaned into the phone's handset.

"It's Dylan Webb . . ."

She went silent. Grimacing.

"Yes, the council member. He wants to talk to Ms. Busken . . . No. Not on the phone."

She looked up at him, then back down.

"He's standing right in front of me."

She listened for a few seconds, then eyed him again.

"She's on a call. She can't—"

Dylan smirked.

"Tell her I'm happy to wait."

She repeated his words into the phone, then listened to the reply.

"It's going to be a long time."

He looked at his watch. "That's fine. I've got the time. I'll wait till she's done."

He sat down on a leather couch, leaning back and stretching his arms wide as if prepared to stay for hours.

"He's gonna wait," she said back into the phone in a semi-whisper. Then a second later: "Yes, in the lobby."

She hung up the phone.

"Her assistant's on the way."

"Wonderful!"

Dylan suppressed a laugh.

Being a pariah had its perks.

* * *

"You really shouldn't be here, Dylan," Laurie Busken said from behind her desk, her wavy blonde hair pulled back in the ponytail she usually wore in private. Even her scowl couldn't diminish the former Ms. Utah's beauty. Her skin appeared permanently bronzed, and with high cheekbones, a small button nose, and emerald eyes, Busken and her willowy figure turned heads wherever she went.

Dylan closed the door behind him and sat in a wooden chair across from her. Large windows over both Laurie's shoulders opened up to the river. Her spacious corner office was far more impressive than he'd expected.

"Well, you've refused to answer my calls, so I had no choice."

"You're the lawyer, not me. But the lawyers at city hall warned us to avoid you. That we could all be witnesses if we talked to you."

"Yeah, and if you're deposed, all you need to tell them is that I said it happened exactly like I said it did."

Her eyes were facing the top of her desk, so Webb stopped talking until she looked right at him.

"Laurie, I'm being railroaded," Dylan said, raising his voice. "I don't know why, but this is all bullshit. Praying for me? Are you serious?"

"That was Curtis speaking, not me."

"Right, but what you said was just as bad."

She stared back at him, clearly hesitant to say more.

"What do you need, Laurie?"

The front edge of a barge appeared in the window over Laurie's left shoulder, heading east.

"What do I *need*?" she repeated, eyes crinkling.

From what Jackson had said, she was one of the driving forces behind the resolution. Five was a long way away, but if he could flip even one of the ringleaders, maybe he could turn things around.

"Yeah, what do you need to be convinced it happened like I said it did? To come to my defense?"

"Well, the police need to say it—and I mean loudly and clearly—and then I'm good. But I'm not your problem. I'm trying to stay out of it and get my work done, as hard as that's become."

Work to Laurie Busken meant commercial real estate, which was why they'd often agreed to disagree on development. To be in this corner office with that river view, she clearly was succeeding in her day job. Framed photos on a bookshelf behind her showed an international clientele resembling the United Nations. *Who knew so many wanted to do business in Cincinnati*, Dylan thought without saying it.

"Well, who's the problem then?" he asked instead.

She grimaced.

"Who isn't? The Republicans. The mayor." She paused. "Kane. Jackson."

"Jackson?"

Webb had assumed the mayor all along. Of course, Kane. Pete Stack wouldn't want to stand up to Kane. Plus, while Stack hid it well, Dylan always sensed a competitive streak below the surface.

But Jackson? He'd confided in Jackson.

"Oh, yeah. He didn't say much at first. But then he led the charge for this morning."

Dylan's face tensed up.

"He said it wasn't right that you're embarrassing us all. The lying and drug use. And that you made it worse when you used the police shootings to curry favor. That's how he convinced Spiller to switch and make it unanimous."

Dylan ground his teeth while fuming inside. There went the guy he trusted most.

"Anyone else to be concerned about? The chief?"

After passing in front of both windows, the boxlike cabin of the barge disappeared, a slight wake behind it.

Laurie shrugged. "He doesn't believe your story, of course. But no one does. He thinks you'll resign in a few days. Honestly, everyone does."

"So what can I do?"

"Like I said, if the police say it happened, then you're all good as far as I'm concerned. Probably a few others too."

He shook his head. Awaiting a clear statement from the police would doom him.

"Laurie, I could feel it the moment they started asking me questions that night. They hate us because we're trying to change the place." She'd been a strong ally on some use-of-force reforms. "They love that I'm hung out to dry. They could easily do the same to you."

She shrugged again.

"Maybe so. But what else would you expect me to say?"

That you trust me, he thought to himself.

But his short time in politics had taught him that was too much to ask.

Chapter 60

Rodney Stone swore that his Mustang aged a few weeks every time he navigated down Warsaw Avenue toward downtown. The East Side would never put up with its main arteries left this decrepit.

Mercifully, the bumps and potholes of the steep, curved hill ended as soon as the road levelled off and transitioned into the viaduct. The ancient bridge that connected Cincinnati's West Side to downtown had finally been upgraded a year ago, which allowed for twice as much traffic and a smooth ride. And with it, much faster driving.

Stone veered into the right lane, the river off to his right and the stadiums and downtown rising ahead of him through the soggy gray air. The viaduct crossed high above a hodgepodge of railroad tracks and industrial sites that made up one edge of the long-segregated neighborhood known as the West End. Stone knew it well. He'd grown up on its tough streets, then spent years watching prisoners in an old West End slaughterhouse the county had converted into a jail. The top floors of that jail loomed off to his right.

His phone vibrated in his right pocket.

Having too often seen the carnage that texting and driving wrought, he normally would've let his phone be, but he was running late for Maggie Coyle and didn't want her to leave.

He thrust his right hand into his pocket, dug out his phone, and held it by his knee.

After a few swipes, an unrecognized number appeared at the top of his screen. A non-Ohio area code.

He pulled the phone closer to read the words.

Hello.

Ellipses appeared, indicating another message was on its way. Still driving one-handed, he looked back up.

Another vibration.

Stone . . .

He looked back up. Then another vibration.

He looked down a third time.

Look behind you.

He glanced at the rearview mirror but saw nothing but cars some distance back.

Thump.

A violent jolt whipped his torso to the right while his head shot to the left, directly into tiny shards of glass exploding away from what used to be his window. From his forehead to his chin, a hot pain seared his face as if it were in flames. His left eye went instantly dark.

He instinctually turned in the direction of the collision—his left—but the view was blocked by the red siding of a large van only inches from his face. The van's hood was a yard past the front of his own car, angled sharply into his lane. With the window gone, the van's engine roared in his left ear.

He jammed his right hand against the steering wheel to sound the horn, pumping it twice.

But the van kept pushing, overpowering him so that he was careening out of the right lane and in the direction of the river.

He abandoned the horn to grip the steering wheel with both hands, then forcefully jerked it to his left. Stone had survived in life by ensuring that he could physically overpower just about anyone, but the size and force of the van overwhelmed his Mustang. Then a second violent collision confirmed this was no accident.

Just as he reached the brake pedal with his right foot, his car slammed into the concrete barrier guarding the side of the road.

Any hope that the barrier would save him disappeared in an instant.

Not because the new thick concrete didn't hold.

It did.

But as he collided into it, the Mustang jolted upward from back to front, somersaulting, throwing his body up and forward along with it. For a moment, looking straight down through his front windshield, the top of the concrete barrier raced by, directly beneath him. As he soared over the edge, his old stomping grounds whizzed by in a gray blur far below.

Then, upside down, the free fall began.

Chapter 61

Maggie Coyle looked at her phone for the third time.

Her mug sat empty as she huddled in the corner of the popular coffee shop on Central Parkway, just north of downtown and only three blocks from the courthouse where Fritz Ventre had last been seen.

Not only was Rodney Stone twenty minutes late, he hadn't responded to her two text messages asking where he was.

She dialed his number. Again.

Straight to voicemail. Again.

Something was wrong. Ex-cops respond.

She'd ignored the blaring of multiple fire trucks a few minutes back, but now she assumed they were connected to the empty chair across from her.

She called her best contact in the city's Emergency Communications Center, where both police and fire calls were dispatched.

"Hey, Maggie, what's up?"

"You just had a major fire run out of downtown. Multiple engines. Can you find out what for?"

"Sure. One sec."

Silence followed for half a minute.

"Jesus, Maggie."

"What happened?"

"Never seen it before."

"What's that?"

"Crazy scene. Terrible accident on the viaduct."

Maggie shuddered, suddenly breathless.

Stone was coming from the West Side. Which meant he would've been coming over the viaduct, same route she took every day. Accidents happened there regularly—if less so after the upgrade.

"How bad?"

"Real bad. A car flipped over the wall."

Jesus. She couldn't recall that happening before.

"As in off the bridge entirely?"

But Maggie already knew the answer.

"I'm afraid so. It's now a burning heap in the railyard."

She tried to say something back. But no words came out.

Rodney Stone was dead.

Chapter 62

Arms outstretched, Kai leapt as high as he could.

Heaved from feet beyond the key, the ball was arcing down at the perfect trajectory. Several feet above the rim. Several feet from his hands and closing quickly.

He'd never pulled one off in an actual game, but with his summer growth spurt, Kai had dunked alley-oop passes in practices all fall. He was the only guy on his undersized team who could do so, helping immensely in his quest to make the starting lineup.

This one was textbook.

But as he reached the highest point of his jump, something hard collided into him below his knee. High up and defenseless, he somersaulted almost completely upside down. Just before crashing headfirst into the floor, he thrust his left arm above his head and against the gym floor. It didn't slow the fall, but at least it ensured that his right shoulder hit first instead of his skull.

All went black. Pain shot through both his left wrist and his right shoulder, which had taken the brunt of the fall. A guttural moan escaped from deep within his throat.

He opened his eyes, then squinted to make sense of the view from flat on his back. Steel rafters high above. A circle of blurred faces and wide eyes much closer.

A whistle blared from a few feet away.

"Give him space!" Coach yelled. The circle of faces widened slightly.

"Slayton!" Coach yelled, loud enough that it penetrated the ringing in Kai's ears. "What the hell was that?"

Slay? Kai thought. *Was it Slay?* He'd seen nothing but the floor, then the ceiling.

Above and to his right came Slay's voice, almost in a wail.

"I'm so sorry, Kai. I didn't mean it."

Slay never apologized. For anything. And he was bad at faking it now.

Then his voice got a lot closer. Kai rolled his head to his right to see Slay's nose, sweaty peach fuzz and snarled lips only inches away.

"Motherfucker, where were you at lunch today?" he whispered so that only Kai could hear him. Then without hesitation, he said far more loudly, "I'm so sorry. I got caught under you and couldn't move in time."

A new voice penetrated his left ear.

"Y'okay, Kai?" It was Coach.

Kai cleared his throat. His shoulder throbbed in pain.

"I'm not sure, Coach. Let me lie here for a second and see."

"Take as long as you need. I'll call the nurse."

Slay was still in his right ear. "I'm so sorry—"

"Enough, Slay. That was a cheap shot. Get to the damn locker before you do any more damage. Back to practice, guys."

The faces surrounding Kai turned away, then the circle of bodies dissipated.

Slay stayed right where he was. The menacing whisper returned.

"You fuck around anymore, and you won't be jumping at all. Ever—"

"Slay!" Coach yelled from a few feet away. "Get to the locker room now, or I suspend you from the damn team."

He stood up, pushing Kai's right wrist hard into the floor in the process.

"Yes, Coach."

Chapter 62

"We were able to run the plates. Looks like it was a former sheriff's deputy. Before my time."

Sam, Maggie's cameraman, had picked her up and driven her to the scene of the accident. They were now huddled in a parking lot near where a Ford Mustang—a twisted and charred wreck—had crashed down onto an old, unused railroad spur.

A jittery police communications officer was briefing four reporters, all eager to air images of the mangled wreckage. Maggie had long ago stopped covering traffic accidents—let the whippersnappers grab it for their resumes—but she wanted a front row seat for this one. Still, she hung back, not wanting to stick out.

"Do you have a name?" another reporter asked.

"The deceased's name is Rodney Stone," the officer said, her eyes bouncing between the various reporters.

An older reporter piped up. "Oh, he's some kind of private eye these days."

Two others nodded.

"*Was,*" one of them interjected with a smirk.

"I didn't know that," the officer said. "Sad to hear."

"Solo accident?" another reporter asked.

"Several 911 calls that came in said it was a collision. Stone and some van ran into each other, which propelled him right off the road."

"That's one hell of a collision," the first reporter said. "I've never seen a car fly off the whole viaduct before."

The cop nodded. "We haven't either. It may be the lower wall—"

She stopped short, knowing this was a slip.

"Wait, do you think the new viaduct isn't safe?" a third reporter asked, realizing they now had a ratings-spiking angle to this macabre scene.

"I didn't say that. Just that we haven't seen a car go over before." Too late. The spokeswoman knew it.

"Where's the van?" Coyle asked.

The cop shook her head.

"We don't know. It left the scene, that's for sure."

"No license plate?"

"Nope. No one was close enough."

"And did you get any description of the collision? As in, *who* did the colliding?"

"Two of the callers said that Mr. Stone's car swerved into the van's lane, hit the van, then veered sharply the other way and couldn't recover. And that he'd been swerving for much of the viaduct. Sadly, it has all the markings of texting and driving."

Maggie shook her head. This was a setup, and the 911 callers were likely part of it.

"Are you going to look at his phone records to confirm it?"

"Doing that now. But we actually found his phone fifteen feet from the car." She pointed to a small circle of tape to the wreck's right. "This tells us it was loose in the car. Which is consistent with those reports."

The officer's eyes widened. "Hey, guys, maybe have this story be about the dangers of texting and driving instead of scaring people about the new viaduct, huh?"

"Good luck with that one," one reporter said.

Maggie knew her absurd business well enough to know that the "viaduct may be dangerous" story was about to lead the 6 p.m. news.

But that's not why her blood was racing. As she stared back at the wreck, far greater worries ate at her.

First, the only witness who could confirm Dylan Webb's story had disappeared. And now the guy who was getting to the bottom of that disappearance had been offed.

WEDNESDAY

Chapter 63

"I saw it all over the news," Dylan said, feeling sick to his stomach. "So what the hell do we do now? Who do we tell?"

Dylan was in his council office when Grimes called, filling him in that the former sheriff's deputy who'd driven off of the Western Hills Viaduct was also the private eye he'd hired to look into Dylan's case.

"Well, the police obviously know. They're calling it an accident— texting and driving."

"That's bullshit, and you know it."

"Slow down, cowboy. I agree. My point is, if the cops have already reached that conclusion, there really isn't anyone to tell, now is there? Since that's who we *would* tell."

"I mean who do we tell *about it all*. That he was looking into the homeless guy who saw me at the ATM. And now both are probably dead."

"Dylan," he said slowly, followed by a long pause.

"Yes?"

"Do you think the cops are on your side right now?" Grimes asked, like a parent trying to calm a child's tantrum.

Dylan paused, all his conversations with various police officers coming to mind.

"No, I don't."

"Well, I don't either. At least, some of them."

"And *some* is all it takes," Webb said quietly.

"Exactly."

"So what do we do about it?"

As he asked the question, the door to this office opened. Gabby's head popped through the open doorway, her eyes wide.

"Hold on," Dylan said into the phone before pulling it away from his ear.

"Did the mayor change his mind?" he asked.

Minutes before, the mayor had cancelled the day's council meeting.

"No, different topic," Gabby said. "We just got the strangest email."

"Strange how?"

She shook her head.

"Just really strange. And it's about your case."

Chapter 64

It stuck out immediately.

Fifteen minutes after ending her third live shot under the Western Hills Viaduct in twenty-four hours, Maggie Coyle was back at her desk, scrolling through a long list of unread emails on her screen.

Then she froze.

Forty minutes prior, an email had arrived from the address WebbBeingFramed@gmail.com.

Webb being framed.

While *she'd* suspected it, not a single person had made such a suggestion, either publicly or privately, since the scandal had started. But there it was.

The subject line took it a step further: *The Missing Homeless Guy*

She clicked. Only two lines.

He was at Tri-State Storage a few days ago. Near the highway.

She immediately switched to her browser and googled Tri-State Storage. Three entries down, Google Maps displayed nine different locations for the business, eight of which looked to be large warehouses. Five were near one of the four major highways running through and around Cincinnati.

She was printing out the map and the locations when a new email popped up.

Another tantalizing sender account.

DruggieWebb@yahoo.com.

That address and the subject line brought her back to her riverside walk with the tanned, tattooed guy in the Escalade. She'd forgotten all about it.

Proof of Webb's Buying Habit

Must be him.

She clicked.

Chapter 65

"What do you make of that?" Dylan Webb asked Grimes after forwarding the email from WebbBeingFramed@gmail.com.

"Depends."

Dylan choked on some of the Diet Coke he had just sipped down.

"Depends on what?"

"Who have you told about the homeless guy?"

Webb racked his brain.

"Well, I mentioned it in that TV interview."

Silence from Grimes.

"Okay. But did you mention that he was missing?"

"No. I didn't know that then."

"So who have you told that he's *missing*?"

He remembered his chat with the mayor. And Jackson. "Maybe I told a couple of my colleagues. But they thought it was a joke. Other than that, no one."

Silence.

"So what are you going to do about it?" Dylan asked. "Get another private eye?"

More silence. Then a sigh.

"Did you really tell your colleagues?"

"I did."

"Why the fuck would you do something that dumb?"

"Because I was trying to convince them not to kick me off the council!"

"And how did that work out for you?"

Dylan let seconds of silence answer the question.

Then a deep breath huffed through the phone.

"Mr. Webb," Grimes said, speaking more formally than he ever had. "A man is missing and likely dead because he was a witness to your abduction. Now a second man is dead who was looking into it. You yourself said you cannot trust people in the police department on this. So I am here to tell you that you *cannot* trust a soul on that council. Whatever is going on is deadly serious. And anything you say to *anyone* is gonna bounce around this town so fast, whoever we don't want to know it will know it just as fast."

"I understand now."

"Say nothing else but to me."

"Okay."

More silence, so Dylan repeated his prior question.

"So what are you going to do about it? Another private eye?"

"No way. I don't want to get anyone else killed. Let me take a closer look at this email."

Chapter 66

"Honey, you're not gonna eat *again?*"

Kai nibbled at the spaghetti in front of him, moving the meatballs around with his fork more than he actually ate them. His younger brother, Jamelle, hadn't helped matters, wolfing down his helping and already sitting in front of the television in the family room.

"I already told you about my fall in practice, Ma."

Her head cocked to one side.

"You can ask Coach how bad it was!"

But she knew him too well. As bad as the bruises were on his shoulder and wrist, his roiling stomach had nothing to do with Slay's cheap shot.

Stopping through the school computer lab before practice, he'd set up the new Gmail account and drafted two identical messages. He'd then hunted down the email addresses he needed: the councilman and that reporter who'd interviewed him.

He'd stared at the screen for minutes, the cursor fixed over the send button. Not only would these emails cross the line into betraying Slay and whoever was at that warehouse, but they also risked getting him arrested for the original robbery itself.

In the end, the guilt he'd been feeling for days overcame the fear. So he'd finally tapped the mouse's button with his index finger, sending off the two emails.

A brief moment of relief had accompanied doing the right thing. Then practicing with his sore shoulder had provided a painful distraction from it all.

But once home, the tension reignited with a fury, Slay's snarling whisper still echoing in his ear. The fear of being nabbed for the kidnapping.

The walls were closing in.

"Oh, I see that it was bad, Kai."

"Huh?" he asked, looking up from his plate. "What was bad?"

"Your fall. Those bruises."

"Oh, yeah. It really hurt."

"Of course. But you ate fine last night. So I'm confused why that would keep you from eating your dinner *tonight*."

"It just is, Ma. I think I need to go lie down."

Chapter 68

"C'mon, Maggie. This is not a story. This is part of a coordinated takedown, and you know it."

Maggie Coyle and Dylan Webb faced off in a mostly empty restaurant that hung off the edge of Price Hill, a short walk from her condo. Downtown shone in the distance, to his right and her left. After she'd called and described the basics of the email, the rattled councilman had begged for a meeting. So they chose the West Side this time.

As she always did back in homicide, she didn't blink as she studied every part of his face. This guy was either a very good liar or truly being railroaded.

"But is this true? Is this really you?" she said, gesturing toward the table. "Stuff like this doesn't appear out of thin air."

Spread in front of them both, among her glass of wine, his can of Diet Coke, and some butter-drenched bread sticks were four pieces of paper she'd printed out in the studio. They'd been attachments in that second email. Dates and dollar amounts ran from top to bottom—the name "Dylan Webb" appearing again and again.

But it was the shadowed logo appearing throughout that had especially sparked his ire. A simple double P, which lent damning credibility to all the numbers involved.

He waved his hand toward the pages.

"These have nothing to do with my abduction. Or the nonsense that I made it up."

They were printouts of PayPal receipts. And they made it clear that Dylan was the one paying: $400 here, $600 there. Every month or two for several years.

"But," she said, pointing to one of the places where his name appeared, "is this you?"

"I don't know how you got those, but yes."

"And what were—"

"I told you, I regularly smoked pot then."

"And you paid your dealer over *PayPal*?"

"It wasn't a dealer. Just a friend who always had some. I'd reimburse him regularly."

He spread out the sheets and scanned them.

"That last one's from February, a few years back. Shortly before I started campaigning. As I told you, that's when I quit."

He was good.

"Or maybe that's when you started paying in cash?"

"That's absurd!" he said, open palms flying upward.

"Not absurd at all. It actually would've been the smart thing to do." She leaned forward. "Most people don't stop using cold turkey. But they definitely come up with other ways to pay when they need to, or when they need to hide it."

"Well, I'm not most people. As I said, I quit when the campaign started."

"Can I put that on the record?" Maggie asked.

His eyes bugged wide.

"Please tell me you're not going to do a story on this. This has nothing to do with anything. You already broke this earth-shattering scoop about my past drug use, remember. And don't tell me a whole lot of people you know don't smoke pot, or worse."

"Of course they do," she said, smiling. Including lots of cops she knew, along with much of the city press corps.

"Well, are they getting it for free? I mean, you have to buy it, right?"

She took a sip from her glass, her eyes not leaving his. Time to drop the hammer.

"Dylan," she said, pausing for effect. "I have a source who says it has *everything* to do with the abduction."

"Huh? Who?"

"The same person who sent me these."

He leaned back as she took another sip.

"He says you were getting shaken down for a lot more money once you were on the council. And you refused to pay the higher amount."

"And that's why they abducted me?"

"It's not a wild theory. I'll admit I thought he was full of it at first. But these are pretty impressive receipts . . ."

His face was now beet red, splotches overrunning his cheeks.

"And they make it plausible that you didn't even know it was coming. So you didn't make it up, but that could still be the reason it all happened."

"Of course," he said quietly as his shoulders sagged, reminding her of interviews right before the perps confessed. "Just perfect. I didn't know about it, but it's still unsavory enough that I have to resign."

Stone-faced for a moment, Dylan suddenly leaned forward with a new burst of energy.

"I'm telling you the truth, Maggie," he said, fist hitting the table. "Who's your source? Some kind of drug goon? Is that who you're going to believe over me?"

"Trust me, cops like me get tons of good information from unsavory people. Few bring proof like this."

"But they were before my—"

"It's about the pattern of buying, Dylan. Which backs up the story."

"Except that I stopped buying when—"

"Or moved to cash. How in the hell would this guy have these?"

"I've been wondering that myself. Maybe he's the one who sold to my friend."

"And how would he *get* these from your so-called friend?"

The redness now spread to his neck and ears.

"Trust me, I'm wondering that too. Either way, I'm telling the truth. This is all some elaborate takedown. From my front door a week ago to these emails tonight."

They stared at each other for seconds, an awkwardness Maggie interrupted.

"I so want to believe that."

"Bullshit," he said, now gripping his empty Diet Coke can. "It's pretty clear no one does. The sight of a politician going down is too good for any of you to pass up. And whoever is doing this played you all perfectly: create a scandal, then a feeding frenzy, light up Twitter with some hashtag that goes viral, all to destroy me. And you guys can't help yourselves."

She nodded and finished her glass of wine.

To believe Webb required her to believe one hell of an elaborate plot. The far simpler story was the drug-buying one.

But he was still making a good case. And selling it well.

Too well for her to go with the story. For now.

THURSDAY

Chapter 69

Dylan Webb's cell phone vibrated at six in the morning, shaking against the top of his bedside table loudly enough to wake him.

It was Gabby, far earlier than she'd ever called. Not a good sign.

"Have you seen the *Enquirer*?"

He sat up in bed, legs hanging over the side.

"Gabby, I just woke up. I haven't seen anything."

"Well, take a look!" She was yelling through the phone.

He sighed, having stopped looking at all news outlets days ago. "Just tell me what it is."

"Well, it looks like someone kept receipts of multiple transactions you made a few years ago. Over PayPal. And sent them to the paper. And they're saying they look like repeated drug buys."

"Jesus," Dylan said, his head suddenly aching as if someone had hit it with a hammer. "I can't believe they didn't even call."

"Didn't *call*?" Gabby asked. "But are they real?"

He sighed again.

"They are. Maggie Coyle showed them to me last night, and I convinced her they weren't a story. Nothing new from what's already out there. Whoever sent them to her also must've sent them to the paper."

"Dylan," Gabby said, followed by a long silence.

"Yes."

"I don't think you can keep this up. I don't think *I* can keep this up. It's too much."

"Gabby, you and I both know tons of people who used to smoke pot. And they clearly paid—"

"Just stop, Dylan." She'd never spoken to him that roughly before. "The article is suggesting that it was your refusal to keep paying that led to the abduction. That makes it very different from anyone else."

"And who do they have saying that?"

"They call them 'sources.' No names."

"That is such bullshit."

"Maybe so. But I don't see a way out. We are gonna get crushed today. Crushed. I haven't even told you how bad it is. The other council aides look at *me* like *I* committed a crime! All the other staff too. Even my dad thinks it's time to step down. None of this is worth it."

"Gabby, this all happened like I said it did."

"Except that you were buying drugs."

"Two years ago!"

A long pause.

"So you never refused to pay?"

"No! I never bought any after we started the campaign. They're digging up something from my past and trying to tie it to this. But it's totally unrelated."

More silence. She was coming around.

"Well, how can we prove that?"

His phone beeped as another call came in. One of the talk radio stations, no doubt calling about the story. He usually went on live with their morning deejay whenever they asked.

He let it keep ringing.

"I'm trying. Believe me."

"How can I help?"

"You can't. But Grimes is taking a close look at that email. Hopefully he turns up something."

His phone rang a third time. Florida.

"Let me get this."

"Okay," Gabby said.

He clicked over.

"Dad?"

"Mom's on too." He was on speakerphone.

"Dylan," Mom chimed in. "We're worried about you."

Ever since he'd entered politics, his parents had never questioned Dylan's judgement. They were apolitical—hands off—simply standing by him. And that had been their posture since the abduction, in their nightly phone calls. But their tone now suggested this was about to end.

"Let me guess. You saw the article?"

"We did," Dad said.

"What's happening, Dylan?" Mom again. "It just keeps getting worse."

They both sounded hesitant to say more. But they were calling this early for a reason.

"Is there anything more you're not telling us, son?" Dad asked.

"Nothing, Dad. Nothing."

"Dylan, maybe it's time," Mom said, always the more direct of the two.

Dylan closed his eyes and took a long breath.

"Time for what?"

"To step aside," she said, saying things Dad wouldn't want to. "I mean, city council doesn't seem worth all this. Maybe this would all just go away if you—"

"Mom, that's the whole point. Whoever is behind all this wants me to quit. That's the whole goal. So I just can't give in to this. I can't let them win. I just can't."

A long silence on the other end of the call. He could picture his parents looking at each other. Whispering. Mom urging Dad to back her up. Dad urging her to move on.

"Son," Dad finally said. "You know we trust your judgment. But we just ask you to take a step back. Is it worth all this? There'd be no shame in walking away. Go back to the firm and forget all this other stuff."

"Dad . . . Mom . . . I just can't do it. I can't let them win."

"But what if—"

Mom cut herself off.

More silence. Then Dad returned.

"Okay, son. We hear you. We stand by whatever decision you make. You know that."

"Thank you. Love you both."

As they hung up, Dylan's arms were shaking. Even his parents were losing faith.

Chapter 70

Dark wood panels, bland portraits of old male partners, and antique chairs and couches made the lobby look like every law firm would've looked fifty years ago.

But only the Windsor Firm—Cincinnati's oldest and most respected law firm—appeared this way now. As stodgy as it was, Windsor had the market cornered when it came to Cincinnati's old money. Fourth Street's go-to firm. Windsor also had first dibs on the Ivy League–educated law grads who returned home after graduating.

And one of those elite grads was the guy who'd consumed more marijuana in more forms than anyone Dylan Webb knew, prompting his visit.

In order to avoid gawkers, Webb wore his dad's old Stetson as he walked from the elevator to the receptionist on the other side of the hall.

"I'd like to meet with Graham Mundy," he said, hat tipped forward.

"And your name?"

"Tell him it's Webber. D. Webber."

Whether high or drunk, or both, Graham always called him "Webber" when they used to party—usually in the form of a deep-throated, drunken yell you'd hear in a fraternity basement.

She dialed a number and repeated the name.

"He said he'll be right down." She looked up. "It may take him a moment. He had a bad fall the other day."

Webb waited for ten minutes, hard eyes from the old portraits staring down at him. Most of them were faded black-and-white photos, serious men long since passed. But on one end came a few of the firm's modern-day rainmakers, whose portraits displayed both modest grins and a little color. In a concession to modernity, the firm even allowed one woman to make an appearance. The old men in black and white would be livid if they knew.

* * *

Entering from a side door, Mundy looked twenty pounds heavier in the gut than the last time they'd seen each other. Older, too, with his prominent chin appearing to jut out even further than it used to. Billing more than two thousand hours a year while throwing himself all in to the Cincinnati party circuit was taking a toll.

But it was the black left eye and deeply bruised cheek beneath it that made his appearance so startling.

"Webber!" he said as if they were at a party. "C'mon back!"

Dylan said nothing until the two were in Mundy's office, the door closed behind them.

"To what do I owe the pleasure?" Mundy asked as he sat down at his desk in an impressively spacious office. As rough as he looked, his elite, old-money Rolodex and glad-handing charm made him a successful lawyer where it counted most—bringing in clients and keeping the more junior lawyers busy day and night. He'd risen to partner as quickly as anyone does at Windsor. Webb always shook his head when he saw Mundy listed among Cincinnati's elite lawyers—if only people could see him at 3 a.m. each Saturday morning.

Webb brushed off the jovial greeting.

"I think you can guess why I'm here. But first, what the hell happened to you?"

He chuckled, rubbing long fingers through his shock of wavy light-blond hair. "Honestly, I don't even remember. Crazy night on Friday. So many of our big clients are from out of town these days, wilder than we ever were. So I woke up Saturday morning looking like this." He pointed to his eye. "The good thing is no broken bones."

"Jesus, Graham. When are you gonna stop?"

He shrugged. "You kidding? I couldn't deal with the work schedule here if I couldn't enjoy myself after hours."

Webb said nothing as Mundy leaned back. The guy was headed for a fall.

But Mundy's other comment also piqued his interest.

"Out of town? Where from?"

Mundy shrugged. "All over the world at this point. Europe. The Middle East. Asia. Seems like I've become the partner designated to show them a good time when they're here. But they definitely like to drop big money—both on the firm and on the town—so I'm not complaining."

He smiled, but his young face from only a few years ago looked far older.

"So why, amid all that you're dealing with, are you here?"

"You have to know!"

"I don't."

"Have you seen the paper today?"

"Nah. I was at a late dinner with some clients." He winked. "Why?"

"Well, check online and see for yourself."

Mundy swiveled in his chair to face a monitor on the side of his desk.

"*Enquirer?*" he asked.

"Yep."

He typed a few keys, waited a moment, then leaned in, eyeing the screen.

"Holy shit!" he said, running his hand through his hair.

"Holy shit is right. How the hell did the paper get their hands on *your* PayPal account?"

Mundy kept reading, scrolling with the mouse.

"My account? How do you know it was my account?"

"Because you're the guy I'd always reimburse. Remember?"

Mundy was still facing the computer monitor, the view of his profile accentuating how swollen his face and black eye were.

"Of course. This is nuts. Jesus, this would crush my practice if it ever came out."

Webb shook his head. "How in the world did someone get these from your account, Graham?"

Mundy kept scrolling, shaking his head. "No clue. No one should be able to access it."

"Well, someone did."

"You sure this isn't someone else? I remember you smoking stuff that I didn't buy."

"Almost everything I ever got was from you. That's your account, Graham. I checked mine to make sure, and the dates and amounts all match up." He folded his arms. While they'd spent some time in dark, musty rooms together, he didn't know the guy well. Or trust him. "I still want to know why it's at the top of the *Cincinnati Enquirer* website."

Mundy swiveled back, a frown replacing the frat boy smirk that had dominated their chat so far.

"Well, maybe someone hacked my account."

"And how would they have known what was in your account? To even look there?"

"I have no clue, Webber. It's bizarre."

"It's worse than bizarre. It's part of an effort to destroy me." He studied Mundy's face. "And Graham, why would the person who shared this with the paper bother to hide your name? Why would they protect you?"

Mundy crossed his arms.

"I don't like your tone, Webber. Why would I risk my whole career to out your drug buys?"

"Maybe you didn't have a choice." Webb gestured in the direction of Mundy's black eye. "Maybe someone forced you to."

"That's ridiculous. Someone must have hacked in." The smirk returned. "And to be honest, Webber, you're a member of the city council, not the US Senate. It's not like you're handling state secrets over there."

Webb ignored the insult.

"But how would they know to hack *your* account? Did you tell people I'd reimburse you for your stash?"

Mundy looked up toward the ceiling, which momentarily hid the extent of the damaged eye.

"Who would I tell that to?"

"You're pretty mouthy when you're high, as I recall."

He laughed. "That's true. But if that's when I told someone, that could be any number out of hundreds of people." He paused. "But in all seriousness, I don't think I told a soul."

"How about the person you were buying from?"

"Why would I have done that?"

"Did you?"

"No!"

Webb stared at him for a good five seconds before standing up.

"Are you done with the deposition, Dylan?"

"For now. But I'd like you to think hard about how someone would've known that I was paying *you* for marijuana. Because someone is using your receipts to destroy me."

Mundy leaned forward. "You come in here barking orders, Webber. I'm trying to be patient. But it seems like all the questions around your supposed kidnapping are your bigger problem, don't ya think?"

Heat flushed through Webb. "Listen, I've got press already asking who I bought from. I'm happy to share my source anytime."

Mundy's hands shot up. "Fine. Let me see if I can figure it out."

"I'll let myself out."

"Please do. But keep your head down. You're persona non grata around here."

"Oh, I am everywhere."

"Yeah, but you were *here* long before you got yourself kidnapped."

Webb chuckled.

Mundy was right. There probably wasn't a Windsor client Webb had pleased since the day he set foot in city hall.

Chapter 71

Cameras and microphones crowded city hall's third floor. Reporters huddled outside Dylan Webb's council office as he holed up inside. The PayPal story had generated the largest media frenzy since the abduction itself.

Dylan ignored media calls for an hour, only answering when Grimes's number popped up on his cell.

"It's time."

"Time for what?" Dylan asked.

"Time to step aside. I saw all those cameras mob you as you walked to your office. That drug payment story is the last straw."

Webb slumped deep into his chair.

"But it's—"

"I'm your lawyer. Listen to me. You need to step aside—"

"But—"

"And it may also be your way out."

"I don't get it. If their whole point is to get me to resign—"

"Would you let me finish a goddamn sentence? That drug story is too much. Someone is trying *too* hard to get rid of you, and there's got to be a reason."

Grimes hadn't spoken like this before—all in on Webb's narrative. Webb took a deep breath and listened.

"Plus, stepping aside may be the best way to reveal what their endgame really is."

"Okay. You've got my attention."

"Finally! My team's looked through city and state law, and the best part is that you don't have to formally resign. You can voluntarily agree to be suspended from the office. You still get paid. But they will replace you pending any trial."

"And then what?"

"If you're ultimately found guilty, or plead guilty, then that's it. You stay off the council. But if somehow you're acquitted, or they drop the charges, you get back on."

"And what happens to my seat while I'm suspended?"

"The council replaces you. And that's—"

"The way we figure out what they're up to."

"Exactly. You mentioned to me that you're sort of a swing vote on a lot of issues there."

"Not sort of. I am."

"On which issues?"

"You name it. Police reform. The budget. Zoning for development projects."

"Anything more specific?"

"Yes. All these things get specific pretty fast. I can show you five-to-four votes going back since I arrived. I'm basically the swing vote on all of them."

"So if this is all a setup, do you think it's about one of those issues?"

Webb had stewed about this question for days.

"I do. The police reform stuff is the most high profile, which would also explain the hostility of the cops from the get-go. And it's coming up quick."

"So if they replace you with someone who doesn't agree with you, police reform may go away?"

"Yes. Completely dead."

"I know it's complicated, but how do you get replaced on the council? Is there a special election?"

"No. It's a weird system. At the beginning of each term, every council member designates who on the council they want to select as their successor."

"And who did you pick?"

"All the Democrats basically agree to list all the other Democrats on the council. That way we choose collectively."

Silence.

"But I can always change that designee whenever I want to."

"Don't change a thing. If this is all about a plan to replace you with someone they want, then this is something someone thought out. And that's the key step."

Webb nodded. Made sense.

"Whatever you say."

Dylan quietly exhaled.

Stepping aside—the one thing he never considered—suddenly felt liberating. No longer fearful of the next revelation. And doing something they wouldn't expect.

Going on offense.

"I'm sold. When can we do it?"

Chapter 72

Maggie spent the first fifteen minutes back in the studio fending off Rick Temple's fury for not running with the PayPal story. After he stormed away, Maggie reopened the email from the day before, staring at it for a few minutes.

Then she typed slowly.

Thank you for the information.

After the email about Tri-State Storage had arrived the day before, she'd looked into the basics of the company, and she planned to poke around some more when she had a free moment.

But far more important than where Ventre had been a few days ago was the identity of the email's sender. Who would know that information? What else did they know?

She glanced down at the email's subject line again.

"The Missing Homeless Guy"

She did a quick search of all coverage of the Webb abduction. While there'd been some chatter about a witness at the second ATM, her interview was the only one that had delved deeply into that interaction.

As she'd thought, no outlet had publicly reported that the witness was missing. Some cops surely knew it. Maybe Webb had told others. But who else would know that?

Then she dug up the video of her interview with Webb. Rewatched it several times.

Webb's words had been vague: "At the ATM near the courthouse, a man saw us. He didn't know it was a mugging, but he saw us."

"How do you know?" she had asked.

"Because he asked us for money," Webb had responded.

She played it back again.

That was it.

While Fritzy had asked for money, neither Webb nor she had described him in any other way. Neither of them had called him "homeless." While some might assume someone asking for money was homeless, most would need more details to reach that conclusion. In her own notes, she had written "panhandler," not "homeless." And not a single story referred to the witness as homeless.

But the email did.

Again, cops would know that. But who else? And how?

She started typing.

First question: *"How long was he there?"*

She stared at the screen for several seconds. Then typed again. *"Where is ventre now?"*

She returned to the email and reviewed the lone sentence in its body:

"He was at Tri-State Storage a few days ago. Near the highway."

Her quick search had revealed multiple Tri-State facilities, most near highways.

But this person described it as one location, near "the" highway.

The wording made clear that the sender knew little about Tri-State Storage, the company.

Instead, the sender had been on-site. And must have seen Ventre there.

"A few days ago," she mouthed to herself.

Days.

It had not been an instant decision to write this email. At least two days had passed, meaning it had been a difficult decision. Perhaps guilt drove it. Perhaps fear. Perhaps both. But something was wrong, and it tore at the sender.

This person was on the inside. Involved. But involved in a limited way. And didn't feel good about it.

But "inside" of what? Involved in what way? Was he or she now in danger too?

"I can help you. Would you like to talk?"

The shorter the better. If this person was afraid, more questions might chase him or her off.

As she pressed send, her cell buzzed. Her old friend in traffic.

"You find it?"

"I think so. One of our traffic cameras picked it up as it entered downtown. All beat up where you'd expect."

"Get a license."

"Sure did. Address too. But it's weird."

"It's all weird at this point. Fill me in."

Chapter 73

Maggie turned onto the quiet, tree-lined residential street in Montgomery, one of the pristine East Side suburbs of Cincinnati. Wide driveways and well-manicured lawns followed one after the next, with equally attractive homes behind them.

This couldn't be right. She was wasting valuable time.

Five houses in, she slowed, double-checking the addresses on the mailboxes against the address on her notepad.

She stopped in front of 1086, a modest yellow ranch house dwarfed by hulking new builds on both sides.

Again, this made no sense.

She stepped along the walkway that bisected the well-groomed lawn, reached the front door, and rang the bell.

Silence for a few seconds, then light footsteps. Slow ones.

The door opened, revealing an elderly White woman, no taller than five feet, grinning up at Maggie.

"Hiya, young lady."

"Hi there," Maggie said, looking back down at her notepad. "Are you Wilma Petersen?"

"Sure am," the woman said pleasantly. "You're that lady on the news. I recognize ya. How can I help you?"

"Well, I'm looking for a van registered in your name. Although I think there's some type—"

The smile collapsed into a frown.

"What's wrong?"

"How did you know? I'm just so upset," she said, shaking her head, which tossed her white curly hair to and fro.

"About what?"

"What happened."

"With?"

"My van. Hold on."

She disappeared for a minute, then reappeared with a long coat. "Come with me."

She stepped outside and hobbled along a second walkway that led to the side of the house, then to the back. Maggie followed close behind.

As they reached the corner to the back of the house, she turned back toward Maggie.

"See what I mean?"

Two steps later, Maggie did.

"Sure do."

A red van sat directly behind the house, at the end of the driveway that curved around from the other side. The van's front right bumper had a sizeable dent. Long scratches lined the entire right side, along with two more dents that looked to be crushing both doors shut.

Maggie looked at the license plate. Same one her friend from traffic read over the phone. That match and the damage on the van's right side confirmed this was the vehicle that had sent Rodney Stone over the viaduct.

"I don't have the money to fix something that bad."

"What happened to it?"

"I don't know. This is how they brought it back."

"Who's they? Did someone steal it?"

"No. I rented it out."

"You did? To whom?"

She shrugged. "I don't know. The app does it all for you. The renters pick it up and return it. And this is how it came back."

"What app?"

"It's called VanShare. They do all the work for you, and it makes a little money to boost what I get from Social Security. When my husband died, I had no use for his old work van until my son-in-law told me about this."

Maggie nodded. She'd vaguely heard about this. Like an Airbnb, but for cars.

"Did you let VanShare know about the damage?"

"Of course. They left the van here overnight looking like this, so I filled out the damage form first thing this morning. Uploaded photos. But I haven't heard anything back."

"How long did you rent it out for?"

"About a week."

"Can I look inside?"

"Of course."

It was obvious as soon as they opened the driver door. The van had been wiped clean professionally. Still, Maggie took dozens of photos of it all, both the clean inside and the dents on the outside.

"Who's your contact at the company?" Maggie asked as she put her phone back in her pocket.

"I don't have one. It's all through the app."

"Okay. Let me know what they say. And I'll try to help figure out who did this."

Her phone vibrated in her pocket.

"What now?" she asked, Rick Temple on the line.

"You need to get to city hall right away."

"Why's that?"

"Dylan Webb is making an announcement."

Chapter 74

Dylan Webb held back the smile beaming inside.

The press had been after him all day about the PayPal story. Now crowded together on the city hall steps below him, they'd have a new story soon enough.

And while no council member dared watch in person, each had an aide in the crowd. They'd no doubt be texting details back to their bosses as soon as Webb started talking. One intern was not so subtly taping it with her phone.

Cowards.

But he wasn't going to let them ruin the moment. For the first time since that gun was aimed right at his stomach, Dylan was in control.

Grimes's idea was perfect, as was the script they'd worked on all afternoon.

"Thank you for being here, everyone. I want to say a few words about my case, and about my status here on the city council."

Gabby's cryptic press release had simply noted that Webb would provide an "update." Enough to get the media there, but with no indication of what he would say. They'd expect something about the drug buys. The PayPal account. But the mention of his "status" perked them all up.

Something new was afoot. Something bigger.

"I just got off the phone with the mayor. And I want to share with you all that I told him . . ."

He paused for a moment. Notebook in hand, Maggie Coyle was jogging along the sidewalk to get there. Webb felt a pang of guilt for not tipping her off, especially when she was the only reporter who hadn't bitten on the PayPal story. But this was an announcement he needed everyone to hear at the same time. That would guarantee they'd all lead the news with it. But he at least could wait for her to get there.

She joined them and took out her notepad.

"Tomorrow will be my final day in this office. My attorney and I have decided that given the ongoing controversy, and the possibility of a trial, it's best for me to step aside."

"He's quitting," someone whispered in the crowd, loudly enough for Dylan to hear. Most began texting on their phones, updating their producers and editors on the big news.

Webb waited for silence, then continued.

"As I told the mayor, and as I've said since the first day of my campaign, city hall must spend all its time fighting for the good people of Cincinnati. If I'm not able to do that, then I shouldn't be taking up one of the precious nine seats charged with doing that work. In the end, it's not about me, but the office, and the people."

He gestured at the windows two stories above him. The council offices.

"And if all my colleagues are doing is ducking questions about me, then they're not doing the people's work either."

Reporters were scribbling every word down.

"Second, an indictment seems imminent, based on this absurd theory that I made up my abduction. While that allegation could not be more false, I can't take any chances. My lawyers and I will need to work every hour of every day to clear my good name."

Heads shook among the press subtly, but enough to notice. Disappointment. They were hoping for some kind of confession or apology, not more O. J.-style denial.

"So, effective tomorrow, I'll be stepping aside to mount the strongest defense possible."

Hands immediately shot up in the air.

"Do you deny that those are your payments?" the young *Enquirer* reporter who'd written the PayPal story yelled out.

"At the advice of counsel, I'm not talking about anything that's in any way related to my case. But we will have our day in court on all that nonsense."

Four other similar questions came his way.

Same response.

Then someone yelled out the question he'd been waiting for: "Then why resign?"

He cupped his hand over his right ear.

"Excuse me?" he asked, drawing out the question he'd hoped would come.

"Why resign? Doesn't that make you look like you're guilty?"

"I know it may look that way to some. But in the end, what matters is what happens in court. And that good work be done in the building behind me." He paused. "But let me clarify one thing—a technical point. I'm not resigning the office. I'm voluntarily suspending my seat."

The wide-eyed looks across their faces confirmed they had no idea what that meant. With one exception.

"Which means you keep getting paid for as long as the suspension runs," Maggie Coyle blurted out.

Groans from the reporters. Now they had their story.

"Not exactly," Webb said. "Under state law, under a suspension, if I'm acquitted at some point, I get my seat back. And you're right; I do also get paid, in theory, but I've already told the city manager I will be donating every penny of that back to the city hall coffers for as long as I'm suspended."

"And if you win your case?" another reporter asked. "Will you get that salary then?"

"Nope. If I wasn't working for the people, I wouldn't deserve it."

A few reporters shrugged. There went that juicy angle.

Webb kept an eye on Maggie Coyle. Of everyone there, she was the most likely to know what he was up to.

On cue, she asked the other key question: "Who do you hope will take your place?"

He took his time answering.

"It's up to my colleagues. But this recent drama aside, we've built a lot of momentum here at city hall. I don't want to see it interrupted.

I hope they'll replace me with someone who shares my values on the issues that I and the people of this great city care about."

More hands shot up as more questions were shouted his way. But he was done.

"That's all I've got for today, folks. Thank you."

Mission accomplished.

* * *

"What the fuck was that?"

The mayor barked into Webb's phone as he climbed the two flights of marble steps back to his council office.

"What do you mean? I told you I was stepping aside."

"Yeah. Resigning. What's this suspension bullshit?"

"I never said resigning. And what's the difference anyway? You and the others get what you want. The story's over. You don't have to keep answering all those calls and emails you were whining about. And if they prove their case, and I made this shit up like you think, then I'm out."

"But—"

"You know the news cycle. As soon as you start talking about my replacement, that's the new story. I'm already old news. Take the win, Mayor."

Silence.

Then a dial tone.

Dylan leapt the final three steps to reach the third floor, feeling rejuvenated. The mayor's anger confirmed that this was the right plan.

Chapter 75

"Clive wants to see you."

Dylan Webb's first buoyant mood in more than a week evaporated as soon as his law firm's receptionist said the words.

"When?"

The firm's leadership had always been supportive. Not just of his broader public life—which clearly had pissed off some clients and cut into his billable hours—but over the past week as well.

But that was about to end.

"They said whenever you get here. So now. Meet them in the main conference room and I'll tell them you're here."

Them.

Even worse.

Five minutes later, Webb found himself across the table from the management committee's five members—three men, two women. Clive Johnson, the managing partner with the Gordon Gecko-styled black hair and pin-striped navy suit, sat in the middle, arms folded.

"So you're stepping down from the council, we heard?" he asked, annoyed.

Webb had kept them posted throughout the ordeal in emails and phone calls.

"I am. Suspension, actually. The day flew by so fast I wasn't able to give you a heads up."

"We noticed," Johnson said.

Helene Lewis, the head of litigation and Dylan's direct boss, shook her head.

"Dylan, that puts us all in an untenable position. We've been patient. We've stood by you. We've fended off questions from clients and turned over things the police asked for. But you stepping down from the council complicates this in a way that we have to change our posture as well."

This is a law firm, Dylan thought. *What happened to innocent until proven guilty?*

But he kept that to himself, forcing a smile instead.

"You guys have been incredibly patient. I can't thank you enough. It's made a huge difference. I just need a few—"

Clive Johnson shook his head.

"We can't, Dylan. We have a reputation to worry about. And we think it best to do the same here as what you just did at city hall."

"And what's that?"

"A leave of absence. Unpaid. Until the smoke clears. And permanently if you're ultimately found guilty."

Dylan nodded. At least this was better than being fired outright.

"But what about the cases I'm working on?"

Helene shook her head.

"Dylan, you haven't billed an hour in weeks."

He winced. No more cutting words could be uttered in front of a law firm's managing committee.

"And even if you had the time, no one feels like they can get good work out of you anyway. Better to keep your distance until this is all straightened out."

The other woman passed a folder across the table, with a pen tucked inside.

"Those are the terms," Johnson said as the folder lay in front of Webb. "After you sign it and take any personal belongings this afternoon, we'll ask you to hand your office keys and keycard to Helene."

Chapter 76

With city hall's clock tower looming behind her, Maggie kicked off both the five and six o'clock newscasts describing Webb's decision to step down.

She kept it bland. Just the facts.

She left her personal analysis out of it: leaving was the smart move, downgrading the drama. The public and media would move on quickly. If Webb made up the abduction, there'd be a trial or a plea deal, and that would be that. But if this was a setup, whoever wanted Webb gone had now achieved their goal, likely ending their attacks on him.

As she entered the newsroom fifteen minutes later, several reporters huddled in the hallway, gossiping about what would come next. Maggie walked right past them.

Politics wasn't her thing, especially at city hall. Solving crimes was.

She logged on and checked her email. Nothing. At least, not from *WebbWasFramed*.

She next called back the customer service line of VanShare. She'd waited on hold the entire drive downtown from Montgomery, never getting through.

Now, after seven prompts and another fifteen minutes, a live woman's voice chimed in.

"May I help you?"

"Yes, please. My name's Maggie Coyle, and I'm an investigative reporter in Cincinnati. Can I speak to whoever at your company handles security?"

"Security?" the woman repeated in a friendly voice. "Has your vehicle not been returned?"

"Worse. One of your vans was used in committing a murder, and I'd like to know who the customer was."

"Oh," the woman said, too calmly. "Let me put you on hold."

While Maggie waited, Emmy called. Not wanting to lose the live person she'd finally found, Maggie ignored the beeps until they stopped.

"Our vice president of operations is not available right now. Can I take your name and number?"

Maggie shut her eyes and took a deep breath. It had been a long day of no answers.

"Listen. I'm not trying to be tough on you personally. But I'm an investigative reporter and former police detective who plans to do a story about how your van sharing service played a role in a violent crime in Cincinnati. One person is dead. I can either run with the story as is, mentioning VanShare by name, or I talk to someone there to see if they might want to be helpful."

"I understand, I'm just passing along—"

"Yes, you are. So please pass along to whoever you talked to what I've said."

"Okay. I will."

Ten minutes passed. Emmy tried again, but Maggie again didn't answer. Instead, she texted: *Will call in five.*

Then came a click.

A young man's voice came over the phone.

"Hi, this is Sham Patel, head of operations. How may I help you?"

Maggie reexplained who she was and the situation. "I'd like your help in identifying who rented that van so we can stop a crime in progress."

"I'm sorry, ma'am. We can't release that type of customer information to anyone."

"Even amid an ongoing crime?"

Odd laughter came over the phone. "I'm sorry, did you say you are an active police officer? Do you have a warrant?"

She shut her eyes again. *Patience.*

"Wait. Do you want me to involve the police? Because I am happy to go that route. Let's do this: I'll call the police, invite them into the story, film them delivering the search warrant, interview them as they do so, expose your security and background check policies—"

"Okay! Okay!"

"—or you could look into one rental and help me identify who rented a car through your service."

"Without ever mentioning our involvement?"

"Now why would I do that?"

A long pause.

"Let me see what I can do. Do you have the name of the person who rented out the vehicle?"

She gave him Mrs. Petersen's information, then called Emmy as soon as they hung up.

"Hey, sweetie. Ready for our big date tomorrow night?"

"Mom!"

The daughter of two cops, Emmy had never been a worrier. And she'd always had street smarts. So the fear in her voice meant something was going on.

"What's wrong?"

"I'm pretty sure someone's been following me ever since school got out."

"Where's your dad?"

"He's not home yet."

Chapter 77

After lugging three boxes of personal belongings into his parents' condo, Dylan sat down on the living room sofa and made his phone calls.

The first two led to messages.

But to his surprise, call number three hit pay dirt.

"You did the right thing, Dylan. I feel terrible about all this, but you know how rough politics can be."

Even though they agreed on most matters of substance, Dylan had learned over time that Pete Stack was ambitious as hell and could be as slick as anyone on the council. Dylan leaving clearly was a relief to him. Every word he'd said was disingenuous bullshit, but there was no point in arguing.

"I appreciate that, Pete. I was calling to say I enjoyed our work together, even when we had our ups and downs. I hope you guys can find someone who will keep us moving in the same direction."

A chuckle.

"Us?"

"I mean, the city. Keep things moving in the same direction for the city."

"No offense, Webb, but you really hurt our cause."

"What do you mean?"

"The guy pushing for criminal justice and police reform turns out to be a criminal himself? And lies about it all? Big help that is. It may take a while to get anything done, if it isn't already dead."

Webb didn't take the bait.

"All the more reason to pick the right person. Our little coalition of five was pretty committed. It was never just me."

"Dylan, you're not hearing me. Your little episode has spooked everyone. Your stances are all toxic now. You should see our emails."

Dylan shook his head. Such spineless posturing.

"Believe me, I saw them all. Worse ones than you got, I imagine. Either way, let's try to keep things going."

"Hey, Dylan. Thanks for the call. We'll do our best to overcome the damage."

Dylan next dialed Laurie Busken, which also went to voicemail. He asked her to call him back.

Jackson called back as he wrapped up that message. Dylan clicked over.

"Hey, friend. I saw the news and your call. I think you did the right thing, for yourself and for the city."

Jackson sounded graceful again, as if he hadn't been part of the effort to force him out.

"Thanks. It wasn't easy. But my hope is that you guys can replace me with someone who will keep our important work going. Despite the way it ended, I always enjoyed working with you."

"That's kind of you to say, Dylan. I agree. And we will look hard for someone who can fill your sizeable shoes."

"Do you know who you guys will be looking at?"

"We're getting started. You'll see it in the paper tomorrow. The mayor asked me to lead the effort to come up with names. For now, though, I can't say anything. And Dylan?"

He paused.

"Yes?"

"Please understand, while I appreciate the call, I hope you won't say anything about who your successor should be. That would greatly complicate things."

"I get it. I'm only calling you privately."

"I mean even privately. With me or anyone else. Let me put it this way: If word got out that you were pushing for anyone, or even a certain approach, that would doom that approach."

"Is that so?" Dylan asked.

"I'm afraid it is. Be well."

Chapter 78

Maggie was racing just under eighty miles per hour, west toward Indiana, when Dan picked up.

"Where are you?" she asked.

"You know me, always racking up overtime. What's up?"

Dan, her ex, was two years from retiring. The more overtime he could squeeze into these final years, the higher his annual pension.

"Dan, you need to pick up when Emmy calls, especially when you know she's alone."

They generally kept their distance when it came to parenting. He was a good dad. So saying anything only added to the tension that had torn them apart from the earliest days of their marriage.

"Mags, back off. Emmy's a grown-up, and she's as safe as can be."

Maggie didn't want to reveal too much. Dan was buddies with all the higher-ups at CPD. While a straight arrow, he was also a talker.

"Well, she thinks someone's watching her. And I've been digging into something that might involve some pretty dangerous people."

He laughed.

"C'mon, Mags. I'm the cop here. You're running around covering that goofball councilman who can't get his story straight."

She bit her tongue. Dan loved reminding her of why things hadn't worked out.

"And next time you talk, you might tell him to support the blue. After all, we're the ones who protect people from the alleged perps he keeps talking about."

"Let's worry about Emmy right now. I'm ten minutes from your place."

"Stop! I'll be home in an hour."

"And then I'll leave, but in the meantime, I'll be there. At least see what she's worried about. Get home faster if you can."

Maggie got off the highway at the last exit before the Indiana border. Under their collective bargaining agreement, Cincinnati cops had to live within the county. So a huge number of them lived in Harrison—the town furthest from Cincinnati that was still in the county, and just within the state. The far, far West Side.

Four turns later, she reached one end of Dan's street and called Emmy back.

"I'm down the street," she said. "Which car followed you?"

"The white one. Kind of old. It's across the street now, a couple doors down. Careful, Mom!"

She drove past a few cul-de-sacs, then slowed down. A white Toyota idled in the distance on the left side of the street. A thick head was visible slightly above the passenger seat. She parked on the street's right side and got out of the car, one hand in her purse.

Chapter 79

"Webb?"

The mayor sounded tipsy. He spoke amid lots of chattering voices all around him. No doubt at his usual downtown watering hole, surrounded by those who made a living via the good graces of city hall. But it was earlier than usual.

"Yes?" Dylan said, phone in hand.

"Can't you go away, Webb? Just do the city a damn favor and go away!"

Feeling cooped up in the condo, Dylan had headed back to the Walnut Hills Frisch's to eat another Big Boy and fries.

The mayor called. But with nothing to lose, it was time to punch back.

"I did go away, Mayor. I'm out, just like you asked."

"Then stay the fuck away from the process of replacing your ass. You're the last person anyone wants to hear from."

Even with audible laughter around him, the mayor was both drunk and pissed. Maybe an opportunity.

"Why would you care, Mayor? The embarrassment I caused you is gone."

"Who resigns in disgrace and then has the gall to meddle in who replaces him? This is why no one has ever liked you, Webb—"

"Wait." Some drunken voice interrupted the mayor. A man's voice. "Is that Dylan Webb on the line?"

Another man yelled out: "Webb!"

Others howled in response.

A scratchy sound came through the phone before it went quiet. Webb could picture the mayor cupping his hand over the phone and barking at those around him to shut up.

"Sorry about that, Webb. I'm obviously not—"

"Webb!" someone else yelled out, laughing as they said it. "Fucking Webb!"

"Mayor," Dylan said, far more loudly, "back to your question, there's no disgrace here. I'm gonna prove that things happened as I described. And of course I care that things I worked on—that we all worked on—continue. You should too."

"Don't tell me what I should care about." He was now slurring his words. "And just go the fuck away!"

"Yeah!" a drunken voice yelled through the phone, right before the call ended.

Chapter 80

Kai's plan was to check the new email account back in the computer lab at school.

But as his brother watched a cartoon in front of him, he didn't even hear the words. The email was all he thought about. The prospect of a response. No way could he wait until tomorrow.

He used his phone's browser to enter the new Gmail account.

One new email. From the reporter. He tingled all over as he opened it.

Thank you for the information.

How long was he there?

Where is ventre now?

I can help you. Would you like to talk?

The last line hit home. A single word bringing a surge of relief.

Help.

She knew he was worried. That something was wrong. He so wished he could tell someone what was happening. Tell her.

But accepting any help also meant risking being arrested for kidnapping. And she was a reporter, so his face would be all over the news. So as much as he needed it, getting help from her might also be a trap.

He reread the email again, then typed a series of responses in his phone.

You're welcome.

I don't know. Seemed like for some time. He was hurt bad. But then the place was empty a few days later.

I don't understand the next question. ventre?

I don't need help. I'm trying to help you. I only want to use email.

He pressed send.

Chapter 81

Two car lengths behind the white Toyota, gripping her gun handle firmly within her purse, Maggie stepped over to the driver's side of the car.

The thick head in the driver seat didn't move. There'd been no cover to shield her approach, so he must've already seen her and likely watched her whole approach.

When she reached the rear bumper, two narrow eyes were glued on her through the driver side mirror. His window was down, meaning he wanted to hear her.

"Get out of the car!"

Two large hands rose through the window.

"Stay calm, lady," the man yelled back.

Maggie recognized the deep voice.

"Get the hell out of the car."

Hinges squeaked as the door opened. Two black boots swung out of the car and onto the pavement. The hulking man stood straight up, facing her, hands lifted to his sides.

It was the thug she'd walked with in the park days ago—the one who'd later sent the email.

"Remember me?" He smiled, revealing perfect white teeth.

"Of course. What in the hell are you doing here? Following my daughter!"

"I needed to meet again. Alone. And I had a feeling you'd come."

"I could have brought the cops with me. Or her dad might've—"

"It worked, didn't it?"

She let go of the gun and lowered her purse.

"Either way, you followed my daughter from school! That is totally out of line."

He lowered his arms. "We want to know why you didn't run with the story."

"Because I didn't have enough information to go with."

"The *Enquirer* didn't agree."

"I don't take my lead from them."

"The other TV people sure did."

"I'm not those other TV people either."

"True. You're much older than they are."

She flashed a sarcastic smirk back his way. "Wiser too."

He nodded.

"Yes. The most respected. That's why I came to you in the first place. And it's why I'm back."

Her phone began playing a Taylor Swift song. The ringtone for Emmy's calls.

"Aw, how sweet. Is Emmy checking on you?"

Chills pricked along both arms. He knew her name.

"Don't mention her again."

She texted Emmy back—*All is fine. I'll be in in a minute*—then looked back up.

"Whether I mention her again or not, she seems like a great kid."

The kind words didn't dilute his menacing tone, but she didn't take the bait.

"So what the hell do you want?"

"Simple. What do you need to report the truth about Dylan Webb?"

"And what's that?"

"What I told you at our last get-together—that he refused to pay his dealer and that's why he was mugged."

"Well, if that's the story, I need more than old PayPal receipts that tell me nothing about that."

"Like what?"

"Why do you even care? He already resigned. He's out. Humiliated."

"He ducked out so he didn't have to answer for the truth. People want the truth to come out."

"And why do *they* care?"

"To make an example out of him. So no one else will stiff them like he tried to do."

"But even that story is basically out there. The *Enquirer* hinted at it."

"Hinted isn't enough. And you carry extra weight in this city. You're the closest to the story—the one who revealed his drug use to begin with. Who better to close the loop?"

"That's true." She smiled at the absurd flattery, running with it. "Do you really want me to cover that angle?"

"I do."

"Then I need a pattern. You need to give me someone beyond Webb. Someone else who's part of it. And with better proof than two-year-old PayPal receipts."

He grimaced. "Another customer?"

"If it's as big as you say, there must be at least one you can give up. Someone else who doesn't pay, maybe? Someone people will know. My producers would be all over that."

Whether or not Webb was part of it, this guy's broader narrative about a VIP drug-selling ring was a hell of story, if true. Might as well push a little.

"And any more on Webb you can get me would help. Old stuff is old news at this point. Try something from *after* he was on the council."

"He was paying with cash then."

"Well, I need something to back it up."

He stared at her for a few more moments. Sizing her up.

"Okay. I'll see what I can do. Look for more emails."

"Oh, I will."

He got back in his car and drove off. The license plate was covered, of course.

Maggie walked toward Dan's front door. While she'd maintained calm during the conversation, her pulse was racing now, her legs shaking.

He could've done all that through a phone call. Even an email, setting up a meeting at a neutral location.

This little rendezvous was about sending a message. Keep playing along. Don't pursue other angles about the Webb kidnapping.

And diving deep into her personal space was classic intimidation.

She knew the tactic well, but still couldn't stop shaking. Once they involve your daughter, the truth was, intimidation worked. And she couldn't call the police to help.

FRIDAY

Chapter 82

It was the first knock on his door in days.

"Can I talk to you?" asked a quiet voice.

Looking at the oval, umber-hued visage of Councilwoman Michelle Easley, Dylan set the heavy cardboard box down on Gabby's desk. They'd packed up most of the office over the prior hour—his last morning at city hall.

"Of course. Come on in."

Councilwoman Easley and Gabby hugged before she stepped into his office. She shut the door behind her, and the two sat down. As always, she wore a perfectly pressed, brightly colored pantsuit—orange the choice of the day. But the long pixie cut, with locks of straight black hair flowing across her forehead, was a new look, to go with her hazel, almond-shaped eyes.

"I just want to say how sorry I am about all that's happened."

While the words were sincere, her visit was a surprise. He couldn't recall another face-to-face meeting like this during their entire time on the council together.

"You may be the first person to say that and mean it. Around here, at least."

"I can only imagine how abandoned you feel, especially by people in your own party."

Michelle was the daughter of one of Cincinnati's best-known public figures, a minister and civil rights icon who also happened to be a lifelong Republican. While she'd followed in his Republican footsteps, she wasn't political by nature. She largely stayed out of the limelight, spending less time at city hall than the others.

"It's been a whirlwind. From fearing for my life, to being attacked publicly, to being cast aside by my own colleagues."

"I've been praying for you," she said. "And I'm sorry I didn't call you back sooner."

He nodded. Despite an initial text, she hadn't called back once.

"Party didn't want you to?"

She shook her head.

"No. I don't talk to the party folks much anymore. I just didn't know what to believe. It didn't seem like something you'd make up. But you also really don't know someone, y'know? You and I have been on this council together for almost a year, but we've barely spoken. For real, at least. Plus, lawyers said if we talked to you, we might end up as witnesses."

"But you're here now?"

"Yes. Seeing you pack up all alone made me sad. For you. And for the city. I looked back at all you've done, and I see now that you cared, even when we didn't agree. Your service comes right from your heart."

For that moment, her kindness made him forget everything else.

"Thank you."

"Dylan, I hope they replace you with someone who's the same way. Puts the city first."

"That means a lot," Dylan said, smiling. "Me too."

He studied her face for a moment. Was this an innocent trip of civility, or was there another aim?

"Are you hearing anything?" he asked.

She waved off the question. "C'mon. You think the Democrats would fill me in on your replacement? I haven't heard a word except that Councilman Jackson will lead the search. He's been hosting endless visitors all week, and he's doing a press conference later. They telling you anything?"

Dylan chuckled. "You know more than I do! In fact, the mayor yelled at me for even asking about it."

"Drunk?"

"Of course."

"He yelled at me too when I hesitated on the resolution. He even tried calling my dad."

"Ha! I guess we're in good company."

"Well, like I said, I hope they pick someone like you. We need good people in public service."

She stood up.

"Good luck to you. May we both enjoy our retirements."

This was Easley's final term.

She walked into the other room of the council office and hugged Gabby again before heading back into the hallway.

Dylan watched her go, regretting that he'd never taken the time to get know her long ago. *For real*, at least.

Chapter 83

Coffee cup in hand, hunched over her desktop, Maggie inspected the new email one line at a time.

It narrowed things down a bit.

First, whoever had emailed her wasn't a cop. Or any other type of investigator.

I don't understand the next question, the sender had written. *ventre?*

She'd name-dropped Ventre for one reason—to see if the sender knew the name. Or that it even was a name. The responder didn't seem to know.

This was definitely someone on the inside, not a cop.

But another line made clear he was on the periphery of that inside.

I don't know. Seemed like for some time. He was hurt bad. But then the place was empty a few days later.

The sender had only seen Ventre once. Her guess was he was already hurt at the time.

But then the sender had gone back to "the place" days later, only to find it empty.

Why the first visit? Then the return visit to an empty place?

What especially made no sense was why the leaders would allow someone on the periphery to see Ventre at all.

She looked at the last line again: *I don't need help. I'm trying to help you. I only want to use email.*

The sender was obviously scared. Of what he'd seen. Of the people behind it. But also, perhaps, of being seen by Maggie.

She took another sip of coffee as she reread it one more time. Then she reread the first email.

She jotted notes down on her reporter's notepad.

(1) involved

(2) recognized Ventre as "homeless"

(3) periphery

(4) scared

She finished off the coffee as she stared at all four points.

"That's it," she said out loud.

Only one thing made sense.

She wrote one more word down, in all caps, at the bottom of the page. Then circled it.

KIDNAPPER.

Chapter 84

Before shutting his final, packed-up box, Dylan took a long look at the framed photo lying on top. His swearing in, Mom and Dad by his side, friends gathered behind. Standing upright and with his hand on a Bible, he'd pledged then to uphold the Constitution and the City Charter, so help him God.

The most exciting event of his life. Followed by months of invigorating work upholding that oath and serving the city. And he'd made a difference, far more than with any case he'd dealt with at the law firm.

And all of it would be gone in hours. A photo capturing all that promise, buried in a box. Now just a time capsule of his former life.

His phone rang. Grimes didn't even let him say hello before jumping in.

"Who d'ya know at Silverton High?"

It took a moment to process.

Silverton. A small, diverse, working-class community outside the city. Had its own separate school system. He'd spoken once to the high school as a candidate, trying to convince as many kids as possible to volunteer for his campaign. A dozen did.

"A friend of mine growing up teaches social studies there." As he spoke, he shut the two top flaps of the box, covering the photo. "Why?"

"Have you talked to them about your abduction?"

"She sent a nice text when it happened, and I wrote back. But that's it." Dylan was losing his patience. "*Why* are you asking about Silverton?"

Dylan pulled a large piece of masking tape over the box top, sealing the two sides shut.

"Because I had some tech guru in Louisville take a close look at that email you got. It was sent from Silverton High School. So either your friend knows something about your abduction, or someone else there does."

"My friend would've just called me."

"Of course. It was also sent in the early afternoon, so it could very well have been a student."

"But how would a high schooler know about . . ."

He froze, a lump forming in his throat.

"Gabby?" he asked through the doorway.

No answer.

"Gabby!"

She came in from the third-floor hallway.

"Yes?"

"I need a Silverton yearbook right away!"

"As in the high school?"

"Yes."

He looked at his watch. It was two minutes before noon—only five hours left before time was up. And he had a major decision to make by then.

"And we need it by three. A friend of mine works there. I'll connect the two of you."

He then remembered Grimes was still on the call.

"We'll get the yearbook and take a look."

"Perfect. Keep me posted."

Chapter 85

Just after noon, as Maggie drove west to a luncheon of women ex-cops, the call came in from a 415 area code. San Francisco.

"Is this Maggie Coyle?" the voice asked after she picked up.

"It is."

"This is Sham Patel, of VanShare. We talked yesterday."

"We sure did! You find anything?"

"Yes," he said with enthusiasm. "The person who rented the van was named Diego DeLeon."

The name rang a bell.

"Hold on."

She reached for her purse on the passenger seat, pulled out her reporter's notebook, and flipped through it. She sighed when she got to the page she was looking for.

Diego DeLeon was the same name tied to the gray van from the Queen City Cash video. And the same poor guy the cops had found halfway decomposed in the Price Hill apartment Rodney Stone had called in.

"Diego DeLeon is dead."

"He is?"

"Yes. How did you get his name?"

"That was the name entered into the app when he rented the vehicle."

"What day was that?"

"Four days ago."

"Jesus! He'd already been dead for a week by then. Did you verify it somehow?"

"Of course," he said defensively. "That was also the name from the driver's license they used."

"And how do you view the license?"

"They upload a photo of it to the app."

"And then you verified it?"

"Yes. Nothing was flagged."

Maggie pulled off the highway as she approached the restaurant where she was meeting her friends.

"Well, since he couldn't have been the one who paid for it, how'd they pay?"

"One sec."

The pitter-patter of typing came through the phone.

"They used a credit card."

"Okay. And the name on the card?"

More typing.

"There was none."

"A credit card with no name?"

"I'm afraid so. It was a prepaid card."

She rubbed her hand through her hair, trying to douse her rising temper. But she couldn't resist.

"So someone can photograph a dead man's license and then use an anonymous credit card to pay for your services?"

"I hate to break it to you, ma'am, but we're in the age of cryptocurrency. People pay for things anonymously all the time, and it's getting worse."

He was right. What a nightmare.

"Thanks anyway."

Chapter 86

"Got 'em!"

Minutes before four, Gabby rushed into Dylan Webb's city council office—now empty except for the furniture—clutching a white plastic bag.

"Great. Was Leslie helpful?"

"Totally. She's the only reason I was able to get these out of the library."

She tossed three Silverton High yearbooks onto the conference room table.

"What should I be looking for?"

"Probably best if I go through them. Can you bring up the police sketches of my kidnappers on your phone?"

"Of course!"

He grabbed the most recent yearbook. From both their appearance and their conversation, the kidnappers felt like they were in their mid-teens. Seventeen. Maybe sixteen. Not younger. So he opened the book and turned through pages of young smiling photos until he got to the sophomore class.

"Here you go," Gabby said, holding up the two sketches on her screen.

Webb stared at them for a few seconds, then shut his eyes, conjuring up memories of the duo who'd started this nightmare ten days ago.

Of the two, he had a far shakier recollection of the guy in the back. Only two features stuck out. One was that damn Bears hat, which had obscured the kid's hair and shadowed most of his face in the darkened back seat. And given how threatening that kid's words had been, he'd avoided looking back the entire ride. The other feature was how tall he'd been when they'd approached the ATM. He was at least a few inches taller than Dylan, making him at least 6'2".

As he looked at the sketch now, it still seemed useless.

While the kid in the front had worn sunglasses, several elements of his face—high cheekbones, receding chin, a few pockmarks, and that peach fuzz—had remained clear in Dylan's mind since the abduction.

Dylan looked at that sketch again on Gabby's screen. It held up well. So that's the face he looked for.

Standing over the table, he leafed through the hundred or so sophomores at Silverton from the prior year. This year's juniors.

He stopped at a white teen with a short-cropped fade. Jared Connell. Some resemblance. But his cheeks were a little too round, his ears slightly too big. He would've noticed those big ears against the short hair. No. Wasn't him.

Another sophomore had a similarly shaped head and some decently high cheekbones. Cameron Mooney. But a few group photos showed he was taller than most of his classmates. And definitely taller than the guy who'd pointed a gun at Dylan from his Hill Street sidewalk.

He turned to the juniors.

No one came close for four pages.

He hit the fifth page. And froze.

The second kid in the second row.

His cheekbones leapt off the page. High, nearly jutted.

His chin receded.

And his cheeks bore a few pockmarks. Acne.

The kid's hair was different than the sketch—slightly longer on top. Almost bushy. Hair dipped further down in the back. But kids changed their hair styles all the time.

The other features were dead on.

He looked at the name.

Michael Slayton.

Fingers trembling, he paged through to the junior class's group photos.

Michael Slayton made three more appearances. Average height for his class. Maybe 5'8" or 5'9". Just as he remembered him from outside his Jeep's passenger door.

Neither thick nor thin, but wiry. Muscular. Someone you wouldn't want to mess with.

Moments from the abduction flashed through Dylan's mind, sending his pulse into overdrive.

The gun at his chest.

The first ATM.

The drive down Columbia Parkway.

The pleading.

The second ATM and the homeless guy.

The blindfold.

His hands over his head to divert the bullet from his skull.

Throughout, that hard face now staring at him. Michael Slayton had been only feet away.

"Are you okay?" Gabby asked. "You're sweating."

"That's him!" Dylan said, index finger now pointing at Slayton's chin from an inch away. "That's the guy from the front seat. The one with the gun."

"Are you sure?"

"I'm sure," he said. "It's him."

He sat down in the chair as if he'd just run five miles.

"That's him."

Chapter 87

Judge Thomas McIntosh.

The email arrived while she was at lunch. But from the subject line and its sender—DruggieWebb@yahoo.com—Maggie Coyle knew she had a huge scoop.

No one in the county had created a more tough-on-crime brand than the Honorable Thomas McIntosh, a former prosecutor turned judge. Back when Maggie was on the force, cops loved when cases ended up in front of Judge McIntosh. And she had too.

But since leaving, she'd soured on him as a grandstander who filled up the jail by over-sentencing and publicly humiliating nonviolent criminals for his own political gain. His clerks made sure to alert the press whenever he planned to deliver a scripted tirade from the bench as he sent a shackled defendant off to a long sentence. And the press always obliged. The benefit was mutual: McIntosh always made for a good show, an easy day at the office for reporters. And those shows always got him reelected, no sweat.

This email delivered the promise of a new kind of show. Maggie's eyes widened at the opening line: *Judge McIntosh has been buying a variety of drugs for years. He pays in an elaborate way, but you'll see all of the details attached below.*

It felt credible. McIntosh was extra hyped up all the time—talking louder than everyone else, bouncing in his chair—so maybe drug use explained it.

And far more than Dylan Webb, this *was* a story, given how many thousands of people McIntosh had thrown the book at for the very type of drug activity this email accused him of.

The attachments revealed years of payments. Well-disguised, but the seller had clearly kept a good record.

She typed up a list of questions she'd need filled in.

And this still didn't prove much when it came to Dylan Webb.

But by following up on this tip, she'd leave the impression that she also was going to throw Webb under the bus along with McIntosh. For Emmy's security, leaving that possibility open was critical.

In addition to the list of questions about McIntosh, she typed up one final sentence:

My boss says I need one other buyer to put this all together. Two may be a coincidence. Three is a pattern.

She pressed send, pleased.

Already bored with the Webb story, Rick Temple had been bugging her about a new story. This would be a biggie.

Chapter 88

"Should we call the cops?" Dylan Webb asked out loud, Gabby listening in across the table.

"No," Grimes said back through Webb's cellphone, which was set on speaker so they both could hear him. "This may be the only guy who can prove that you've been telling the truth all along, and he's looking to be helpful. Let's try to talk to him in person and get every detail we can before he finds himself in a room surrounded by cops who have it out for you and won't want egg on their face."

"Fair enough."

"And you're sure you couldn't identify the guy in the back seat?"

"I looked through all three yearbooks. No one stuck out, mainly because I never got a great look at him. But the guy in the front seat, that's definitely him."

"Well, now that we have his name, we need to approach him when no one else is around, and in a way that doesn't spook him. The other guy in the car is probably watching him like a hawk."

"You think go to his home?"

"Sure. Get whatever detail we can out of him, then chase down everything we can to confirm it all. We *then* announce it to the world. Hell, you may not even get indicted if we do this right."

Webb beamed, still giddy about their find.

But Gabby remained stern. "Are you positive Slayton would be the guy emailing you?"

Webb looked back at the photo of Slayton, reliving the conversation in the car.

"I told you already, the kid in the back was a true thug—kept threatening to kill me and kicking the back of the seat. No way he writes that email. Slayton was the one who was calm the whole time. We had a rapport going."

"I trust your gut," Grimes said through the phone. "But we should send an email back so we know 100 percent. I'll send a draft."

"Okay."

The clock on Webb's phone indicated it was ten past four. Less than an hour to go.

"Rusty, you still think I should step aside, right?"

"Absolutely. You don't want them to know you're getting to the bottom of it. And don't forget, who they replace you with might clarify what's behind this."

Webb heard the words, but something had been bothering him all afternoon. Which was why he'd asked the question.

Stepping aside still made sense. But letting Curtis Jackson, Stack, the mayor, and the other jackals replace him made him sick.

"True. But Rusty, and you might not like this, I want to do things a little differently than we first talked about."

He looked at Gabby.

"Can you give us a minute?"

Chapter 89

Ten minutes before five.

Ten minutes to go.

Dylan and Gabby had loaded every remaining box into his car. The office was now spotless, ready for whoever stepped into his shoes. He scanned it one last time, then joined Gabby in the third-floor hallway before locking the door behind them.

"I'll drop off the keys at the clerk's office," he said.

"Okay. See you downstairs."

Webb walked down the hallway. As his shoes clipped the marble floor, the echo was drowned out by the mayor's loud, tipsy voice from the night before, replaying in Webb's head.

The disrespect. The anger.

One door remained open near where the hallway cornered left. Michelle Easley's chief of staff typed away even as the other offices were closed for the weekend.

"See you later," Webb said.

"Take care of yourself, Councilman," she said back, smiling up from her desk.

Dylan turned left, passing the closed doors of council members Jackson and Stack. They and their staff were gone. But their words still made Dylan boil inside. Neither couldn't care less about what they'd worked on together. Or how Dylan had approached his public service. Or what he still hoped the city might do. They'd made that perfectly clear in those short phone calls. They wanted him to butt out.

All three sets of double doors to city council chambers were wide open. The grandeur of the room within reassured Dylan about what he was about to do. Grimes had hated his idea at first, but Dylan had worn him down. If he never came back to city hall, this was too important a decision to get wrong. Part of his legacy. Plus, they still could get what they needed.

He'd grown so used to all the nastiness, he'd forgotten what mutual respect felt like. And sounded like. So at the time, the conversations with the mayor, Jackson, and Stack felt like business as usual.

But one conversation changed that.

"See you later, Mr. Webb," a friendly voice said from within the chambers.

Dylan craned his neck to look through the last open doorway. An older man with round glasses, a three-inch-high Afro of curly white hair, and a tousled gray beard leaned against a mop, smiling his way.

"Take care, Rocky."

Rocky had scrubbed the floors at city hall for decades. Dylan and he had often overlapped after hours, finishing their long days at the same time. Rocky always had a lot to say, often slowing Dylan as he tried to close up and head home. But Dylan listened enough to know that Rocky had four kids and twelve grandkids, was a widower, was a huge Reds fan, and lived on the economic edge in Avondale. Still, he'd never had anything but a wide smile and warm greeting for Dylan, even when he'd been too busy to look up.

"Sad to see you go, sir, and best of luck. They won't keep you down!"

"No, they won't, Rocky. Thank you and stay well."

Seconds later, he entered the small clerk's office and laid three office keys on the table.

A deputy clerk reached out and took them.

"Gabby gave us everything else we needed," she said. "So you should be all set."

Dylan checked his watch. Five minutes until five. Too late for anyone to change things.

"Actually, there's one other thing I need to do."

"What's that?"

The Fifth Vote

"Can you hand me my successor designee form?"

The clerk's eyes widened. The form was something only council members' staff would ask about, and only on the first day of their terms. The simple document that determined who named each member's replacement should he or she leave before the term was over.

"Okay. One minute."

She walked into another room, reappearing a minute later.

"Here you go."

She laid the single sheet of paper in front of him.

The top was dated December 1 of the prior year, in Gabby's handwriting, while his signature was on the bottom. He hardly remembered signing it then, amid a long stack of papers, and with all the excitement of inauguration day, capped off by a speech he'd given with the whole city watching.

And of all the documents of that first day, this wasn't a form that required a lot of thought anyway. Democrats had done the same thing for decades. They designated the other Democrats on the council as their joint designees, so the group of Democrats who remained on the council together decided on the replacement. Designating one another was like a blood oath of party loyalty.

He looked at the names on the list, written in blue pen, again in Gabby's handwriting.

Verna Spiller
Curtis Jackson
Bob Stack
Christian Kane

Although Kane had already rubbed him the wrong way, he hadn't hesitated in listing all four at the time. Again, it's what you did. And they'd all been excited to work together on their robust agenda, so this form was part of that initial rapport. In it together.

"Can you pass me a pen?" he asked.

"Of course," the deputy clerk said back.

She took a blue ballpoint pen from a tall coffee mug on the desk.

"Actually, I'll take that one," Dylan said, pointing to a thick black Sharpie that was also in the mug.

"Okay."

"Much better," Dylan said as took the cap off.

He eyed the paper for seconds, then lifted the tip of the Sharpie to the left margin. He skipped Spiller and started with Jackson, who'd led the charge. He crossed out the name slowly, pressing down hard so that the unbroken, thick black ink would leave no doubt. He did the same with Stack, then Kane, then went to the top and crossed out Spiller.

When he was through with her, he stared at the white space beneath Kane.

It wasn't just the way she'd said the words, but the expression on her face that made it clear she'd meant every word: "Your service comes right from your heart."

Then she'd unintentionally closed the sale with the next line: "And I hope they replace you with someone who's the same way. Puts the city first."

Something no one else had said since the entire ordeal began.

He'd never bothered spending time with her. Person to person, at least. Why not? What had his hurry been? So much time to have done so, but he'd wasted it.

Dylan placed the black tip on the paper and, using the best penmanship he could muster, wrote a new name.

"Here you go," he said, passing the form and the pen back to the deputy clerk, whose eyes dilated even wider than before.

Two flights of stairs later, as he walked out of the building and ignored the first phone call, Dylan Webb was still beaming.

Councilwoman Michelle Easley would get her wish.

So would he.

Chapter 90

An elbow clipped Kai's chin, the latest in a game full of hard fouls, called and uncalled.

Kai snapped, uncorking a roundhouse back where the elbow had come from.

Crunch.

The minutes that followed were a blur of shoves, punches, and shouts among players, coaches, and parents in the stands.

When he was finally pulled away from the scrum, Kai's bloody knuckles and the opposing center's mess of a face made clear that he'd socked him right in the nose.

"Get your butt to the locker room, Kai!" Coach yelled, bugged-out eyes flaming with rage.

"But Coach, the kid was—"

"I don't care what he was doing. That's part of the game. You *never* slug someone like that. Now get out of here."

Of course, Coach was right. The contact hadn't been worse than most other games.

The opposing home crowd booed loudly as Kai walked past the basket on his way out of the gym, only feet from two men mopping blood off the floor. As he entered the locker room and the door closed behind him, he could still hear the chants from the mostly White crowd: "Thug! Thug! Thug!"

He'd avoided looking up at his parents in the stands. They'd be shocked. Even worse, they'd be disappointed. He'd never gotten a technical foul in all his years playing ball, let alone into a fight. Worst case, this might risk his scholarship to Miami.

While his parents wouldn't understand, Kai knew exactly why he'd lost his cool. After using a towel to wipe the blood off his knuckles, he sat on the end of a long narrow bench and took his phone out of his gym bag.

No emails had come to the new Gmail account. But that didn't keep him from writing a new one to the reporter.

I've been thinking about it. And I would like to meet. But I need to be very careful. What's the best way to do it?

Losing control on the court crystallized his new reality. Agreeing to be part of the robbery had started a chain of events he couldn't stop. His life was going to change for the worse no matter what he did. And now the guilt of it all was eating away at him to the point where he was no longer himself. To the point where he'd knocked someone nearly unconscious in front of hundreds of onlookers, including Ma and Dad, who'd spent every day teaching him to be better than that.

The tension within was too much to bear.

Time for something new.

The reporter had offered help, and the pool of blood on that gym floor confirmed that he sure needed it.

He felt a tinge of relief as soon as he pushed send.

SATURDAY

Chapter 91

"Why me?"

Michelle Easley asked the question as she and Dylan sat at the busy counter of Sugar 'n Spice, the iconic diner in the heart of Cincinnati's Black community. In jeans and a pink sweater, she was more casually dressed than he'd ever seen her, with the exception of parade routes.

While he'd ignored numerous incoming calls the night before, he'd left the councilwoman a message at 5:30 p.m. to fill her in on his decision. She'd called back and asked to meet for breakfast.

Webb rested his fork on his plate, thinking through his answer.

"Hey, is that the infamous Councilman Webb you're hanging with, Michelle?" the aproned, elderly Black man yelled from behind the counter, five feet to their right.

"Sure is, Sonny."

Expecting the worst, Dylan cringed at the glee on Sonny's face, whose curly white hair on the sides of his bald head shook as he laughed.

"Councilman, we've been cheering you on from here—you need to know that!"

"Really?" Dylan asked, surprised.

"Oh, yeah," Sonny said, slapping a greasy spatula against a skillet below, steam rising in front of him. "Someone's got it out for you, that's for sure. Why the heck would you make up something like that?"

Dylan chuckled; his mood lifted. "That's what I've been saying!"

"Well, we see you, man. We got you. Stay strong."

"Thank you," Dylan said. "I so appreciate that."

"Hear that a lot, I bet," Michelle Easley said.

"Are you kidding?" Dylan asked. "It's been the opposite. Skeptics all around."

"Please don't tell me you think Twitter and talk radio represent the real world. I've heard what he just said from so many. You need to spend more time with real people, Dylan. Get out of the bubble."

Dylan nodded. Even sitting at the counter was putting him at ease.

He devoured a piece of bacon before returning to her question.

"Michelle, you asked why you," he said. "Because you were the only one who showed any decency as well as a commitment that city hall should be about public service—including the decision of who replaces me."

"Well, I appreciate that," she said, frowning, "but you just made my life far more challenging. I'm getting calls nonstop. Three from Curtis alone, who's livid. Then the mayor, first thing this morning. I wish you'd at least given me a heads-up."

"I understand that. I apologize, but it was the only way. And I know you'll handle it well." He chuckled. "Plus, you're now the most powerful person in the city! Remember how I was the swing vote on everything?"

"Of course," she said, chuckling. "'Especially when you and I disagreed."

"Well, whoever replaces me will basically decide what moves forward and what doesn't. And now that's all up to you."

"Believe me, I've already figured that out, which explains all the calls I'm getting." She took a sip from her coffee mug. "But you can be sure I will take this responsibility seriously."

"That's why I picked you, Councilwoman."

As Dylan scooped up a forkful of scrambled eggs, Michelle leapt to her feet, embracing a professionally dressed woman who'd approached from another table.

"Councilwoman, I still can't thank you enough!" the woman said, holding Michelle's hand.

"Of course, Vanessa. Was happy to do it."

"Well, it will really make a difference for the community. Give my best to your parents."

"I surely will. Give mine to yours as well."

The woman looked closely at Dylan, who was watching from his seat. He recognized her, largely from the unique way she braided her hair, thick strands flowing in all directions. She'd testified before the council at some point.

"Wait, is that Councilman Webb?"

He looked her way and nodded politely as he swallowed.

"It sure is," Easley said with gusto.

"Councilman, my husband and I prayed for you. We saw that interview on Channel 5 the day after you were robbed—we could feel the pain you were feeling. I'm sure it was difficult, but you spoke for so many who can't."

She reached out and hugged him.

"Thank you so much. If I helped others in any way, I'm glad."

"You surely did. We hated seeing you step down. The press and those members of council needed to leave you alone!"

He laughed. "I wish they had. Thanks again."

She walked back to the table where she'd come from.

"How's the bacon, Mr. Webb?" Sonny asked from behind the counter. "Need any more?"

"It's great, Sonny! But I've had more than enough. Eggs are perfect too."

"Let me know when you change your mind!" Sonny yelled over the sound of bacon sizzling.

"See?" she asked.

"See what?"

"You look like a different person than when you walked in here. We gotta get you out more with regular folk."

"Well, I have time for that now, at least," he said.

She shook her head, frowning. "Dylan, that's the point. You had time for that before too. You just didn't use it right."

He finished off the second half of the egg, her words weighing him down.

"Do you have any preferences?" Easley asked when he was done.

"Preferences?" he asked. "For what?"

"Who I pick to replace you."

"Councilwoman, I'm not here to give you those preferences. But the one thing I'd ask is that you keep me apprised of the process."

"Okay."

"And if someone starts coming on too strong, be sure to let me know."

"Oh, I will."

They sat for another thirty minutes, talking with Sonny and three other customers who walked up to say hello.

Chapter 92

Kai's right wrist almost doubled in size by midnight, aching so much he tossed and turned until early in the morning.

When he awoke at ten, he was relieved to be the only one left in the house. At least he didn't have to face his parents again. The drive home had been hell. The only thing worse than lectures from Ma and Dad was their complete silence.

He wrapped his purple wrist in a cold, wet towel, then picked at a bowl of cereal with his left hand. Between bites, he typed away on his phone to open his new email account.

Two new emails awaited him.

The first came from the councilman himself. But it was from a private account, not the one Kai had sent the email to.

Thank you for the important information you sent. We will do our best to find the man.

What else can you tell us of what you know? Can we talk?

Dylan

"Dylan."

Like they were friends. Just like in the car.

Kai had relived so much of the conversation in the weeks since. Even as he'd threatened the man's life with his best impersonation of TV street thugs, the councilman had responded politely. It was one reason Kai felt so much shame.

He jumped to the second email. From the reporter. It had arrived twenty minutes before.

Thank you for writing back. I would like to help you. And I know how to be careful.

Anything you say to me will be off the record (a secret between you and me), and a reporter never reveals who they talk to. To anyone.

I will meet you wherever and whenever you want me to.

It was one thing to ask one person for help. But two?

At least now he had a choice.

Kai looked back at the councilman's email, then the reporter's. Who could he trust more?

Kai had seen enough on the news to know the councilman was desperate. He needed to bust Kai to prove that he had not made up the crime. The more public Kai's guilt, the better for him. The sooner the better, as well.

The reporter faced less pressure. She promised secrecy. And she was a former police officer. She always seemed fair in the stories he'd seen. She could give him advice on the best way to handle it all, including how to get out of the situation.

He closed Councilman Webb's email and replied to the reporter's.

SUNDAY

Chapter 93

It was a quiet weekend.

Too quiet.

No political appearances. No Monday committee meetings to prepare for. The calls had died down once Dylan had stopped responding. Poor Michelle Easley—she'd be getting all the incoming.

And there'd been no reply to the email Dylan had sent Saturday morning, copying and pasting the draft Rusty Grimes had sent to him late Friday night.

A Sunday evening dinner with a tipsy Grimes broke the monotony.

"We've had someone watching Slayton's house since yesterday morning," Grimes said as they huddled in a fancy, smoke-filled restaurant on the Kentucky side of the Ohio River.

It looked like Grimes's law office. Surrounded by dark wood and more heads of dead animals, Grimes spoke in between bites of a hulking slab of steak. The uneaten half still lay on a plate in front of him, next to a glass of bourbon—a glass he'd already emptied once. Webb and Gabby picked at salads while sipping Diet Coke.

"Find anything?" Dylan asked, impressed to learn of the surveillance.

"Not really. Just a typical kid. He plays basketball for the high school, so he didn't do much Saturday before playing in a game that night. Rode the bench most of the game. Then he spent today at home. From what we found, he lives with his mom, who's on disability. No siblings. No father, at least since he was really young."

"Any criminal record?"

"A few fights. And he was once put on juvenile probation for shoplifting at a Walmart. Unarmed. Nothing like this."

Gabby shook her head. "Well, he sure picked a heck of a starter crime!"

Grimes chuckled. "True. Armed kidnapping. From zero to a hundred quick!"

"Hold on, guys. We don't know who put him up to this. And that's probably *why* he went from zero to a hundred. So let's wait to see what he says before passing judgment."

Grimes shook his head. "Passing judgment? I try to keep my politics out of stuff, but you libs really are soft, ain't ya? This guy threatened to kill you, made you beg for your life, cost you your job, and now you're taking his side?"

"I'm not taking his side. His life is about to be ruined—the next decade, at least. But I could tell throughout the incident, *he* wasn't the one to worry about."

"But he held the gun!" Grimes said before coughing on a piece of steak.

Dylan waited for the coughing to end.

"Yes, which is probably why I'm here now. Trust me, he was the cooler head of the two. But more importantly, this is bigger than either of them. We need to figure out who's behind it all."

Grimes, chewing on another mouthful, said nothing back.

"So what can we do if he doesn't respond?" Dylan asked.

Grimes finished his bite before taking another swig of bourbon.

"Someone needs to meet with him in person, then build some trust to keep him talking."

"And who should that be?" Gabby asked.

Grimes shook his head.

"I'm still figuring that part out."

MONDAY

Chapter 94

Jungle gyms.

Swings.

Slides.

Squeals and giggles.

The sights and sounds brought Maggie back a decade.

Having been at the scene of too many playground injuries, she'd watched like a hawk whenever Emmy was playing. But she always tried to maintain calm so her daughter and her little friends could enjoy themselves.

It'd been the perfect example of balancing her roles in life. Being a cop meant you saw too much of the world, usually the worst parts. Being a mom meant you tried to shield your daughter from most of it—even on a playground—without seeming to.

Maggie had the same instinct now, watching a dozen kids swinging and hanging from every piece of equipment imaginable, parents sitting yards away on benches, talking or looking down at their phones. But she again held back.

Ten minutes in, she forgot the kids completely.

He was tall—six feet at least. Thin. With a well-ironed sweatshirt tucked into holeless jeans, he was better dressed than most teens these days. He appeared over a slight hill, emerging from a grove of pines, the opposite side from where Maggie had parked.

She smiled at the out-of-place Packers hat and cheap sunglasses—a rookie's attempt at a disguise.

Based on Webb's description, this was clearly the kid from the back of the car. Which surprised Maggie because Webb had said he'd been the scary one.

He tried to look cool as he neared, but failed, scanning to his left and right.

Just like she'd taken extra care not to be followed here, she rapidly eyed the surroundings one last time. No one was watching.

Still planted on the bench, she casually raised her right hand to shoulder height to confirm she was the one he was looking for.

He approached to within a few feet, then stopped.

She stood up.

"Hi there. Thank you for meeting me. I know this isn't easy."

"Are you Maggie Coyle, from Channel 5?"

"I am."

"I recognize you."

He flashed a quick smile, one that made him look well younger than his height.

"Where should we go?" he asked, so quietly it was hard to hear.

"Let's walk," she said. "And don't worry, no one is following."

That appeared to calm him.

At his suggestion, they were at the entrance to French Park in Amberley Village, an upper-middle-class suburb north of Cincinnati. The heart of Cincinnati's Jewish community. She doubted he lived there, but he probably lived in one of the half-dozen diverse working- and middle-class neighborhoods in the vicinity.

They walked into the park, past a few older couples walking their dogs.

"What happened to your hand?" Maggie asked. The bandage wrapped around his right wrist and palm made for an easy warm-up question.

"Basketball game," he said.

"Tough rebound?"

"Sort of."

"I played power forward at St. Agnes. So I know the feeling."

"Try being center!" he said, flashing that youthful smile again. "But it's why I could meet now—no practice!"

They walked for a few seconds in silence, so she broke the ice a second time.

"My guess is you don't want to use your real name. So what can I call you?"

"Call me Aaron," he said, pointing to his hat.

She kept her gaze forward. Looking right at him would make him more nervous.

"Okay, Aaron. I'm going to be very straight with you, and you don't have to say anything. From your emails and the situation, my guess is that you're one of the two people who kidnapped Councilman Webb."

She could see him shudder, but they kept walking.

"And now, you've discovered something about it that's made you more scared than at first. Something worse is going on than a simple robbery. And you regret taking part in it."

His head tremored even more. He reached up and wiped his left cheek.

She stopped and turned toward him. The sunglasses and hat couldn't hide a face of anguish.

"And I want you to know that reaching out to me is as brave a thing as anyone could do. And I am going to do my best to help get you out of this mess."

Tears now trickled down both his cheeks. As she suspected, there was a lot pent up within him that needed to come out. He'd been battling this alone for a week and a half. A guilty conscience. Fear—of getting hurt, of getting caught.

He reached out and hugged her. And through sobs, he started talking.

"My parents taught me better than what I did. I can't sleep. I can't tell anyone. And now something terrible is happening that *I* started."

In police work, confessions often came out in an explosion of emotion. Weeks, months, or years of stress pile up, then unleash all at once. Reality dawning that life would never be the same.

The difference here was that Maggie found herself in a bearhug with the person confessing as opposed to watching the meltdown across a table while a camera captured it all.

"I know, and I'm here to help," she said over his sobs, embracing him for a few more seconds.

"What can you do? I made a terrible decision. I've ruined my life."

Sticks crackled in front of them.

Maggie froze.

Then came a growl, followed by the sound of women talking. Seconds later, four women, two with golden retrievers, two with large poodle mixes, appeared on the path. One of the poodles eyed Aaron, continuing a low growl.

The four women stopped talking as they walked past, no doubt ogling the odd scene. Seconds later, they disappeared in more trees as their conversation picked back up.

Maggie took a step back and looked up at Aaron.

"It's not over yet. I've seen many people come back from bad decisions by doing the right thing."

She smiled.

"And reaching out like you did was definitely the right thing."

Using the sleeve of his sweatshirt, he wiped tears from his cheek.

"Thank you."

"But Aaron, to help you, I'll need to know everything that happened."

He nodded. "I know. I haven't told anyone anything, but I'll tell you."

Over the next twenty minutes, as they walked deep into the park, he shared all the details. Jotting down notes, she interrupted as little as possible.

A school classmate—he wouldn't say what school or the name of the classmate—approached him about making quick money by holding up some rich guy he knew about. He assured "Aaron" it would be easy, but he also framed it as a dare. He pushed and pushed. In the end, Aaron didn't want to be seen as a coward, and he needed the money, so agreed.

"I knew it was stupid, and for some reason, I wasn't even convinced it was real," he said. "Just talk."

The classmate wasn't a good friend but an acquaintance. The tough kid from school. They knew each other from sports.

The day of the robbery, Aaron told his mom he was going to an extra basketball practice and would be home later. But after practice ended, the other kid drove him downtown, then up to the top of Mount Adams, parking near a big church.

"Immaculata?" Maggie asked.

"I don't know," Aaron said. "But it's the big one you can see from the highway."

She wrote down *Immaculata*.

According to Aaron, the other kid kept checking his phone as they sat in the parked car. After about fifteen minutes, he said it was time.

"That's when I started to get super nervous. It was really happening."

"Did you know he had a gun?"

"I did. I saw it in his pants, then I asked him about it. He said it was just to scare the guy—that it wasn't even loaded."

They got out of the car and walked down the sidewalk of a steep hill. Near the bottom of the hill, a Jeep passed them. The driver appeared to look at them. The Jeep then turned left and parked in a spot just down the hill. They watched as the councilman got out and walked into his house.

Exactly as Webb had described.

"So you missed him?" Maggie asked.

"I thought so at first, and I thought maybe it was over. But Sl—I mean, the other kid—he said it was fine. So we waited behind another car on the hill, one up from his Jeep."

Maggie wrote as he talked: *Knew would come back out.*

"And he was right. Only a few minutes later, the councilman came back out of his house. He reached into the car to get something, and that's when we got him. The poor guy had basically trapped himself."

"You call him the councilman. Had you ever seen him before?"

"Well, when he later told us he was a councilman, I remembered seeing him on TV."

"But not in person? Or before that?"

"Never. All that stuff they're saying that we were selling him drugs is so stupid. We held him up like he said. And I've never sold a drug in my life. Or used one. My ma warned us about drugs all growing up."

From zero drug use to an armed abduction, Maggie thought. What a tragic decision this kid had made.

"Did your friend appear to know who he was?"

"Ma'am, we may play ball together, but he's not my friend."

"Okay. Well, the guy in the front seat. Did he seem to know?"

"He didn't act like it. But I can't say."

Aaron described the next hour almost identically to Webb's account. The ATMs. Their meandering conversation interrupted by Aaron's threats of violence. The homeless guy at the second ATM. The blindfold. The drive back to Mount Adams. Leaving him on the hill.

"He was actually calm most of the time. Talked a lot, but calm. Kept telling us about the work he was doing. He only seemed really nervous at the end, with that blindfold on. But even then, he told us to lower the seat so we wouldn't stick out."

"And after you left the car?"

"We ran back to our car, drove back down that steep hill, dumped his stuff in a garbage can, then went home."

"Why'd you dump his stuff there?"

"It's just what he said we should do. So no one could trace his cellphone to us."

"And you guys didn't take his credit cards?"

"Slay said he took some to get more money later."

"Did you happen to see any receipts from the ATM?"

"I think they came out, but I was too worked up to pay close attention. I know we didn't take them."

"One other question before you go on. What kind of car were you in? Was it a car you'd seen before?"

"It was some beat-up old thing. White. A Toyota, I think. Not the one he usually drives. I don't know where he got it from. And I've never seen it again."

Aaron next described being dropped off at home, then going straight to his bedroom, knowing his mom would suspect something was wrong if she saw him. He didn't sleep the whole night.

"What happened to the Bears hat?"

"I left it in the car, along with the jacket he gave me to wear. He must've gotten rid of them."

"He brought both?"

"Yes. He said it was to be safe. And when I saw those police diagrams a couple days later, I was glad I'd worn them. Those could've been anybody."

He went on to describe seeing Ventre at the warehouse, beaten. He shared as many details of the men as he could remember.

"That's when I knew this was much worse than a robbery. I barely saw the homeless guy when he interacted with us at that ATM. Maybe two seconds. But someone still grabbed him. Which meant that someone else must've been watching what we were doing. Or Sl—I mean the other guy—told them about him right away. Then, when I saw that everyone was saying the councilman made it all up, I realized that that homeless guy was the only person who saw us with him. The only person who could back up the councilman's story."

Except for you, Maggie thought.

"I'm afraid you're right," she said instead.

"Have you been able to find him?" Aaron asked.

"No. Although we know who he is."

Aaron stared straight ahead, saying nothing. Guilt clearly weighed on him.

They were heading back toward the parking lot now.

"Anything else you can recall?"

"Not really, except that he's watching me like a hawk. He knew I'd skipped out on lunch when I went to that warehouse. The next day, he threatened me not to say anything."

"Have you ever gotten any money?"

"Not yet. He says it's coming. But I don't even care anymore. That's blood money."

The faint sounds of the playground returned as they neared the entrance to the park.

She stopped walking and faced him.

"Aaron, listen to me. And this is important. You need to act like you *do* care. And now that we've talked, you don't need to do any more investigating of your own. Outside of the homeless guy, you are the one person who knows that what the councilman said is true. So from now on, I'll do any of the investigating we need. You act like you're a guy with no regrets who wants to get your money."

"Okay. I'll do my best."

"Are you sure you can't tell me the name of the person who got you into this mess? It would make this a lot easier, and you said he's not your friend."

"Ma'am, I'm trying to help as best I can, but I'm not ready to go there yet. You know what happens to snitches, right?"

"I understand," she said, content at all she'd gotten from their first meeting, as well as the rapport they'd built. No need to push for more now.

"Well, if anything else comes up, or you remember anything else you want to share, send me an email. And I'll do the same. Thank you for putting your trust in me."

As they stepped out from under the trees, his eyes darted around again. Playground. Parking lot. Lawn of grass beyond.

This kid was scared.

"Don't worry," Maggie assured, patting him on his shoulder. "No one's watching."

Chapter 95

Due north and up the hill from downtown, even as many of its better-off residents flocked to the suburbs, the neighborhood of Avondale remained the beating heart of Cincinnati's Black community.

And not just because it occupied its geographic center.

Looming over both sides of Reading Road, the busy corridor running right up the gut of Avondale, were a half-dozen of Cincinnati's most iconic Baptist churches. And even though many of the parishioners and their families had moved out of the city, they returned to those churches every Sunday morning.

Along that avenue of churches, none matched the stature and history of Calvary Baptist. Long-ago Southern transplants created the city's oldest congregation more than a century before. And amid the great migration north, its membership grew rapidly, ultimately moving into the former German Gothic synagogue at the crest of Reading Road. With its multiple towers, renovated red-brick surface, and pristine stained-glass windows, Calvary looked out over Avondale like a fortress over a valley below.

But even more than its architectural grandeur, the true draw of Calvary was its dynamic pastor, Dr. Calvin Easley. Hailed as Cincinnati's most powerful orator and preacher, he led a congregation of thousands, from everyday folks from down the street to the region's most important civic leaders.

Dylan Webb had visited Calvary numerous times, but unlike other church leaders, Pastor Easley never let political guests speak. Still, his large and devoted following made him one of the city's most potent political forces. Just a moment of recognition in a Calvary pew bestowed a huge political benefit, boosted further when Dylan shook every hand as parishioners left the church.

Today's visit had an entirely different purpose. And unlike on Sundays, the church's parking lot was empty when Gabby and Webb pulled in just after four on Monday afternoon.

Gabby rang a doorbell at a humble side entrance, and an older man answered with a polite grin.

"Hiya, young lady." Gabby had grown up in this church, which was how Dylan had first met Pastor Easley during the campaign. "Come on in."

The man ushered them through a long hallway to the back of the building. After rounding a corner, he led them to a closed wooden door and knocked twice.

"Send him in," a voice said from within.

The words may have been simple, but the baritone voice sent butterflies churning through Dylan's abdomen. Michelle Easley had been the one who'd called Dylan an hour before, asking for the meeting. But it was her dad, the pastor himself, speaking now.

The man opened the door, and Webb and Gabby walked in, the door shutting behind them.

Behind a wide desk, Pastor Easley looked far different in an open-collared shirt and dark gray suit than his Sunday black robe and always-colorful stole. But he also looked angry, a fire Dylan had seen at protests following high-profile police shootings but rarely in person.

From a chair on the far end of the room, Councilwoman Easley—in a bright pink pantsuit today—stood to greet Dylan, but the pastor shooed his daughter back into her seat.

"No time for small talk, Michelle. Please have a seat, Councilman."

Then he hugged Gabby. "And great to see you again, young lady, although it's been a while, if I'm not mistaken. There's a chair for you too."

He turned back to Dylan, glaring.

"Councilman, what kind of mess have you gotten my daughter into?"

"What happened?" Webb asked.

Michelle shook her head, looking uncharacteristically frazzled. Altogether different than their Saturday morning breakfast.

"Nonstop calls," she said. "Requests for meetings. Demands of who to pick. It's been more intense than anything in my time on the council. The mayor and Curtis are demanding to meet in person, and you know how forceful they can be. Chairman Myers"—the chairman of the county's Republican Party—"is demanding to meet also. And the tone from all of them is over the top. Even threatening."

Webb had assumed this was why she'd called an hour ago.

"I am so sorry, Michelle. I didn't—"

The pastor's long arm shot high in the air, reminding Webb of one of his sermons.

"Young man, this may not be Sunday, but you are still in the house of the Lord. Please don't say anything that you and I both know is not true. You picked her to play this role because you *did* know this would happen."

He stopped talking and stared directly at Webb for a few painful seconds.

"Didn't you?"

"I knew it was a hot potato. But this sounds more intense than I would have guessed."

"Young man . . ." He raised his arm again. "More than you can possibly imagine, I've been around. And I know what's happening here. I've been watching all this closely. Your entire sad downfall."

Dylan felt the urge to defend himself, but the pastor kept going.

"You suspect that someone set you up so they could replace you, don't you?"

Webb nodded, once again in the principal's office. A very wise principal. He also felt a tinge of relief, hearing someone else echo his narrative.

"Yes, I do."

"So to interfere with that plan, you handed all this to my daughter."

"I wouldn't put it that way. I wanted to put it in the hands of someone with integrity. Someone who clearly was not involved. Michelle was the only one who fit that bill."

A long pause.

"Son, I respect what you've done, but you should've been straight about it with her."

Dylan nodded, then looked the councilwoman's way. "You're right. And for that, I am sorry."

Another long silence.

"You should know I, too, am getting calls from pastors and other community leaders about who she should pick."

"I'm sorry to hear that as well."

Pastor Easley leaned back, rubbing his thin fingers through the tufts of white hair curling off the sides of his otherwise bald head. The back-to-back apologies seemed to set him at ease.

"So now the question is, what can we do about the dilemma we find ourselves in?"

"Well, let me know who—"

"The way I see it," the pastor said, interrupting, "we now have a perfect bird's-eye view of what whoever did this to you really wants."

"So you actually believe I was set up, Reverend?"

Easley laughed, gleaming white teeth on full display.

"Of course I believe you, son. When you minister people as long as I have, you become an able judge of character. You know when people are lying, and you know when people are incapable of lying. You buzz in and out of my church so fast, you probably didn't think I was sizing you up . . ."

He eyed Dylan for a few seconds.

"But you don't think I'd let you sit in my church before an election if I didn't believe you were a man of character."

"Thank you, Reverend. That means a—"

"From the day they questioned your story, I've told Michelle that someone had it in for you."

The councilwoman nodded. "Yes, you did," she said.

Easley chuckled. "And whoever it is, they seem to want something real bad."

Dylan nodded. "Yes, they do."

"So as much as you've handed our family one big hot potato, it also gives us an opportunity. As I was saying, we now sit in the driver's seat. So what are we going to do?"

"See what names people recommend to Michelle?"

Pastor Easley shook his head, smiling again.

"Son, we can do even better than that."

"We can?"

"Yes. Michelle, tell them what you were thinking."

The councilwoman sat up straight, the same poise she showed at every council meeting.

"We thought the best approach would be to create a highly public and formal selection process. Anyone can suggest a candidate, but they must do so in writing. And at some point, we release a short list of candidates to the public, asking for more written feedback. Then we make our selection."

Webb grinned.

"So we force the whole thing out in the open?"

"Exactly," the pastor said. "Smoke them out."

"Don't you think that might scare them away from their original plan?"

"Not a chance. Someone is investing a lot to get what they want. My guess is they've enlisted a lot of people, and they're close to achieving their goal, whatever it might be. You threw them a curveball, but the calls to us make clear they're not about to give up now."

Dylan sat up straight, mind whirring.

"I keep thinking it's all about stopping the police reform we were so close to achieving. The chief and his people are all so against it, and from the beginning of this, I could tell this was an opportunity to get rid of me and kill it."

Pastor Easley nodded. "Well, now we'll see, won't we?" he asked nonchalantly.

"You don't think so?"

"As I said, I've been around a long time. And in that time, I've learned that there's one thing that makes people so relentlessly pursue a plan like this."

"And what's that?"

He held his hand over his desk, palm up, rubbing his thumb against his second and third fingers.

"Money. Lots and lots of money."

Chapter 96

Back at her desk, Maggie Coyle reviewed the notes she'd scribbled down in her car after "Aaron" had walked away from the playground.

Basketball.

"SL."

Center.

Aaron had shared a lot of information, but none more important than these offhand nuggets.

She turned to her work desktop and opened up Google Maps, honing in on French Park to recall which neighborhoods ranged within walking distance. She jotted down the five in the vicinity: Golf Manor, Reading, Deer Park, Silverton, Pleasant Ridge.

Then she walked to the far corner of the newsroom where the sports guys hung out. As always, the one she needed was there.

"What's up, Mags?" Barry Knight asked in his always booming voice, looking up from a desk buried in papers and empty cans of Monster. He still had makeup on from the 5 p.m. broadcast.

"Hey, Barry. I need a quick favor."

"Oh boy, who's in trouble?" Barry asked, guffawing even louder than he'd spoken.

Barry was a cad, but after thirty years in sports, he was also an institution.

"No one. But you may be able to help me find a basketball player I'm looking for."

Barry hyped high school sports more than any TV guy in town. He kept up daily with football and basketball coaches across the region, who all hoped to get a few precious seconds of footage on his previews or recaps. And being featured as "Barry's Game of the Week" was the most exciting thing to happen to a high school all season, short of winning a state championship.

He clapped his hands. "Now *that* I can help you with!"

"Do you have team rosters?"

He rolled out a drawer from a file cabinet beside his desk. "Have I got rosters? You bet I've got rosters! Photos too."

"Photos?"

"Yeah, the coaches send signed photos every season. What team you looking for?"

She looked down at her list.

"I need Golf Manor, Reading, Silverton, Pleasant Ridge, and Deer Park."

"Well, Golf Manor and Pleasant Ridge are part of Cincinnati public schools. So those kids could go to any number of schools. But sure, I've got all of 'em."

He reached into the file cabinet, leafing through folders and dividers.

"Here's Withrow," he said, pulling out a manila folder and laying it on his desk. "The Tigers are strong this year."

Maggie's heart thumped as she eyed the folder. She was getting close.

"Here's Reading . . . and Woodward."

He dropped two more folders on the desk.

"The Falcons!"

He looked up at her as he lay that folder down. "What was the other school you needed?"

"It depends. Who are the Falcons?"

"Deer Park."

"Then I still need Silverton."

"That's right," he said, turning back toward the filing cabinet. "The not-so-mighty Hawks of Silverton. Now that's a team that's struggling."

Seconds later, Silverton's folder lay on the desk.

"Oh, and you'll also need Walnut Hills."

He hunted that folder down, handed it to her, then sat back in his chair.

"Anything else you need?"

"Just to borrow these for the next hour."

"Sure thing!"

* * *

Maggie eliminated the three Cincinnati public teams right away. Bigger schools, their teams' centers all towered over their teammates. At least 6'2" or taller. No way Aaron from the park played center on Withrow, Walnut Hills, or Woodward.

That left the three smaller schools.

She scanned back and forth between the Deer Park photo and roster. A diverse team. Players of all sizes. But no one resembling Aaron. She looked at each name just in case—no name began with the letters "Sl."

The Blue Devils of Reading had one player around Aaron's height. But he had thicker shoulders and forearms, along with traps bulging out from his neck. Although the sweatshirt had hidden his upper body, Aaron was skinnier. The long hug had confirmed more bone than muscle.

Plus, this kid was listed as one of the team's forwards. Not a center.

She picked up the last folder.

Silverton. The date on top made clear it was the team photo from the year before.

Two rows of players. Not an impressive group. "The not-so-mighty Hawks," Maggie whispered, echoing Knight.

The only center listed in the photo was a gangly and tall White kid—at least 6'5".

But it was the kid standing next to him who drew Maggie's attention. Similar hue to Aaron. Not that tall—six feet at best. Thin too. And a youthful smile.

She looked down at the name.

Kai Brewer. A junior. A forward.

She looked back at the center. A senior from the year before. Kai Brewer was the second-tallest guy on the team then. He easily could've grown a few inches and moved over to the center role now that he was a senior.

She looked at the expression again, remembering Aaron at the park. Had to be him.

She quickly scanned the names of the other kids on the team, looking for a first name starting with "Sl"—the name that Aaron, or Kai, almost spilled when they were talking.

The players in the back row were all standing. Along with Kai Brewer and the center who'd graduated, four players were listed:

Devon Murphy, F, Senior

Jesus Guzman, F, Sophomore

Shaquille Smith, F, Sophomore

Sloan Turner, F, Junior

Sloan.

She took a look at the photo. Caucasian. Flabby cheeks. A few inches shorter than Kai Brewer.

She turned to her desktop and opened the folder she'd kept on Webb. She found the sketch of Webb's abductors. The one that was supposed to be Kai was so general, it could've been anyone. But the one of the kid in the front seat was more distinctive. But the sketch looked nothing like Sloan Turner.

She moved to the front row, all seated.

Josh Ellington, G, Senior

Trey Cummings, G, Freshman

Quinton Mace, G Freshman

Michael Slayton, G, Sophomore

Slayton.

Michael Slayton.

She looked back up at the photo.

Looked at her screen.

Same high cheekbones. Same recessed chin. Noticeable acne and pock marks.

Same guy.

Pulse pounding, she clenched her fist.

She had them.

Kai Brewer and Michael Slayton of Silverton High School—Dylan Webb's abductors.

Chapter 97

Headphones on, and the door to Slay's small bedroom closed, the sound at first came through as a muffled interruption to the rap blasting through his ears.

He ignored it once.

Then a second time.

On the third, he got up from his bed, removed his headset, and opened the door.

"Michael!" yelled out his mom, the only person who called him by that name.

"Yeah, Mom, what is it?"

"There's a man at the door for you."

The hairs along his arm stood up. No one ever came to their home.

"Who?"

"Some lawyer. He says it's important."

Slay looked at his phone. Seven forty.

Why would a lawyer stop by in the evening? Couldn't be good.

"One second."

He reached under the mattress of his unmade twin bed.

They'd let him keep the 9mm pistol after the robbery for moments like these. He'd hidden it under his mattress ever since. Loaded. He grabbed it now and tucked it under the waistband of his jeans, over his right buttock. He pulled a baggy gray sweatshirt on and down over his waist.

"Michael!"

"I'll be there in one second!" he yelled back.

He walked down the short, dark hallway to the kitchen, where his mom spent every hour of the day when she wasn't sleeping. Except for meals at the kitchen table, they hardly interacted.

She looked up from her wheelchair, stringy gray hair cascading over her face.

"Where is he?" Slay asked.

"Front door."

"Did he say what he wanted?"

"Just to talk. Said he wanted to help you. Seemed like a nice man."

"Talk about what?"

"He didn't say. Go ask him yourself. And don't tell me you're in trouble again."

Slay shook his head.

He walked into their barren living room and approached the front door. Visible through a window to the left, a tall figure with short black hair stood waiting on their narrow front porch. In a suit and dark coat, he looked like lawyers Slay had seen at the courthouse. Or worse, some type of cop.

Whoever he was, Slay didn't recognize him from the people involved the robbery. Too clean.

He opened the door a few inches with his left hand but didn't unlatch the chain connecting the door to its frame. With his right hand, he reached down and grasped the pistol—still in his waistband—by its grip.

"Who are you, and what do you want?" he asked through the narrow gap.

"Is this Michael Slayton?" the man asked in a friendly Southern twang.

"Yes, it is. Who are you, and what do you want?"

"I'm a lawyer. And I've been sent here to help you."

"Help me how?" he asked.

"Help you get out of the mess you're in."

"What mess? I'm just a high-school kid minding my own business."

The man looked through the gap in the door.

"Michael, we both know it's not that simple."

Slay tightened his grip on the pistol. He'd shot at some cans in the woods to practice, but never at a person before. But there was a first time for everything.

"Okay, if you're a lawyer, who's your client?"

The man smiled.

"I can't go there yet."

Slay's pulse raced.

This guy had to be a cop. If they'd discovered that he'd kidnapped the councilman, they'd send a cop right away. A well-armed cop. Wouldn't they?

He lifted the gun out of his waistband and held it behind him, bending the tip of his forefinger over the trigger.

"Mr. Slayton?" the man asked.

Slay peered out the window again. A plain gray sedan was parked on the street. No one else looked to be in it.

"You alone, Mr. Lawyer?"

"I sure am."

He reconsidered. The cops would never send only one person to arrest a suspect for armed kidnapping. They would've already knocked the door down.

"How do I know you're not a cop?"

"Well, I know all sorts of details the cops don't know."

"Like what?"

"Like that you were civil to the councilman throughout the hour."

Slay smirked. Kai had been panicking so much in the back seat, he'd decided to play the good cop throughout. Funny that the councilman had been saying he was the nice guy.

"Civil? To who? What are you talking about?"

"Michael, we both know who and what I'm talking about."

Slay said nothing. This guy knew. No point playing dumb. But why was he here now?

"So?! He told a lot of people that. I even saw that on TV."

"And it was the councilman's idea to put the blindfold on. So you wouldn't get caught."

Slay nodded. He hadn't seen that reported anywhere.

"And you told him you weren't going to be friends when it was all over."

Slay moved his finger away from the trigger, smirking. Yes, he'd said that. The councilman had been working so hard to impress them that he'd grown annoying. Was talking *too* much. That line had been Slay's attempt to shut him up so he could concentrate on each step of the plan.

"Okay, okay. So tell me how you know all this. Did the councilman tell you?"

"Listen, we know you're scared."

Slay shrugged. He wasn't at all scared. Hadn't been scared of anything since his dad had walked out when he was seven, forcing him to man up at a young age. He was eager to get the rest of the money he'd been promised, and that was about it.

He was about to push back, then hesitated.

"Of course I'm scared," he said back softly, using his best country club voice—where he'd worked for years as a caddy, taking orders from rich people while learning how to feign politeness. Still, some members had complained he looked too rough, and he was ultimately let go.

He tucked his gun back under his waistband.

"We can be of help."

"You can? How?"

"You don't have to let this ruin your life. And we can get you out of danger."

Danger? What was this fool talking about?

"Thank you," Slay said, again playing along. "It's getting very scary."

"We know. And we can help. We just need to know about the people behind what you did. They're the ones who will go down for this. Not you, if you help us find them."

No fucking way, Slay thought. They were already livid that Kai seemed so unreliable. Snitching would be signing his death warrant. Far worse than what they did to the homeless guy. He knew the trip to that warehouse served multiple purposes, including spooking Kai. And him.

"I don't know that much. But you really think if I get you details, I'll be okay?"

"If you help us find the big fish, for sure."

"Okay. I'll do my best."

The man reached toward the door, something small in his hand.

"Here's my phone number. And you can use this email from now on."

The corner of a business card appeared in the gap in the doorway.

TUESDAY

Chapter 98

Maggie Coyle stood at the same city hall location where Dylan Webb had announced his departure days before. But she got there early this time.

"Thank you all for coming," Councilwoman Michelle Easley said, kicking off at ten sharp.

No one at the station could remember the last time the low-profile councilwoman had held a solo press conference. Maggie had convinced Rick Temple to let her cover it.

Stylishly dressed in a mustard-yellow pantsuit, the councilwoman spoke without notes.

"I wanted to fill in the public on the process I'll be undertaking to fill the vacancy left by Councilman Webb."

For the next ten minutes, the councilwoman walked through the kind of open process the press had been asking for for decades. Orderly. Fully transparent, as opposed to backroom deals. Firm deadlines.

As she spoke, an aide handed Maggie and the others a piece of paper spelling out a detailed timeline.

After she stopped talking, questions flew immediately.

"So anyone can recommend a name?" a radio reporter asked.

"Yes. But it must be in writing, along with the signature of the person recommending the candidate."

"What about your colleagues on the council?"

"Same rules apply to them. Mayor as well."

A few reporters chuckled. They'd all be livid.

"What do they think of your plan?"

"You'll have to ask them. This is the first time I've outlined it."

"Party chairs and insiders also have to follow the rules?" another reporter asked.

"Same rules, whoever it is. And all names are due this Friday."

She repeated the email to which people could submit their recommendations.

"And how about those advocating for candidates that have been submitted?" Maggie asked. "You're obviously getting a ton of calls to push for certain people."

"That's one reason I chose to do it this way. My phone's been ringing nonstop since Friday. I will no longer accept those calls. If you want to advocate for a candidate whose name is on the list, send it in writing. Same email address. All public."

"And that's how everyone has to do it?" Maggie asked.

She nodded. "Again—same rules for everyone."

"Why?" a woman's voice yelled out.

"Why what?" the councilwoman asked.

Maggie looked over and saw that the questioner was a long-time columnist for the *Enquirer*. Someone who'd been around the block even longer than she had, covering city hall when she was a young cop.

"Why have you chosen to do it this way? This couldn't be more different than any appointment process we've seen around here."

The councilwoman smiled.

"I'll take that as a compliment. I thought about this all weekend. Prayed on it Sunday. But especially given the way this seat became vacant, I think I owe it to the citizens to do this right. This is the public's seat. Not one party's. Not one group's. So if it's the public's seat, we should of course fill it in the most public way possible, seeking as much input as possible."

Maggie held back a laugh.

It was the perfect soundbite. And politically, the perfect answer. The public would eat it up.

But that's not why she was amused.

If you were Dylan Webb, and you suspected all of this was about replacing you with a hand-picked successor, the process Councilwoman Michelle Easley had laid out was also the perfect strategy to smoke it out.

Chapter 99

Dylan, Grimes, and a new lawyer—Hugh Stabler, a former FBI agent from Louisville—huddled back in Grimes's conference room, debriefing.

"Whatd'ya mean, he was hard to read?" Grimes asked, interrupting Stabler almost from the outset.

"Well, he *said* he was scared, but he didn't seem scared. In fact, he was tough as hell. Like he didn't scare."

"Why do you say that?" Dylan asked.

"His eyes, man. Mean-lookin' eyes. And he didn't flinch throughout it all. My guess is he had a gun in his hand the whole time and was deciding whether to use it."

"Jesus," Dylan said. "But he said he needed help?"

"Yes, he did."

"No mention of the emails?" Grimes asked.

"None. Like we agreed, I didn't bring them up, and neither did he."

"But he wasn't surprised by the visit?"

"If he was, it didn't show."

Grimes shook his head. "I sure as shit hope we knocked on the right door."

Stabler nodded. "My gut says we did. Anyone who kidnaps a guy at gunpoint is gonna have some toughness to him. But if he wasn't the one emailing us, he played it off so well. It's gotta be him."

Webb relived the scene in the car. The trash talk from the back. The calmer tone in the front.

"No way was it the guy in the back. It's got to be him."

Grimes turned Dylan's way. "And he hasn't emailed you yet?" he asked.

"Nothing."

"He texted me a few minutes ago, Rusty," Stabler said as he looked down at his phone. "He wants to meet again. What do you want me to tell him?"

"Ask when."

Stabler typed on his phone, then ogled the screen for several seconds.

"He's writing back . . . He says tomorrow. Should I ask him what for?"

Grimes thought for a moment.

"No. Don't want to spook—"

"Hold on." He looked at his phone longer this time. "He says he wants out. That he thinks they know he's been communicating with us. And that his life's in danger."

Webb leaned forward in his chair. "I knew it!"

Grimes shook his head. "Or he's playing us."

"What should I say?" Stabler asked.

"Put a question mark," Grimes said. "Then ask him where and when we should meet."

Stabler typed it in. After several seconds passed, he looked up.

"Three o'clock. And you're not gonna believe where he wants to go."

Chapter 100

It was the most relaxed Kai had felt in weeks. Since before it all began.

He'd slept well, knowing he finally had someone to talk to. A professional who knew exactly what to do, and who'd keep his secret.

Plus, Slay hadn't been at school, setting Kai at ease all day. At the end of the lunch hour, without a pang of worry, he'd sent the reporter another email from the computer lab. He wanted to meet again—there was more to share.

When the final bell rang at three, Kai slung his backpack over his shoulder and walked out of the school's main entrance, as opposed to the door that took athletes to the gym. Coach had cooled off a bit, said he'd let him know Friday when he could return to the team. But for now, he remained suspended.

Kai didn't mind, and not even the steady drizzle could dampen his spirits. Home was three small streets and one busy boulevard away. He walked the first two streets and most of the boulevard at his normal, long-striding pace, head down to avoid the rain.

Well down the boulevard, consecutive cars hit puddles at just the wrong time, sending water splashing his way. His jeans drenched from the thigh down, Kai stepped to his right while glancing left to see if any more cars were close. And that's the only reason he noticed the gray van.

It was well behind him, but its tinted front windows stuck out. It also was driving more slowly than the other cars, hugging the right curb. Even as his frayed nerves fired away, Kai's first thought was that he was being paranoid. Still, the next intersection was only twenty feet away, so he decided to take that side street instead of walking the additional block to his own street.

Keeping his gaze straight ahead, Kai skipped to his right—to the edge of the sidewalk—as he closed on the intersection. The van reacted immediately, its engine revving into action and tires squealing.

Kai broke into a full sprint, racing diagonally over wet grass to the side street, then running past two small houses that fronted the street.

The van's tires screeched as it made the sharp right turn behind him. Then came the unmistakable roar of the van door rolling open.

Kai sprinted past a third house, options racing through his mind.

Even though home was a block away—accessible through the yard across the street that abutted his back yard—it wouldn't be safe there. And heading home might endanger Ma and Jamelle.

At the same time, he was on a cul-de-sac and fast approaching its dead end.

Unlike the others he'd passed, the next house was set back from the street, a driveway into the lot. Kai veered right and sprinted down the driveway as voices shouted behind him. At least one person had left the van.

"Stop," that person yelled out. "Police."

Kai flinched.

Ma had trained him for as long as he could remember: Never run from the police. Turn around. Raise your hands. Look them in the eye. Show respect. Without her saying it, it was clear the constant reminders were about keeping Kai safe.

But if these *weren't* cops, but part of Slay's group, Ma's wise steps of precaution could get him killed.

The voice was far enough behind him that he slowed and shot a glance back. One guy was chasing him. Short. Muscular. Tan, maybe Hispanic. He wasn't in uniform, but Kai knew that cops patrolled neighborhoods all the time in street clothes.

The van wasn't far behind the guy. Gray, with those tinted windows. Also, no police markings. But again, cops used unmarked cars all the time. He'd heard stories about it—it was how the cops jumped out on drug dealers and caught them before they knew what hit them.

Cops or not? Kai had no clue.

Casting Ma's warning aside, he kept running. He'd take his chances. Better to piss off the police than be nabbed by the people who'd brutalized that homeless guy.

The driveway ended at a large wooden fence, the top of which looked higher than the rim of a basketball hoop. But from teaching himself to dunk, Kai knew he could carom off the fence to push himself an extra foot in the air, then grab the top.

He planted his right foot hard into the fence, lunging up. But as his wet shoe hit the slick vertical board, his foot slipped immediately. His shoulder and outstretched arm crashed into the hard wood a foot short of the top, and he nearly lost his balance as he hit the ground.

"Stop," the voice yelled again from behind. "Mr. Brewer, we want to talk to you! Put your hands up."

A chill ran down his spine. They knew his name. And this guy even sounded like a cop.

He took a deep breath. Maybe it was time to give up. If he was trapped anyway, why risk angering them even more, or being shot? He began to lift his hands.

Then he saw it. Three feet to his right, and one foot up from the ground, a large knot in one board opened a hole that went clear through to the other side.

A perfect foothold.

He leapt in the direction of the knot, jamming the front of his right sneaker into the hole. Arms already up, he pushed against the knot, and this time the sneaker held long enough for him to reach over the fence and grip the top firmly with both hands. With pain piercing through his wrist, he pulled himself up and threw his legs over in a single motion, then landed in a squat position on the other side.

A half-second later, a collision shook the boards of the fence so hard some of them cracked. Kai looked up to see several fingers shoot up over the top of the fence before disappearing just as quickly.

Crack. Something snapped on the other side of the fence.

"Shit!" a man cried out in pain, confirming that whatever broke was part of his body.

Fearful the van would circle back to the new street and intercept him, Kai scampered to his left and through the backyard he had jumped into. He raced away from the boulevard, backyard to backyard, shrouded by houses on one side and fences and bushes on the other, with an occasional low fence to climb over.

Chapter 101

The phone indicated the call was from Calvary Baptist. Slowing from a jog to a walk, Webb picked up right away.

"We got something," the baritone voice said.

"You do?"

"Sure do," Pastor Easley said.

"I'll be right up."

"No, you won't. We don't need anyone seeing you driving onto this lot. I'll meet you."

* * *

Thirty minutes later, Webb and Pastor Easley sat in Webb's parents' condo as rain poured down outside so hard they couldn't see the Kentucky side of the river.

"I can't believe someone dared call Michelle even with all she laid out," Webb said. "And so fast, too!"

The pastor shook his head. "They didn't call Michelle. They reached out to me through one of my congregants. He asked if I'd take a call from Curtis Jackson."

"And did you?"

"Yes. He wants me to meet with him, the mayor, and some others."

"Did he say exactly what for?"

"To share feedback on Michelle's pick. And that some very important people had a strong interest in this process that I'd want to know about."

"And what did you tell him?"

"At first I told him they should follow Michelle's process. That I wasn't involved. But he pushed back hard, saying it was an opportunity for the city to get things right, and an opportunity for both me and the church. So I knew this was our opening."

Webb nodded.

"So you set up a meeting?"

"Sure did."

"Where's it going to be?"

"The church, of course. My home field advantage."

"Is Michelle going to be there?"

"No. I'm keeping her away from this. But you're gonna be there."

"I am?"

"Well, watching at least. That room you sat in the other day has a camera in every corner . . ."

Webb laughed.

"Like I said, home field advantage."

Chapter 102

Maggie passed the Michelle Easley announcement onto another reporter so she could cover the bigger story of the day.

That story brought her back to the same county courthouse where she'd talked to the homeless vets a week ago. Spotting her, two of them said hello as she scampered up the front steps. With the rain, she'd have to film the live shot from outside the main entrance doors, where an overhang would keep her and her cameraman dry. She didn't have time to straighten out the frizz in her hair, but the story was big enough that Temple would forgive it.

The email from DruggieWebb@yahoo.com had come through around the time that Easley had made her announcement at city hall. And it was such a doozy that after hours of frantic work, she'd now go live at five, five thirty, and six.

Karma was a bitch, but it also made for great ratings.

As the camera's light turned green, Maggie took a deep breath. She'd rehearsed the first sentence a half dozen times. So much was riding on it. Not just for the story, but to complete her end of the bargain. To assure Emmy's safety.

"While the city learned more about former Councilman Webb's pot buying habits yesterday, it turns out he's small fry compared to several well-known gentlemen who work in the building behind me. Channel 5 has obtained documentation of years of secret drug purchases by Judges Tom McIntosh and Barry Feist, both well known for handing out tough sentences for drug dealing."

She paused as the studio aired past clips of the two judges chewing out defendants sitting in front of them. Then she walked through the extensive drug-buying details of both men. Like the first email, the new email had included years of evidence. Together, the duo had spent thousands of dollars buying not marijuana, but cocaine. She held up pages of printed out transactions as she spoke.

"When confronted with this evidence, both McIntosh and Feist refused to speak with me and referred me to their lawyers, who wouldn't return our calls." She grinned. "But have no doubt, we will keep calling, and we'll fill you in on what they have to say."

She ended with a grim face until the camera's light turned red, then let out a long breath.

"You nailed it," Sam said.

"You think?"

"Oh yeah. Now how in the hell did you get all that stuff on them?"

She still felt guilty about the whole thing—pushing a story that, although true, also helped protect her family.

"You know the game," she said, smiling. "A reporter never reveals her sources."

Her phone buzzed from her pocket. Probably Temple calling. He was the first person powerful people called to complain about one of her stories.

So she reached into her pocket and pulled her phone out.

It was a number she didn't recognize.

"Hello?"

"Who'd you tell?" a voice yelled.

"Excuse me? Who is this?"

"It's Aaron. From the park. Who did you tell?"

Chapter 103

Deep into the trail in French Park, rain pelting down amid the darkness, the tall figure appeared from behind a tree for an instant, then stepped back behind it.

Flashlight in hand, Maggie approached the tree, then circled the thick trunk, almost bumping into him.

She hardly recognized him.

No baseball cap. No sunglasses. Shivering. Scowling.

A scared kid.

"You made a promise," he shouted, a voice full of fear as opposed to anger. "So I told you everything."

"Slow down. What happened?" she asked, taking a step back.

"What happened is you told someone. About me. About what I told you."

"I didn't tell a soul. Nobody. Like I promised."

"Then how do they know?"

"Who's they?"

He threw his hands in the air.

"I don't even know. They said they were cops. Followed me in a van as I walked home from school, then chased me down a street. I escaped, but they looked for me for the next hour."

"They said they were cops?"

"Yes!"

Didn't sound like standard plainclothes behavior, but some undercover guys pushed the envelope in certain neighborhoods.

"And you ran?"

"If I were sure they were cops, I wouldn't have." He sounded sincere. "But if these were the people behind the kidnapping, I didn't want to end up like that guy in the warehouse . . ."

She nodded. He'd made the right choice.

"So nobody bothers me for weeks, but within a day of our meeting, someone's chasing me?"

She racked her brain. The only person she'd talked to since their conversation was Barry in sports, getting those photos. But she hadn't revealed a thing.

"I get it. And I'm sorry. But I'm telling you, I didn't say a word. And I wasn't followed."

He stared at her, his deep breaths slowing.

"Can I ask you one question?" she asked in a softer tone.

"What?"

"Did the other guy—the one who put you up to this—act different since we met?"

"No. He wasn't even at school today."

"Well, that's pretty different."

"Maybe, but he misses school a lot."

"He knows where you live, right?"

"Yes."

"So he doesn't show up at school today, and then you're followed as you walk home."

He stared back for a few seconds. "So you think he knows we're talking?"

"I don't know if he knows a thing about me. But he may suspect you're talking to someone."

"But I haven't been. Just you."

She pulled her phone out of her pocket. "Give me one sec."

Detective Shirley Meadows answered on the second ring. "Hey there!"

"Shirley, I need your help on something, and you can't tell a soul."

"Coyle, do I ever tell a soul when we talk?"

"Fair. Do you know if there's been any progress on the Webb abduction? Any leads on who did it?"

Meadows laughed. "Are you serious?"

"Yes, I'm serious."

"You just broke a huge story about how Webb's scandal is tied into judges at the courthouse, and you're still asking me about his so-called kidnapping?"

Maggie had already forgotten about her big story an hour ago.

"So they're not looking into it?"

"Maggie, that case is done. Unless they go after him for filing a false police report. But the only lead on that crime is the former councilman himself."

"You're sure?"

"Honey, I'm sure."

"Thank you. I'll give you a call tomorrow."

She looked up at Kai.

"Well, it definitely wasn't the cops."

"How do you know?"

"Because that was a cop, and if they were onto you, she would've known. They still think he made it up."

Kai shook his head. "Which means the people chasing me were the people from the warehouse."

Maggie nodded. "I'm afraid you're right."

And, she thought but didn't say, *how the hell would they know?*

"So what do I do now? Where do I go?"

Maggie at first had no answer. Then she had an idea.

Chapter 104

Slay was back at home. In his room. Door closed. Exhausted.

The three men had made him sit in the back of the van for hours as they circled the neighborhood, looking for but never finding Kai. They'd pumped him for information throughout the ride, growing ever angrier, even when he was the one who'd told them Kai may have snitched. Given how mad they were, he was relieved when they'd dropped him off.

They said they'd call him later with a new plan. So when Slay's phone buzzed, he'd planned to ignore the call.

Then he saw the number and picked up. Before he could say a word, Kai yelled through the phone.

"Slay, did they not get you?"

It was an odd question for someone he'd been pursuing for hours.

"Who?"

"The cops," Kai said breathlessly.

"No. Why?"

"Because they tried to grab me off the street as I was walking home from school. I barely got away. Jumped a fence and kept running and hiding. Holy shit! They almost got me."

Slay didn't know how to respond. Kai really thought they'd been cops.

"So they didn't come after you?" Kai asked.

"No, dude," he said, trying to sound casual. "I was at practice anyway, but I haven't seen any cops."

"I don't get that. Why would cops come after me and leave you alone? How would they even know to go after me in the first place?"

"I have no idea. Why are you so sure they were cops?"

"That's what they yelled when they chased me. And who else would it be?"

"I have no idea. Either way, where are you now?"

"Staying with a cousin in Kentucky. Someone I can trust."

Asking for more details would seem suspicious, so Slay held back.

"And what did you tell your parents?"

"Same thing. I stay with him pretty often. They wouldn't think much of it."

A long pause.

"You going to go to school tomorrow?" Kai asked.

"Was planning on it. You?"

"No way. I'm going to lay low over here. Especially now that I ran, I'm not going anywhere near school. Or home."

Slay shook his head. Kai really was convinced the cops were after him.

"Want my help?" Slay asked. "Need me to pick you up or anything?"

"No. I'm good. But thanks. Call me tomorrow and let me know if they come around school again."

"Will do."

Kai hung up.

Slay immediately called back his main contact from the van.

"What do ya want?" the man asked gruffly.

"I just heard from him."

"From Kai?"

"Yes."

"Where is he?"

"Hiding out in Kentucky somewhere."

"He told you that?"

"Yes. He's convinced it was the cops chasing him down."

"Really?"

"He really is. Says he's going to lay low for a bit."

Slay hesitated to say what he was thinking. They'd be pissed, but he went ahead.

"And I know I told you I thought he may be a snitch, but after the call, I'm not so sure."

"What the fuck do you mean you're not so sure? You had us chase him around the whole night. And Munoz broke his ankle from that fence. And now you're not sure? Are you fucking kidding me?"

"I know. I know. All I can tell you is that he's convinced the cops are chasing him. He's hiding out from them. And he called *me* to tell me all about it. That doesn't sound like what a snitch would do."

Seconds of silence on the other end.

"So you're saying you were wrong?"

"Maybe."

"Then who was that guy who came to your house?"

"I have no idea. But I guess we'll find out more tomorrow."

"You're damn right we will. And we'll also ask your man Kai some tough questions whenever we get our hands on him."

Chapter 105

Dylan opened his eyes and sat up, a grating sound piercing his ear.

He found himself on his parents' couch facing the television set, which was still on. The football game was now in the third quarter. He must have dozed off.

The noise came a second time. A long buzz, which he now realized was his parents' buzzer. The one visitors pressed from the lobby. Which was odd, since he hadn't had a single visitor since he'd moved over here.

He walked over to the receiver next to the condo's front door and pressed the red button.

"Who is it?" he asked.

A crackly voice came through.

"It's Maggie Coyle. I need to speak with you right away."

Even hearing the name made him seethe. He'd stopped watching local news, but Gabby had called to fill him in on Maggie's big scoop tying his robbery and past weed buys to the far more serious cocaine buying of two tough-on-crime judges.

"And why in the hell should I let you up here after that hatchet job?" he asked.

"For one, I can explain all that. But more importantly, I know one of your kidnappers reached out to talk to you."

How in the hell would she know that?

"Come on up."

* * *

The moment she walked in, Dylan knew something big was happening. In addition to being soaking wet, the usually cool and confident Maggie Coyle looked frazzled, a glassy stare in her eyes.

He grabbed a blanket from the closet and handed it to her as they sat down on the couch.

"Thank you," she said, wrapping it around herself. "I need to swear you to secrecy, Dylan. I'm going to tell you something you can't even repeat to Gabby, or to your lawyers."

"Okay."

"I've been talking to one of the two kids who held you up."

Dylan sat up straight. "You have? And he admits it?"

"He does. The whole thing. Your entire story checks out, minute by minute."

Dylan's anger flared again.

"Then why the hell would you—"

She held her hand in the air.

"Stop. You getting mad is going to waste our time. He's a source, and like you would as a lawyer, I protect sources. I'm only telling you because he gave me permission."

"He did? Why?"

"Because we need to know if you've put him in danger."

"Me? How?"

"He said he wrote to you, like he did to me."

"That's true. I got an email about a week ago."

"And he said you wrote him back?"

"Yes, Grimes drafted something, and I sent it."

"And?"

"Didn't he tell you?"

"Tell me what?"

"We never heard anything back. So we paid him a visit."

Maggie shook her head.

"That's what we were worried about."

"That we went to his house?"

"No. That you went to the *wrong* house. Who do you think wrote you?"

"His name is Michael Slayton. Lives in Silverton and goes to high school there. He was the kid in the front seat."

"I knew it," she said, in a resigned tone.

"What?" Dylan asked impatiently.

"Slayton didn't write you. He's the dangerous one! And by knocking on *his* door, you endangered the guy who's actually trying to help."

Webb slumped down in the couch.

"But the guy in the back—"

"Was scared shitless. He admitted he was talking a big game, but he's more of a freaked-out kid than a hardened criminal. Slayton's the one who put him up to it all. And he's the connection back to whoever was behind this."

"Shit." Webb put his head in his hand. "Where's your kid now?"

"He's home. But only after being chased by the bad guys for hours. Thanks to that visit to Slayton."

"Is he safe?"

"I think so. We think we convinced Slayton that he never snitched, then watched his parents' house for an hour before sneaking in the back door. But that's why I'm here—to be sure. What did you say to Slayton when you visited?"

"It wasn't me. It was a lawyer from Louisville. A partner of Grimes. Ex-FBI. He just knocked on the door and said he could help."

"And what did Slayton say back?"

"That he was scared and needed help."

"No mention of emails?"

"Not a word. The whole point of going there was to confirm the hunch that it was him. We knew if we were wrong, it posed a risk."

"And?"

"Based on the conversation, we thought it was him."

"Well, it wasn't."

"I get it!" Webb said, raising his hands in the air. "We fucked up."

She nodded. "So how did you leave things with him?"

"Funny you should ask. The lawyer left him a card, and he texted back earlier today that he wanted to meet tomorrow."

"And you agreed?"

"Yes, we did. They're meeting at three. But speaking of meetings, there's another meeting tomorrow you're going to want to know about. And this time, I need to swear *you* to secrecy."

He filled her in on the meeting planned for Calvary Church, which they'd be able to watch by video.

"Wow. You *have* made progress. Do you think Pastor Easley would let us tape the meeting as well?"

"Who knows? Let's check in the morning."

WEDNESDAY

Chapter 106

Kai awoke, knowing he needed to stay home from school. But Ma would pose a major obstacle to that plan.

He'd snuck in the back door at 9:30 the night before, telling Ma through her bedroom door that he'd been at a friend's house and his phone had died. He'd then gone right to bed, shivering under the covers until he fell asleep. Waking with a slight cough would help him make his case.

"What were you thinking, Kai? Of course playing basketball in the rain was going to get you sick," Ma said as Jamelle got dressed for school.

"I know, Ma. It was dumb, but I wanted to stay in shape. Coach says I might be back next week."

"Either way, your cough sounds pretty mild. You're going to school. I'm not about to reward your bad decision-making."

"But Ma—"

"You're going, and that's the end of it. We're leaving in ten minutes."

She and Jamelle walked to the kitchen as Kai sat back on his bed, brainstorming.

His phone rang.

Slay.

"You sound bad, dude," Slay said after Kai greeted him.

"Sick as a dog. Those fucking cops did it to me, chasing me through all that rain."

"So you're still in Kentucky?"

"Yeah. Haven't moved. Feel like shit. Let me know what happens at school. And if they come back around."

"Will do."

He hung up, determined not to walk out his front door in case they were watching.

He'd only resorted to this once before, but he had no choice. He walked into the bathroom, leaned over the toilet, stuck his finger deep in his throat, and threw up.

Chapter 107

Not only did Pastor Easley approve of Maggie taping the meeting, but he was ebullient about the idea.

So at eleven, Maggie arrived at Dylan's condo to set up a desktop computer and large monitor to watch the meeting together online. But the equipment would also route the footage directly into Channel 5's control room to ensure the best quality for later editing. Sitting on the Webbs' dining room table, the screen was split into four rectangles, each offering a different view of the pastor's office.

As Easley promised, the meeting started promptly at 1 p.m. after a knock on the door.

"Come on in," the pastor said from behind his desk.

Councilman Curtis Jackson was the first person to enter the room, followed by two others neither Maggie nor Webb recognized. A fourth man—tall, broad-shouldered, with white hair and a trim white beard—looked familiar, but Dylan couldn't pinpoint where from. All wore suits.

After polite greetings—the three other men each introducing themselves as attorneys—they took their seats.

"Where's the mayor?" Easley asked, standing behind his desk.

"He couldn't make it," Jackson said. "Wasn't feeling well."

"It's one in the afternoon. Figured he'd be able to recover by now."

Jackson ignored the jab and got the meeting started.

"Well, Pastor, you certainly find yourself in an interesting spot."

Easley raised his hand high in the air. "Gentlemen, before we discuss matters of such public importance, let us pray."

For the ensuing two minutes, all five men bowed their heads for a prayer, which Easley delivered with as much passion as if facing five hundred parishioners on a Sunday morning.

He closed on a high note: "May God bless our discussions today, making them fruitful for all involved and a positive step for the community we all love. Amen."

"Amen," the four men repeated.

Easley looked up from his desk and eyed Jackson.

"Interesting spot, you say?" he asked, laughing. "I guess I can blame my daughter for this one. But I'm used to it, as you know."

"He's a cool customer," Maggie said to Dylan as they both leaned toward the screen. "Totally at ease."

"The man's been around," Dylan said as he kept his eye on the monitor.

"So how can I be of help, Councilman?" Easley asked.

Usually laid back, Jackson looked uneasy.

"Well, Pastor, as you know, the mayor assigned me the task of finding a replacement for Councilman Webb."

"I understand that, but that was before the councilman handed my daughter the assignment."

"Of course. But in preparing my committee, I spoke to numerous people who have a strong interest in this selection. And I wanted to be sure you knew where sentiments lay about the ideal candidates to replace Webb."

"Whose sentiments?" Easley gestured at the other men in the room. "Are these gentlemen members of your committee?"

Webb chuckled at the question.

"No, they're not. The committee disbanded once your daughter took over. But they represent people who have the strong interest I mentioned."

The pastor leaned forward over his desk, eyeing the three White, well-dressed men one at a time.

"And I can see just how representative they are. But what, pray tell, is that interest? The welfare of our children? Improving police-community relations? Better job opportunities?"

The man next to Curtis Jackson, the one who Webb recognized, leaned forward. With his dapper white beard, he looked like the senior of the trio.

"We have an interest in seeing all those things happen, Reverend. And more. Which is why we want just the right person to replace the disgraced councilman."

Dylan cringed at his new moniker.

"One council appointee can do all of that at once?" Easley asked, now holding his chin. "You must have some truly impressive people in mind."

"We think so. And that is what we were advising Councilman Jackson here before your daughter was put in charge. No offense."

"None taken. I happen to think she's the perfect person to be in charge." He winked at Jackson. "No offense."

Councilman Jackson nodded. "Michelle and I have always enjoyed working together."

"She agrees. And I'm meeting with you today in that spirit. But you gentlemen need to get more specific. I'm a simple preacher, not a politician. I need to know precisely what you want me to do."

The man sitting to Jackson's left reached into a small satchel and plucked out a manila folder. He removed a single sheet of paper and gave it to the councilman.

The white-haired man spoke again. "Reverend, we've taken the liberty of suggesting three names for you to consider. All three would be acceptable."

Easley studied all three men, one eye squinting.

"Acceptable, you say? Pass that on over here."

Jackson stood up and handed the paper across the desk. Easley looked down, shaking his head.

"You're kidding me, right? You'd be okay putting Malcolm on the council?"

Curtis nodded. "Yes, we're comfortable with him."

"And these other two? Really?"

"They are both strong candidates, in our opinion," the bearded man said. "All three meet the bill."

"The bill . . . I see."

Easley stared at the paper for another twenty seconds, creating an awkward silence. Then he stood up.

"Curtis, I'd like to speak to you alone. Gentlemen, I'm going to ask you to leave now."

The councilman held up his hand, stammering. "I'm sorry, Pastor, but these are my—"

"It's fine," the white-haired man said, cutting him off. "The pastor is right. Some things are better left discussed among just two people."

"Exactly," Easley said. "You three can wait in the chapel. Down the hall."

The three men walked out, while Curtis Jackson remained on his feet.

"Pastor, with all due respect, I don't think you understand how powerful those men are. And who they represent."

Easley sat back down, his wide grin returning.

"You're right. I don't. And that's why I wanted to ask you that in private." He waved the paper in the air. "I think we both know these three have no business being on the city council. Which means that man with the white beard must be mighty powerful for you to agree."

Curtis leaned back defensively. "I think you should give them more credit than—"

"Don't bullshit me, son. I know these three—nice people who do what they're told. Which means we both now know what's really going on here. And if I'm going to help you, I want to make sure I understand it. I have a reputation to maintain in this town. A standard to uphold. I need to understand what's at stake before we go any further."

"Understand it? Is that all?"

Easley leaned back in his chair.

"You know that's not all. To tell you the truth, I want to seize the same opportunity you are seizing. That the mayor, these men, and some of your colleagues are seizing through this decision."

Jackson nodded. "I assumed that's why you agreed to meet."

"You catch on quick, young man. How much are they paying you?"

Curtis leaned back in the chair, holding both hands up.

"Oh, they're not paying me a thing. But they will be very supportive of my campaign for mayor if we can shape the right council."

Dylan fumed. What a gutless sellout his former ally was.

"Well, that's a form of payment, isn't it? Making you mayor?"

"I see it as helping me perform public service. And lift the community. And my guess is that they're willing to do the same for you, perhaps by making a contribution to this church, or to other causes you care about. You heard what he said, right? He wants to help on the issues you mentioned."

"And what is it *they* want?"

"Simple. They want one of those three picked for city council."

"Of course. But for what purpose?"

"I'm not at liberty to say. And I don't think you want to know."

Easley laughed again, waving his hand forward.

"You are such a fool!"

Easley paused, slowing down.

"Let me reword that to be more respectful. I am *not* a fool. Unless I know what their purpose is, I don't know how valuable my decision is to them. And not knowing our value is exactly how all the rich White people of this town get richer while we do their bidding for peanuts on their dollar. It's why they live in new mansions in the suburbs while we settle for their old houses in the city. And they've been doing it to us for years. Why? Because we never know what our value really is. We never even ask!"

"You don't have to lecture me, Pastor."

"Apparently I do, because you want me to cut a deal without knowing its real value. I don't work that way."

He paused, staring right into Jackson' eyes.

"I want a piece of it."

Dylan, sipping a Diet Coke as he watched the screen, choked when he heard the line.

"You want what?" Jackson asked.

"I want a piece of the action. I don't want some one-time payoff like you're getting. Or that others on the council are getting. I want a *piece* of it. I'm talking equity. If this is so valuable to them, they can share their value with the only person in the city who can make it happen."

"Pastor, be reasonable. That's not how this works."

"Well then, they don't get their council member. I've got a whole congregation of fine people who would make better public servants than these three"—he sneered down at the paper—"and I am happy to announce one of them tomorrow."

The two men stared at each other for an awkward half minute.

"Are we finished?" Easley asked. "Because I've told you my bottom line. I need to know the purpose and the value, and I want a cut."

Curtis stood up, sighing.

"No, we're not finished. Let me go talk to them."

Easley stood up and patted him on the back.

"I'm so glad to hear that. I'll be back here in twenty minutes. I'll expect to see you here, with the one who's in charge. The others don't need to return. This needs to be private."

They both left the room, the pastor patting the councilman on the shoulder.

* * *

Dylan and Maggie sat in silence for seconds. Stunned.

Maggie stood and stretched her arms before Dylan finally spoke.

"Now that was something."

"It really was. You might need to make some popcorn for after the intermission."

Dylan chuckled, then noticed that he'd missed a text while watching Easley's performance. It was from Grimes.

Slayton says you need to be at the meeting.

Webb texted back right away.

What? Why?

He says you need to show to confirm that this is legit.

Jesus. You think it's safe?

Stabler's a pro. He'll have a gun on him.

"What is it?" Maggie asked. "You look like someone died."

"That someone might be me. You know that meeting I mentioned? With Slayton?"

"Yes."

"Apparently he's insisting that I be there too. Hold on—"

Dylan typed back to Grimes: *A gun? Well that's reassuring.*

"That sounds risky as hell," Maggie said.

Grimes wrote back: *You're meeting on a riverboat. Public. It may be our last chance. I think you need to go.*

Dylan looked up. "Grimes is right. If the whole point is that we're helping this guy, and we think he's the one emailing us, then how could I refuse? That would raise a major red flag."

"Sure. But when we know that he *isn't* the one emailing, and he suspects that his buddy is, it could be a trap."

"I've gotta do it. The guy I'm with is former FBI. He'll be armed."

"Your call. But if anything is off, let me know right away."

"Why? What can you do?"

"I still know a lot of cops who can help when I ask."

"You think they'd rescue me?"

Maggie laughed. "Well, I'd keep your identity a secret until after you're free."

"Gee, thanks."

Chapter 108

Five minutes after Webb left the condo, Maggie watched Pastor Easley reenter the room. Curtis Jackson followed him in a minute later, with the white-haired, bearded guest a step behind. The three sat down.

"Did the council member explain my position to you?" Easley asked, all business.

"He did."

"And?"

"I think we can put something together along those lines. Your participation would be of great benefit."

"Equity?" Easley asked.

"Equity," the man confirmed.

Easley looked back at Curtis. "See, Councilman? I knew there was a reason to keep talking."

The man stood up and handed Easley a folder.

"The councilman said you wanted to understand the purpose. This explains it all very well."

Easley pulled open a drawer and lifted a pair of bifocals onto his nose. Then he opened the folder and scrutinized it, flipping through a page every few seconds.

"Now this is what I'm talking about," he said. "Big."

The man nodded. "Yes, it's big. Turn to page eighteen. Look at that spreadsheet. I believe it communicates the value you were asking about."

Easley flipped through a few more pages, stopped, then leaned toward the page.

"*Very* big. Never seen numbers like this before."

"No, you haven't. And I talked to those I represent. They are prepared to include you as a silent partner, with one percent equity."

Easley looked up, steely eyes peering out over the bifocals. Dead serious.

"One percent?" he asked, no emotion in his voice.

"One percent. And if you look at the last column on page eighteen, and do the math over time—"

"And *who* is it that you represent?"

"I'm sorry, Pastor. I'm not able to share that with you. That's part of the terms of the silent partnership."

"Sir, I know every person in this town. Enough to know there are some you don't want to do business with."

"Well, let me put it this way. The major investors in this project are not people you know. But let me assure you they are good for their commitments."

"From out of town?"

"You can say that."

Easley nodded, casting a wry grin.

"And that's why it's so much money?"

The man nodded. "You catch on fast."

"I've read about this," Easley said, leaning forward. "Foreign investors parking big money in American real estate. Way beyond the Upper East Side. Who knew they'd come to our little city?"

"I can't say any more," the man said, in a tone that made clear Easley was on the right track.

Maggie wrote down "foreign investors" in her notepad. Unlike Easley, if this was a trend, she hadn't heard of it.

Easley pivoted abruptly. "And I assume this is no less than the mayor is getting, and other silent partners?"

"We're not at liberty to talk about other silent partners."

"C'mon, Rev," Jackson said. "Be reasonable."

"Gentlemen, I am not a greedy man. I simply want what's fair. And for the role you are asking me to play, I want to be treated the same as others."

The bearded man lifted both hands in the air. "I will put it this way: You are on *at least* equal terms with our other silent partners."

"Including the mayor?"

A long pause. Easley's eyes fixed on the bearded man.

"Yes, including the mayor, once his term has ended."

Jackson's head spun toward the bearded man, clearly surprised by the revelation.

Easley laughed.

"As I told you, Councilman. You gotta ask for your value." He turned back to the bearded man. "For what you are asking me to do, one percent is a fair arrangement."

"Wonderful," the man said. "I've already asked my firm to draft up the documents. They should be ready by tomorrow."

"Same as the mayor?"

"The exact same."

"Wonderful."

"And do you know who you will be selecting for the council seat?"

Easley picked the single sheet of paper off the table and looked once more at the names they were suggesting.

"So any of the three serve our purposes?" he asked, holding up the folder. "They'll support this pivotal effort?"

"Yes, they will," the bearded man said.

"You're positive?"

"If they are on that list, I am one hundred percent positive."

"Then I must say, gentlemen, that all three are outstanding candidates. But I would like to consult with my daughter to make our final decision. I'll let you know at the same time I see those documents you mentioned."

All three stood up.

"Sounds like a plan," the bearded man said.

The councilman watched as the two others shook hands.

Chapter 109

As many times as he'd watched the old river boats paddle by, Dylan Webb hadn't been on one since he was a kid. A Mother's Day brunch. Outside of special occasions like that, Cincinnati's old riverboats were basically tourist attractions for out-of-towners. Leaving from the Kentucky side of the river, they were usually short trips, cruising downtown then heading a few miles east before turning around and coming back.

So the red-and-white Queen City Belle felt like a bizarre place to rendezvous with someone who'd mugged him. And definitely not something a tough hometown kid would come up with.

At five before three, Dylan and Stabler walked up the long-sloped ramp as a folksy rendition of "Rocky Top" played from the boat's hull. A few seniors, surrounded by families and kids, walked in front of and behind them.

"He said to meet him on the dining level," Stabler said as they stepped off the ramp and onto the riverboat itself. "But only after the boat leaves."

Dylan looked up at the top floor. "Sounds good. Let's head up there for now."

The duo walked up two flights of steps to the boat's uncovered top deck, then crossed to the far side.

Scanning across the river, Dylan could see his house perched halfway up Mount Adams. The colorful houses below his along Hill Street appeared far bigger from here than from the street, as their lower floors stretched straight down the hillside, almost to Columbia Parkway.

He zeroed in on the Schunks'—his next-door neighbors. The biggest house on the hill, and the place where he first learned the cops were telling people he was making it all up. Now he was about to meet with the guy who could prove his every word true.

A bell rung out from the boat's stern. After the fifth gong, a voice yelled, "All aboard," from up front, followed by a long and deep toot from above. The immense red wheel at the stern began rotating.

Dylan's economic development brain immediately kicked in as the Queen City Belle crept away from shore: This was a pretty nifty setup. The city should use the riverboats far more in its tourism marketing than it did.

"Any word?" Dylan asked as the Belle passed beneath the blue steel of the Roebling Bridge, the identical twin of the Brooklyn Bridge, only smaller.

"He said he'd text me," Stabler said, yelling over the din of the traffic crossing the deck above, "but nothing yet."

They passed by the Reds stadium, then in front of Cincinnati's full skyline. It was an eclectic mix of sleek twenty-first-century skyscrapers towering over classic old buildings that were among the nation's tallest when built a century ago.

"Still nothing?" Dylan asked.

"Nope."

Dylan spotted Grimes's law firm with its fancy outdoor patio, then the more modest windows of his own firm. A block to the left, he spied the building where Laurie Busken worked, eyeing the corner offices near the top. She was probably in one of those offices now.

One block further rose the old Central Trust Building. With its white brick facade and ornate tower that looked like it'd been shipped right from Greece, the old bank was still the signature building of the skyline. Which made it the fitting location for the Windsor Firm, where he'd visited his old seller, Graham Mundy, the other day.

He shook his head, recalling those old portraits watching over disapprovingly as he'd waited for Mundy. What an oppressive place.

Then it struck him.

Most of those portraits were of men long since gone, but some of the firm's current leaders also made appearances at the end. Today's rainmakers.

And one of them, he now recalled, had a striking white beard. Just like the guy who'd met with Easley. The one who'd looked so familiar a few hours ago. The one who'd carried himself as the leader.

Stabler tapped his shoulder. "He just wrote. He's on the second floor now. Inside. Let's go."

"One sec."

Dylan pulled out his phone, googling the Windsor Firm. He pushed on the button taking visitors to the "Our Team" page. A photo of the team's managing partner appeared atop a group photo of the management team. None looked like the guy with the white beard.

Another tap on the shoulder. "C'mon. What could be more important than this?"

"Hold on," Dylan said impatiently. "Almost done."

He scrolled down further, looking at each department listed.

He opened up corporate. Eight names. Five men. None familiar but Mundy, who looked a lot better in his photo than he did the other day.

Environment—which at firms like Windsor meant anti-environment. Three men. All younger. None with a beard.

Real estate. Second-to-last department, listed only before taxation. He opened it.

And there he was—the man from the church meeting, pictured in his white-maned and bearded glory.

Sebastian Gray. Senior partner. Chair, real estate committee. At the Windsor Firm for decades, including a stint as its managing partner.

The close-up of his face triggered more detailed memories. Dylan had seen him in the audience at some zoning hearings, although he'd dispatched more junior people to the podium to testify. That's how associates gained needed experience while partners like Gray racked up billable hours without getting their hands dirty.

And the name Sebastian Gray had appeared on documents for projects that had come before him. One of the key players making big projects happen in town, representing the who's who of banks, developers, insurance companies, construction companies, and other deep-pocketed businesses. The type of rainmaker who'd earn a place on the Windsor wall. And when Mundy had said that Dylan was *persona non grata* at the firm, a real estate big shot like Sebastian Gray would've thought that more than anyone.

The third tap on his shoulder was far more forceful.

"It's time!"

"Okay," Dylan said too loudly, motivated more by his big find than the impending rendezvous. "Let's go talk to him!"

They walked down one flight of stairs into a large dining room.

With most of the passengers remaining outside, the room was largely empty. One large family took up a whole table, downing drinks and snacks they'd brought on board, while an older couple chatted quietly at another table.

The one other occupied table sat in the far corner—a single person facing the other way, his hair obscured by a baseball cap.

"That's got to be him," Stabler whispered.

The two walked over to the table with the solo guest, Stabler tapped him on the shoulder, and he turned to face them.

Dylan's stomach knotted.

Even with the sunglasses off—revealing the narrow, mean-looking eyes Stabler had described—everything else about this kid's face looked the same. The peach fuzz, the thin cheeks, his fade. The pockmarks. Seeing a guy who'd held a gun on him for an hour sent his pulse racing. He was suddenly back in the car, every moment between then and now gone.

The kid stood up. Dylan did a double take, struck by how small he was. No more than 160 pounds; 5'8" at most. Yet this kid had made Dylan beg for his life for an hour. Something about their physical mismatch sparked rage all over again.

"Mr. Council Member. Thank you for meeting. I want you to know how terrible I feel about everything that's happened to you."

He reached out to shake Dylan's hand.

Dylan initially reached forward, but he pulled his hand away at the last moment.

He tried to smile but couldn't. Tried to think of something polite to say but couldn't.

"Mr. Slayton, what you did to me was absolutely horrible. Horrible. You have no right to threaten *anyone's* life. To do it for an hour is downright sick."

Stabler put his hand in front of Dylan as if stopping an impending punch.

"Hey, man! This is not the time."

Of course he was right, but seeing the kid in person was overwhelming Dylan's rational side.

"No, this *is* the time! What this guy and his buddy did to me should never happen to anybody. Ever. And he needs to hear that directly from me."

The kid nodded, his steely eyes blinking.

"I understand. It's one reason I called."

The family eating snacks looked in the direction of the conversation. They weren't speaking loudly, but the intensity of the conversation was drawing attention.

"Maybe we should head outside," Stabler said quietly. "A little more privacy."

"Fine with me," the kid said. He stood up and walked toward the back of the boat.

They exited a side door onto a long, narrow outdoor deck that ran along the Belle's starboard side. They were two-thirds of the way toward the boat's stern, with no one visible in front of them. The large wheel was spinning fast not far behind them, drowning out their conversation from others.

Peering over the side of the boat, leaning against a railing that reached his lower chest, the kid removed an e-cigarette and started sucking from it.

"So why did you call us?" Stabler asked.

"You're the one who knocked on my door, remember? And you said you could help me."

"I did."

"Well, I need that help now. Bad. I'm in trouble. This has gotten much bigger."

Dylan tried to calm himself as the other two talked, focusing on a small harbor of mangy looking sailboats the Belle was passing.

"How so?" Stabler asked.

"It was supposed to be a simple robbery. To embarrass the council member, I think. They offered to pay me a lot of money to do it. Sounded so easy. But now they're chasing my friend, and I'm afraid they're going to kill us both."

He smoked the e-cigarette nervously, fidgeting with it between puffs.

"So you knew I was a council member the whole time?"

"Of course. They showed me your photo, told me where you would be and when, told me to find someone who could help me with the robbery, and gave me the exact route to go to."

"Wait, they told you which ATMs to go to?"

"Yes. It was a very specific plan, and we did exactly what they said. Then they followed us the whole way, even grabbing the receipts we left behind at each ATM. Again, it was all to make you look like a freak so you'd resign. We thought once they paid us, it would be over. But it's never been over. They've kept a close eye on us every day since, clearly worried we may talk. And that's why I think they're going to kill me. And my partner."

He sounded credible. And scared. But this might also be fishing—seeing if Kai Brewer had already ratted him out. So Dylan continued to play dumb.

"And who's your partner? He seemed a lot angrier than you did."

The kid chortled.

"He acts like a tough guy like that. But he's also really scared too. Heck, he was scared the whole time."

"And he hasn't told anybody?"

"I don't think so."

"Did you tell him we were meeting?"

"I didn't. But I can if you want me—"

A bang interrupted the kid, causing Dylan to jump. He turned to see the old couple from the dining room struggling to open the door—it was on a tight spring and must've slammed shut on their first attempt. Dylan stepped toward the door, grabbed the handle, and opened it for them.

"Thank you," the man said. "And excuse us."

The woman did a double take as she looked up at Dylan.

"Do I know you from somewhere?" she asked.

"I don't think so, ma'am. Just visiting relatives from out of town."

"Well, maybe one of them looks like you," she said smiling.

"Thank you again."

She took a step forward before turning his way again, pointing.

"I know it now. You're that councilman, the one who said you were mugged."

"Ma'am, yes, you—"

She shook her head, frowning.

"I was so disappointed."

Dylan could see Slay watching the conversation from a few feet away.

"Well, I'm sorry—"

"Those snakes on the council should've waited for the investigation to conclude. Why would anyone make something like that up? Politics is so awful. I'm so sorry you felt like you had to step aside."

For a moment, he forgot all about Slay and Stabler feet away from him.

"I can't tell you how much that means to me, ma'am. It's been a rough two weeks."

She reached out and clasped Dylan's hands, smiling up at him.

"Well, young man, I hope you stick with politics. We need more people like you. And I loved that you spent so much time trying to tell those two crooks what you were doing at city hall. That was such smart thinking. Probably why they let you go."

"Okay, honey," her husband said, wrapping his right arm around her left. "I'm sure the councilman wants to keep talking to his friends here. Let's leave them be."

The two hobbled away, disappearing toward the front of the boat. Dylan moved back in place against the railing.

Stabler picked up the conversation, turning toward Slayton. "You asked about your friend. Well, you can tell him if you want to. And we're prepared to do anything you need us to do to get through this safely."

The kid nodded. "I so appreciate that. The first thing—"

The door opened again behind Dylan, then slammed shut. But to avoid being recognized, he didn't look back this time.

It was a decision he immediately regretted.

A large hand grabbed the back of Dylan's belt and lifted him up over the rail while another pushed him hard between his shoulder blades. He plunged thirty feet down. Arms spinning, unable to right himself, he smacked face first into the gray water of the Ohio.

Before he could surface, a body hit the water above him, crashing against the right side of his head and neck.

All went black.

Chapter 110

A sharp pinch under his right armpit brought Dylan to. Then a similar pain bore into his left.

He opened his eyes to find them only inches above the brown waterline, remembering now that he was in the Ohio River. He was pinned back against something that was keeping him afloat.

He tried to take a breath of air, but instead he swallowed a mouthful of water that tasted the way sewage smells.

As he gagged violently to clear his throat, both armpits were squeezed even tighter, and someone—he could hear the person breathing—pulled him straight up, then back. First his back, then his legs, dragged along a hard surface. At the release of his armpits, his upper back and head banged down onto that same solid surface.

Thick legs and a torso stood above him as he coughed out the last of the foul river water.

"Got 'em!" a voice said a few feet behind him. "Let's go."

The sound of an engine revved up loudly to his left, while the legs above him bent to an angle, the person sitting down against something.

The engine revved louder, its pitch rising, and Dylan could feel both himself and the surface he was lying on lift then accelerate to his right. The movement caused his entire body to tumble left, until a boot crashed down on his right shoulder, pinning him back against the hard surface.

"Don't move," a low voice growled at him from above.

Dylan lay still, looking up at the gray sky above him. The boat suddenly lunged up, then fell, the back of his head banging against the deck as water splashed over his face. Seconds later, it happened again. Waves that had felt like small chop on the large riverboat were tossing this smaller boat around far more forcefully.

After a few more hard bangs, Dylan figured out how to time it right, lifting his head just after the boat rose in the crest of a wave to avoid banging it in the troughs. That's also when he noticed someone grunting a few feet to his right with every wave.

The man sitting over him chuckled. "You're getting the hang of it better than he is."

For minutes, Dylan concentrated on the routine: boat lifts, lift head, boat descends, splash. Boat lifts, lift head, boat descends, splash.

His neck began to ache just as the engine's pitch lowered again, the boat slowing.

"Pull up there," the guy above him shouted to whoever was behind the wheel.

The boat slowed to a near stop before the engine turned off completely. They drifted forward, the only sound now the whooshing of water against the boat's sides.

"There they are."

Leafless tree branches appeared ten feet above, curling and twisting over them like thin, outstretched arms.

This was not a dock.

The boat lifted again as the bow ran aground, then stopped completely.

"Stand up," the voice commanded as the man's large hand reached under Dylan's armpit, then pulled up forcefully.

"Here, use this," another voice said from several feet away.

Dylan planted his other arm and lifted enough to see that they were in a large Boston Whaler that was pulled up against a muddy shore under a thick line of trees.

Before he could observe anything else, a hand from behind pulled something soft over the top of his head, then down over his forehead and eyes.

Everything went black.

"Now walk straight ahead."

A hand clamped down on his right arm, shoving him forward. He took three steps.

"Now step down."

He did what he was told, stepping off the boat and into what felt and sounded like watery mud.

"Walk forward."

Suction from the thick mud almost swallowed his shoe on the first step, but his second landed on more solid ground.

A minute later, the hand tugged his arm to stop him.

"Get in," the captor said as he pushed him up and sideways into a vehicle.

"And sit there." A hand pushed him sideways into the seat.

The door next to him rolled closed—he was in a van or SUV, not a car.

Two doors slammed shut in front of him, the engine turned on, and they drove away.

Chapter 111

Something was wrong.

Maggie had sent Dylan a text message right before three, as she drove downtown from his parents' condo. He'd responded immediately with a simple okay.

Once at the studio, she'd reviewed the tape of the church meeting, replaying key parts and taking copious notes.

At 4:00, she paused the video and checked her phone for an update. Nothing.

He was still on the boat, and the meeting probably hadn't ended. Still, her anxiety about the rendezvous grew.

All good? she texted, hoping he was checking messages.

But the words remained green on her screen, meaning they were never delivered. Dylan's phone had either died, or he'd turned it off. Not smart, but maybe the FBI guy had told him to. Still, her angst grew.

She tried to distract herself by reviewing more of the tape, but by 4:15, she couldn't concentrate. She looked at her phone again. The prior message remained green.

She sent a third text.

You okay? Let me know as soon as you're done.

These words, too, remained green.

She called his number, which went straight through to voicemail. "Dylan, it's me. When you get this, call me right away."

She searched online for Rusty Grimes's law firm, then called the main number.

"I'd like to talk to Mr. Grimes," she said after being patched through to his assistant.

"May I say who's calling?"

"It's Maggie Coyle."

The assistant chuckled. "Ah, Ms. Coyle. I'm sorry."

"Why's that?"

"Rusty has a rule. He never takes calls from the press. I don't even need to pass along the message, since I already know the answer."

"Listen. I'm calling because his client Mr. Webb has disappeared."

"C'mon, ma'am. This isn't the first time one of your type has tried something like this on me. I can promise you he won't want to talk to you."

Maggie balled her fist in anger, trying to keep her voice from boiling over.

"Young lady, maybe think of the call this way. I'm an ex-cop. And that's the hat I'm wearing at the moment. *Your* client has not responded to me for almost an hour and a half, and my years as a detective tell me that he's in grave danger. Put me through to Mr. Grimes."

"Okay," the assistant said, all confidence fading. "I'll do it right away."

Grimes jumped on the call seconds later, dropping the good-ol'-boy coolness she'd seen so often in court.

"You haven't heard from him either?" he asked.

"I haven't."

"My guy was supposed to text me on the half hour and hour. Nothing. My texts to him aren't going through. And I just got off the phone with the riverboat. The cruise is almost back, but the manager checked with the captain, and he says no one meeting their description is on board."

"How about Slayton?"

"Same. No one who looked like him was on board either."

"But you're sure they got on?"

"Yeah, ma'am. My guy texted me at 3:02. They were on board and pulling away from shore. Nothing else since."

A chill shot through her. All her instincts had told her Webb joining the rendezvous was a bad idea. She should have argued more.

"Well, what do we do now?"

"I've got them scouring the boat, but my guess is they're not on board anymore."

"Which means they could be anywhere."

"'Fraid it does."

After they hung up, Maggie opened her email's inbox and searched quickly for one email in particular.

Once she found it, she called Kai's number, but he didn't pick up.

Chapter 112

For the first time, Dylan thought they might actually kill him.

Strapped to a wooden desk, he'd spent the past hour assuring himself that his life wasn't in danger. While he still ached from having a body land on top of him, and he was bruised from the rough boat ride, these were professionals—not reckless, amped-up kids. It was all a bluff. They wanted something, but it made no sense to actually kill a prominent political figure. That just didn't happen in twenty-first-century America. And this was Cincinnati, Ohio—not Brooklyn or Miami.

But the third punch to the face crushed that confidence.

These were not blows meant simply to scare him. And ominously, the two people in the room—the thick, goateed brute in front of him, and the interrogator behind him—didn't care how much damage they were doing, or how much evidence of that brutality they were leaving. They already had passed a point of no return.

Still, Dylan made a commitment: As bad as it gets, don't give up either Maggie or Kai Brewer. They knew the truth, and he needed them to stay alive.

Brushing off questions about Kai proved easy, since he'd never met or communicated with him.

The interrogator moved on quickly, focusing on Maggie.

"What did she tell you?" he asked for the third time.

"What I already said—that I was full of shit. She never believed me."

"Then why did you two talk so much?"

"I wanted to convince her, but it never—"

From a foot away, the beefy, tattooed henchman uncorked a fierce uppercut that struck Dylan's right cheek, the hardest blow yet.

Salty liquid gushed throughout his mouth, gagging him. He hacked up some from his throat, then spat a chunk of it to the side. Thick drops of blood landed on the top of the wooden desk while even more stained the floor below.

"Jesus. Didn't you see her last story on me?" he asked, spitting out more blood. "That bitch crushed me. My guess is it was exactly what you'd hoped for. Do you really think we were working together?"

The thug unloaded again, ramming the front of his knuckles hard into Dylan's forehead.

"Shut the fuck up with your questions."

Blood now flowed into Dylan's right eye. He blinked rapidly to clear it.

"The truth is, I tried hard to get her to believe me. She never did. That's when I knew I was finished. That's when I quit."

The brute stepped toward him, fist clenched. Dylan tilted his head, preparing for another punch. But it didn't come. The guy walked past and out of his line of sight, but his heavy breaths were only feet behind.

"And why switch who picked your replacement? What was that about?"

New topic. His denials must've worked.

"I was pissed. The Democrats had treated me like shit. Councilwoman Easley was the only—"

Fingers suddenly grabbed a handful of his hair and pulled it straight up. His entire scalp felt like it might rip off.

"Ahhhhhhhh!"

After five seconds of agony, the pressure released.

"Don't give us this bullshit about hurt feelings. Why did you switch?"

The fingers tightened around his hair again but didn't pull up.

"I told you. The Democrats treated me like shit. So I—"

The hand pulled straight up, harder and higher this time.

Dylan yelled out even louder.

"Stopppp!!"

It went on far longer than before. Dylan lifted himself in his seat to minimize the pressure, but that only led to a harder pull from above.

"Why did you switch?" the questioner asked again.

He closed his eyes. Images of the church meeting flashed through his mind. Pastor Easley. The bearded man. Curtis Jackson. That meeting was why he'd walked onto that riverboat with so much hope that this would all soon be over. That he'd be vindicated. In all the drama, he'd forgotten about it.

But a new reality set in.

This might not be about Maggie and Kai at all. Those were the warm-up questions.

He'd only been summoned to the riverboat after that meeting was well underway. And now they were trying to confirm whether the meeting with Reverend Easley was real or a trap.

Chapter 113

Maggie stuck to the fast lane the entire way up Interstate 75, never dropping under eighty miles per hour.

It was a shot in the dark, but it was the only one she had. If it's where they'd interrogated Fritzy, why not take Webb to the same place?

Her search last week had revealed nine Tri-State Storage locations around town. Kai hadn't answered her call minutes ago. But back in the park, he'd described driving north and west of Silverton to reach the one where he'd seen Fritzy. Ten minutes, he'd said. Maybe fifteen.

From the map of locations she'd looked at, that left only two options.

Reaching the exit, Maggie lurched two lanes over and decelerated from eighty to fifty before running the light. Three turns and three streets later, she parked outside a large steelworkers' union hall, the last building before the first of the two Tri-State Storage sites that fit Kai's description. She got out and peered around the building's corner to see the warehouse.

Kai had said it was empty the day he visited alone. But against the early evening dusk, lights were on inside. And a car and a van were parked outside.

That alone wasn't enough to call in the cops. Already on thin ice, a false alarm would crush her credibility. She needed something more.

She left the cover of the labor hall and crossed the open lot. Twenty feet from the vehicles, she could make out the basics. A dark, beat-up Ford Coupe of some sort, which she didn't recognize.

And a van.

A gray van. Tinted windows.

She moved five steps closer, snapped a photo of its license plate with her phone, then scampered back to her car. She grabbed her reporter's notebook from the passenger seat and leafed toward its halfway point.

She found the page she was looking for—*Queen City Cash* was written at the top, underlined.

Halfway down the page came her notes from the video. Then the words: gray van, tinted windows. HGY 1842.

She looked back at the photo she'd just taken: HGY 1842.

They matched.

This was the same van that had nabbed Fritzy outside of Queen City Cash. And the same van that was registered in the name of Diego DeLeon—the one that Rodney Stone had also tracked down and called in.

She was definitely in the right place, which meant Dylan must be inside.

Her pulse quickening, Maggie called Meadows.

"Hey, you," Meadows said after picking up, chuckling. "You still tracking down Webb's kidnappers?"

"Shirley, I don't have time to explain, but you need to dispatch the best people available up to the Tri-State Storage facility off I-75, exit 15."

She read the exact address.

"Are you serious?" Meadows asked, instantly in emergency mode. "What for?"

Maggie chose her next words carefully. If she described it the wrong way, no one would show up.

"This time someone *has* taken Webb hostage. Not the kids he bullshitted about, but people far more dangerous. You know that drug ring I exposed on last night's news?"

Nothing excited the chief more than a high-profile drug bust. Not the street dealers, but the middlemen and bosses at the top.

"Yeah. It's all anyone's talking about over here."

"This looks tied to that."

"Wow. And how do you know they have Webb?"

"He told me he was meeting with them, and now he's disappeared. His phone is completely dead."

"He met with them *after* your story? That fool can't stay out of trouble."

"Yeah, but in this case, he may be leading you right into a major bonanza. I've traced them to this warehouse, using a vehicle associated with the drug gang."

"You sure?"

"Shirley, I'm absolutely positive. I'm looking at the vehicle right now." She read the license plate number. "And if you check the plates, you'll see it's registered to someone found murdered a week ago. This is a dangerous crew."

"I'll see what I can do."

"Hurry. Webb is inside, and he doesn't have much time."

They hung up.

Maggie removed her Glock from her purse, confirmed it was loaded, and stepped out of her car.

The safe option was to wait for whoever Meadows sent, but her gut told her she was already dangerously late to the scene. If something bad was happening inside, she needed to disrupt it as soon as possible.

Chapter 114

At some point, the man behind Dylan shifted from yanking his hair to striking him in the back of the head. The pounding was blurring the room around him. And an intense ringing in his ears now drowned out everything else, including the interrogator's questions.

"I can't hear you!" he cried out. "Say it again!"

"Why did you pick her?"

He'd already answered this. Twice.

"I told you! She was the only one who'd shown me any respect. It was a way of getting back at the others, and I trusted her to find a good person."

It's what he meant to say, anyway. Between his battered face and ringing ears, he couldn't tell if that's how the words sounded.

"And her dad?"

Don't give it away, he kept telling himself. In a fog, it was the clearest thought he still had.

"Her dad? What about him?"

"Did he put you up to it?"

"The preacher? No! He had nothing to do with it."

A punch crashed directly into his left ear.

"Stop!"

"Not 'til you tell us the truth. Why did you bring him in?"

"I *didn't* bring him in. It was a last-second decision about *her*, not him. He had nothing to do with it."

He braced for another blow.

Seconds passed.

Nothing.

No punch.

His mind raced about what was coming next. No doubt it would be worse.

Seconds more.

Not another punch.

Not another question.

Silence.

Chapter 115

Her first two throws accomplished nothing.

Maggie got back down on all fours and crawled forward through the overgrown grass, inching closer to the warehouse from its side. The growing darkness shrouded her, which was good, but it also meant she couldn't see the ground beneath her.

Five seconds later, she paid the price. As she put weight down on her left hand, something sliced deep into the lower part of her palm. Grimacing, she reached down and felt a curved shard of glass—likely from a broken bottle—sticking out. She pulled the piece out and stretched the sleeve of her shirt over the wound to stem the bleeding. It was drenched with blood in seconds.

This was a serious wound, but she didn't have time to worry about it now. She'd processed enough crime scenes to know that every minute mattered for the victim's survival. Even without a way to get into the building, she could at least distract the thugs inside long enough for the cops to get there.

She stood up, reached into her pocket, and flung another fistful of gravel as hard as she could toward the facility's wall and lit-up window. The small rocks pelting the metal and glass reverberated louder this time.

Seconds later, light exploded from within the warehouse as a metal door swung to the right of the window.

Maggie squatted low in the grass.

"What the fuck was it?" a gruff voice asked.

"Sounded like rocks against the wall here. By the window."

The shadows of two large figures moved in front of the window. One leaned over.

"Here they are. Bunch of gravel from the driveway."

"What the fuck? Who would—"

"Maybe just some kids causing trouble."

"Right in the middle of all this?" This voice came from in front of the door, meaning a third person was outside. "I doubt it. Look around."

Maggie pulled the remaining gravel from her pocket. This time she aimed her throw well to her left, toward the highway. The metallic side of the warehouse clanged again as dozens more rocks struck it.

"Down there!" yelled one of the figures.

The two men ran along the warehouse's side while the third walked in front of the window.

"More gravel—nothing else!" one yelled back.

"Keep going around," the man in front of the window said. "They probably ran toward the highway."

Good. Two people heading around the warehouse. One posted up front. Hopefully enough distraction until—

Glass crackled on the ground only feet behind her.

Maggie whirled around to see a hulking figure closing in on her quickly.

She jumped to her right as the man lunged behind her, grunting as he fell head and arms first to the ground.

"Over here!" he yelled out to the others from the ground.

Maggie raced to her right, away from the other three. She was out of the grass in seconds, onto the parking lot in front of Tri-State Storage. Bright floodlights suddenly clicked on, illuminating the entire front of the warehouse.

"She's out front," another voice yelled.

Maggie was plenty fast. The problem was the math. If even one of her three pursuers were faster, she'd never make it back to her car. So she sprinted in front of the warehouse, past the van and car, and headed left behind its other side, back into darkness. A thick tangle of tall grass, weeds, and brush grew only feet from the warehouse's side, so Maggie plunged into them.

"Other side," a voice yelled between huffs, well back. "She's on the other side."

With sharp branches and what felt like thorns ripping at her clothes and skin as she went, Maggie ducked her head and rushed deep into the brush, diagonally away from the warehouse. The roar of cars and trucks along the highway grew louder. The highway was her best escape.

Small lights and beams danced behind and around her. At least two of her pursuers had flashlights. Smartly, they had also stopped talking back and forth.

Calling on her academy training, she zigzagged as much as the terrain allowed, trying to throw them off her trail. The highway traffic was close to deafening now, inspiring her to run faster toward it. If she could just get to the berm—

Oof.

Her left foot kicked hard into a thick object lying on the ground. It gave a little, but not before she fell chest and face forward over it, water splashing up onto her stomach. From its feel and smell, it was a large truck tire.

She pushed herself up with both hands, pain coursing through her sliced palm, then stumbled forward, almost tripping for a second time as her right foot awkwardly kicked the front end of the tire.

The beams of lights were larger now, and more concentrated in their aim—circling within a few feet of her.

Her hands hit the rusty wire first, but not soon enough to stop her whole upper body from colliding into a tall chain-link fence. She bounced off it and fell hard to the ground.

She climbed back to her feet to see the flashlights now aimed her way from no more than twenty feet. One beam closed on her face, blinding her.

Only two options were left: give up, or grab the Glock holstered under her jacket.

But she never got to make the choice. A large hand grabbed her right shoulder, spinning her ninety degrees to her left. Two thick arms then wrapped around her neck, squeezing so tight she couldn't breathe.

"You couldn't leave it alone, could you?" a familiar voice yelled into her ear, barely audible over the roar of the traffic from beyond the fence.

Bone and muscle from the powerful forearms crushed her throat.

The beams from the flashlights blurred, faded, then disappeared.

Chapter 116

At first, Dylan assumed they'd be right back, so he sat still and waited. Even as his head and upper body throbbed in pain, he soaked up every moment of solitude. A chance to regain his strength.

But the men didn't come right back.

A minute passed.

Then another.

Something was happening. Something they hadn't planned on. This was his chance. The one he never had in the Jeep.

He pulled at the cords binding his wrists behind him and to the desk. They didn't budge.

He tugged his arms in opposite directions, trying to slip the cord over his right wrist, then his left. Neither way worked.

He tried kicking his legs. But cinched tightly to the legs of the desk, they didn't move. Nor did the cords loosen.

But as he thrashed his legs around, the desk shifted a few inches along the cement floor.

Amid all the violence, he hadn't noticed: the old wooden desk was heavy, but not bolted down.

He leaned as far forward as he could, then pushed himself back. The desk slid an inch or so, but not enough to help.

He tried shifting his weight from left to right. The desk leaned slightly, its left legs lifting a few inches off the floor.

He tried again, thrusting his hips to the left and his torso and head to the right. The legs now rose a few more inches, tipping the desk up about twenty degrees.

He rested for a few seconds, then tried a third time. He leaned even further to his left side, then threw all his mass to his right as forcefully as he could. This time the desk tilted up far higher as its legs slipped the other way along the cement floor.

Dylan's momentum carried him all the way to the floor, the desk crashing down next to him. While its legs remained intact, still tied tightly to his legs, the wooden desktop shattered in two as it hit the hard floor. The cords around his wrists slackened, and with some wriggling and tugging, he freed his arms from the desk, although they were still tied together behind him.

He rotated his body so that he was lying flat on his back. Arms painfully pinned behind him, he kicked the legs of the desk as hard as he could against the cement, hoping to break them off.

On the third kick, the cord around his right leg finally loosened. He kicked even harder. It loosened some more—enough that he might be able to slip his ankle down below the bottom of the desk leg.

He started to—

Bang!

Light spilled into the small room as the door burst open and slammed against the wall.

"Come look!" a man yelled to another, amused. Dylan recognized the voice of the interrogator from minutes ago. "He's really asking for some pain now, isn't he?"

Dylan looked up. A man about his size walked past the open door into the room—slick guy, with a brown leather jacket, jeans, and shiny black hair. The larger enforcer from earlier trudged in behind him, fresh blood on his arms.

The enforcer laughed. "Fuck yeah, he is."

Dylan's newfound energy collapsed at the duo's entrance. All hope, gone.

A third guy, almost as big as the second, followed them in. But what stuck out most was a fourth person, slumped down limply, held up in the newcomer's tightly wrapped arms.

A smaller figure, the body was clearly a woman. With her head dangling down, tousled brown hair covered most of her face, but not enough to hide the rough shape she was in. Thin trails of blood ran along her cheeks and neck. Her left sleeve was stretched up and around her hand to form a ball of oozing red blood. Her blue jeans were ripped in multiple places, as were the sides of her gray, hooded windbreaker.

The man tossed the limp body to the ground. Splayed on her back, legs twisted and arms above her head, the frizzy hair that once covered her face fell away, revealing the blood-stained face of Maggie Coyle. Her eyes were cloudy, frozen open in a haunting look.

"Jesus Christ," Dylan shrieked. "You killed her?"

"Calm down," said the guy who'd tossed her down. He leaned down and put his hand an inch from her lips. "She's breathing. Just out for a few minutes, thanks to a sleeper hold. Most of that damage she did to herself."

The interrogator stepped toward Dylan, looking down disapprovingly. "But if your answers and hers don't match up, neither one of you will be breathing soon. Sabo, clean up this mess. We've got work to do."

The big guy who'd roughed up Dylan earlier leaned over and righted the entire desk, Dylan included. He refastened Dylan's wrists to what was left of the desk, then tightened his loose leg.

From the floor, Maggie groaned, then coughed loudly. Her eyelids closed, opened again, then fluttered. She stared straight up at the ceiling for seconds, gathering her bearings.

"Welcome back, missy," the interrogator said with a sneer.

She rolled in the man's direction, her bleary eyes looking up at the interrogator first before focusing in on Dylan.

"Oh my God. What have they done to you?" she asked.

"Not a word back," the interrogator said to Dylan. "Only we ask the questions."

Maggie turned the other way to spot the guy who'd brought her in.

"You!" she uttered. "I did everything you asked."

He shook his head. "You did. We loved your story. And then you had to come out here."

"Shut up!" the interrogator said, talking to his colleague. "Sabo, take care of her too."

The big guy stepped over toward Maggie, positioning himself behind her.

"Please stand up."

"I can't."

"Okay. Well, I'll help you."

He reached down and tugged her up by her arms.

"Easy," she yelled out, grimacing as she got to her feet.

"I gave you the chance to do it on your own," he said as he pulled her wrists behind her. He turned to his colleague.

"Hand me more cord from that desk, will ya?"

Chapter 117

Dylan watched as they pounded Maggie—tied to an aluminum folding chair several feet to his right—for the same details they'd demanded of him.

Why'd she keep talking to Dylan? Had she talked to anyone else? What did she know about Reverend Easley? Despite some hard punches and their rising anger, she answered the questions well, and consistent with Dylan's answers.

She was tough as hell, never losing her cool.

Then came the curveball.

"How did you know to come here?"

"I'm an investigative reporter," she said, stalling. "I had a hunch."

"To come to a warehouse? And *this* warehouse in particular? Bullshit!"

The thug slapped her across the face.

"Leave her alone!" Dylan yelled out.

The interrogator whirled his way, pulling a gun out from his waistband and pressing the barrel hard against Dylan's head.

"You wanna be a hero, Councilman?"

As scared as he was, witnessing them beat Maggie had sparked an inner rage.

"C'mon. Are you really going to kill a council member and a well-known TV reporter? That would bring more heat than ever and blow up your whole plan."

"You don't think we will?" The interrogator clapped his hands. "Hell, the people who hired us don't understand why you're still alive now! Tony, bring out the other guy from the riverboat to show him what I'm talking about."

"Sure thing."

The guy who'd carried in Maggie stepped out of the room.

As he watched it all, one question kept cycling through Dylan's head: Just who were these people, and who was behind them? Whatever they wanted from city hall, they were inflicting a level of brutality that seemed so over-the-top for the politics of a midsize Midwestern city. And for a white-shoe local law firm.

None of it made sense.

"Thanks to her big scoop," the interrogator continued, "all anyone knows at the moment is that you were buying drugs from some drug ring. And that she exposed it. People get killed in those circumstances all the time, whoever the fuck they are."

The man walked back through the door, dragging a body by the arm.

"Here ya go," Tony said smiling. He pulled the man to the middle of the room, then let go of the arm. The limp body slumped to the floor on its back.

Dylan jerked his head back as his stomach heaved.

Hugh Stabler. Lifeless.

"Like I said, don't try us," the interrogator said, returning the gun to his waistband.

Dylan bit his lip to keep from saying any more.

The interrogator leaned over Maggie. "Now answer my question: Who told you to come here? That we'd be here? Only a few people would know about this place."

"It was just a—"

The thug grabbed a handful of her hair and pulled it straight up. Maggie screamed in pain.

"Okay! Okay!" she blurted out. "He called himself Slay!"

The thug loosened his grip on her hair.

"Slay?" the interrogator asked.

She didn't answer.

"Pull again!" he yelled.

The man's fingers tightened again.

"That's what he called himself!" she screamed.

"Who?"

He pulled upward.

"The guy who told me," she yelled. "Slay!"

Both the thug and the guy who'd carried in Maggie looked wide-eyed at the interrogator. This was a revelation.

"When?"

"Days ago. He told me you guys used a warehouse off a highway. To beat up that homeless guy. He even gave me the address. So that's why I headed up here."

"Fuckin' Slay," the guy at the door muttered.

"Bring him in here," the interrogator barked. "Sabo might have to work him over too."

The guy at the door smirked. "Happy to—that little punk."

"Don't do anything stupid. This bitch has been bullshitting us up to now. This may be more of it. But get him in here so we can see."

The man walked out the door.

"So when did you last talk to Slay?"

"I think it was yesterday, or maybe—"

"What's that?" the interrogator asked, interrupting.

The large guy lifted his hands in the air. "What's what?"

"I hear a vibration. Maybe a phone."

"We took theirs, but they're waterlogged anyway," he said, gesturing to Dylan and the lifeless Stabler. Then he patted his pocket. "And it's not mine."

"It must be hers," the interrogator said, pointing. "Check."

The goateed brute reached down and patted Maggie's windbreaker.

"Got it. And yes, it's vibrating."

"See who's calling!" the interrogator said excitedly.

He took an iPhone out of her pocket and walked it over to the interrogator. "Here."

The interrogator's squinty eyes widened as soon as he looked at it.

"Well, isn't this interesting," he said, cackling. "Your friend Kai is calling you, Ms. Coyle. Now how on earth would you two be in communication?"

Maggie's head fell, saying nothing.

"I say we let it ring through, then text him back," the interrogator said, enjoying his good luck.

He held up the phone for a few more seconds, then walked over to Maggie.

"What's your passcode, Miss?" he asked gently.

Maggie glared back at him, pale lips pursed.

"Tell me your code," he growled.

The big guy lifted his fist high in the air. "Want me to make her do it?"

"Actually, no. We need her face to look exactly as it does now. Please hold it up for me for a few seconds."

The big guy grabbed Maggie's hair and pulled it back, forcing her head upright. The interrogator held up the phone, screen facing her from a few inches away. He then turned the phone back his way.

"We're in, thanks to the genius of modern technology. Now let's see what young Kai wants."

He typed into the phone and waited for a response.

"Well, isn't that nice? He's sorry he couldn't answer your call earlier. And he just sent you the address for the building right next door to this one. Sure is a nice kid for having been so rough on our councilman here."

He typed into the phone again.

"Sabo, go tell Tony we don't need Slay after all. We know now who this lying bitch has been talking to."

Sabo let go of Maggie's hair and stepped out of the room.

"Now," the interrogator continued, "let's see if we can convince your friend Kai to meet up with you somewhere nearby, shall we?"

Chapter 118

Cinched to their chairs, Dylan and Maggie watched in horror as the interrogator texted back and forth with Kai, joyfully filling them in on every word Kai wrote back.

He ultimately coaxed Kai into meeting in thirty minutes, a few blocks down the road. He pocketed the phone and looked back Maggie's way, smirking.

"You made that far too—"

"Don't move!" a muffled voice yelled loudly from outside. "Police! Put your hands up."

One gunshot rang out, followed by a fusillade of shots along with loud clanging—bullets hitting the side of the warehouse. Then came a loud bang.

"Freeze!" a new voice yelled, this time from inside the building.

More gunfire crackled, far louder this time, followed by screams.

With a thud, a large mass fell to the ground just outside the open doorway. It was Sabo, the thug, flat on his stomach, his bald head and goatee appearing in the doorway in a widening pool of blood.

"Shit!" the interrogator yelled, lifting the gun from his waistband as he spun toward and then jumped behind Dylan.

"Don't move a fucking inch," he snarled in Dylan's ear, clenching the back of his left shoulder as he pressed the cold barrel of the gun into Dylan's already bruised right temple.

A series of heavy thuds sounded from outside the door. Footsteps.

"There's no way out," a deep voice boomed from the hallway.

"Bullshit!" the guy behind Dylan yelled, pushing the gun so hard that Dylan's neck twisted left. "I can off a councilman and a reporter in two quick shots if you don't clear a way out for me."

"We're not going anywhere," the voice yelled back. "All your compadres are dead. If you don't want to join them, drop the gun and walk out."

"I'm not dropping shit," the interrogator yelled, his quaking voice undermining the defiant words.

One side of a squarish black object appeared in the doorway from the left. Dylan recognized it from the SWAT ride-along he'd done six months ago—a ballistic shield that would stop any bullet the guy behind him might fire.

"Now I'm going to step out here so we can talk eye to eye," the voice from the hallway said. "Don't do anything stupid."

"You need to clear the way for me or I'll kill them both."

"We can talk about that," the officer in the hallway said calmly.

The shield moved to the right as a large figure eased into the doorway, thick leg armor completing the bulletproof package. Two eyes appeared in a clear window near the top of the shield, with the top of a thick dark helmet sticking out above.

"Welcome, asshole," the guy behind Dylan yelled. "Now you see how easily I can kill them both. So clear your other men out before I shoot."

"It's just you and me," the officer behind the shield said. "You're not going to shoot either one of them. And the only way you're getting out of here alive is if you put that gun down and walk away."

The gun at Dylan's head began shaking, and the guy was now panting as if he'd just sprinted a mile. It was time to speak up.

"This may be your—"

"Shut the fuck up," the guy said, fingers clawing into Dylan's left shoulder.

"Sir, let me handle the negotiation," the officer behind the shield said gently.

Seconds of silence passed.

"Ms. Coyle, you look pretty rough over there. Are you okay?" the officer asked.

"I'll be fine, sir," Maggie said, her strong voice sounding like a cop once again. "Nothing an old SWAT member can't handle."

"Ex-SWAT, huh?" the officer asked in a friendly tone.

"Shut up, both of you," the interrogator said, breathing even harder.

Another moment of silence.

"SWAT all the way, sir," Maggie said with gusto. "Thumbs up. Ten."

"I said shut up!" the interrogator said. "Or he gets it!"

While he heard the words, Dylan was distracted by what Maggie had said and the way she'd said it. Some sort of verbal cop ritual—the SWAT equivalent of "Semper Fi."

No one spoke for seconds, which, judging by his even faster breathing, rattled the interrogator even more.

Then the room exploded.

From Dylan's right came a simultaneous clanging of metal and an ear-splitting scream from Maggie.

The pressure against both Dylan's shoulder and head instantly vanished as the interrogator whirled Maggie's way, yelling at her.

"What the—"

His question was interrupted by a thud and even louder clanging, as Maggie, still in the chair, toppled the other way and onto the cement floor.

Three flashes and ear-shattering cracks exploded from the doorway, with the accuracy of the shots evidenced by blood spattering across the right side of Dylan's face. The interrogator flopped face forward into a twisted heap as the gun flew out of his hand, spinning feet across the floor before coming to a stop. Blood gurgled out of the dead man's head and back.

"All clear!" the officer yelled loudly. He repeated the words again, at normal volume, into a radio.

Seconds later, two men in dark street clothes and black mesh caps and a man and a woman in SWAT body armor ran into the room. Dylan recognized them as the same officers who stood guard at city hall chambers meetings every week, watching the crowd while listening stoically to voluminous political hot air. Prince had once told Dylan that the police officers assigned to council meetings were among their most elite SWAT members. He hadn't been exaggerating.

The woman and the officer from behind the shield ran to Maggie, and two others ran to Dylan, freeing them quickly.

"Still remember our signals, eh, Ms. Coyle?" the first officer asked as Maggie stood up.

"Some things you never forget," she said, a weak smile emerging on her otherwise exhausted face.

The fifth officer, who stood in front of the door, talked into a radio.

"We got 'em. You can send in the chief."

Chapter 119

Two life squad units patched up Dylan and Maggie's wounds on scene and assessed that neither had concussions.

So rather than being transported in ambulances, the ride back downtown reminded Dylan of the ride away from his law firm weeks ago.

Deputy Police Chief Patrick Prince drove the same unmarked SUV while Dylan sat in the back. Darkness. Awkward silence. Relief.

The only difference was that Maggie Coyle was sitting next to him, and Chief Reinhardt himself was sitting in the front passenger seat.

Dylan broke the silence.

"Chief, I can't thank you enough. Those guys were on the verge of killing us."

The chief nodded.

"Drug gangs will do that, Webb. You were in bed with some very dangerous people."

As tired as he was, Dylan fumed at yet another accusation.

"Chief, I think—"

Maggie reached her bandaged left hand in front of Dylan.

"Chief, those men may be tied to a drug ring. But they also are tied to something bigger happening right now."

The chief's oversized head whirled around, first glaring at Dylan, then Maggie.

"C'mon, you two. Give your imaginations a rest. Coyle, you kicked ass back there, and we appreciate the tip, but don't turn this into something it isn't. You and I have been down this road before, and it won't end well for you."

Dylan's body tensed, but Maggie jumped back in.

"Chief, we have direct proof that all of this, including the original kidnapping, were part of a broader corrupt plot. Buying off city hall support for a major project of some sort."

He shook his head. "I told you to give it a rest, Coyle."

The chief's tone made it clear the two had a history. And that the chief had once been her boss.

"Chief," Maggie said, "we've got proof. Including a videotape. And it's going to get out there either way. You can either be the hero who busted it, or the guy who had it under his nose the whole time but never saw it."

He didn't respond for a few seconds.

"Where?"

"Where what?"

"Where's that tape you mentioned. I'll need to see it."

"At the station. Uploaded and ready for editing. We can go straight there, and I can show you."

"You guys aren't in any condition—"

"They cleared us both and said we need to check in again tomorrow," Maggie said. "Let's do this now."

"Head to the station," the chief said to Prince.

Prince shook his head. "You sure?"

"I'm sure. Let's at least take a look at what she's got."

"One other thing," Maggie said. "Do you know Reverend Easley?"

"Of course. Who doesn't?"

"Give him a call. He should join us there."

"I'm running out of patience, Coyle. He hasn't exactly been friendly to my department. Please explain to me why he should be there."

"Trust me, you're going to want him there. And when you call him, be sure to ask him to bring the folder."

Chapter 120

Back at the studio, huddled in a conference room with the shades pulled down, the chief, Prince, Maggie, Easley, and Dylan played back the church meeting on a monitor that covered the entire back wall.

They were mostly silent, the two cops occasionally interrupting with short, gruff questions, or asking Maggie to replay snippets of the conversation.

When it was over, the chief let out a long sigh, laying both hands over the table's edge. Strands of hair spiked up in varying directions, out of place in a way Dylan had never seen before.

"Well, that pretty much speaks for itself. So, who was the guy in charge? The one with the beard?"

Maggie answered first.

"We haven't had time—"

"His name is Sebastian Gray," Dylan said, jumping in. "Runs real estate for the Windsor Firm. A big deal in town. Represents the city's most prominent banks and developers."

The chief took notes as he spoke—something Dylan had never seen him do before, at least when Dylan was talking. Finally, he was listening.

Maggie looked over at Dylan, surprised.

"But you didn't say anything."

"I thought I recognized him, and then I confirmed it when I got on the riverboat."

Reverend Easley nodded. "I knew he looked familiar. I've seen him at fancy functions in the past. Windsor supports just about everything."

"And the other two?" the chief asked.

"Probably lawyers too. Or clients. Shouldn't be hard to find."

"So what's in the folder, Reverend?" the chief asked.

All eyes in the room watched as Easley passed the folder across the desk.

"I think you all may have heard of it. It's been in the paper of late—a project called Pristine Village. And it's clear from what's in here—"

"Jesus Christ," Dylan cried out. "They ruined my life over that monstrosity?"

"As I was saying," Easley said, annoyed by the interruption, "you'll see that the amount of money at stake here is huge. The stake they were willing to give me for picking a council member was worth millions over time."

The chief opened the folder and thumbed through it.

"I've heard some of the business types talk about this, but I had no idea it was this big."

"It's not just a project," Dylan chimed in. "It's a whole neighborhood of them. Years of development. Years of work. Billions in contracts. All assuming they're able to kick out the thousands of people who live there now."

But Dylan didn't mention one other thing he was thinking. In the taped meeting, Easley had raised the issue of foreign money. Gray hadn't denied the suggestion. That moment brought Dylan back to his conversation with Graham Mundy and all those foreign clients he'd said he'd been entertaining. Was this all a lot bigger than a Cincinnati scandal?

Easley slapped Dylan on an already bruised back, interrupting his train of thought.

"And that, young man, is why they needed you out of the way. One honest man in a den of thieves is the dangerous one. Isn't that right, Chief? Which makes him an endangered one."

The chief looked thoughtfully at the minister, a man who'd railed harshly against him in the past.

"You're a good judge of character, sir. Do you think that fellow was being truthful about the mayor being part of it?"

"Oh yes. I have no doubt the mayor has a stake."

"Unreal," Dylan said, recalling the meetings and phone calls with the mayor since the incident. The unsolicited advice to resign from the get-go. The humiliation. The yelling. And in the end, it had nothing to do with politics. It was all to grab a golden parachute as he ended his final term.

The chief said nothing for a few moments, then stood up, Easley's folder in his arm. Prince did the same.

"What are you going to do, Chief?" Dylan asked.

"Look into it all, obviously. But this is much bigger than my department. We'll gather what we can, then call in the feds."

"How long will that take?" Maggie asked.

"A few days. And, Coyle, I'm going to need you to sit on that tape until—"

"Chief, I can't sit on that! This is a huge story."

"Coyle, you air that tape before we've swooped in, and every document we need to make anything stick will be gone. You were a cop once. This is a lot bigger than one night's ratings and your station's profits."

"I'm sorry, Chief. There's no way we can wait on this."

He exaggerated an eyeroll.

"You don't learn, do you? Is Rick Temple still your boss?"

"Yes, he is," Maggie said.

"Okay. I'll talk to him, then."

Chapter 121

"Well, there goes one of the two guys who could vouch for my story."

Icing their wounds, Dylan and Maggie were watching the 11 p.m. news from their respective bedrooms while talking over the phone. At 11:04, the station scrolled through the names of those killed in the raid, displaying small headshots as they went.

Dylan and Maggie recognized four of the five. Max Sabo and Tony Castro were the heavies. Felix Tomasky was the slick interrogator, killed at the end. Neither recognized the fourth listed. But the fifth listed was Michael Slayton, shot down in another part of the warehouse.

"You okay?" Maggie asked softly.

"You mean, am I traumatized about the fact that he's dead?"

"Yeah. You've been on an emotional roller coaster."

"It's jarring. I mean, I was talking to him eight hours ago. But I'm pretty convinced his schtick at the riverboat was an act. Part of the trap. Which basically means he kidnapped me twice."

He paused to take in a deep breath, putting Slayton behind him.

"How are you and Emmy? I mean, that other guy was the one who followed her, right?"

"Yes. Relieved isn't the right word. She's still shaken up, but at least we know the threat is gone."

"Good. And is Kai safe?"

"Yes. Home safe and sound. But given that he's now the only witness who can vouch for what happened to you, we need a plan to keep it that way. Especially given how this story is playing out."

By early evening, every news station had arrived at the warehouse, breaking into prime-time shows to report that five suspects had been

414

killed in a shoot-out, with one SWAT officer shot in the leg. Then at eleven, with sirens still flashing in the background, each reporter kicked off the evening news with a live shot from the scene. They all echoed the same narrative for drama rarely seen in Cincinnati: Police had broken up the gang that had been selling hard drugs to Councilman Dylan Webb, two well-known judges, and potentially others. The raid turned into a gunfight, leading to the violent deaths of the gang's leaders.

"They took your scoop and ran with it," Dylan said. "Not a whiff about corruption."

"Nope," Maggie said. "I tried to convince Temple to at least hint that there was more to the story, but he ran exactly what the chief told him to. And the other stations were already chomping at the bit on my story, so this was an easy sell."

"So how long did Temple agree to sit on the video?"

"He gave the chief two days."

"Jesus, a lot can happen in forty-eight hours."

"Believe me, far too much."

THURSDAY

Chapter 122

It took far less than forty-eight hours.

The chief summoned Dylan and Maggie to police headquarters at eleven the next day. A uniformed cop met them out front, then walked them into the conference room where Dylan, Prince, and Moses had had it out nearly two weeks ago.

The chief entered, Prince walking in behind him. All four sat down. The chief took off his white, hard-brimmed hat and carefully placed it on the table, his thick wheat hair back in top form. He pursed his lips in a way that made clear that the prior night's interlude of informality was over.

"We talked to Mr. Gray first thing this morning," the chief said, frowning.

"Whoa," Dylan said. "You got to him fast."

"Actually, he and the firm's managing partner called us early yesterday evening, before we reached out to him."

"He called you?" Dylan asked, thrown for a loop. "What about?"

"Not me. I didn't hear about it until we wrapped up." He looked at Maggie, then back at Dylan. "He called to report a crime."

Maggie let out a long breath, dreading what was coming. "And what crime was that?"

"Attempted bribery by the pastor you had stop by last night."

"What?" Dylan cried out, slapping his hand down on the table. "That's absurd."

"Son, you tell me how absurd this sounds. The moment you switched your successor designee form over to Michelle Easley, they knew that a shakedown was coming. Putting it in a single person's hands was a red flag."

"I gave it to her—"

"Pastor Easley," the chief interrupted back, loudly, "then called Councilman Jackson and asked who in the city had shown a serious interest in the vacancy. Sebastian Gray and his team show up at the church, and the next thing they know, the pastor is demanding equity in their project in order to select a councilman they prefer."

"But he was just—"

"Son, they were so confident that this was the gameplan, they taped the whole meeting through Sebastian Gray's phone. To protect themselves. And I gotta tell you, those tapes don't sound at all good for Reverend Easley. You can listen to them for yourself."

"Is it any different than what we watched last night?" Maggie asked.

"No, but it sure sounds different once you hear Gray's side of the story. Go watch for yourself. We're talking to Jackson this afternoon. If he confirms this all, your pastor is in a world of trouble."

Dylan slumped in his chair. "You can't be serious, Chief. They walked in there looking to get themselves a council member, and in only minutes agreed to pay whatever Easley asked for."

The chief's face turned red.

"I couldn't be more serious. They smelled a shakedown coming, went along with the meeting, and got it all on tape."

"What time did they call you, Chief?" Maggie asked.

He sneered her way. "I'm not here to answer your questions."

"And why didn't they call you before the meeting?"

That one got him.

"They meet with people all the time, Coyle. Hell, these guys . . ." he gestured toward Dylan, "criticize them when they *don't* meet with community leaders. So while they suspected trouble, they weren't sure, but went into that meeting prepared for the worst."

He stood up, putting his hat on his head, adjusting it so it was perfectly straight.

"Webb, this was a courtesy meeting so you know where things stand," he said, looking at the wall and not Dylan. "While your drug gang connection isn't pretty, I'm assuming you're not implicated by any of this, but I'm also not the prosecutor. My advice is that you fill in that attorney of yours, in case you have exposure."

Dylan's head still hurt from Grimes cursing him out an hour ago for last night's meeting with the chief and today's. But the chief had insisted—no lawyers.

"Have you told Easley yet?" he asked.

"We haven't told him a thing. And if *you* tell him, you'll be adding another potential criminal charge to your name."

He walked out of the room, Prince trailing behind.

Maggie and Dylan walked out of police headquarters.

"This is insane," Dylan said. "We can't let Reverend Easley take the fall for this."

"Well, what can we do?" Maggie asked as she unlocked her car remotely.

"You're the expert."

"I know. And I'm stumped."

Chapter 123

Taking the chief's threat seriously, Dylan waited all afternoon for the inevitable phone call.

It came minutes past four.

Fumbling with his new phone, Dylan picked up on the third ring.

"Michelle, I'm so sorry."

"Did you know?" she asked quietly.

"Yes, they told me just before noon. But they warned me that if I said anything, they'd charge me with obstruction of justice."

A painful silence followed.

"Dylan, he stepped up to help you. To support you. To bail you out. And this is what he gets in return?"

"I know, Michelle. It's so wrong. I feel absolutely terrible. I already talked to my lawyer, and he's happy—"

"They took him out of the church—*his church*—in handcuffs," Michelle said, far louder now. "A man who's done all he's done for this community, treated like a dog."

"I'm so sorry."

"Are you? You knew but said nothing."

Dylan almost repeated what he'd said before, but he held his tongue. It wouldn't help.

"Did anyone see? Was there press there?"

When the cops really wanted to screw someone, they tipped off reporters to the arrest.

"Thankfully, no. No one was around. But handcuffs on my father? In his own church?"

"Terrible. Did they charge him yet?"

"I don't know. He still hasn't come back."

"Well, we can only hope that he convinces them of the truth."

"Dylan," Michelle replied, still seething, "no one's interested in the truth. Haven't you learned that by now? Some powerful people are cornered. And when that happens in this town, look out. A whole army of other powerful people will stand up to protect them, and they're willing to destroy anyone who poses a threat to them."

Dylan nodded. That was exactly what was happening. They'd tried to take him out, and now they were taking out a giant like Calvin Easley.

"Dylan . . ."

"Yes?"

"When the cops pulled up, my dad told me to send you something."

"He did? What is it?"

"It's an audio file. From his phone. He said to get it to you and that Maggie Coyle. That you'd know what it was. Can I text it to you?"

"Of course. Send it through."

* * *

"Easley sure is a savvy character," Dylan said to Maggie as they caught up ten minutes later.

"He's been around, so my guess is whenever he meets with police, he's getting a record of it."

From the first thirty seconds, it was clear that the audio file Michelle sent was of last night's meeting at the television studio. Pastor Easley had recorded every word of the conversation they'd had with the chief and Prince.

"But how does it help us now? They were basically listening to *us*. I don't remember them saying much back besides asking some basic questions."

"Believe me, as a reporter, you can't record things enough. I'll listen through it again. You never know."

Chapter 124

Aching all over, Dylan knew he couldn't handle his usual hilly jog.

Still, restless as hell, he went for a long walk instead. Limping slightly as he went, he headed over to Eden Park, navigated a wooded trail down into Mount Adams, then hobbled up to Mirror Lake, which he circled three times to complete a mile. After figuring out how to play music on his new phone, he listened to some old Eagles' songs that usually calmed him. But they didn't do the trick, largely because he expected a call or text from Michelle Easley at any moment.

At the end of the fourth lap, two quick tones interrupted "Take It Easy" as it played in his ear.

The message came from a 614 area code. Columbus—not Michelle Easley. And a number he didn't recognize.

But the message itself was even more unexpected.

They're in a panic. Don't stop.

He looked up and around, as if he needed to hide this message from onlookers when there were no onlookers.

Who is this? he wrote back as he stepped into a classic white gazebo just feet from the lake trail.

The quick reply: *Doesn't matter. Don't stop. You've got them.*

Got them how? he answered.

Seconds passed.

They never thought you'd fight this hard. They didn't think it would get this bad.

. . .

And now you caught them in the act.

Small drops began pelting the gazebo's roof. A breeze blew through, usually the sign of more rain to come.

This person knew a ton, so Dylan couldn't resist.

Who is this???

Doesn't matter, came the response.

They weren't going to say.

The rain picked up as he decided how to respond, going with, *So what do I do next?*

Seconds passed, building to at least a half minute. Dylan shivered as the gusts stiffened, but he didn't look away from his screen.

Ellipses appeared, then a new message: *Dive deeper into Gray. He's the center. Literally.*

Dylan limped back up the hill, rain fading in and out. As he reached the overlook, the expected call came from Calvary Church.

"Dylan?"

It was Michelle.

"Hey there. Any word?"

"They let him go. He just got back here."

"Any charges?"

"Not yet. He gave his side of the story, and they seemed to listen."

"Who'd he meet with?"

"The chief, Deputy Chief Prince, and some investigators. They seem to want to make it all just go away. Like one big misunderstanding where each side unintentionally assumed the worst of the other."

Dylan laughed out loud. "I bet they do."

"But there's more. They say part of making it go away, given what's happened, is that I can't be the one to name your replacement. That our role has now become too tainted."

Dylan glared up into the gray sky.

"Are you kidding me?"

"That's what they said."

"That's outrageous!"

"I know it is. But it's also what they implied would get him off the hook. Before anything goes public. It cleans it up, they said."

Dylan thought back to the text messages he'd received.

They're in a panic . . . You've got them . . . Now you caught them in the act.

"And is the chief the one who said this all to him?"

"Yes, apparently he did most of the talking."

Silence.

"Dylan, I'm trying to think of any good reason *not* to do what they're suggesting. For my father's sake."

"Michelle, you're the one who said earlier that a whole army will stand up to protect this town's elites when they're in trouble. This has *got* to be part of that."

"It may very well be. And if it was me, or anyone else but my mother, I wouldn't even think about doing it. But I'm not going to let my father become a public spectacle."

Dylan sighed, reliving how painful it had been to be that public spectacle.

"I understand, Michelle. Can you at least buy some time?"

"They gave him time. They want an answer by the end of the day tomorrow."

"Okay. I'll get back to you with something by then."

Dylan hung up, not nearly as confident as he'd sounded.

FRIDAY

Chapter 125

"That doesn't leave us a lot of time," Maggie Coyle said as she and Dylan huddled in her usual corner booth of the West End Frisch's. He'd just filled her in on Pastor Easley's dilemma as well as the out-of-the-blue text messages.

"Why do you think I wanted to meet so early?" Dylan asked, holding a shriveled piece of bacon in his left hand. It was 6:35 in the morning.

"What'd you learn so far?"

Dylan had spent the evening looking into Sebastian Gray, the bearded Windsor rainmaker.

"Basic stuff. Gray lives in a fancy mansion in Hyde Park. Part of every elite Fourth Street group and club there is. Active in politics, but he and his wife seem to give to everyone regardless of party. His adult son pitches in too."

"What do you mean by everyone?"

"City hall. County officials. Statehouse officials. Governor. Anyone who can play a role in getting his deals through. I'd forgotten about it, but he gave to my campaign early on as well."

Maggie shrugged.

"So he gave to lots of people and is an East Side millionaire. How does that make him different than all the other big shots in town?"

"It doesn't."

"Remind me what the texts said."

Dylan pulled them up, then read the one about Gray out loud: "Dive deeper into Gray. He's the center. Literally."

"'The center.' 'Literally.' What could that mean?"

"That he's in the middle of it."

"Right, but of course, we already knew that. That text is trying to tell you something different."

Dylan chewed on a third piece of bacon, thinking.

"'Dive deeper,'" Maggie said.

"That's right."

"Which means go beyond the basic stuff."

"Like what?"

"Where'd Gray go to law school?"

"Harvard."

"Impressive."

"Yes. Law review and everything."

"Then what?"

"He clerked for a federal judge in New York, then moved back here to work at Windsor."

"Anything special about the judge?"

"Not really. A respected district court judge. The judge died about five years ago. Overall, pretty typical of a Harvard law student, and would've made him an easy hire for Windsor."

"Okay. How about college? Where'd he go?"

"Notre Dame."

"But of course. A good Cincinnati Catholic boy. St. Joseph's too, I bet?"

The most elite of the East Side Catholic schools. Where Dylan went. Christian Kane too. So many others who ran the town.

Dylan shrugged. "I don't know."

She chuckled. "C'mon, Dylan, this is Cincinnati. You surely know that what high school you went to is the single most important fact about you."

Dylan laughed at the inside joke, which also happened to be true. When people in Cincinnati asked what "school" they went to, most answered with the name of their high school, not college. Heck, people shared what grade schools they went to.

"Apparently not for Sebastian Gray," he said. "He only lists Harvard in his bio. But you're right. He probably went to St. Joe's or one of the other schools out where I grew up. I swear Windsor starts recruiting them out of high school."

That reminded him—Graham Mundy also graduated from St. Joseph's a couple years ahead of him. He probably knew a lot about Gray. And he hadn't followed up since their terrible meeting.

"Definitely not my experience at an all-girl West Side school. We had to claw for everything we got."

She took a few short sips of her coffee, then put the mug down.

"Well, let's divide up the schools and see what we can find. Dig up anything else you can, and let's reconnect at eleven."

"Sounds good," Dylan said, grabbing the bill and standing up.

But Maggie stayed in her seat.

"I've got one more thing I need to tell you," she said. "And you're not going to like it."

"What's that?"

"I'm interviewing the chief today. About the drug bust."

"Are you serious?" Dylan asked, fuming.

"I am. Temple and he have been talking, and he offered to do it as an exclusive. No news producer would say no to that. And he knows it boxes me in."

"And you agreed?"

"What am I going to do? Let some rookie who knows nothing do the interview?"

"So you're going to run with a story you know isn't true?"

She stood up and stepped away from the booth.

"Let's just say if I do it, I can contain it. No one else will."

Chapter 126

Professionally homeless, Dylan spent the morning at the offices of Gabby's father's law firm, sharing a conference room with her as they dove more deeply into Sebastian Gray.

They stumbled onto a variety of tidbits beyond what Dylan had dug up the night before.

Gray was a leader in the Friendly Sons of St. Patrick, a huge fraternal group of Cincinnatians of Irish descent. He taught a course in real estate law at the University of Cincinnati Law School, publishing a number of articles over the years. He was involved in a number of local charities, including the Comfort Center. And he'd married a woman named Penelope Adair, from a large and wealthy East Side family. She'd gone to Michigan after graduating from St. Mary's, a prominent all-girls Catholic School on the East Side.

But what high school *he* went to remained a mystery, even though St. Mary's was informally considered the sister school to St. Joseph's.

Checking whether Gray was a St. Joe's grad was easy enough. Dylan called and asked the alumni affairs director, who regularly sought him out for contributions.

"No. We have no trace of a Sebastian Gray in our system," she said after looking up the name. "He didn't go here."

The other three schools were tougher. When Gabby called and tried to pry the information loose over the phone, only one of the schools agreed to even look. No luck. And nothing online turned up any connection to the other two big schools.

"Does he have any siblings?" Gabby asked.

"Good idea. Let me check."

With Gabby looking over his shoulder, Dylan typed the words *Sebastian Gray* into his laptop, along with the words *Cincinnati* and *sister*. The only thing that showed up was an event where he and his wife were honored for supporting the local Catholic nonprofit Sisters of the Poor.

"Dylan, type in his name and the word *brother*," Gabby said. "If there's a story about *her*, that's how he would be listed."

"True."

Dylan followed her suggestion.

A story finally came up.

An obituary.

Dylan pored through it and called Maggie right away.

Chapter 127

Dylan Webb called twice in five minutes, interrupting Maggie's prep session for the interview with the chief, which was scheduled to start in an hour.

She picked up on his third try.

"His older sister went to St. Agnes!" Dylan blurted out before she could even say hello.

"Really? When?"

Across the conference room table, Rick Temple's bushy right eyebrow jolted up a half inch. He'd grown tired of her continued conversations with Webb and was far more interested in the chief's take.

"She graduated in 1974," Dylan said,

Maggie stepped out of the conference room, signaling to Rick Temple she'd be back soon. He responded with a full eye roll, pointing to his watch.

"A generation above me," she said, heading toward her desk. "What's her name?"

"Eleanor Gray. Eleanor Mitchell after marrying. She died five years ago. Cancer."

"Sad," she said, "but I've never heard the name."

Then the obvious struck her.

"Dylan, you know what that means, right?"

"Yes. That's why I called. Despite going all in on the East Side once he got to Windsor, Sebastian Gray is a West-Sider. Where would he have gone—"

"St. Tim's. He has to have gone to St. Tim's. St. Agnes and St. Tim's go hand in hand."

"I thought St. Tim's grads wore it with pride. They bleed scarlet. Why would he make it so hard to find?"

"Easy. Less so these days, but for generations, word on our side of town was that the West Side background hurt you getting ahead in the business world, which was dominated by East Side money and decisionmakers."

"Really?" Dylan asked. "That's nuts."

"Dylan, when one side of town has looked down on the other for generations, of course people would think that. As a young lawyer, Gray probably heard that as well. So someone like him, doing well in the world, moves east and hides it."

"Well, he sure acted on it," Dylan said. "He screams out East Side in everything he does."

"Yeah, given his success, he probably thinks that was part of the reason."

Maggie sat down at her desk, mind racing. She'd looked up Gray's bio earlier, so she reopened it on her computer.

"He graduated from Harvard in '83. So if he went to St, Timothy, that would make him class of '79."

"Yes, it would."

Hairs lifted on her arms as her mind kept racing.

"Dylan, how old do you think the chief is?"

"Maybe late fifties. Early sixties."

"Exactly," she said, typing a new search on her computer. "Which means he graduated right around the same time."

The new screen popped up.

"*Chief Buck Reinhardt '77 honored as St. Timothy Alum of the Year.*"

"He did!" She yelled. "Class of '77, and not hiding it. Unlike Gray, the chief is damn proud of his West Side roots."

Silence as they both clearly were asking the same question in their minds.

"But it's a big school, right?" Dylan asked. "I mean, I went to St. Joe's and all, but I can't say I knew most of the people two years below me. Almost any of them, really."

"True. Same with St. Agnes." She shut her eyes, thinking about her days back in school. "We pretty much stuck to our class, and as seniors, we definitely didn't spend a lot of time with the sophomores."

She pressed her memory of those days. Who in school had she known that much younger? The few faces came to her. Then the names. A couple sophomores, now that she thought about it. Even a freshman. All from—

"Dylan, read me that text message from yesterday. One more time."

"Hold on. I'm putting you on speaker." A click sounded, followed by a few seconds of silence. Then he spoke into the phone more loudly than before. "It says 'Dive deeper into Gray. He's the center. Literally.'"

"That's what that text may have meant," she yelled, remembering Sebastian Gray's size in the meeting with Easley. At least six feet tall—not a huge guy weight-wise, but on the bigger side. "'The center. Literally.' If Gray was the center of the St. Timothy football team, then he definitely would've known the chief, who was the star running back in his time there."

Maggie's heart pulsed into overdrive. People were starting to look at her from other desks.

Dylan picked up her train of thought. "And if the chief knows Gray that well, then—"

"He lied his ass off in our meeting when he acted like he didn't know who he was," she said in a whisper. "And the next day's meeting with us was a sham. He was helping an old friend get out of trouble."

"Or worse, he was part of the plan even earlier."

"Right," Maggie said, "and either way, with that tape from Pastor Easley, we'd have him dead to rights."

More silence as her mind whirred.

"Here's the thing. We need full-proof evidence that they knew each other."

Silence again.

"Maggie, where are you doing your interview with the chief?"

"His office. Why do you ask?"

A chuckle through the phone.

"Oh, Maggie, I know just the place where you can get that proof."

Chapter 128

The chief's starched ivory shirt and navy-blue uniform jacket were made for TV, displaying far more medals and badges than two days ago.

"Welcome, Maggie," he said as he pulled the thick wooden door open.

"Thank you, Chief. We appreciate the opportunity. This is Sam, my cameraman. He'll just take a few minutes. Where do you want us?"

As with the uniform, the layout of his office made clear that the chief was no stranger to this type of long-form interview. To the left of his desk was a small sitting space with two short couches facing one another.

"There you go," he pointed. "Have a seat."

Maggie moved quickly in her three-inch heels, making sure to grab the couch that would allow Sam to aim his camera toward the chief's desk and the bookshelf behind it without drawing attention to it.

"Thank you," she said, sitting down slowly and crossing her legs.

"You've stayed in pretty good shape, Coyle," the chief said as he sat, his hazel eyes probing up and down.

The chief's open ogling of her figure made her stomach churn, but the consultants would be pleased. The white blouse hugged her chest, and a blue pencil skirt fell just below her knees. She'd taken twenty minutes—fifteen minutes more than usual—to straighten her hair while finessing curls at the ends. She'd also added enough blush and lipstick to hide every hint that she was closing in on forty-five, as well as the bruises and scrapes from the other night.

She ignored the comment.

"Let us know when you're ready to go, Sam."

"Will do, Maggie."

Upper right, Dylan had said. She didn't want to look directly over, but she could see a few frames out of the corner of her eye. Most importantly, she'd told Sam where to look, and to take in as much as he could. As close up as possible for as long as possible.

"Another minute and we're good to go."

The chief squinted.

"So you finally quit this Dylan Webb wild-goose chase, Coyle?"

"As Rick Temple told me yesterday, it's time to move on. Sounds like the whole Easley thing is pretty complicated, so it's back to my original story about the drug gang. That's why we appreciate you doing this long interview."

"Of course. You're pretty stubborn, and we both know that's hurt you in the past. Glad you've finally learned when to stop barking up the wrong tree."

Maggie seethed at the words—they both knew he'd destroyed her career for telling the truth—but she forced a smile through the anger. "Painfully, yes."

"Ready to go, Maggie."

"Okay. Give us a countdown."

"3 . . . 2 . . . 1 . . ."

"Chief, thank you for meeting with us. And congratulations on the big raid the other day . . ."

Chapter 129

Michelle Easley called Dylan at 3:45.

"We're down to the wire," she said. "Anything change?"

"Michelle," Dylan said slowly, "we are very close to blowing this whole thing up."

"Very close? Like in the next hour?"

"Maybe."

"And exactly what's gonna blow up?"

"I probably shouldn't say much until we confirm it."

Silence.

"Dylan?"

"Yes?"

"We trusted you completely, which is why my father's in this mess in the first place."

He had to tell her something.

"Okay. I just don't want to overpromise."

"Just tell me."

"When we met with your dad and the chief and revealed what was happening, the chief acted like he had no idea who the guy your dad met with was."

"You mean Sebastian Gray? I know. I listened to the whole meeting after sending it to you. And you're right, the chief definitely left that impression."

"Well, we think we've discovered that that's not true."

"Really?" she asked. "So they knew each other?"

"Very likely."

"How well?"

"We're talking way back. Playing high school football together."

"Didn't the chief play at St. Tim's?"

"Yes."

"Wow. That's as deep a bond as it gets in this town."

"Exactly. A blood bond."

"So that would mean the chief lied straight up to you all when he saw who my dad met with."

"He sure did. And thanks to your dad, we have that lie on tape."

"And if he lied about that . . ."

She paused, so Dylan completed the thought.

"Then he's up to no good—either helping his old friend once he got caught in a scandal, or worse, he was involved even earlier."

"So how can you confirm this in time so my dad can make the right decision?"

"That's happening as we speak."

Chapter 130

The chief milked every second of the interview. The fact that Maggie was tossing softballs clearly made him enjoy it all the more.

"Those two judges are owed the same fair trial as any other defendants," he explained, "but if they are found guilty, it will be one of the lowest moments in the history of this community's criminal justice system."

"Are you able to comment on any others caught up in the scandal?"

"Well, of course, there's Dylan Webb. Allegedly. Of course, you've talked to him at length." He paused, letting the dig stick.

"Any others?"

"We're looking now. Unfortunately, the best information was lost when that gang decided to go Butch Cassidy with this country's finest SWAT team."

"You mentioned Dylan Webb. Is this what was behind his incident?"

He nodded.

"Mr. Webb looks to have made some remarkably bad decisions, and he was up to his ears with some very dangerous people. He's lucky to be alive. We also have reason to believe one of the people killed the other night was one of the people in the car with Mr. Webb. You might show your viewers the face from the deceased and the police sketch, and they'll see the similarity."

Maggie clenched her jaw. They really were tying up all the loose ends.

"So yes, it all seems connected."

"And what will happen with his case?"

"We'll send it all to Prosecutor Magwood for him to decide."

Her heart drummed about her next question—the furthest she'd go down this road, and beyond the scope the chief and Temple had negotiated.

"And there's nothing else you know that can explain what happened to Councilman Webb? No other theories?"

"Nothing credible," he said, deadpan.

Good. That was all she needed.

"Chief, I want to go back to the raid. Why do you think your men did such a great job dealing with such a dangerous crew?"

She knew where he'd go with this invitation. His favorite topic.

He smiled broadly.

"I'm so glad you asked. And I know you know the answer. Here at Cincinnati Police, our core operational value is teamwork. Your team is everything. Your teammates are everything. So you each play your role within that team structure. And whatever your role, you look out for everyone on your team. And," he slowed down, "nobody knows that better than our SWAT team."

"I've heard you talk about this philosophy many times. This goes back to your playing days, doesn't it?"

His West Side eyes beamed with pride.

"Oh yes. No place taught me about teamwork more than St. Tim's. Our coach then, God rest his soul, and the coaches now, drill it into every freshman from the first two-a-days on. The *team* is everything. Your teammates are everything. Fight for your team and those teammates, and you won't lose."

Her nerves picked up again. She needed more, but the further she went, the riskier this got.

"And you were a star running back, right? All-state? So you probably learned that better than anyone."

He leaned forward intensely.

"Yes. Those big guys up front are everything. No one on the team matters more. I think of them like the breachers on our SWAT team, opening things up for everyone else to do their jobs. Then the receivers and the quarterback pitch in in key ways. Every play, that teamwork is what matters. And when it works, when the members all work together, it's magical. Far more than my own accolades was the fact that we won state three of my four years. And were undefeated in the last two. Now that's teamwork."

"Trust me, Chief. Growing up on the West Side, I heard about those years as early as I could understand what football was."

Nostalgia and Scarlet pride were driving all his answers. And blinding him.

"Outside of this police force, it's still the finest team I've ever been on. To a person."

He paused, pivoting.

"But back to your question, those teams also shaped my leadership approach ever since. Up to and including that raid the other night."

"And of course, like a good team leader, you were on-site for it all."

"Yes, I was. Even had a few bullets whiz by."

"And *that* is why you're still chief after all these years."

He shook his head, false modesty no doubt on its way.

"Maggie, again, I'm still chief because of teamwork. And the first-class team we've built. And, yes, I'm damn proud of that."

"Thank you, Chief. I can't think of a better way to end our conversation."

The chief nodded, then waited a few seconds to be sure they were done.

"Mics are off," Sam said.

"That was fun, Coyle. Rick assured me you'd play nice, but that was even better than I expected."

"Of course," she said, piqued that Temple would've said such a thing.

"Sam, you still need some B-roll, right?"

Sam had been moving around the room for most of the conversation, and he was now behind her.

"Sure do. Just keep talking, and I'll get some additional angles of you guys talking. Again, sound is off."

They talked for another ten minutes as Sam moved around the room, grabbing a variety of shots.

"All set," he finally said as the bright light on his camera went dark.

"We're good to go, Chief," Maggie said, standing, shaking his hand, then walking straight for the door. "Thank you again."

Chapter 131

The text from Maggie Coyle came through at 4:45 p.m.

Dylan Webb immediately called Michelle Easley.

"We got him. Tell them 'hell no' on any deal."

"Before I do that, tell me what you got?"

"Everything we need."

"Dylan, I need details."

"I haven't seen it yet, Michelle. But Maggie Coyle is telling me that. And no one has a better read on this than she does. Tell them no. Watch them squirm."

"Okay."

Dylan next called Rusty Grimes and filled him in on the first piece of good news since the riverboat.

"What do we do next?" Dylan asked.

Grimes walked through a remarkably simple plan.

After they hung up, Dylan scrolled through his messages. Fortunately, he'd received far fewer than just weeks ago.

He stopped at the 614 number and texted back.

He was indeed the center. We got him.

Ellipsis appeared after a few seconds.

A thumbs-up emoji came back his way.

Dylan stared back at the phone, weighing his next words. Should he go there?

Acting on a hunch, he'd done a little research as Maggie conducted the interview. He'd racked his brain all day. Only one guy Dylan personally knew might know intimate details about Sebastian Gray. He was Gray's long-time law partner—the one with a very big drug problem. And a quick search uncovered that that partner had married a woman who'd spent her first twenty-eight years in Columbus. A 614 area code.

Dylan had also recently seen evidence that this person may have been roughed up, black eye and all. He'd blamed a fall at a party, but what were the odds?

And please thank Graham for me.

No response for a few seconds.

Then another ellipsis.

Then a second thumbs up.

MONDAY

Chapter 132

Even with his stomach fluttering, Dylan grinned as he sat down at the large, oval oak table.

Rusty Grimes and County Prosecutor A. J. Magwood were polar opposites in what they did and how they appeared, but their mammoth offices were nearly identical. Dark wood and heads of dead animals everywhere.

Rusty and Maggie took seats to Dylan's left and right, sinking into deep-cushioned chairs far more lush than anything at city hall.

At 9 a.m. on the nose, the tall county prosecutor loped in, wearing a charcoal suit, a red tie, and his signature leather boots. For a guy in his late fifties, he still had the boyish looks of a surfer, with wavy light-blond hair, a high forehead, and an always deep tan. But a hawk nose with flared nostrils and a prominent bump along its ridge balanced those youthful features with a dose of the aggression that sent more people to death row than any prosecutor in Ohio.

A toothy smile greeted Grimes.

"Rusty Grimes!" he called out loudly. "It's not often I get a call from you *inviting* me to a meeting."

Rusty hoisted his round body out of the chair and the two shook hands heartily.

"Believe me, it's not a call I'd ever thought I'd make."

Magwood nodded at Maggie, still grinning.

"Coyle, that was one powder puff of an interview you granted our illustrious chief the other day. I wish you treated me that gently even once!"

She chuckled.

"I figured after roughing up your favorite judges, I needed to even things out."

His blond eyebrows bounced up and down.

"If there's one thing I've learned in politics *and* law, it's that people are always projecting. And those two buffoons are the best poster children of that I ever saw."

His eyes turned to Dylan, smile fading. Still, Dylan stood, and the two shook hands.

"I'm surprised you'd want to meet under the circumstances, Mr. Webb. Unless, of course, you're here to plead guilty. But your call."

Dylan was about to speak, but Grimes cut him off.

"Believe me, A. J., you'll be glad he's here when we're through."

"Is that right?" Magwood asked, turning his back on Dylan and walking to the other side of the table.

"You'd think I'd bring a client to talk to you otherwise?" Grimes asked.

Magwood never answered because the door to the conference room opened. In walked one of Magwood's top lieutenants—a guy Dylan saw on TV all the time handling the office's highest-profile crimes.

"Rusty, I believe you know Zeke Long. The man takes perfect notes, so every word you all say better be true. Sit down, everyone."

All five took their seats, but somehow Magwood's chair left him towering over everyone else. Elbows on the table, the prosecutor opened his palms upward, his big teeth making an encore appearance.

"Okay, gentlemen, what's so important I had to cancel my golf game?"

"A. J.," Grimes replied, looking around the room before gesturing at a freakishly big elk. "We are about to bag you the two biggest trophies of your life."

* * *

At Grimes's prompting, Dylan walked through the abduction, the cops' instant skepticism, and the immediate political pressure to resign. Maggie filled in the prosecutors on Fritz Ventre and the deaths of Diego DeLeon and Rodney Stone.

"Such a shame about Stone," Magwood said, frowning. "Came from nothing to become a good law-and-order man. But I thought that was an accident?"

"Making you think that was the intent," Maggie said. "But the license plate of the van he collided with was registered to DeLeon," she went on.

"And DeLeon was the same guy whom the other van was also registered to?" Zeke Long asked.

"You got it. The one that was used to nab Fritz Ventre. What are the odds?"

"But you say DeLeon is dead too?" Magwood asked.

"Yes," Maggie said. "And he was already dead when the second van was registered in his name."

Long looked up from his notes. "This is awfully complicated. Does it all connect together at some point? Where are these big trophies you mentioned?"

"Getting to them real soon," Grimes said, winking. "And this connects a lot better than most of your cases."

Dylan next explained his decision to resign from the office and the switch to Michelle Easley.

Long smirked. "You know, Mr. Webb, we've been watching you like a hawk. That was the slickest move of all."

"Thank you," Dylan said, unsure how else to respond to the cryptic comment. "It felt like the right thing to do, but it also gave us the best way to see what was really happening."

"Mm-hmm," Long said, looking down as he took notes.

"I assume we'll get to that at some point," Magwood said, growing impatient.

"Right now, in fact," Grimes said. "Within days, as we'd expected, deep pockets approached the councilwoman's father for a meeting. And we got that whole meeting on tape. Maggie, take out your laptop, will ya?"

"Sure thing," she said, pulling it out of her bag.

Maggie played the opening of the meeting, which Magwood interrupted as soon as the bearded man entered the room.

"Is that Sebastian Gray?" he said, leaning forward. "Of Windsor?"

According to Dylan's quick research the night before, Gray had been a loyal donor to Magwood over the years, cohosting a number of fundraisers along the way.

"Sure is," Grimes asked. "Didn't I tell ya these were big trophies?"

Magwood's eyes flared open. "Rusty! You're talking about one of the most respected lawyers in town."

"Maybe so, A. J. But just watch."

Maggie, who'd paused the tape, started it up again. At the moment where Easley chewed out Curtis Jackson, Magwood hit an open palm against the table.

"That Calvin Easley is over the top, isn't he?"

Maggie paused the video on a frame where Easley's mouth hung wide open and right hand soared high in the air.

"You know him?" Grimes asked.

"Oh yeah, I know him," he said, stone-faced. "Your friend Jackson seems spooked by the whole thing, doesn't he, Webb?"

"He definitely looks uncomfortable."

"Keep going," Grimes instructed Maggie.

The two prosecutors' expressions remained frozen as they watched Sebastian Gray pass Easley the folder and agree to the minister's terms after the brief chat about the size of the project and where the money was coming from. Minutes later, the recording ended.

"Anything else?" Magwood asked, sounding as if he regretted skipping his golf game.

Unphased, Grimes had Dylan and Maggie summarize the shootout and the two meetings with the chief that had followed that evening and again the next morning.

Grimes twirled his finger and looked at Maggie.

"Let's review another tape, shall we?"

Magwood winced.

"You guys taped the chief of police?"

"We did," Grimes said. "It's legal as long as—"

"Trust me, Grimes, I know when it's legal and when it's not. Just surprised you'd do something like that. Keep going."

Maggie played the audiotape of the meeting.

When it ended, Magwood shrugged. "The chief didn't say much. Neither did Prince."

"Interesting, huh?" Grimes asked.

"I can't say that it is. He was listening to you." He looked at Dylan. "And after your past two weeks of high drama, I'd say that was generous on his part."

"Sure," Grimes said. "But he also made it seem that he didn't know anything about it or anyone who was involved."

"He said he knew Calvin, but not Sebastian Gray. But maybe he was playing coy." He looked at Maggie. "I mean, did you reveal everything you knew when you interviewed a witness or a perp?"

Grimes answered before she could.

"A. J., *you* saw Sebastian Gray's face and blurted out his name right away. The chief watched him for close to an hour, didn't react at all, then *asked* who he was. Then, when Webb here said his name, he *still* left the impression that he didn't know him."

Magwood bounced his head left and right as if he was weighing the issue.

"Let's move on."

The hope buoying Dylan a few minutes ago was fading fast. Magwood appeared to be going south.

"A. J., what if it turns out that the chief actually knows Sebastian Gray well?"

"Well, does he?" Magwood asked impatiently.

"And what if I told you the chief came back the next morning and informed Maggie and Dylan that he'd met with Gray, and that he'd now concluded that Easley was the one doing the bribing—not Gray?"

Zeke Long squinted. "And you're saying they know each other well?"

"That's what I'm saying," Grimes said.

"Where's your proof of that?" Long asked.

Grimes twirled his finger one more time.

"Next tape, please."

Maggie called up another file, the chief's face appearing across her screen.

Magwood waved his hand.

"I told you, Coyle, I already saw this interview."

"Not all of it, you haven't," Grimes said.

She pushed play, and the time stamp made clear they were well into their conversation.

A close-up of the chief captured him waxing nostalgically about his football days: "Oh yes. No place taught me about teamwork more than St. Tim's. Our coach then, God rest his soul, and the coaches now, drill it into every freshman from the first two-a-days on. The *team* is everything. Your teammates are everything. Fight for your team, and those teammates, and you won't lose."

"Stop!" Magwood said loudly, glancing at Dylan, then back at the screen. "I only came to this town for law school. I grew up in a village an hour east of here, right on the river. A thousand people on a good day. Not a penny to scratch together among all of us, let alone the money to field a football team. I've heard this 'We Bleed Scarlet' versus 'We Bleed Blue' shit so many times from you guys and your fancy high schools I could puke."

Grimes guffawed. "I couldn't agree more, A. J., but that's not the point."

"Well, what is?"

"Just keep watching."

Maggie pushed play again as the chief leaned forward and continued:

"Those big guys up front are everything—no one on the team matters more. I think of them like the breachers on our SWAT team, opening things up for everyone else to do their jobs. Then the receivers and the quarterback pitch in in key ways. Every play, that teamwork is what matters. And when it works, when the members all work together, it's magical. Far more than my own accolades was the fact that we won state three of my four years. And were undefeated in the last two. Now that's teamwork."

It struck Dylan more on this second viewing than it had last night. The words were powerful, but it was the passion on the chief's face that really cut through. He believed deeply in what he was saying.

Maggie fast-forwarded through her question, then slowed back down, the chief back on the screen: "Outside of this police force, it's still the finest team I've ever been on. To a person."

Maggie pushed pause again.

Magwood jumped back in. "Okay, so the guy loved his teammates."

"To a person," Grimes said, emphasizing the last word.

"Yeah, I heard that part too. Like I said, I hear that shit every day. What the hell's the point?"

Maggie fast-forwarded to the moment where Sam asked for B-roll. The camera scanned around the room with the audio cut off.

Magwood shrugged. "B-roll? Is that it? I don't get it."

"Ten more seconds," Maggie said impatiently.

The camera zoomed in on the chief for a few seconds, then toward Maggie. Legitimate B-roll.

Then the view swung to the right. The camera zoomed in.

Toward the desk, then over it.

A broad shot of the bookshelf.

Then closer in. To one shelf. Second from the top.

For a moment, the photo of the chief being sworn in appeared, blurry but recognizable. Then the camera veered a few feet more to the right, zooming in even more.

The picture was blurry at first, a fuzzy mix of people, faces, and blobs of scarlet and white.

Then things came more into focus. Details of the faces emerged. The outlines of the people sharpened. Their outfits became clear.

It was a team of football players—boyish faces on big bodies— proud as can be. Each wore the scarlet uniforms of St. Tim's. Each held his white helmet at his side.

"Yeah, that's the chief," Magwood said, pointing to the screen. "I saw this photo in his office a few years back. So?"

The view of the team grew even larger, now taking up the whole screen. Blurry again for a moment. Then sharp again.

"Stop there," Grimes said.

Maggie pushed a button.

"Bring it over here," Magwood said. "My eyes aren't that good." Maggie carried the laptop around and placed it in front of him. "See if you recognize anyone else," she said. "I'll give you a hint. The face directly behind the chief's, to the right. Blond hair, a lot like yours."

Magwood leaned in. Squinted.

"I see him now," he said, again with no hint of enthusiasm. "Sebastian Gray. Funny. I'd never pegged him for St. Tim's. He doesn't leave the impression he's a West Sider."

"A. J., he didn't just go there," Grimes said as if ending a closing argument. "Sebastian Gray was the star center of that football team. Not good enough to make the Notre Dame team, but good enough to be recruited. And he started both years that he and the chief overlapped."

Dylan nodded. The sports guy at Maggie's station had dug up some incredible old stuff on Cincinnati high school football back in the chief's day—things no internet search would ever find. Gray had been all-city his sophomore year, opening up huge holes for the state's most decorated running back, Buck Reinhart. This was the photo taken right after they won the state title.

Magwood leaned back in thought, eyes narrowed.

"And you're telling me that forty years later, the chief is supposed to instantly recognize a guy whose ass he looked at for two years in high school?"

Dylan felt ill. This was a replay of his initial meeting with Prince, Mustache, and Buzz Cut. Unending skepticism.

"C'mon, A. J.!" Grimes said, turning red in the face. "That's a deep bond that never goes away. Hell, the chief himself said it."

"He was grandstanding there, just like I would," Magwood said, gesturing toward Maggie's screen. "Who knows if he really knows Gray anymore?"

"A. J., first off, *you* can know by opening a special grand jury to look into all this corruption," Grimes said, practically yelling. "And second, the chief said his team was the finest group of people he's ever known, to a person. Hell, he called his offensive line his 'breacher.' Then he meets with the guy at the center of it all, who was also *his* center, flips the whole narrative, yet still never tells us he knows him?"

Magwood stared at the huge elk head looking down on him from one wall.

"This is the decorated and highly respected chief of police we're talking about. An icon. And you want me to go after him because of an old football photo? All to build some building?"

Dylan couldn't hold back. Magwood had stumbled into his wheelhouse.

"Gentlemen, this isn't just a building. It's an entire neighborhood of new development—housing, retail, and commercial. Numerous buildings, and more than a billion dollars in investment. Years and years of work. A whole lot of people stand to make their entire careers out of this development—and get filthy rich in the process. It's why they could offer Easley what—"

Magwood held his palm up.

"Simmer down, guys. Time's a wasting. You got anything else?"

Grimes took a few deep breaths, which sounded the same as loud snores.

"One final thing," he said quietly.

"Make it good."

"The chief is trying to say this all was part of a big drug bust and not corruption."

The prosecutor looked over at Maggie. "Yeah, which dovetails with the story *she* told the whole city about."

Maggie sat straight defensively. "There clearly was some drug ring out there, and some of its members were involved here as well, probably as hired guns. But that's not what *this* was about. And Dylan's robbery in particular."

"And how do we know that?" Magwood said. "I mean, you were the one who aired his drug payments. Jesus, Webb, did you really use PayPal?"

Again, Dylan couldn't hold back.

"That had nothing to do with—"

"We have a witness," Rusty said, yelling again.

"A witness to what?" Magwood said. "No one witnessed a thing, except for that homeless guy you talked about."

"This witness can attest to everything Councilman Webb said. Every moment of the robbery. Every word uttered. Even the beating of the homeless guy after. And he can make it crystal clear that it had absolutely nothing to do with drugs or drug use or anything else."

Zeke Long scrunched his cheeks up against his deep-set, dull eyes.

"Who the hell would've witnessed all that?" he asked.

Dylan sat high in his chair. "The guy who sat right behind me the whole time."

"Wait, one of your kidnappers?" Magwood asked. "How in the hell?"

Grimes jumped back in.

"He reached out to Ms. Coyle and is now represented by the Moore Firm. He's ready to testify to everything Dylan said, along with other aspects of what we described, assuming you're willing to take it easy on a kid who made an enormous mistake that he's regretted ever since."

"He's a good kid," Maggie said. "And he'll be a game-changing witness."

Magwood ignored her comment and looked back at Grimes. "Anything else in your bag of tricks?"

Grimes opened his beefy hands in front of him. "That's all I've got. We just ask that you take a good hard look at—"

"Any other questions, Zeke?"

"None, sir."

The two prosecutors stood up in unison.

"Thank you for your time," Magwood said, and the two left the room.

MONDAY, ONE WEEK LATER

Chapter 133

It was the same queasiness that he'd felt back in the Jeep a month before.

Blindfolded. Doors closed. The muffled voices of Slayton and Kai arguing only feet away. About him.

It wasn't just the fear but the total loss of control. A coin in midair. His fate in the balance.

But this time, it lingered for days. And even though he wasn't trapped in a vehicle, there wasn't a thing he could do to impact the decision.

Even worse than in the Jeep, he couldn't hear a thing. Grimes said that's how it worked when a prosecutor weighed a case, but it was still hell.

And the inaction meant everything else in life was stuck in place.

No job.

No politics.

No social life.

And nothing to be done but wait.

Dylan first occupied himself by moving back to Mount Adams. With Slay dead and Kai now on his side, home was safe again.

He then picked up a few books he hadn't gotten to in years. But amid every few pages of progress, the uncertainty gnawed at him. He powered through two books over five days but then stopped trying.

His physical wounds had healed enough that he jogged his old route again twice a day. But even as he ran, he dwelled on everything. He weighed it all so intensely that at times he'd slow to a fast walk.

More than anything, he relived the ninety minutes with A. J. Magwood, second-guessing himself ruthlessly.

Should he have pushed harder? Spoken more? Emphasized certain points more forcefully?

Then he played back every word out of Magwood's mouth. Each tough question—each skeptical expression.

Grimes had assured him that Magwood's MO in a meeting like that was to push back. To probe and push at every weak spot. Playing devil's advocate was part of any good prosecutor's process, but that didn't necessarily reflect his true feeling.

Dylan imagined the politics that must have been weighing on the prosecutor, with an election only weeks away. Magwood had expressed it in so many words. Politically, he had no reason to help Dylan. The no-brainer move was to pile on a tainted councilman who'd been caught buying drugs and lying about it. Going after a legendary police chief, the icon of one side of town, was political suicide. Taking down one of the kings of the business community, and perhaps others he was tied to, would no doubt dry up financial support.

Also distracting Dylan was all he didn't know.

The 614 number never texted him again. He'd written once, with no response. That silence could mean many things. If it really was Graham Mundy communicating through his wife's phone, he could either have gone dark to protect his role at the firm, or he could already be cooperating.

He'd kept up with Maggie, who was back to covering run-of-the-mill crimes, but she didn't say much. And she never mentioned what happened to Kai.

"This is how these things work," she said at one point. "Grand juries are secret, so no one knows a darn thing until we know it. And anyone talking to the prosecutor isn't allowed to talk about it to anyone else."

In the meantime, everything else had frozen in place.

Michelle Easley had made no announcements about Webb's replacement, and she refused to comment whenever asked. She didn't call Dylan back after he'd tried her once, so he never tried again. Calvin Easley didn't call either.

Waiting for a ninth council member, city hall ground to a halt. Only ceremonial and noncontroversial matters advanced.

And the Cincinnati Police Department fell quiet. No announcements about sending Dylan's case to a prosecutor. No announcements about prosecuting Cavin Easley. Nothing.

Nine days after the meeting with Magwood, Dylan's parents talked him into visiting them in Florida.

A day later, Dylan bought a ticket for the next day.

Twenty minutes after that, Grimes called for the first time in days.

"Any news?" Dylan asked.

"You have a pressed suit?"

"I do. What's up?"

"Prosecutor wants to meet. At three."

"Any sense of what about?"

"None. We'll know when we get there."

Chapter 134

"Thanks for coming by so quickly."

A. J. Magwood stood as Dylan and Rusty Grimes entered the same room where they'd met ten days before. A new man—beefy, raven-haired, in a gray suit—was with Magwood, but he stayed in his seat.

"My calendar's pretty free these days," Dylan said, forcing a nervous smile.

"I can imagine," Magwood said grimly. "Have a seat."

A moose head right above him, the prosecutor stared across the table, looking into Dylan's eyes, then at Grimes, then back to Dylan.

"Well, you sure have fucked things up, Webb."

Grimes jolted up straight in the chair.

"C'mon, A. J.," he sputtered, droplets of spit landing on the pristine table. "My client's been through too much already to be ripped again, by you or anyone else. Just tell us the bad news, and we'll deal with it."

Magwood kept his gaze on Dylan.

"But he has, Rusty. He's fucked everything up."

Dylan stared back, numb.

"I don't know what you want me to say."

"You don't have to say anything . . . " Magwood said, pausing.

Seconds more passed.

Then slowly, a smile emerged across his face, revealing his squarish, perfectly white front teeth.

"Except to keep telling the truth."

"That's all I've been—"

"I know you have. Just keep doing it. Tomorrow, in front of the special grand jury."

"Wait, are you saying you believe him now?" Grimes asked.

Magwood laughed.

"You catch on quick, Rusty. This man has fucked everything up . . . *for this office*. Things were quiet around here. I'm cruisin' to a drama-free reelection. Then, after ten days of looking into all this, every damn part of his story checks out. And now my team tells me we need to pursue indictments against Chief Reinhart, Sebastian Gray, the mayor, two council members, and a bunch of other business big shots caught up in the largest corruption scandal in modern memory, not to mention the sloppiest effort to take someone down in this town's history."

Dylan clenched his fist as he let out a long breath.

"So others confirmed it all?"

Magwood nodded. "They did."

"Who?" Grimes asked.

"Well, I can't reveal details of what was said in front of the grand jury, but Cal was a big help. Explained it all."

"Cal?" Grimes asked.

"Yes. Calvin Easley and I go way back, beginning with my first church visit decades ago. There's no more honest man in this town than Pastor Easley. They went after the wrong person when they messed with him."

He stopped talking, but Dylan and Grimes stared back, waiting for more.

"And you guys were right. The young man, Kai Brewer, was credible. It all checked out. He was so helpful, and so remorseful, and we've worked something out with him so he can move on with his life."

"So you confirmed that they meant to take me out?"

"Yes. And we had someone from inside the firm come forward." He winked at Dylan. "Someone you know. The whole thing was basic at first, driven by out-of-town clients who, shall we say, engage in a far more aggressive form of business than anyone around here.

The plan was to make you look like a fool with the robbery, then pile on with your past drug deals, which they'd uncovered in his emails. Then have your city hall colleagues drop the hammer for you to quit. When you wouldn't, those foreign clients took things into their own hands. And it went downhill from there."

"You keep saying these *clients*. Who are you talking about? Like the pastor said, this seems to go way beyond—"

Dylan had largely forgotten about the guy in the suit, but the man spoke up now.

"Sir, I can only say so much, but those clients are why *I'm* here."

He passed a card across the table. The words *Federal Bureau of Investigation* appeared in matter-of-fact small print across the top.

"Oh," Dylan uttered without meaning to.

"Your pastor was onto something. Cincinnati, St. Louis, Minneapolis, Louisville—you name it. Midwest cities like yours have become the next stop in the mass cleansing of global dirty money. Through big real estate deals first and foremost."

Magwood spoke up. "I called these guys in as soon as I watched Easley raise the idea of foreign money, and when Gray didn't push back."

"Money laundering?" Dylan asked, the FBI agent's jarring words still echoing in his ear. "In Cincinnati, Ohio? C'mon."

The FBI agent nodded.

"Believe it. Laundering in Manhattan and South Beach has become too easy for us to spot. And it's saturated. So they're looking for new and cheaper places to park and wash their dirty money. So the projects that keep accelerating around here—the ones you've been voting against—there's a whole lot of dirty money in them."

"Dirty money?" It still didn't compute. "From whom? From where?"

He cracked a faint smile. "Oh, you name it. Drug cartels and mobsters. Corrupt foreign officials. Sanctions evaders. Anyone looking for a place to clean ill-begotten funds. Towns like this turn out to be the perfect place—hidden, for one thing. But even more than the big cities, the powers that be get drowned by the money, from billable hours through fancy law firms, big commissions, campaign cash, fat bank deposits, and bribes that most local officials can't say no to. And the front line for it all is that little zoning committee you sit on, where they almost always get their way over the folks who actually live in the communities where the money goes."

The anxious faces in that damp Lower Price Hill auditorium now flashed through Dylan's mind. True roadkill in the world he was now hearing about.

"And as you experienced," the FBI agent continued, "the guys behind all this don't respond well when they're told no."

"Think about it," Magwood said. "From start to finish, what happened to you probably felt much more like some kind of orchestrated takedown in Eastern Europe or South America. Well, that's because that's how these guys conduct business."

"I'll say," Dylan said, before going quiet as a knot returned to his stomach. Suddenly, all that he'd faced and seen—the violence, the brutality, the gaslighting, the intensity of it all—made sense. Along with what had happened to Rodney Stone, Hugh Stabler, and—

"Did you find Fritz Ventre?"

Magwood winced. "We found his body. Buried in a shallow grave behind that warehouse. Beaten terribly."

"Awful," Dylan said, remembering the brief interaction at the second ATM. Eyes full of life despite whatever challenges he'd endured.

"Yes. And without his quick thinking at the check cashing place, you may never have figured this out."

"Or worse," Dylan said. Maggie had explained she only knew she was at the right warehouse because of the van's license plate, which she only knew because of Ventre.

A door opened from the right, and in walked a youngish woman, with glasses and strawberry-blonde curly hair, wearing a sharp brown pantsuit.

"Guys, meet Monica," Magwood said.

She smiled and nodded her head.

"Monica runs our special grand jury. Tomorrow, she's going to ask you to walk through everything you told us the other day, and then some. The nine good people on that grand jury have heard from other witnesses for the past week, and they are there to listen to your story. So take all the time you need."

Magwood stood up, as did the FBI agent.

"I'll leave you guys to prep," the prosecutor said.

"And what about the bigger stuff?"

"We'll let this play out," the FBI agent said, "treating it as a local case as if we know nothing about the deeper connection. But once our prosecutor here does his thing, we'll use that leverage and see who we can get to talk, and where the money trail leads. Your contact is already being cooperative. This is going to be a huge case across the whole country. Most officials on the front lines of these decisions don't react the way you did. They can't say no. But because you did, we finally have a way in. We owe you a huge thank you."

The two walked around the table, Magwood reaching out to shake Dylan's hand. "You remember how I said there was no more honest guy in this town than Calvin Easley?"

"Yes, sir," Dylan said, standing.

"Well, you're right up there with him, which is the only reason we're here today. Thanks for having the guts to stick it out."

The duo turned and walked out the door.

Grimes started to say something, as did Monica, but Dylan couldn't hear either one. Too many thoughts and images were racing through his head.

He sat back down, only then noticing that the arms and back of his chair were moist with sweat.

"Webb," Grimes said, his voice muffled.

Dylan shut his eyes, then took in a long, deep breath. The images slowed, then faded completely.

He exhaled.

"Y'okay, Webb?" Grimes asked, his twang now coming through more clearly.

Dylan was suddenly back in his Jeep looking down an empty Oregon Street.

Giddy. Energized.

It was over. He was free.

He reopened his eyes.

"I'm great!" he said, louder than he intended.

He turned toward Monica, who looked back at him with an awkward grin.

"Let's get started."

MONDAY, ONE WEEK LATER

Chapter 135

In a mere fifteen minutes, A. J. Magwood had turned the entire city upside down.

Standing alone behind a podium, the prosecutor announced the indictments of Mayor Willie Ames, Sebastian Gray, another Windsor partner, two associates, and five leaders in various development businesses who would've profited from Pristine Village and were part of the scheme. The charges varied from conspiracy to abduction to bribery to felony murder, and a diagram to Magwood's left demonstrated how all the players connected together. One First American Bank vice president, a board member of one of the developers, also faced a charge of tampering with evidence—he'd wiped out any trace of Dylan Webb's two kidnappers from the bank's ATM videos. And Stephanie Walker's boss, also on the board of a major developer, was arrested for having furnished the precise details of the planned date, knowing exactly why Sebastian Gray needed the information.

There wasn't a single mention of foreign involvement. As they'd told Dylan, it was big—but it would be framed as local.

Magwood then announced a separate indictment of Chief of Police Buck Reinhardt for obstruction of justice, with potentially more charges to come as an investigation into the chief's knowledge of the broader plot continued. When asked about charges for other individuals—council members, senior police officials, business leaders—Magwood hinted that more might be coming.

Two days later, they did.

The two council ringleaders pushing for Dylan's resignation—Curtis Jackson and Christian Kane—were indicted for bribery, having vacuumed up huge contributions to force Dylan out while handpicking the successor they were instructed to. No evidence pointed to knowledge or involvement of any other council members. Apparently two complicit Democrats were all that were needed to begin the political dominoes toppling.

Maggie Coyle watched it all from the press well in Magwood's modest communications office. But she didn't ask any questions, nor did she do any reporting. It wouldn't be right, given that she'd spent three hours with the grand jury, walking through everything she knew about the case. It was already clear then that, prodded by Magwood's lawyers, the six women and three men were gung ho to indict.

By Wednesday, Dylan Webb was reinstated to the city council. But now there were *two* vacancies to fill, Jackson and Kane having resigned Tuesday. Then, Friday at 5 p.m., four weeks to the hour that Dylan Webb had walked out of city hall, Mayor Willie Ames released a one-sentence statement that he was resigning effective immediately. The mayor used her so little in the vice mayor role that people largely forgot about her, but Verna Spiller was the city's vice mayor. For the coming months, pending a spring special election, she would serve as Cincinnati's interim mayor.

As for replacing Jackson and Kane, the remaining seven council members all agreed that they would use what they called the "Easley process" to gather feedback on names to consider. All out in the open. But rather than a single council member, all seven would vote on the two successors, and all seven amended their successor designee forms accordingly.

It took multiple meetings for Maggie to explain it all to one of the station's newest reporters—who'd arrived weeks before from a Chattanooga TV station—but she did a fine job covering it in the end. Each time, with hair, makeup, and an outfit that the consultants would no doubt gush over.

The one part of the story Maggie saved for herself was the chief's downfall. Along with the footage of his humiliating arrest and appearance in court, she spliced in long clips from their final interview together to brutal effect.

She'd spent years avoiding any confrontation with the man who'd ruined her career, paranoid that he could do it again whenever he wanted.

It turned out, when that direct confrontation finally occurred, it ended his career, not hers. So she felt like she'd earned the right to air that story herself.

SATURDAY

Chapter 136

It was the first of three stops Dylan had planned for the day. Far fewer than most Saturdays before the kidnapping.

They'd agreed to meet at Maggie's Frisch's in the West End, not his in Walnut Hills. Still, he'd been on television all week, so the woman inside the door greeted him like he was a regular.

"You're that councilman, aren't you?" she asked, flashing a warm smile.

Dylan grinned, happy to have his old title back.

"I am. Dylan Webb. I'm meeting with Maggie Coyle."

"She's not here yet, but I'll take you back to her booth," she said, leading him through the sparsely crowded restaurant. Several customers looked his way as he walked past. One waved. Another grinned.

"I'm so glad you're back," his guide said. "Never made any sense to me that you would have made something like that up."

"Thank you. All the trust and empathy from the community helped me get through it."

"It's like those rich people thought we were all stupid," she said, stopping at the corner booth he and Maggie had shared weeks ago. "Here you go."

"Thank you again," he said.

A teenager in a Frisch's uniform approached the table with a large plastic pitcher of water. The name "Jorge" was emblazoned on his name tag.

"Welcome, council member," he said nervously before pouring water.

"Thank you, Jorge. I appreciate your service."

Jorge beamed back.

The warm welcome reminded Dylan of those precious weeks following his election. Smiles. Congratulations. Kind words. Genuine moments that had soon disappeared once he got caught up in the harried, cold form of public service he was now committed to retiring. Now that he knew better.

As he waited, Dylan tore small pieces off the napkin's edges, then rolled them into small balls—a habit he'd had since middle school whenever he waited nervously for something, or someone. He downed his first glass of water within two minutes.

He couldn't see the door. But as Jorge refilled his glass, he heard the high-pitched squeak of the front door opening, followed by a friendly greeting. Maggie was a regular, so he assumed she'd arrived.

But it was Kai who appeared first, his head high above a booth. With no hat, a collared shirt, and a wide grin on his face, he looked as youthful as Maggie had described, despite his height.

Maggie emerged from behind the wall of the booth, to Kai's left. Her hair was wet, frizzled in the same way it was back in the warehouse. She was dressed as if she had been working out.

When Kai first spotted Dylan, the teen's grin faded, and his face tightened. His upper body sagged.

Sensing how nervous he was, Dylan stood up and took five long steps toward him. Unlike with Slayton in that riverboat cafeteria, nothing held him back. He *wanted* to meet him.

Maggie stepped forward.

"Councilman Webb, let me introduce you to Kai Brewer."

"Hey there, Kai," Dylan said as he shook his hand firmly, looking right into his eyes. "I'm so glad you're safe and that we can spend some time together."

Kai's lower lip trembled, but his eyes didn't waiver from Dylan's. "Mr. Webb, I am so deeply sorry for what I did to you. I have relived it every day since. I am so, so sorry."

Kai's hand still in his, Dylan reached up with his left and patted Kai on the shoulder. Then he placed his left hand over Kai's right wrist, squeezing gently.

"Kai, I know how much you regret it. I can feel it. And I forgive you. Just as important, let me thank you. You showed incredible courage and character by coming forward to Maggie and then to the prosecutor. You risked your life to do the right thing. And by doing so, you saved mine, and you helped this city get to the bottom of something that was much bigger than both of us. We were both victims without knowing it."

They looked into each other's eyes for a few more seconds, silent—intense—but not at all awkward.

"Have a seat, you two," Maggie finally said.

The three sat down. And even though Dylan didn't eat a thing—he was saving his appetite for later—they talked for the next hour.

About Kai's parents—their anger at the robbery, but pride that he'd come forward.

About the deal that he and Magwood had struck, and all the community service he would be doing.

About Magwood's call to Miami to convince the school's president to keep Kai as an incoming freshman next year. The president agreed.

About his goals in school, which were still murky, but revolved around either public service or journalism.

About tonight's basketball game, his first time back as a starter.

Dylan enjoyed every minute.

While he kept it from Maggie and Kai, as they'd sat down, vivid images from the robbery played back in Dylan's mind. Details of Kai. Being cornered by him on Hill Street. At the second ATM. Walking by Fritz Ventre. The angry words from the back seat, from under the down-turned baseball cap in the rearview mirror.

Dylan assumed Kai was doing the same.

But as breakfast ended, as he'd hoped, something changed.

Those images faded.

The name Kai Brewer conjured up something else.

A boyish smile. A nervous humility. A kind, soft-spoken voice. Soulful eyes.

An earnestness like his own.

A future.

They'd pushed the reset button.

As Dylan walked to the front door, the kid from the back seat was gone.

* * *

The press conference started at 9:30.

Just Dylan at the podium, no notes, and a small bottle of water. Getting hungry now but holding out from even a snack.

Every station was there, featuring their ace reporters, forced to work Saturday because of what they expected Dylan Webb to announce.

The speculation had begun midweek and exploded on Friday after the mayor's statement. So much so, Dylan felt compelled to address it.

Excited just to be back, he hadn't spent that much time thinking about it. But by late week, he'd made up his mind. It was clear what he needed to do. The sooner he announced it, the better.

The special election for mayor would unfold rapidly. A primary the next spring, then a run-off between the top two vote-getters in May. Signatures would be due within a month. With all that had happened, it was obvious he'd be the favorite to win, giving him the chance to clean up the mess at city hall.

It'd be a perfect feel-good story. A phoenix rising from the ashes. One honest guy prevailing over a web of corruption, then taking over the place.

Given the time crunch, today was the day he'd announce his plan.

"Thank you for being here," he said as the lights from the cameras shone his way. "This will be brief."

He dedicated a moment of silence to the three men killed in the plot against him.

Maggie was standing off to the side, not covering the story, but obviously curious. She hadn't brought it up at breakfast, nor had she mentioned that she would be coming by.

"I wanted to call this press conference as soon as I could after yesterday. The mayor's decision—the right decision, by the way— leaves a void of leadership at city hall at a time when the city desperately needs strong and honest leadership. The longer that void remains, the more the uncertainty will linger. And that only holds back the great people and great communities of this city that much longer."

All the eyes in front of him were intense with anticipation. Willie Ames had been Mayor for so long, a new leader of the city was a big story. An exciting moment. A pick-me-up after weeks of dreary news. A new path for a frustrated city. A new hero.

"So I am committed to not let things linger. Today, I want to announce . . ."

He slowed down his cadence. Took in a deep breath of air so his voice would resonate more loudly.

"That I have no plans to run for mayor in the upcoming special election. My only plan is to seek reelection in the next council race, as I'd always planned to do."

Mouths opened wide. A few gasps. In the corner, Maggie crossed her arms, a playful grin on her face.

"I'm sure you're all asking why. And the answer is that in the past four weeks, I've learned enough to know I'm still new to this. I've got a lot to learn. About city hall. About politics. About myself. Even before this incident, people were urging me to run for mayor. And I'll admit, I was thinking about it. And maybe I'll be mayor someday, maybe not. But this is not the time for me to take that step. Most important, this is bigger than me. It's about the people of this great city, what is best for this city, and who is best positioned to bring us all together."

The surprised looks remained. But his next step, he hoped, would dilute the uncertainty.

"In the last four weeks, I've also come to see that there is a person who is *not* new to this, who doesn't need to learn the things that I do. In fact, this person has taught me the most important lessons I've learned since I arrived at city hall. And this is the person I hope will run in the special election. After talking with her last evening, I believe she will be doing so."

A long pause.

"She is ready to go. Now. She is ready to lead. Not as a step to some other office. Not as an ego trip. But because the city needs her type of leadership—anchored in integrity, grace, humanity, compassion—now. If anyone can bring this badly broken community back together, lifting us one at a time, it's she. So I for one would be absolutely honored to serve with Michelle Easley as the next mayor of this great city."

The press didn't budge. Blank stares.

Definitely not the big news they were eager to report.

Their producers had sent them to cover the story of a council member who had been through hell and was rising to become mayor. A tidy narrative.

This was not that. Their looks made clear they didn't know what this was.

They didn't know Michelle Easley well. Neither did much of the city, primarily because she was the rare political leader who didn't spend most of her time seeking attention.

And there had never been talk of her being mayor. But with Dylan's support, they all knew instantly that she'd become mayor in a matter of months.

Hands jolted into the air.

But Dylan raised his hands as well, cutting off questions that were already coming.

"Sorry, folks. No questions today. I have nothing to add, I'm a little tired, and I'm very hungry. Take care, you guys."

He stepped away from the podium, a bounce in his step.

He couldn't remember a decision he felt better about.

* * *

Famished, Dylan walked to city hall's parking lot and climbed into his Jeep, which—no longer the scene of an active investigation—

the cops had returned two days before. He'd spent hours scrubbing away the residue of dark fingerprint power that investigators had left all over the interior.

He drove to Central Parkway, then crossed Vine Street to formally cross into the city's East Side. But after passing the courthouse, then the jail, rather than heading up Columbia Parkway and east out of downtown, he veered left.

North.

Up the hill into Avondale.

At the hill's peak, Dylan passed the imposing red brick facade of Calvary Baptist. He took it in for a few seconds, but he kept driving. He and Calvin Easley had had a nice visit the morning before, and what he planned to do—and he'd be back there tomorrow morning for the main service. The pastor wanted him to say some words.

But where he was heading now felt equally important. Not only because of his empty stomach, but because of a deeper hunger for something else. More than any moment, his last visit to this place had shown that he'd been doing so much wrong during his time in office, at least after the first few heady weeks. He hadn't understood what the essence of service was all about. Not because he'd forgotten, but because he'd never really known.

He'd felt the urge to return ever since. It had been growing daily, peaking into a full craving as he'd spent recent days holed up and isolated, waiting to hear from Magwood.

Finally, today was the day—so much so that he was starving himself so he could truly enjoy it.

Minutes later, he drove into the packed parking lot, squeezing into one of only two spots that remained in the back of the lot. He'd driven by the pink awning so many times without thinking much about it, but as he walked below it now, it put him at ease.

He entered the double doors of the diner and stepped inside.

A dozen heads turned his way, and the sizzle and steam from behind the counter dominated the place.

"Mr. Webb," one man yelled out from a booth along the wall, and Dylan walked over and greeted him. "So glad you're back on," he said. "We were pulling for you, and good people always come through."

He asked the man his name, and the names of those he was sitting with.

"Thank you, Lincoln. Maybe not always, but in this case, I'd like to believe that's true."

They chatted for a few minutes before Dylan ventured to a new table where someone had called out, and he started a new conversation with a new group.

"C'mon, folks!" The familiar voice yelled out from behind the counter behind him. Laughing, but loud. "Let the man through. He's here to eat the best eggs and bacon in the 'Nati, not gab with you all!"

Dylan finished his conversation, shook two more hands at the end of the counter, then sat down in a seat that Sonny had reserved for him.

"Take a seat, Councilman," the aproned cook and owner of Sugar 'n Spice said.

"Please, Sonny. Call me Dylan for now on."

"Okay, Dylan. Take a seat. How do you want them?" Sonny asked, face gleaming with sweat.

"Let's go scrambled today. Shredded cheddar on top, with some onions and peppers tossed in. Bacon on the side."

"Coming right up, Dylan."

For the next two hours, long after the eggs and bacon were gone, Dylan chatted with Sonny and at least a dozen customers who came by and said hello. Gabby Moore joined him forty minutes in.

Most conversations started with the drama at city hall. The robbery, the doubts, then through the events of the prior days. The exciting prospect of Michelle Easley becoming mayor, someone everyone he spoke with knew and admired.

But then Dylan shifted to other topics with each visitor.

He pivoted to *them*. To *their* lives.

Their kids. Grandkids. Jobs. Churches.

Their ups.

Their downs.

How *they* were doing. How *they* were feeling.

And phone in his pocket, with nothing scheduled for the rest of the day, he listened to every word.

Each conversation was full of laughter. Some included hugs. A few involved tears.

They were the most fulfilling two hours he could remember.